M000307324

THE
PRINCIPLE OF MOMENTS

THE
PRINCIPLE
MOMENTS
OF

ESMIE JIKIEMI-PEARSON

First published in Great Britain in 2024 by Gollancz
an imprint of The Orion Publishing Group Ltd
Carmelite House, 50 Victoria Embankment
London EC4Y 0DZ

An Hachette UK Company

1 3 5 7 9 10 8 6 4 2

Copyright © Esmie Jikiemi-Pearson 2023

The moral right of Esmie Jikiemi-Pearson to be identified as
the author of this work has been asserted in accordance
with the Copyright, Designs and Patents Act of 1988.

All rights reserved. No part of this publication may be
reproduced, stored in a retrieval system, or transmitted
in any form or by any means, electronic, mechanical,
photocopying, recording, or otherwise, without the
prior permission of both the copyright owner and the
above publisher of this book.

All the characters in this book are fictitious, and any resemblance
to actual persons, living or dead, is purely coincidental.

A CIP catalogue record for this book is
available from the British Library.

ISBN (Hardback) 978 1 473 23419 2
ISBN (Export Trade Paperback) 978 1 473 23420 8
ISBN (Audio) 978 1 473 23423 9
ISBN (eBook) 978 1 473 23422 2

Typeset by Input Data Services Ltd, Bridgwater, Somerset

Printed in Great Britain by Clays Ltd, Elcograph S.p.A

www.gollancz.co.uk

To the Black women who wrote a way to the stars,
and showed me how to dream the future.

The Beginning

This is a story we are hesitant to tell, though it is true we are many lifetimes removed from it now.

We record it because it is our history, and through our history we illuminate our future, and through this ritual of illumination we find the power to shape that future. We find precedent. We find order. Indeed, the old mandate rings in our ears—Order is the Architect.

How we repent for that naivete now, after the fact.

It is with regret that we must inform you this tale survives solely in fragments, salvaged at great personal risk. As for its ending, that is clearest of all, having only just come to pass.

Perhaps this is not such a bad thing.

Perhaps this is a tragedy.

Perhaps that is for you to judge.

But we digress—and there will be time enough for that later.

Here, then, is how the story starts.

In the beginning, there were no heroes to speak of. This, we call the Dead Age, as it preceded the Age of Life; the Life that our heroes would later restore after overcoming so much peril.

During the Dead Age, shadows reigned and no plants grew.

During the Dead Age, the rain fell as acid and poisoned the rivers, souring the oceans and drying the land. Creatures with twisted limbs and savage mouths ruled the jagged crags, their many-hundred eyes and wicked spines glinting in the sun's red light.

During the Dead Age, the planet was in pain, as the talons of these creatures dug ever deeper into Her flesh, and the acid rain scorched Her past all recognition. Where once She had been blue, and brightest pink, dappled with jewelled purple and lush, lively green, She was now muted grey, carbon-black, and crumbling.

She had forgotten Her own name—all She knew of Herself was the agony.

Soon (by a planet's standard—so not very soon at all by ours), She grew weary of being corroded, grew weary of the pockmarks and lightning strikes and tectonic shudders, grew weary of the effort it took to push hot magma out of fresh wounds, weary of each split of scar tissue and each gout of boiling blood forced from beneath Her mantle to harden over Her tender skin.

So, She carved from the earth three heroes who would rid Her of this monstrous blight, find the Life She had lost, and bring it back into the light.

From the shadow. From the river. From the mountain.

A shield. A sword. A crown.

Adesola. Sensit. Dandeyi.

Three heroes. One prophecy: save the world.

'A Complete, Annotated History of Chasca, Including Relevant Translated Mythologies. Chapter: Scroll the First' by I. Nisomn, ex-acolyte of the Aonian Archives.

(Archivist's note: This text by I. Nisomn is the only remaining source at our disposal regarding the mythos of that strange planet, Chasca, forgotten by the universe but not forsaken by its scholars, it would seem. This key episode details the origins of the first of three prophecies, of which two have purportedly come to pass, and which all, as reported by Nisomn, foretell great calamity, and can only be thwarted, or fulfilled, by three brave heroes. The author, Nisomn, was one of our most promising acolytes, with an affinity for preservation that saved many a crumbling volume. Though we mourn his flight from the Guild, we wish him luck with whatever endeavour it was that he felt could not be completed within our hallowed halls.)

The Middle

Much of what we now know relies on the word of those closer to it all than we were: visions written down, memories extracted, lifetimes preserved and transcribed. It is clumsy, but we have always been clumsy. We see that now. If only . . . But, no. Even we must learn from our follies, grave and blood-drenched as they are.

By this time, the time of the child's birth, the Age of Life brought into being by our Heroes was almost over, almost dead, its founding heroes and their deeds long relegated to halls of myth and the opening verses of the planetary epos. Though it had lasted millennia, its peace was dealt a mortal blow by the inevitable arrival of the Second Prophecy, and killed forever by the great and terrible betrayal at its heart.

Here, then, is the story's gracelessly recollected middle.

Once, there was a girl born amid chaos.

It was the dying day of that same civilisation our three heroes had fought to begin, so long ago. As the child took her first dust-choked breath, ideals shattered and monuments crumbled, but her eyes remained stubbornly shut, firelight glimmering off eyelids sticky with fluid, brows faint and indistinct—so she did not see the violence of the world for what it was.

(Yet . . . Did not see the violence of the world for what it was *yet*. Later, she would. Later, it would be written in the stars; every single one of them a part of it. *Empire*. But not yet.)

The girl's mother gathered her to her chest with shaking arms, pushing sweat-soaked hair from her face and gazing at her daughter with a blind sense of all-encompassing wonder. She marvelled at the child's waving hands, curled into fists, fingers as delicate as the bones of a bird, wrists chubby and dimpled, thinking *if only her father could see her now*.

But her daughter's father was dead and had died protecting them and all he loved from ruin, so it was a difficult thought, to say the least, and one she pushed quickly aside.

(That idea of absent family, of missing heritage—of not being quite sure what to *do* with that idea, of pushing it quickly aside—would turn out to be a recurring theme. A sparking pattern in her neurons and the neurons of her progeny; a line in a prophecy; an echo of that violence writ in starlight.)

The cracking of stone and the deadened sound of falling ash faded into the background as she moved her fingers to the artery running along the side of her daughter's neck. A sudden flutter against her fingertips—more like a moth's wings beating than a *heart*—filled her chest with giddy laughter, and *oh*, it was so easy to marvel at this new life, this child that might not see the sunrise, and yet was so full of light, simply because she did not know what the sunrise would bring.

Her mother knew though, so she pulled herself to her knees. She had never felt pain like this, yet she stood, because if she did not then her daughter never would. The palace was collapsing, the hallways groaning and crashing down around her, but she walked on, her daughter cradled in her arms.

There was no ship waiting for them in the atrium, so the

queen drew in a breath and spoke one into being—word and will coalescing into metal and fuel and a chamber of ice made for sleeping.

The effort nearly killed her.

And so, the queen of a planet whose people had fought the bloodiest civil war in three millennia pushed her daughter into the only holding pod of the conjured spacecraft, closed the hatch, and watched it launch.

And so, the queen of a planet whose people had fought the bloodiest civil war in three millennia—and destroyed themselves in the process—collapsed to the granite floor of her castle and wept.

For her daughter, who was the sole heir to the throne, and the last hope of their people.

For her daughter, who was already hurtling across the galaxy towards a new life, inside a cryogenics unit where she would sleep for year upon year, until the time was *right*.

For her daughter, who would grow up abandoned and confused, never to inherit the crown that was her birthright.

Excerpt of a vision relayed by a trustworthy source whose identity cannot be revealed at present.

(Archivist's note: You must excuse my poetic licence. Artistic liberty is something I am rarely afforded, and this tale begs to be transformed into scripture; everything about it is epic.)

The End

And now for the ending, the part we are most familiar with and can at least tell in its entirety.

This closing is many years removed from both the beginning and the middle—perhaps this is why we failed so astronomically in anticipating it—but it draws them to completion nonetheless.

It is not impartially told; that would be nigh on impossible with a story like this.

On the contrary, we see the importance of sentiment now. Of empathy in our history telling. Of an open heart.

That was, after all, what you opened this volume in search of, wasn't it? A story. Well, this one is about people, of course, and the incredible things they are capable of when faced with equally incredible, seemingly unconquerable injustice. It is a story about a girl and her friends, and how hard times made heroes of them, whether they wanted to be or not. It is a story of loss, and adventure, of daring, and of courage burning bright in the bleakest of times. It is a story about love.

And this is how it ends.

Part One

'We turned the Earth, our home, into a wasteland, and left. Now, we have arrived here, alighting upon a wasteland with no other choice but to make it our home. Like a fable, nature has given to us what we gave back to her, and so we must rise to the task of turning this desert into a soil rich enough that we may begin to sow within it the seeds of our future.'

From the diary of a human settler on Gahraan, born aboard the ark ships, killed during the Emperor's discovery of the settlement.

Chapter One

Asha Akindele was knelt in prayer, chanting the sacred words of imperial petition and invocation that had been graven unwillingly on her memory since birth.

Her heart beat steadily in time with the rhythm, her hands opening and closing to its chorus.

We welcome our Emperor—may He rule forever—into our hearts and into our minds, unflinchingly.

Her mind, however, was somewhere else entirely.

Equations were solving themselves against the pale red backdrop of her closed eyelids like flowers blooming. Each one yielded yet more numbers, spilling out unknown quantities like gems tumbling from a geode, cracked wide open and sparkling in the red noonday sun. Her head hurt—partly from the loud droning of communal prayer, and partly from trying to wrap her mind around complex mathematical theory in the middle of a temple during a deference recitation—but she soldiered on. As always.

Eventually, the service ended.

Thracin bless us, may He rule forever; Divine Right is Divine Might.

Divine Right is Divine Might.

Divine Right is Divine Might.

The maxim of their government and religion and ruler rang out in whispered reverence through the assembled body of worshippers, and Asha mouthed along, playing her part even as she blinked rapidly, her eyes growing reaccustomed to the blue light that filtered through the temple's crystal walls.

Years ago, she'd discovered that the only way to bear all those hours spent kneeling with her head bowed in respect was to close her eyes and discuss, in the privacy of her own mind, exactly how she would leave this planet, given the chance. She had started with the big ideas. Where would she get transport? *Steal it from the Imperial Academy of Aeronautics on the other side of the dome.* How will you fly it? *I'll learn. I'll modify the tablet they give everyone at fourteen to access their timetables and ration points and use it to hack into the Academy files. I'll watch their classes at night, over and over again, and I will learn.*

One particularly vivid fantasy often sustained her: the sight of her own grinning face in the cockpit of a stolen jet, middle fingers up to the rear-view cams, guns blazing as she blasted the whole place to ash—

Someone nudged her, telling her to hurry up. *"Thracin bless us,"* she murmured hastily, rolling up her mat and joining the line of people shuffling towards the exit. The headache looming behind her eyes only seemed to intensify with each step, but the thrill of knowing what she held locked safely inside her mind was worth it. Even if it would never leave the confines of her imagination.

Lost in thought, she accidentally bumped into the person in front of her. Everyone was drawing to a stop. The line of people flowing out the doors had halted. A gasp rippled through the crowd, people stepping back. *What's going on?* After a few moments, through a gap in the bodies, Asha glimpsed the reason for the delay.

A woman had fallen, collapsing between the rows of

worshippers to lie unmoving on the ground. Unconscious due to exhaustion probably. *Nothing too dramatic*, Asha thought. And yet she was reminded suddenly of an image from her childhood: her first day in the weapons assembly warehouse. The boy next to her had touched a delicate, thinly membraned plasma filament without gloves. The slim cylinder had snagged on a fingernail and torn, sagging and spilling its valuable fluid onto the workbench. He had been taken away for punishment, kicking and screaming. She'd never seen him again. All she'd been able to do was stare at the broken energy bar emptying its gleaming contents onto the bench like blood from a corpse.

The fallen woman wasn't bleeding—not yet—but Asha could imagine her blood spilling just like the plasma had, red instead of luminous blue, and infinitely less valuable.

Hulking Lithian guards were already shouldering their way towards the accident, weapons drawn, reptilian limbs bunched with muscle and desperate for a fight. Asha could practically smell the lust for violence rolling off them—that distinctly inhuman stench of scale sweat mixed with the viscous, milky residue of their acrid saliva.

One of them kicked the woman with a clawed foot, sneering as she groaned weakly, tears cutting tributaries down her ashen face.

Soldiers of the Consortium.

A gang of monsters and sadists, who cradled blaster rifles in their similarly clawed hands like they'd been born to use them, teeth sharp and eyes cruel, grease-slick indigo scales glittering in the sunlight—body armour provided free of charge by millennia of evolution on their home planet, Lith, a craggy place covered in sandy rock, not too dissimilar to Gahraan. Her own fleshy human softness was constantly made horrifying in their beady eyes by contrast—lean meat and viscera wrapped in dark brown skin—skin thinner than metal foil, and so much better at conducting pain than electricity.

Keeping her face carefully blank was second nature, the dullness in her eyes less a learned protective mechanism than a by-product of a life lived in terror. A second guard swung back the copper rod he carried as an accessory to his rifle, his arm falling to strike the weeping woman with it. The bright crackle of raw electricity flashed in the dim light, leaping from his scales, turning the woman's soft weeping into agonised screams. Her elbow slipped, lightning-quick in her convulsions, scraping against the polished floor . . . and there it was. Blood. Welling to the surface of a friction burn, of all things.

"What are you?" the guard hissed, teeth flashing in the sun. "*What are you?*"

"Nothing," the woman gasped, as was expected of her. "I am nothing."

The guard unleashed another burst of electricity with a flicker of his forked tongue.

"That's right."

The man who stood next to Asha shook his head in disgust, but even that movement was subdued. His eyes darted around, looking for someone to share in his disdain, in this small act of moral rebellion. She recognised him. He worked two rows across from her in the factory on the textile recycling day. A bit of a troublemaker, in fact—something which had immediately endeared him to Asha, even though the most basic sense of self-preservation should have ensured that it didn't.

She wanted to meet his eye.

Thracin, why was she like this? If her mother had been there, had seen her even *think* about looking at that man, let alone meeting his gaze, she would have dragged her home and beaten her until she didn't have thoughts, let alone eyes to look with.

And Asha wouldn't have blamed her. People who looked back at troublemakers ended up lying next to them on the incinerator floor.

Then the man's eyes darted in her direction, catching her hesitant glance and pinning it down like a spider would a fly.

She froze.

Just look away, she thought. *Asha, just look away.*

She nodded back at him. It was a tiny movement, more like a compulsion, stilted and terrified.

Adrenaline pounded through her.

Stupid girl, she thought. *Stupid, stupid, stupid.*

But of course she had done it.

Asha didn't think a universe existed in which she had not.

The light of the midday suns blazed brightly above her as the temple disgorged the last of her line into its crystal courtyard. Above her, the shimmering hexagons of the terradome that enclosed the oasis-centred settlement were busy filtering out the harmful UV rays and extreme temperatures that were par for the course on a terraformed desert planet such as Gahraan. *Life* was inside this dome, and the four others that clustered together in the barren valley that their great-grandparents had thought fit to start a new world.

Outside, there was nothing but scarlet sand and searing heat.

That should be our motto, she thought wryly. *Never meant to support life but supporting it begrudgingly anyway.*

She glanced at the building behind her. The temple was a glorious, beautiful thing. A beacon of belief and faith—a monument to Emperor Thracin and the empire he had created to save the galaxy and its hundred inhabited worlds from annihilating each other. It shone with its wealth—just like everything Thracin owned (*except humanity*, Asha thought, *except me*)—like the polished chrome barrels of the guns they assembled every day, like the sword he held in all his statues, like the very stars in the sky—each one a sun or a planet that belonged to him, because—what didn't? His, his, *his*, the whole galaxy shining because he decreed it so. Because he liked to cloak depravity in crystal and call it 'salvation'.

Her heart beat faster just to think it.

Careful, Asha. Remember your scripture; Divine Might is Divine Right. Do not forget what you are and what that makes you. Do not forget your place.

She exhaled shakily, eyes closing for the briefest of moments against the sting of hot tears. Because righteousness felt so good for a moment, but when the thrill was gone, fear was all that remained. Fear and rage, feeding each other in a vicious, endless loop, until she could barely tell them apart.

Walking down the slope of the hill and into the main square of the city, she saw imperial priests of the gentle species, Whid, their long, pale limbs enfolded in white robes, congregating by the path opposite the temple, as kids a little younger than her milled around in small groups, unsure of what to do with themselves.

On an ordinary day, they'd all be in the weapons manu-facturing warehouse until their backs ached and their vision blurred, hunched over their stations, putting guns together for Thracin's soldiers, or third-party stakeholders, or distributor chains, or private security firms—an infinitesimal selection of the myriad corporations that propped up the Consortium like a million grasping hands.

Today, though, with working responsibilities cancelled for the Anniversary, the rest of the afternoon was to be filled with

'RECREATIONAL TIME', as their timetables had proclaimed this morning. 'TO BE SPENT IN PRAYER, OR EXERCISE, OR EDUCATION AT CULTURAL SITES'.

Asha had requested 'PRAYER: TO BE COMPLETED WITH FAMILY', just like most of the population, as it meant a few rare, unsupervised hours at home with loved ones. In Asha's case, she would be able to talk with her mother, Iyanda, who she had barely spoken to in weeks aside from mumbled conversations at bedtime, after her own graduation to the adult warehouse had turned their timetables almost identical.

That had been four weeks ago, by the Consortium calendar. The bureaucrats in charge of all such dreary processes on Gahraan had absorbed old Earthern standards, not bothering to complete any research on their own, and settled on eighteen as the age of human maturation. And so, on her eighteenth birthday she'd said goodbye to her benchmates and the slower pace of life in the adolescent warehouse, and joined the ranks of the adult workforce.

The past month had been the most tiring and mentally draining of her life.

So she was grateful for today's opportunity to rest, even if it meant spending half of it kneeling in simpering gratitude to the tyrant who had sentenced her to this life in the first place.

'REQUEST APPROVED', read her wristband. 'ENJOY YOUR PRAYER, IN HONOUR OF THE HUNDRED YEAR PEACE'.

The Anniversary: one hundred years of peace.

One hundred years since Commander Thracin had stood on the drawbridge of his ship amongst the dark rocks of A'lkari, and said, *now, peace*, before crowning himself head of an empire, as if the inevitability of empire wasn't perpetual war with itself and its disparate organs.

17

Asha could have cried at the irony of it.

I spend all day building guns, she thought. *Guns for a peaceful empire.*

What she *wanted* to think, however, was, *Thracin, you are a liar, and a tyrant,* but that was sedition and treason, and she was too frightened. Terrified of the Emperor and his million guns, the guns she built for him, but far more terrified of the thoughts that crowded her every waking second, the thoughts born of her hatred for the throne he had stolen, along with the right of them all to govern themselves. The right to decide *when* they worked, *if* they worked, and *to what end.* The thoughts that said, *one day I will leave this wreck of a planet, one day I will find you, one day I will make you pay.*

But any anger she felt was quickly smothered by a great rolling wave of fear, that pendulum of rage and terror, ever swinging. All she could see now was the woman, convulsing on the temple floor; the troublemaker, trying to make eye contact and finding her, *implicating her,* with a single flick of his gaze.

She felt sick.

And that's why you'll never leave, sneered a voice in her mind that might have been her own, or a priest's, or even the Emperor's. *That is why you will only ever plan, and wish, and dream, and never act. You're scared. You're always too scared.*

Asha scowled as she turned down an alley, grinding her jaw in frustration. She knew she should have conquered the anger by now—the anger at her circumstance, at the system, at the way the world worked, at the way that power and opportunity and *luck,* even, were all held up by inequality at their very foundations—but maybe that just wasn't the way her brain worked, and maybe there was too much to be angry about.

Before she knew it, she was ducking into the alleyway behind warehouse number 7 to stare at a rusted old monument in a small square that most inhabitants of Gahraan had long avoided—for good reason.

At first glance, the monument comprised a melted lump of metal, supported on a sturdy pole that thrust the twisted mass of pipes and jagged-edged plates a few metres into the sky, superimposing it against the faint, tessellating hexagons of the dome that flickered above them. A pathetic beam of sunlight fought through the roofs of the neighbouring buildings, shining on the thing, illuminating the grime and the red dirt blown into every rusty crevice.

A polished plaque at the base of the monument read:

HERE LIES THE ENGINE CORE OF THE PRIMARY SHIP
THE HUMAN RACE EMPLOYED TO LAY SEIGE TO THE
EMPEROR'S GREAT DOMINION

But if Asha looked close enough, she could see faint scratchings on the plates of metal. Letters, or numbers, maybe, written in one of the old Earthern languages. Mandarin, perhaps, or English—both were still spoken occasionally in family homes, amongst others. Spanish, Yoruba, Hindi, French. The ability to read any of those languages had been lost in less than three generations after Thracin came to power—writing of any kind was banned in the human settlement, and the older members of the community had long given up scratching letters in the dust.

And yet the memory of the message inscribed on the engine core all those decades ago lived on.

And now, to the stars.

A few years ago, she had spotted two lines of writing on a thin sheet of metal near the bottom of the core that she had previously missed. It was close enough to run her fingers over, though she didn't dare to touch it. *I wish I could read it for myself,* she had thought at the time, cringing at her own illiteracy for anything that wasn't the sanitised, clinical symbols of Universal Standard and wondering at all the other messages that had been lost, or purposefully mistranslated, and had felt like she was being hit over the head, repeatedly, with a cudgel.

She looked around now, at the grey walls that surrounded her, at the red dirt beneath her feet. This was their punishment, for building ships capable of interstellar travel, for failing to save the planet that had birthed them; an indefinite indenture, working to repay their debt and all of its compound interest, until one day, if the Emperor was to be believed, when they would be free to go out into the stars again and find a future somewhere else.

Work hard and you will be rewarded.

It was the kind of narrative only a certain type of person could subscribe to without it being called self-deceit. She was still figuring out exactly who that was, but she knew with absolute certainty that it wasn't her. That it would likely never be her.

Beneath the engine core, there was another metal plaque nailed into the floor. It was a statement of ownership, a claim to Gahraan, staked by the person who owned the planet, and didn't need it, but wouldn't give it to the people who did, because an investment meant more to him than the quality of a few hundred thousand lives.

"How could we have known," Asha murmured to herself, "that it was *him*?"

THIS LAND IS OWNED BY EMPEROR AI'VAREK THRACIN, GLORY BE TO HIM AND HIS MIGHT, PURCHASED IN THE SIX THOUSANDTH YEAR OF THE GALACTIC CALENDER. INVADED FORTY YEARS AGO, IT NOW BOASTS THE LARGEST MANUFACTURING PLANT IN THE SEVEN OUTER SECTORS.

Asha sighed. This small exhibit was simply a reminder that they stacked machinery parts in a factory all day, their whole lives, and that they would continue stacking those same parts until the resources the empire expended on them became more than the resources they produced, or they got sick, or got back problems, or looked at a guard wrong and were disposed of. It made Asha want to scream, or throw something, or violently stab someone—preferably someone whose name rhymed with 'basin'—but she couldn't. There were a lot of things she couldn't do though, so she was used to it. Oh, but that didn't mean it didn't make her angry. *Angry* was Asha's second skin, one she hadn't taken off in years. It was coded into her DNA, right alongside *survive* and *by any means necessary*.

Asha walked to the opposite side of the small square, where a larger alleyway would take her to the parallel thoroughfare. It was the long way home, but it was still a way. She'd be late, and her mother would be mad, and they'd probably fight and then go to sleep.

Just another day.

Walking through the alley, she turned onto the street. The sun was setting. In the distance, a hazy cluster of buildings at the edge of the dome flashed orange in the pre-dusk light.

The Imperial Academy of Aeronautics. The black and white banners of the Consortium billowed in the breeze, but the school itself was empty—all the students had returned home to celebrate the holy day.

The school did not admit humans, of course. It was a boarding school for the talented children of the galaxy's elite, and its creation had been the catalyst for the indentured servitude of humanity. She wondered if they taught the students that—if they knew the true history of the small planet they called home during the school year.

Here was the version she knew.

Humanity, hurtling through the stars in a fleet of rapidly degenerating generational ark ships, forced to abandon an Earth that had been deemed ninety-eight per cent uninhabitable in the 2070s, had been praying for a miracle, and had found Gahraan instead. Initially, Terraforming had been limited to four key spots—one around each landing site. They had built a new life out of sand and recycled metal, all the while daring to dream of the future. It had been that way for two years. Two years of peace. Of existing on a planet no longer dying under their feet.

Until Thracin had won a war they hadn't even known was happening, finished his unification of all the inhabited worlds in the galaxy, and begun the business of building his empire. First Tetrarch of a council of four, he had crowned himself head of a galaxy-wide association of corporations that called themselves the Consortium and promised to deliver their citizens into a new age of prosperity, driven by competitive markets and controlled by an elite few. By the time humanity had realised Gahraan was an outlying planet of a galaxy teeming with life, three thousand years more developed than they were, it was too late.

They had listened to his victory speech so many times over the years that it had become permanently etched into the mind of every citizen, just as he had intended, and Asha was no different. The words echoed softly in her memory, accompanied by the images her mind created in response to the audio crackling out through speakers in the square, or in the temple, or at home: a tiny figure in front of a huge crowd, lifting a sword to the sky, and then sheathing it in the ground of his stronghold planet, A'lkari.

"And now, peace. A hard peace, enforced by any means necessary.

"We have fought too long and too hard against archaic powers to fall victim to the structures that brought ruin to them. Their

insularity was their failure, their refusal to progress their down-
fall. They believed dogged preservation of the old ways would
save them, but it was only by creating a new path that we were
able to save ourselves. And so, I promise you: this galaxy will be
united forevermore. No citizen will be constrained by the limits
of their kind. No citizen will be without opportunity to better
themselves. For, under my governance, each one among you shall
be the arbiter of your own fates. Work hard for your fellow citizens,
and your fellow citizens will thank you. Work hard, so that the
empire can work harder for your peace. Work hard and you will be
rewarded.

"Let it be so, as I have decreed it.

"Divine Right is Divine Might."

It was the same slogan he'd used when he ordered his troops
not to leave the places they had freed, until his kindly 'liberation'
came to mean 'unending occupation', and his sphere of influence
came to hold the entire galaxy. Before Thracin's ascendancy, all the
planets had been on the brink of mutual destruction, each trying
desperately to protect their territory from alien threat. Thracin
had appeared seemingly out of nowhere, and his campaign to
unite the hundred known worlds under one banner, one system,
one empire that would bring increased profit and abundance
to all, had gained followers so fast that, within a decade, they
were a major player on the galactic stage. Thirty years later, they
had succeeded, becoming an army somewhere along the way.
Universal Standard, previously a mercantile tongue, had quickly
become the standard language of the empire, as all the species
of the hundred worlds—still reeling from the fallout of the war
started by their territorial forebearers—found themselves moving
swiftly into an age of high-volume inter-planetary trade and
commerce—in product, customs, and the imperial rhetoric that
circulated constantly, swapping back and forth and back and

forth until it had seeped into the ground and the stars and all the space in between.

It was only when Thracin sent scouts to scour his various properties for locations suitable for his Imperial Academy of Aeronautics that the human settlement was discovered, and its people enslaved.

That had been decades before Asha was born.

Gazing at the glass windows that glinted in the distance, a familiar feeling rose in her chest. Obsession; hatred. It was hard to tell them apart most days. Usually, she didn't try to, and today was no exception. Instead, she thought about her plan. The one where she would finally have enough intel, enough courage, and enough pure recklessness to cross the mile of desert that separated them, break in, and steal a ship.

It was an impossible dream.

Of course, it was.

But that meant it was safe.

She wondered if the sight of the place would ever stop cutting her so deeply. *Probably not*, she thought, and turned away, jogging down the shortcut past the incinerator to the darker, meaner streets of the Lower Quarter. Her mother was expecting her home.

A figure much too tall to be human was standing in her street.

At first Asha didn't even see them—dark, skulking figures were easily lost in the darkness of the desert at night, and a long, black cloak rendered them shapeless, putting Asha immediately on edge. She froze, watching from halfway down the street as the person knocked on the door to her family unit.

A cold sweat pricked under her arms. They *never* got visitors they didn't know, and her mother was home alone.

Her heart slammed against her ribcage as her mind went into overdrive. Childish fears surfaced first: What if it was an imperial scientist, one of the Magekind, come to snatch her away for one of their sick experiments? She'd seen it happen a few times, but not recently—sleek ships disgorging pale, white-robed people who wielded strange weapons, who took twenty or so humans back with them to run tests on. But this alien's cloak was dark, not white . . . *Shit.* What if it was the government? Had they discovered her escape plans, somehow? What if they had realised how she'd pried back the lines of code and security defences one by one, with an illegally modified tablet as the tool? What if they'd found the hours of footage—*over two thousand hours of classroom footage*—mined from the Imperial Academy of Aeronautics' archives over a period of seven years, and followed it right to her door?

Run, was her immediate thought.

She didn't know where it came from—running got you nowhere inside a militarised dome, besides inside a pair of handcuffs staring down a lethal injection. Should she intervene? Give herself up? Her mother didn't deserve to suffer for Asha's recklessness.

Thracin, she was so stupid. Fear squeezed tight at her throat, and in a painful moment of glittering clarity, she saw all the possible consequences of her thoughtless rebellion land upon her mother, who would do anything to protect Asha—even lie.

Near frantic now with terror, she scanned the visitor's cloak for any identifying signs, but it was so dark she couldn't make out any more details. Maybe she could—

Asha's mother opened the door.

She could see what Asha couldn't: the visitor's face. As she took in whoever it was that stood before her, Iyanda's mouth opened, as though she wanted to scream—as though this person, whoever they were, scared her more than the guards and their guns that would inevitably appear to punish her for the offence of verbalising her fear. And there was a look in her eyes, dark with terror, that made Asha think this cloaked alien at the door might be an omen for the end of the world.

Then the stranger reached out a thin, alien hand, and gently caressed her mother's face, trailing long fingers from her brow bone to her cheek. Iyanda closed her eyes, her whole body trembling—*in fear, or something else?* The stranger's hand dropped.

Asha's heart felt like a stampede in her chest, her body tense and trembling, caught like a fly in a web, torn between action and inaction, her brain too numb with fear to choose.

Then, the automated streetlight above Asha's head turned on, just like it always did an hour before curfew, washing the street in a pale white light. Now, Asha was bathed in a beam of white brightness, her position given away.

Her mother's gaze darted towards the alcove where Asha stood, back pressed against the wall. Her eyes widened.

No, Asha wanted to yell, *look away and I can help you! Look away and he'll never know—*

But it was too late.

Before she could take a step forward, before she could speak, or cry out (or even wish that she had come home half an hour earlier so that she might have at least—at the very, *very* least—been standing next to her mother whilst she experienced a moment that would change the course of her life forever), the cloaked stranger stilled, and turned. Following Iyanda's eyeline straight to where Asha stood, alone and defenceless on the other side of the street.

Inexplicably, she was reminded of a jutting rock that rose from

26

the red of the sand, just outside the dome's eastern wall, that she had observed since childhood. Once it had been strong, and broad, wide enough for a child to have walked across without falling off. But over the years, as the wind had whipped past it, scraping its great dark face with sand and other rocks, with particles of air and dust and time, the rock had grown thinner, and smoother, until it was as she had seen it last—worn down to its dark core, a thin spindle pointing heavenward, the horizon's craggy tooth.

The spindle of a stranger smiled.

And several impossible things happened in quick succession.

From the depths of his cloak's cowl, she saw his eyes, blazing with an unnatural light. And, though she did not know him, though she had never seen him before, though her mind should have told her to run, or hide, or fight, she could only stare back in stunned disbelief, and think, *you took your time. Is it starting, again?* Her left arm felt heavy. *Yes,* she thought. *Yes, I think it might be.*

Before she could understand whose voice it was, so old and so weary, speaking inside her head, the stranger raised a hand and whispered something, and Asha felt an alien coldness descend over her skin, burrowing under it, sending ice through her veins.

"*I am sorry. I am so sorry that it came to this.*" His voice, echoing inside her head, somehow, though his mouth hadn't moved. She *knew* his mouth hadn't moved—

Then, the street in front of her vanished, replaced by complete and total darkness.

Her body felt lighter than air—it barely felt like she had a body at all.

Briefly, she wondered if this was death—if the alien at her front door had killed her with a single glance.

And, truly, she might have died, if the dark had consumed

her for just a moment longer. But through the dimness of her vision, brightness was swarming. Bright light, splitting into colours, then converging again, into images. Images that felt like memories, of people she had never seen, places she had never been, all of them threaded through with light like liquid gold, and juddering with a terrible noise that sounded like the thunderous, rhythmic ticking of an enormous and ancient clock.

She saw a hand, reaching out to her. A young man, his dark skin an ocean of stars, reflecting the blue and purple and silver of the galaxy that hung in the darkness outside the window behind him.

She saw a planet painted in oranges and whites, suspended in the vastness of space, tilting on its axis, imploding.

She saw another figure, outlined in white light, two horns curving from their head towards a sky split by lightning, and she felt a rush of *something* that felt wild and old, and out of her hands.

The person disappeared, replaced by a woman with lilac skin and three eyes opening a door, and saying something. A name. *Ishoal.* Next, she saw her own hands, turning the pages of a book whose alien script danced in the light of a flame, letters changing in the shadows as she watched, dumbfounded, to form a word that felt like coming home.

She saw a chair of wires, and a girl, whose thin face looked remarkably similar to her own, whose eyes, dark in their sunken sockets, held a world of pain.

She watched, from somewhere outside of her body, as they embraced, as she whispered, *sister,* and held the girl's hand to her heart.

There was a flash of light, and something materialised out of thin air, particles of gleaming crystal, luminescent and shining, coalescing to form something heavy and violent, the weight of which rested on her left arm, and felt like a limb that had once been taken from her, restored.

The images faded. Darkness surrounded her. She felt suspended in it, like an insect in amber.

A voice sounded softly in the darkness. The same voice that had spoken in her head, the one that had recognised the stranger at her mother's door. It sounded like a woman.

Everything is about to change. And so must you. I am sorry it had to happen this way. It will be hard. It will be terribly hard, and at times you will want to abandon it all, but you mustn't. I will be there, to guide you. All you have to do is call.

The darkness was lightening slightly, the twilit street coming back into focus. The woman's voice grew fainter.

And, above all, you must remember: courage is the only thing stronger than fear, and love is the thread that holds the atoms of this universe together.

And then Asha was standing in the street, drawing in the same breath she had been when the stranger had smiled at her, aware, somehow, that something had happened to her which she did not possess the ability to understand, all within the space of a singular second.

She blinked once, slowly.

The world restarted.

"What the—"

The stranger was already moving—away from her mother at the doorway and up the street. He disappeared down the alleyway that led to the housing compound behind theirs.

For a moment, all she could hear was her breathing. The hot night air ghosted past her, the grit of sand that had billowed up in her wake sticking to the sweat on the back of her neck. The mouth of the alley transfixed her—a slim channel of darkness into which the stranger had disappeared like a scrap of shadow.

Out of the corner of her eye, she saw her mother's stricken face, her trembling frame. She should run to her, help her inside, close the door, and turn out the lights and try to sleep, until—

Until what, Asha? she wanted to scream. *Until the knock of a reptilian claw on your door, and the punishment that will surely follow for causing such a disturbance so close to curfew? Until you tell her you saw people that don't exist, heard voices in your head, and she won't ever be able to look at you the same again?*

She had to find out what she'd seen. It was like a compulsion. Why had she seen it?

What did it mean?

An image flashed into her mind: the girl, the one who looked like her, who called her sister.

Sister.

She turned away from the path that would lead her home.

"No," her mother breathed, seeing the look on her face, and knowing what it meant. "Asha, no—"

But she was already gone.

Three minerals were chosen by the planet, and into them She breathed the last of the Life She had been hoarding. Red clay, white quartz, darkest obsidian. As hands burst from rock, and eyes blinked out of glinting facets, the planet drew three pieces of shining crystal from deep within Her core. She shot them through with gold and tempered them in herostuff, to make them weapons, and then drew breath and made the first of Her requests from Her fledgling, made-of-stone saviours.

"Speak," said the planet to Her children. "And name yourself."

"I name myself Sensit," the man of clay replied. "For the river that cuts."

"I name myself Dandeyi," the one of quartz replied. "For the mountain that rules."

"And I name myself Adesola," said the woman of obsidian. "For the shadows that protect. For the darkness that conceals."

'A Complete, Annotated History of Chasca, Including Relevant Translated Mythologies. Chapter: Scroll the First' by I. Nisomn, ex-acolyte of the Aonian Archives.

(Archivist's note: Due to Nisomn's recent status as 'vanished', his work is currently under review. The bastard burned most of his notes, though, and this book is the only complete volume he left us, so we're working largely in the dark. The title denotes a 'history', but upon our initial perusal closer resembles a kind of mythological canon compiled from Nisomn's birth planet, Chasca—the destruction of which remains a mystery to the galaxy, and to Nisomn, if his claims of ignorance are to be believed. We suspect, however, that he knows more than he's letting on, and hope to find some kind of confirmation within these pages.)

Chapter Two

[planet: Earth] + [location: London] + [year: 1812]

Obi Amadi was on a mission, insofar as one could describe winning back the heart of the only person who had ever loved him as a mission.

The place was London, the year was 1812. The Napoleonic Wars were spilling blood and cannon smoke over the fields of Europe, while the king of Great Britain had already lost the American colonies and was in the process of losing his mind. The French army had set their sights on Russia and were marching in; a tragically finite stream of summer uniforms spilling onto frozen ground. On a railway in Leeds, the first steam locomotive was building speed and chugging soot-thick steam into a slate-grey sky. Half a country away, the last of Earl Elgin's looted marbles were sliding across polished floors and into storage—an ancient temple dissected and stolen from its natural habitat to stand incomplete in a museum for hundreds of lonely, lonely years.

In the midst of all this history, however, Obi could think of only one thing: his pride, and how to go about laying it at someone's feet.

Most people would probably think of this as *an apology*. But Obi was nothing if not dramatic, and after all this time spent chasing rumours through centuries and across galaxies with nothing to show for it, his pride was all he had. Besides, apologies can be difficult for those owed even one by the world, and Obi was owed a million.

He pondered the idea of sacking it all off and running away as he stood in the relentless London drizzle, watching the passers-by, and drawing the long, black coat he used to conceal his hoodie and jeans around himself more tightly. His trainers were black too, but so worn he doubted anyone would deign to look past the half-attached sole currently letting in rainwater, or the Nike tick. Besides, they'd take one look at his dark skin, shaved head, and strange eyes and assume he was from another place with other, entirely foreign customs.

They didn't need to know that the ocean usually separating him from them was one made of time.

Ladies in lilac-coloured lace held parasols whimsically above pearl-studded curls as children in collared frocks laughed and ran around statues, hiding behind bushes. A father flourished a gold coin out of an inside pocket and bestowed it upon his chubby-fingered son. The smiling boy was pick-pocketed mere moments later but still . . . the casual, carefree nature the families exuded so effortlessly made something stick in Obi's throat. It was the way they seemed to have their own centre of gravity—all of them like contained solar systems spinning on secret axes.

Someone had once remarked that perhaps Obi's axis had been knocked loose.

Shaking his head, he turned away from the milling crowds, slipping into the winding alleyway that would deliver him to Westminster Bridge.

In the winter, London was a city on low exposure, covered in a slate-grey sky. The brown water of the Thames ambled along beneath them, dotted here and there with small sailing vessels, and paddle boats. People strode over the cobbles, heeled boots clacking against the stone, skirts brushing over puddles, and above it all, the abbey rose in the distance, gothic and lovely against the darkening sky. Obi thought, *I have seen you in two different centuries. I bet my father saw you in more.*

A grubby boy interrupted his train of thought, running up to him and flapping a soggy sheet of paper in his face. "Come see the ghost in the British Museum! Tickets for a tuppence, sir, take the missus?"

Though Obi did not plan to make a habit of chatting to urchins, he paused, his interest undeniably piqued. He raised an eyebrow. "A ghost?"

The boy nodded, shaking his soggy handful with renewed aggression. "Of a girl in strange dress," he lowered his voice, "in men's trousers!" Obi raised his eyebrow again. "She speaks in a foreign tongue, too," the boy added. Then his expression brightened under the grime on his cheeks. "Perhaps you would understand it, for she is as black as you are!"

Obi's eyebrows climbed to new heights. Uninformed conclusions aside, that detail was interesting. As soon as he had heard the boy's claim, he had thought it to be a hoax. But for him to be advertising the ghost of a Black child . . . that was certainly abnormal. Perhaps the abolitionists were behind it. *Trying to prove we have souls like them,* Obi thought. But his father's voice echoed in his head: *or maybe Londoners are meddling in things they don't understand, trying to make money, surprising no one.*

For a moment, he considered delaying his mission, and going to the museum. It was unlikely to be a ghost, as he was at least eighty per cent certain they did not exist. But it was, however, likely to be an Artefact.

His arm ached in the biting cold. The seam between metal and flesh almost rheumatic in the chill.

Obi nodded to the boy, and walked on.

Supernatural occurrences in big cities like London were usually one of three things: hoaxes carefully constructed by entrepreneurial circus owners, or the owners of some failing establishment, hoping to lure in more business by announcing the capture of a mermaid, or the sighting of a spirit. On rare occasions they might be the real thing. And even more rarely: they were the by-product or side-effect of a piece of future technology falling backwards through the timeline—sent here, or summoned, or, on occasion, accidentally dropped on the way through.

This didn't sound like a ghost.

It sounded like a hologram.

No. Obi thought. *No, no, no, no, no, fuck no.*

He was here to leave that all behind—the chasing, and the jumping, all that risk for no reward. He'd travelled to the future trying to find so many things. His father, a cure for the disease consuming him piece by piece, biting off another chunk of him with every jump, and he had *failed.* And it had cost him so much. It was time to accept that. Time to try and make a life, a stable life, in *one place.* Even if the thought of that was antithetical to his very existence.

But that's why you're here, isn't it? You're hoping against hope and God, and all manner of other impossible things, that the love of a good person will be enough. Enough to make you stay. Enough to make the feeling, like a knife against your throat, go away. The feeling that begs you to leave, to move, to see the universe in every century, to collect Artefacts like wrinkles on your face, never stopping, never slowing down, until whatever it is that comes for time-travellers at the end visits you and this whole thing is finished. Until you reach the end of time and step off the darkening edge.

He sighed, and strode on. There was no use thinking like that. He was done.

A long time ago, a thirteen-year-old boy laid down to die on the cold, vicious streets of Georgian London. Only a fortuitous combination of the boy's cries, a passing time-traveller, and the inexplicable proximity of a sleeping prince allowed him to survive the night.

The boy was impossible; he was glowing. The boy was Obi Amadi on the brink of combustion. Obi's left arm flickered out of being and did not return. Half of his right eyebrow soon followed suit.

A man in a battered, blood-stained trench coat watched all this from across the street. Nodding to himself, he appeared to come to a decision.

Delicately, purposefully, he took off his coat, and laid it over the boy, placing his hand on the boy's forehead as he did so and whispering something. Then he tucked a folded-up piece of paper into the breast pocket.

The boy twitched, then vanished. Re-appearing almost instantly metres away. This happened several times. The boy was seizing, limbs smacking into the snow as he moved around, unconscious, blinking in and of time.

The man in the trench coat grimaced. He had done what he could to help him, but this was not going to be pretty. He would have felt sorry for the boy, had he not stopped feeling sorry for anyone, himself included, centuries ago on a planet that no longer existed, under the light of its twin moons. The man adjusted his lapels, then stepped sideways into nothingness.

The street lit up, and Obi screamed as his soul Anchored itself to the city of London, saving his life.

Behind heavy cream curtains, in a room where a vase of white tulips sat elegantly on a bedside table, King George IV's only son sat bolt upright in bed, gasping as the image of a boy with eyes the colour of winter rain and skin like dark brown velvet seared itself into his mind.

Carlton House loomed in front of Obi, its Corinthian porticos and Ionic colonnade a grander sight than even the alabaster pilasters and red brick of Buckingham House—his only other point of reference for inner London mansions. *That* building was as engraved into his memory as the inscription above the door. Gold, capital letters that announced '*sic siti laetantur lares*', and Obi laughed every time he read them, though his translation was terrible; the household gods might delight in the situation, but he was considerably less enthusiastic. He was almost regretful that wasn't his destination anymore.

It had been so long.

Three years, to be exact, and the interim hadn't exactly been a holiday.

How do you say to someone: *I'm sorry that I walked out on you. But you reminded me in no uncertain terms that I was alone in this world. So, I left to find the only person I had any reasonable claim to: my father. I thought if I found him, I would understand how to make sense of the world, and my place in it. I even wondered if he would know how to cure me. I searched everywhere, across time. I jumped and jumped through thousands of years, and I lost so much of myself along the way. I didn't care if I lived or died, if that journey or the next would be my last. Because I was so mad at you for what you'd said. But I was furious at myself because it was true.*

I didn't find him.

Will you recognise me? My arm is metal now. So is my left eye, but you won't be able to tell. Three fingers too. Lost a molar, but I didn't bother replacing that. And don't get me started on my bones. I've got more technology in me than exists on this planet, right now. Isn't that incredible?

Will you touch me, again? Will you even talk to me, after all this time?

The fingers of his metal arm clenched into a fist.

He might not have found his father, but all signs pointed to the man being dead anyway. Obi felt the grief pushing upwards through his chest, and shoved it down. He'd suspected it for years. Now it was as good as confirmed, and he was never time-travelling again.

I'm choosing this, he thought fiercely, silencing the voices in his head. *This is a choice, not a failure. And anyway, I'd rather spend time with someone who loved me once, because they chose to, than with a father who was supposed to love me, but couldn't bear to.*

Emerging from behind a beautifully sculpted hedge, he grimaced at the fountain in the courtyard. It was gauche and ridiculous, but at least it wasn't the palace. He recalled his first visit there. The memory was constructed more from what he had been told by others—one person in particular—than any real recollection. The only part of it he knew for sure was his, was the pain. You do not easily forget the way a soul feels when it begins to tear inside your chest, and that had been precisely what Obi had been experiencing; the tearing of his soul as his body prepared to enter the first stages of the Anchoring.

He had also been a complete stranger then, he reminded himself. Now, at least, he was here for a reason. Or two reasons. Two reasons that had become so entangled over the years he had been away that he found them nearly impossible to separate.

Find somewhere to call home; find the man he left behind.

38

Obi forced himself to remember the first time he had stood—lain, collapsed—on steps that looked just like these. Nausea rose in his throat. He choked it down. *Let not the spectres of our past dictate our actions in the present, nor our decisions in the future,* whispered his father's voice in the back of his mind. It was cruel advice in hindsight, but Obi's father had abandoned him when he was only eight years old, and so Obi supposed that he must have been quite a cruel man in general. Cruel or desperate. A familiar melancholy rose up in him. He choked that down, too.

Reaching into his pocket, he withdrew a crumpled, faded slip of paper. The page was torn from a book he had never had the privilege of reading. It had been left to him, one solitary page, by his father, he thought, though he didn't know for certain, and would likely never find out. He'd searched every library he'd ever come across for a copy, but it didn't seem to exist. The first paragraph was circled in what could only be blood. There was a message written on the back in blood, too. Seven words that made no sense. Obi didn't like to read them, or think about them, or acknowledge them, really. So, he didn't. The front was easy, though. The facts of his life laid out in print, cold and non-fictional, and entirely unsympathetic:

PAGE 77 – GUIDING AND ITS PERILS

contracting The Sickness. The Sickness is rare, only affecting those who have not properly been taught their craft by a more experienced Guide, usually a relative or mentor. It is commonly contracted during an Anchoring, as this is when a Guide's physical form is least connected to any realm, and therefore more susceptible to parasitic energies. The Sickness is characterised by the gradual unmaking of the Guide's physical form; limbs may be lost, fingers, even a single eyelash. The stages of the unmaking, i.e. loss of limb, only occur after a Guide has

39

*made a jump. It is unclear why. The Sickness is not contagious. There
is no known cure.*

ANCHORING

*When a Guide turns of age, he must Anchor himself to a time and
place so that he will always be able to return somewhere without
an Artefact* to guide him. He must leave a part of his soul in the
Anchoring Place, or risk never being able to return. Of course, this
means that multiple versions of himself may exist in the same time
in the same general area. If he sees himself, the Guide is strongly
advised to <u>look the other way.</u>*

*(*Artefact: an object that was once, or will be, of massive sentimen-
tal value to persons known or unknown by the Guide. An Artefact
can be commanded to return to its owner by a Guide, and a Guide
only. The sentimental energy of an Artefact can be harnessed and used
to make a jump across space and time to the location of its owner.
Warning: Some Artefacts can be volatile, and cases have been reported
of Artefacts arriving too early in the timeline of their owners. See
page 107: 'Paradoxical Ignition')*

At the bottom of the page, printed in tiny letters was:

THE ORDER OF LEGENDS

The slip of paper had been tucked inside his inner coat pocket
when he had woken, nine years ago, feverish and delirious with
pain, on the icy steps of Buckingham House. He had somehow
wound up inside the curling iron gates, inches from the ornate
double doors.

His pain-muddled brain hadn't noticed the absence of guards.

Or the boy craning his head over the balcony to stare down
at him.

"Who the hell are you?" the boy had half-whispered, half-shouted, his voice rasping on the breeze.

Hardly the beginning of an epic love story, Obi would think later. But nothing about them was conventional, so it seemed to fit.

Nine years, one biomechatronic arm and several misadventures later, Obi had returned to the city, if not to the same house. *Just rip off the bloody plaster. Come on.*

He strode up the final steps towards the doors and executed the appropriate knock with an inappropriate lack of flourish—he was cold, okay—and stepped to the side, out of the sightline of whoever would open it.

The wind whistled through the trees. He felt watched. He put up his hood.

The door opened. A servant looked around in confusion, before leaning against the doorframe and fanning her red face with the cool air. She closed her eyes, enjoying the small break.

That was when Obi raised his left hand and shot her.

There was no bullet—only a small tranquiliser dart, unloaded from a tiny compartment located in his forefinger. *Two left now.* He liked to make his hand into the shape of a gun for vibes, though he realised this was probably inappropriate.

Rushing forward, he caught her as she fell, one hand on the back of her neck to support her head, before placing her gently down behind a cabinet, for a restorative two-hour nap.

A sheaf of papers on the top of the cabinet caught his attention. The daily news, prepared in an official royal document for the person who owned this building, unread. Top story was of course the war. Obi's eyes immediately glazed over in boredom. He turned a few pages. A sketch caught his eye. A low pedestal in a dark room, and a small child, dressed in plain, sterile looking clothes, like something from a modern hospital. The incongruity of it stalled him. He squinted, trying to read the hastily written report in the dim candlelight. He made out the words, "some sort of apparition", "hand passes through it", "light, emanating from a small black box".

Why was a member of the royal family being briefed on—

A noise.

Obi dropped the papers, and darted to the other side of the hallway, tucking his body behind scarlet drapery.

The noise wasn't heard again.

He climbed three flights of stairs in the dark, making his way to the centre of the building, before sliding through a door left ajar by a careless hand.

A golden beam of candlelight spilled into the room from the hallway, falling across the floor, and up the wall opposite Obi, illuminating a painting that made his heart stutter in his chest. A painting that was achingly familiar to him, though he had never seen it before.

Diplomatic brows were drawn into a frown, dark hair swooping over a smooth forehead. A jaw, sharper and angrier than the last time he had seen it, was cast uncharacteristically arrogant over a shoulder, from which gold tassels hung. Badges, and of course, the royal insignia adorned the other.

It was an older face than the one he was used to.

Of course it is, idiot. That's what happens when you don't see someone for three years. They change.

Obi swore softly. Suddenly he wasn't sure if this was even remotely the right thing to be doing. It had seemed right, had seemed like the least he could do, had seemed *decent* of him, until he was eye to eye with a memory he hadn't planned on facing until he had sorted his *entire fucking life out*, and once again found himself wondering what exactly it was one said to a person they had given semi-regular hand-jobs to at seventeen, and maybe loved, but had left before they were really sure.

(Had left because they never wanted to find out.)

The metal fingers of his left arm clenched into a fist.

"Look, I'm sorry," he whispered, unable to stop himself. Compelled to speak by the face in the painting, by the golden light that fell across it like fire from heaven. "I barely know why I've come here. I mean, I do. It's—it's you, it always is, but I . . ." he trailed off. The painting stared back, tall and authoritative and larger than life, but also so much paler and smaller and less *present* than the real thing. "You're so . . ." He closed his eyes tight. "You're my best friend." It was the only thing he could say, frozen as he was by the realisation: *I'm here. So is he. This is Happening.* But at least it was true—perhaps the truest thing about the two of them, after the fact that Obi feared emotional intimacy like most people feared dying early, or the fact that George had once said, *I love you,* to him when they were eighteen, and Obi had replied, *No you don't, no one does,* and George had rolled his eyes and mouthed *fine,* and neither of them had ever come close to saying anything like that since.

It was also true that Obi had loved him back since they had met at thirteen, and that while George had been five years overdue in verbalising the feeling they both knew was there, he might have to wait five more for Obi to be ready to even think about saying it back.

But here was a start.

"I know we said that this wasn't supposed to mean anything." Obi's voice was an echoing murmur in the empty dark. "But I've been reading that book of Ovid that you gave me, and I think, maybe . . . *Oh, I don't know* . . . Maybe I want it to? It's like that one line from *Metamorphoses,* Book Nine, I think, but I can't be certain. Theseus calls to Pirithous, and he says—he says, 'You are more to me—' no, sorry, it's—"

A shadow interrupted the light, throwing a silhouette across the canvas.

"'You mean more to me than myself'," said the prince, who was second in line to the throne of Great Britain. "You who are part of my very soul."

Obi turned around. The shadowy hallway was no longer empty.

"Book Eight," the prince continued, pushing open the door and stepping fully into the antechamber. "Not Nine. It's the battle against the Caledonian Boar. Theseus is telling his . . . his companion, to be careful. He doesn't want to lose him; doesn't want the man he cares most for to leave him for the shade." His face was gaunt, his gaze caustic and cold—so far removed from the dimples and easy smile Obi had once known that he felt the urge to turn and run.

I wasn't dead, he wanted to whisper. *I didn't mean to be away for so long.*

"I imagine," the prince continued, "that he couldn't bear the thought of living in a world where the person he shared his soul with was—" he paused "—absent."

Obi forced his face not to do anything.

"I thought you were dead."

"Well—" Obi started.

"Don't you dare say 'Well, I wasn't'. Don't you *dare*." The prince glared at him, and Obi's body reacted viscerally—this thing they had was muscle memory—his hand flexing and clenching in an aborted attempt at reaching out for some part of George he could hold on to like an anchor—his hand, maybe, or the back of his neck. "It's been three *years*. You lied. I saved your life, and you thanked me with coldness and deception." The prince closed his eyes, his mouth a grim a line. "I cannot even find my anger, anymore." His eyes opened, and Obi realised he had forgotten just how green they were. Just how easily they saw through the theatrics and the persona to settle directly on the truth.

"Why," asked the prince, sotto voce, half-devastated, half something else Obi couldn't name, "are you here?"

Somewhere within himself, Obi found the willpower to break eye contact and step neatly around him. The prince whirled around, raking his hair out of his face.

"You know if you cut it, it wouldn't get in your eyes so much," Obi said, smiling weakly. "You look good, though. Maybe it's the crown, I'm not sure yet. Perhaps I need a closer look."

"Do not do this. Do *not*—" The prince made a choked sound. "You cannot just waltz in here and act like nothing has changed."

"Well, if I can't waltz then it's your fault," Obi said. "You taught me."

The prince took a breath. "We were nineteen-years-old. The way I felt for you—"

"Don't," Obi said, aware he was being cruel, but unable to stop himself. "I've had a really long day."

"You left when I needed you most," the prince replied. "Would it do you such an injury to take something seriously? Do you not owe me at least that? *At the very least?*" His shoulders slumped the slightest bit, and Obi wanted to go to him, to lift his chin with his hands, and say, *hey, everything is going to be alright*. But he couldn't, not now that he'd ruined everything good between them, so instead he bit down a *maybe* and looked up.

"George, I can explain—"

The prince held up a hand. It was a thoughtlessly regal gesture, and it instantly killed the explanation on Obi's tongue. He realised that he had just said George's name aloud for the first time in three years. It was the name used only by those closest to him, an informal name his eccentric father had used since he was a boy. When he ascended the throne, it would change.

Everything would change. *Augustine,* Obi thought. *I don't even know who that is. Who would I be to him?*

The boy who—no, the *man,* who was second in line to the throne, after his father the Prince Regent, who would become, formally, King Augustine I, upon his ascension, stared at Obi with old anguish in his eyes.

"Well, you can't do it here. Come to my rooms, we can get some food brought up." He gestured at Obi's lean frame, at his high, pinched, and jutting cheekbones. "It might do you some good."

And the planet remembered her name. Mother, She had been called once, though She did not know by whom. Struck by this newfound knowledge, and hungering for more, She sent one of Her heroes back in time, to the chaos that churned at the beginning of it all. It was Sensit She sent, and so it was upon Sensit She bestowed the first of Her gifts. A sword, made of crystal, shot through with gold, and imbued with powers that would reveal themselves, in time, and when if he proved himself to be worthy.

'A Complete, Annotated History of Chasca, Including Relevant Translated Mythologies. Chapter: Scroll the First' by I. Nisomn, ex-acolyte of the Aonian Archives.

(Archivist's note: The replacement of 'when' with 'if' in a contested revision to cast doubt on the inevitability of Sensit's worthiness is interesting, in that it implies his worthiness was not inevitable after all. We had thought the title 'hero' assumed as much already and so find ourselves re-calibrating our own definitions of the concept.)

Chapter Three

The air inside the alleyway was cool. Asha's eyes adjusted slowly, her vision still swimming with the images she had seen when she'd locked eyes with the stranger.

The boy with grey eyes. A planet, viewed from space, imploding. A gaunt woman wrapping her arms around Asha's middle and whispering *sister.*

She shook her head, which ached just thinking about it. Now was not the time to be distracted—

A cold, bony hand slammed into her throat and squeezed.

Sharp nails dug into her skin as the stranger lifted her clean off the ground and swung her into the alley wall. She crashed against it, teeth slamming together, head ringing on impact. Bright white light bloomed across her vision as she fought for breath, her heels kicking uselessly at the wall.

Blazing eyes met hers.

"Stop *moving*," came a voice like gravel, "or I shall be forced to separate your head from your body and deprive the third and final prophecy of its chosen warrior."

Asha thought, *whatever the fuck that means,* and kicked him in the crotch.

The stranger jerked backwards in surprise, dropping her instantly. With the sharp movement, the deep cowl of his

47

cloak—already pushed back at an angle during their brief scuffle—slipped and fell around his shoulders.

She saw it almost in slow motion.

The black material falling past papery skin, across which thick black stitches ran in irregular seams, grey-browns and sallow yellows sewn together in patches like a handmade quilt, stretching ill-fittingly over a harshly planed and pointed skull.

The eyes that stared back at her, with a strange mixture of shock and anger, were so blue that Asha felt nauseous—it was a toxic colour, bright and sickly, that seemed to have no edge, fading seamlessly into the sclera, like a sapphire sky into thickening clouds, as though his irises were simply dissolving. And his pupils . . . jagged stars of black burst over the surface of his eyes, like dark cracks on the frozen surface of an icy pond. His mouth was a red gash, the teeth inside it thin, like needles. But strangest of all were the tattoos. Tiny, rune-like images etched into his skin, seemingly at random. Asha saw a pair of overlapping diamonds, a sword, several triangles. Something that looked like a double-headed axe. A crown. Many were faded, though some seemed newer. One, near the bridge of his nose, was still crusted in blood, no doubt from the needle that had recently drawn it.

They gazed at each other. Asha, sprawled on the floor, staring upwards in dumbstruck disbelief, and the stranger . . .

Well, Asha faked reverence every day to stay alive, but years of practice had never brought her this close to the real thing.

"You're really her," he murmured. "Aren't you? The other daughter."

Asha was barely listening. White spots swam in and out of her vision, the back of her head pulsing in pain where it had cracked against the stone wall.

"Get up," came that voice again, and then there was a hand

on her arm, yanking her into a standing position.

Scrabbling against the wall for support, she swayed on her feet, clutching her stomach.

"Who are you?" she asked, her voice weak with pain.

"I do not have time for the confused questions of a child. Your mother should have told you. I told her to tell you everything. Eighteen years, and—" he made a noise of frustration "—there is no time for this."

"No! You have to tell me." She coughed. "*Please.* I heard your voice in my head. When you looked at me, I—I saw things. What did I see? And how do I—how do I know you? *Why is there something inside me that knows you?*"

The stranger's eyes darted to the mouth of the alley, almost as though he were watching for someone . . . or waiting to be discovered.

You're not supposed to be here, are you?

"I'll scream," she blurted. "If you don't explain to me what just happened, who you are, and exactly what you want from me and my mother, I'll scream, and the guards will come running, and I'll say I was attacked by an off-worlder. I'll say that someone was trying to steal from the Emperor."

Silence.

She tried one last time, measuring her words, speaking slowly, as though this would stop him from dismissing her again.

"*What* are you?" She needed to understand what had happened to her when he had looked into her eyes, how she had heard his voice echoing inside her head. "*And how do you know my name?*"

"What I am," he said finally, "is the worst thing that has ever happened to you." His mouth split open in a smile that seemed to Asha equal parts mocking and sad. "But you will call me Sentinel. The Sentinel of the Order of Legends."

His name was nothing to her—another impossible thing in

49

an hour filled with them. But she knew a cult when she heard one. *You will call me Sentinel.* She knew a threat when she heard one, too. *The worst thing that has ever happened to you.*

"Why? What are you going to do to me?"

The Sentinel shook his head. "That is the wrong question. But how can I blame you? Raised in ignorance by a coward, kept in the dark at the cost of—"

"What are you talking about?"

"Not what, *who.* Your mother, who would hide you and doom the galaxy, because she didn't want to see another child get hurt," he sneered. "You would think after the first one she'd be used to it by now. She knew I was coming for you. Did she tell you that?"

"No." she replied, feeling two feet tall. "That—that's not true. She doesn't know you." But even now she remembered his hand on her mother's face. The way her mother's eyes had closed.

"In this galaxy, truth died a long time ago," the Sentinel said coldly. "There are only stories left, and this one we are living is being told by a master. After we die, it will pass into legend. So, all we truly have left is what we hold in our hands." He looked down at her. "And you."

"Me?"

"Listen very carefully to what I am about to tell you." Chills erupted down Asha's spine. "There is something starting—out there." He pointed to the dark purple dusk and the stars beyond it. "Something that has been readying itself for many years, lying in wait for the right person, and I am so sorry to tell you, little girl: you are that person." He pinned her with his gaze. Asha couldn't look away. It was like staring out over a hundred-metre drop into the sea. "I wish that it were not so, because you are not ready, and I am unsure if I can make you ready. But we have run out of time, and so it has to be you, Asha. I don't have

50

time to teach you what it means to be a hero, so you must learn another way."

Asha did not understand.

"When you looked into my eyes, you saw things that have not yet come to pass. The true name for this is a word in a language that is dead now, but we can name it *calling*. You are being called."

"How did you know—"

"It does not matter. You will know in time. But you felt it, didn't you?

His eyes are too blue, Asha thought, nonsensically. *Like a warning on a desert snake's scales: exposure to me will kill you, stay away.* "Felt what?" her voice was a murmur.

"The golden light," he said, then hesitated. "The prophecy."

Prophecy? Asha barely knew what that word meant, but there was a feeling, growing inside her like a fast-acting poison. Cold wrapped around her limbs, her heart beating faster, and in her mind was a huge and darkening sense that something awful and incomprehensible was happening to her. Something bigger than her mind could hold.

The Sentinel reached into his cloak and withdrew a small black box with a slit in the top and a symbol on the side, a triangle with a tiny circle in the middle. It almost looked like an eye. He gave it to her, and she found herself accepting it, too numb with shock to do anything else.

"A long time ago," he said, his voice like metal scraping on rock, "when I was a boy, there was no empire."

That was three hundred years ago, Asha thought. *That is impossible.*

"There was no Emperor, the hundred worlds had not yet been unified, there had not been a galactic war. But there was a prophecy. Born of a planet whose prophecies always came to pass. Unfortunately, it went wrong. A great civilisation fell." He looked pained, as though in telling her this, he was debasing himself. As though this nonsensical story was as sacred as a prayer, and she wasn't worthy of receiving it. "Of that place, and that people, nothing remains. Except me . . . Or so I thought. A few years ago, I became aware of a great power flowing through the universe, looking for something. It eventually led me here, to your mother, and then to you." His eyes bored into hers. "I've been waiting to meet you, Asha. I've been waiting a very long time. The prophecy is born again, and this time it will not fail, *I will not let it*." His voice was a hiss now. "And I know now that chosen people rarely walk into the tempering fires of prophecy of their own accord. Sometimes, they need a push."

He reached out to her, grasping her hand. She recoiled—

But he was only reaching for the box, pressing a small button on its side.

The hologram built itself in front of her at lightning speed, photons swarming from the box to construct a figure, looking at someone past the recording device. The seal of the Consortium rotated benignly in the top corner. This was government footage. The recording showed a young girl. Standing on the ground, she would have only come up to Asha's hip. Deep brown skin took on a blue cast in the hologram's cold light, her big, dark eyes and darker lashes were set into a thin face, with a chin pointed just like Asha's had been at that age, before she'd grown into the strong, angry jaw that adolescence had handed her. The girl's head was completely shaved, which made Asha wince, but she imagined that if she'd had hair, it would have been tightly curled, just like Asha's was. Just like her mother's.

The girl picked something up off the ground and motioned for something else—or someone, perhaps, a person standing past the camera's scope. "Is anyone there?" Her voice was tinny on the old projector, and eerily high-pitched.

I've seen you before, Asha thought. The girl in the hologram was younger, and healthier looking, but there was no doubt in Asha's mind. She was looking at the same person that she'd seen when she'd stared into the Sentinel's eyes and dreamed with her eyes open, preserved in a hologram, recorded a decade or so ago. The woman who had pulled her into her arms and said—

Sister.

"Where did you get this?" Her voice was low.

"It was taken from the Emperor's private databank. It was one of a few files my organisation managed to salvage," said the Sentinel. "That girl is your mother's first daughter." He paused, before delivering his killing blow. "The one she had before she arrived on Gahraan."

Asha's heart stopped. *What do you mean?* she wanted to yell. *My mother was born here.* But the words wouldn't come. Shock and fear constricted her throat, making it hard to breathe. She sucked in air, but it wasn't enough.

"No," was all she could say. "I don't—No—" And all she could see was her vision, like a video, superimposed over reality. A woman, who looked just like her, gripping her wrist, pulling her forward—

The other daughter. That's what he'd said, as soon as he'd seen her up close.

Asha backed away, she wanted to put as much space between her and this man as possible. She didn't know why she'd follow-ed him here. Suddenly her convictions, her desperate need to understand what she'd seen, were gone. She wanted to rewind, to go back to a time when she didn't know any of this.

The Sentinel didn't let her get far. Moving faster than Asha would have thought possible, he grabbed her shoulder, his long fingers digging into her skin.

"You must find your sister," he said. "She is the key; I am certain of it. The one with the power to end this."

"What are you saying?"

"You must find a way off this planet." He stared fiercely at her.

You are desperate, she thought. *You are desperate and you've been desperate for a long time.*

"You must leave this place. Journey through the stars, to the Emperor's stronghold. To A'lkari. That's where your sister is being kept."

A'lkari.

"I'm not going anywhere," Asha spat back. "Why should I believe you? Believe any of this? What makes you think that I'll—"

"You *must* find her. The fate of the hundred worlds depends on it." His face softened, just for a moment. "In time you will understand. And in advance of your understanding, I must tell you . . . I am sorry." He paused. "I must also tell you something else."

The moonlight seemed to carve his face out of the very darkness itself and Asha couldn't help but think it the strangest, oldest face she'd ever seen.

"If you do not do exactly as I say, your mother will die."

Adesola slew demon after demon, culling the creatures from the Mother's surface with savage precision. Her weapon—the weapon bestowed upon her by the planet, the shield of shining crystal and wrought gold—was smooth as one of the facets of the crystal from which she had been born, strong as her will, its edge razor sharp. The shield saved her life as she tried to save Life itself, and so they were bonded. Gatekeeper; protector.

She was alone, as Mother had sent Sensit back in time, and spirited Dandeyi away to the opposite side of the planet, to cut their own way through the demons there. But thoughts of her heroes-in-arms never left her, and in their courage, she found her own.

'A Complete, Annotated History of Chasca, Including Relevant Translated Mythologies. Chapter: Scroll the First' by I. Nisomn, ex-acolyte of the Aonian Archives.

(Archivist's note: A shield of this description has appeared several times throughout myth and, indeed, throughout history. We wonder if there might be a connection—a physical artefact passed down through generations, perhaps—or if it is simply a metaphor for the unspeakable violence often committed in the name of protection.)

Chapter Four

[planet: Earth] + **[location: London]** + **[year: 1812]**

George's rooms were different to the ones he had occupied the last time Obi had seen him. Back then, George had been on the cusp of nineteen, still living with his family at Buckingham House. In basic ways, they were similar—cream curtains, heavy with their gold brocade, hounds and horses painted in oils, family portraits hanging next to ornate lamps, and a four-poster double bed, complete with ivory and crimson hangings and a twisting golden frame.

His eyes settled briefly on the lock on the door, and he remembered turning one just like it, a hundred lifetimes ago, the slow flip of his stomach as he spun around into George's lucid gaze and the tension that had appeared between them one day and grown and grown until—

If Obi closed his eyes, he could almost hear his younger self reading passages aloud from the *Aeneid*, could almost hear the stupid voices they'd put on and the clash of imaginary swords in fight scenes they'd meticulously copied. He remembered standing over George, once, and driving a poker towards his chest, slowing it at the last second so that it came to rest in the hollow of his clavicle. They'd stared at each other. Personally, Obi thought that to be the moment George had realised he didn't always need to be in control, and that maybe he could cede the

56

reins to someone else once in a while, and like it.

In a horrible, brilliant epiphany, Obi realised he had forgotten what it felt like to be a boy, horsing around with another boy, with no one else's opinion present in the room. To be back here was to come full circle—he had grown up sneaking into a room just like this one from the window; he had become a young man with his back against the headboard of a bed just like that one, holding George as he moved against him, trying not to fall in love.

And now he was back; and now he was a man, almost, with a couple of years of shiny new trauma added to sweeten the deal.

George's presence behind him was so loud Obi felt as if he were drowning in unspoken confessions. He did not turn around.

"Do you still have it?" he asked, smothering the desperation in his voice with a nonchalance he did not feel.

"Yes."

"Can I see it?"

"Don't you trust me?"

Ah, Obi thought. *There you are.*

Then, he turned.

"Funny," he said. "I remember someone asking me that question a few years ago. He looked like you. Couldn't have been, though—he was a lot nicer. Smiled more."

George's face was a mask of control. *It fits him well*, Obi thought.

"Do you have *any* idea what I've been through these past few years?" George asked. "Do you have any idea what I've dealt with?" He shook his head—a precise, controlled movement. "No, how could you? You vanished without a trace. All you left behind was that box." He pinched the bridge of his nose between thumb and forefinger. Obi had forgotten that he did that. "I did what you asked of me," George continued. "I never opened it."

Obi closed his eyes in relief.

"Also, you have two arms now. Don't think I didn't notice. Though of course if anyone were ever to leave a place with one arm and return three years later with two, it would be you ... Obi Amadi: the impossible boy, returned. I should make it a national holiday. Which I can do now, by the way."

"Careful, George. Don't let that dashing crown inflate your own sense of self-importance any more than it already is."

"Bastard."

Oh, Obi thought, and hated himself briefly for being excited. *He's mad.*

"Well, according to the rumours, that's you, actually."

George's face flushed an angry scarlet. "How *dare* you insinuate—"

"Oh, relax. I'd forgotten you couldn't take a joke."

That was a bold-faced lie—George took jokes just as well as he delivered them: delightfully cutting, yet tempered always by kindness—but Obi needed to get to that box, and riling George up had always been a good way to get what he wanted in the past. Possibly, he thought, looking at George's furious scowl, things were different now.

"The night you pulled me in from the snow ..." Obi started, then stopped, cringing at his own sudden seriousness. He tried again—a different tack. "I wouldn't have asked, you know. I—I wouldn't have asked you to keep it safe if I didn't trust you." This last part came out closer to a mumble.

"Oh, please," George replied, cheeks flushed. "I was there, and I was convenient. A boy appeared under my balcony writhing in pain, one arm gone, clutching at my nightshirt and begging me to catch a part of his soul as it was trying to leave his body.

And I did, in a *snuff box* that I grabbed from the mantlepiece. I think about it and it feels surreal, but what else was I to do? I'd seen you in my dreams! I wanted to believe it was fate, or God, or something even more incredible, and it was. It was *you*, and it was the beginning of—of *whatever this is*, and sometimes I wish I had never bloody met you, but more often than that I wish we could go back."

He was breathing rather heavily now, green eyes bright like chips of emerald in the lamplight, his hands clenching and un-clenching by his sides, and Obi wanted to say, *go back to what, exactly? Me pushing you away at every turn, because I'm apparently physically incapable being in a functioning relationship? And you, saying that it didn't matter we could never be anything real because you had to be king one day, pretending like this was even close to enough for you, feeling the way that you did.*

But he didn't say that, and George turned away, walking over to his dresser and opening the bottom drawer. When he withdrew his hand, a box rested in his palm.

Three years later and he hadn't opened it.

Had it been it worth it? Obi thought bitterly. *Running into the future pretending like your father was the only reason? Had it been worth all the distance, all the centuries you shoved in between him and you like barbed wire, hoping it would prick and draw blood, until you were both made strangers to each other by the pain?*

Closing the distance between them in a few short strides, George placed the box in Obi's outstretched hand.

"Key, please," Obi said, without looking at him. George reached into his shirt—Obi glanced up in curiosity—and drew a chain from around his neck. A golden key dangled on the end next to a small circular piece of metal with something inscribed on it that Obi couldn't make out. George's face flushed immediately, but he met Obi's eyes, steadily, unabashedly.

Suppressing a smile, Obi took the key on its chain and unceremoniously shoved it in the lock, twisting once. The lid sprung open, and a bright white glow spilled out. Pure points of light scattered across the ceiling and the walls behind them, limned with rainbow, out of focus and soft.

From inside the box rose a bright sphere, so bright they had to squint to see past the glare and make out the miracle at its core, the cluster of little lights that formed it gently rotating around a central source.

"Obi?" George whispered, but Obi was too enthralled by the box's light to respond. This light was *his* light—the light of his soul. Proof that he had one, even if it wasn't all in one piece. And it was safe. Safe with the only person who cared enough about him to ensure it remained that way. He could finally breathe.

"So," he said, snapping the box shut, and looking pointedly around George's bedroom—or bed*rooms*, rather. "You moved out, huh?"

". . .Yes." George looked confused at the swift change of subject, but played along. "As soon as I was of age. I worked with the architects myself, designed it. It isn't complete, though—not for a few years."

Obi whistled through his teeth. "You know this place is ridiculous, right?"

George grinned. "Yes, well, my grandfather says the only two things I'm good for are spending his money and dragging the family name through the mud."

"How is he?"

George turned away—sinking half of his face into the shadows that the candles had failed to banish. "Oh," he said. "You know."

"It's really that bad?"

George shrugged. "He is nearing the end of his life, and his legacy leaves much to be desired. He lost America. He lost his influence in Parliament. While he was King, his ministers became a laughing stock, and it wasn't too long ago the papers were reporting on prominent political radicals being welcome in his profligate son's inner circle." His voice was measured. "He is so ill he cannot tell friend from foe. Politically speaking, he is useless. Constitutionally speaking, he is dead."

"And your father?"

George's eyes darkened, candlelight shining in his pupils. "He is Regent only in title. He spends most of his time with his mistress, throwing parties, drinking himself to death. I try not to see him. Sometimes he writes to me but I can never bring myself to respond in earnest."

Obi was silent. If George had been literally anyone else, he could have said, *is there anything I can do?* But Obi couldn't change anything, and there was no reality in which George's family situation wasn't incredibly messed up, on account of him having been born into the self-serving, poisonous abomination that was the British Monarchy. He had been sentenced as soon as he was born, as soon as he began to be a man, to a complete and total divorce from the emotional support a young person might wish to have from his father, or his grandfather. He knew that, had always known it, as long as Obi had known him. So Obi said, instead, "Well, *I'd* like to formally apologise. For being a dickhead." The last part came out as a mumble, but it was a start.

George blinked again at the second swift change of subject, but looked undeniably grateful for it. "Are you feeling quite alright?" He raised an eyebrow. "It's only that, well, forgive me, but that word sounds distinctly unfavourable." He shrugged, looking a little too pleased. "And I do not believe I have ever had the pleasure of hearing you cast yourself in any other light but the most favourable kind, before." He smiled cautiously, as though he wasn't sure if he was quite allowed, and Obi felt that feeling rising in his chest, hot and surging—traitorous—and so, so *persistent* that thousands of light-years and the icy vacuum of space couldn't make it any less than what it wanted so badly to be.

"I missed you," Obi said, because he was an entire twenty-two-year-old, and if he couldn't talk about his feelings now, when could he?

"Yes, I know," George replied. "You announced it to the entire atrium."

Okay, he was never talking about his feelings again. He blanched. "Do you think anyone *heard*?"

"Besides me?" George smirked. "I know for certain that several people heard. Fortunately for you, I have assured them that retaining any memory of declarations made by strange men in my entrance halls—specifically ones regarding their utterly overwhelming loneliness—is not expected of them, nor something they will see reflected in their salaries. That said, they are being compensated as we speak." A smile played around his mouth. "You are still my most reluctantly kept secret, I'm afraid."

Oh my god, Obi thought. *You grew up while I wasn't here.* What he said was, "So competently handled," only half-sarcastic, walking over to one of the low couches and settling onto it. "But I have notes: firstly, there is a difference between missing someone and being lonely, they're not mutually exclusive, so jot that down. Secondly, can we *pretty please* pretend you didn't hear any of that, because it's actually *incredibly embarrassing*." He scowled—though his feelings were trending closer to barely restrained, completely unadulterated joy, than actual anger or even embarrassment—and settled back further into the plush velvet of the couch cushions.

"Anything else?" George asked, amused, leaning against his dresser, long legs kicked out in front of him, hands braced on the hardwood.

"Oh yeah." Obi grinned. "Do you do that for all the girls—you know, *bribing* and all that—or am I just that special?"

George shook his head, tipping his chin down and whispering, *"all the girls,"* as if to say, *I am exasperated beyond coherent thought and it is entirely your fault.* Then he looked up through the hair that had fallen over his forehead, smiling, and suddenly Obi was fifteen again—falling hard for a prince who made him laugh so hard he cried; who saw the good in him when he couldn't see it in himself. A prince who smiled stoically through the pain of the stress fractures that the weight of a country-sized responsibility caused in his heart.

He looked away, out of the window.

George said, "You want me to say there hasn't been anyone else."

"No," Obi replied, "because that would be stupid. Also, you're not my boyfriend."

George looked sharply away. "I'd forgotten how it feels to—" the tips of his ears coloured slightly "—to talk with you about this. No one else says it so plainly." He shook his head. "And anyway, that is out of the question."

"Oh, I bet it is."

"Obi, *you* said—"

"I know what I said." He tried to meet George's eye, but lost his nerve. "Look, just forget it."

"Tell me how I possibly can, and I will."

Obi looked sharply back towards George. He was glaring at him intensely, accusation writ plain across his face. "You said this was a relationship of convenience, but I heard you in the entrance hall. You said we would never be together because the world did not want us to be, or else it would have made us both commoners, or be born in the year 2000, whatever *that* means, or it would've made you a prince, too."

"George . . ." Obi stood up. He had no idea why he did it—vague notions about them being on equal footing—but he found his feet walking, crossing the room in three long strides, until he stood in front of George, looking up slightly into his eyes. He opened his mouth to say something, literally anything at all, but then he saw—*truly saw*—that the anger in George's face was actually a very deep sadness—and suddenly there was nothing in his head except the past; nothing in his heart except the things he'd thought it had forgotten.

The last time they had stood here like this, they had just been teenagers, not yet adept at dealing appropriately with any emotion—certainly not any even a little close to love.

But they were older now.

George reached up, and touched Obi's face. "Why are you here? Really?"

Obi tried to speak, but he couldn't. "I don't know."

"I won't make this complicated if that isn't what you want."

Obi pulled gently on George's neck, so that they were eye to eye. Their noses nearly touched. "Thank you," he said, quietly. *Tell him,* the voice in his head reminded him. *Tell him you're back for good.* But all he could mumble was, "I'm not even sure what I want anymore."

"I remember what you used to," George said, his voice catching slightly. "I can remind you, if you'd let me. I haven't forgotten."

"I haven't, either." Obi pressed his forehead to George's and looked at the ground. "Wait, George—"

"What is it?" George murmured, mind clearly on other things.

"I'm staying." Obi felt him go tense beneath his hands. "For good this time. I'm not leaving again. That's why I'm here. And

I'm sorry. I'm so sorry about last time. That was wrong, but I want to explain."

George stepped back. "Staying?" his face was a mask. The excitement scrubbed from it by shock, barely concealed. "In London?"

"Yes."

"For the night? Or . . . the week?"

"No," Obi sighed. "No, I'm here for . . ." He shrugged. "I'm staying. Forever."

George looked . . . Obi couldn't read this expression. Halfway between utter disbelief and resignation.

"Obi, I do not think—"

"I'm back, for good, George. And I came here to tell you that. So. There. I said it." Obi sighed. "And don't ask me how, but I'll figure it out." Once he'd started talking, he couldn't stop. "And I know things are different now. Between us. That they have to be, because of who you are, and who I'm not. And maybe you don't feel as you used to, but I think—I think I do—"

"I do." George's voice was quiet, but sure. His cheeks burned red, and he wouldn't meet Obi's eyes. "Obi, you have such terrible timing, but I do. I do."

"Look, I'm not asking you to make a decision right now, or say anything you don't mean. But tonight . . . we can have one night, can't we? Before we have to think of practical things?"

"One night," George echoed. "Obi, you do not understand. Everything has changed, since you left. Everything, and I—"

"One night." Obi said. "Please?"

He asked again because George had never been able to say no to him twice—and it was an out too, for both of them.

One night. No consequences, no conversations.

Obi felt him relax—it was a full-body thing for George, who carried himself like the weight of the world was on his shoulders and humanity itself would perish if he slackened a single spinal ligament. He nodded, stepping forward until his soft hair brushed Obi's forehead, and then he took Obi's chin in his fingertips and tilted it upwards, before kissing him, open mouthed and a little desperate, sliding his other hand into Obi's back pocket and pulling their bodies flush up against each other, so that there was no part of them that wasn't touching.

Obi kissed George like he was water and Obi was ablaze. George kissed Obi like he had everything to give and nothing at all to lose, though that couldn't have been further from the truth. They tangled up in each other, desperate and clutching, breathing hard. Obi groaned into George's mouth, winding his hand into the front of George's stupid lacy shirt and pressing him against the nearest wall. One of his hands slid up the smooth wallpaper, forcing their bodies impossibly closer. George lifted his knee, hooking his calf under Obi's thigh, pressing them together, and then Obi was swearing and lifting him clean off the floor and onto the dresser, ornaments and inkwells and paperweights clattering to the floor. George put a hand on his shoulder, pushing him back.

"What?" Obi said.

"Your shirt," There was red high on George's cheeks, and his pupils, blown dark and wide, seemed to be searching for something in Obi's face. "Why is it still on your body?"

They wrestled out of most of their clothes, Obi grabbing George by the waist, and helping him off the dresser and on to the bed, where he lay, looking for all the world like a painting of a young man rather than the real thing. Obi could imagine the title: *Prince in a circlet of gold laid low by a treacherous heart.* Obi was reminded of the fact that sometimes George felt far away and untouchable. But no, actually, he was right there, practically begging Obi to put his hands all over him. So he did just that, fitting himself against the planes of George's body, pressing him into the sheets, twisting his fingers into his hair.

The ice-cold front that George put on for other people had fallen away, leaving him warm and pliable under Obi's hands. Obi felt a heavy heat pool in his stomach.

Is this what you wanted? whispered a voice in the back of his head. *Back where you were three years ago, still a secret kept by a prince, nowhere to go and no one to go with, because the one person who loves you is tied to this place by the blood in his veins and the crown on his head. In a few years, he will be a king. And what will you be?*

Obi pulled away, the heat of George's mouth obvious in its absence. He gazed at George's shoulders, broader than before. His jaw, his red mouth, the traces of stubble that had barely been there three years previously. He dragged his gaze past the long, smooth column of his neck and his rosily flushed cheeks, all the way to his eyes. They were old eyes. Older than the twenty-two-year-old to whom they belonged.

George leaned forward, not noticing his hesitance, and kissed him slowly. "Wake me up before you go tomorrow morning," he said. "I want to say goodbye this time."

Obi felt something inside him melt—the last chip of ice surrounding his heart, his resolve, maybe.

"I'm not going anywhere. We can see each other whenever we want now, remember?"

George looked away.

"Okay, I will," Obi said. "I promise. Happy now?"

George nodded. "Yes."

Sensit fell backwards through time at Mother's behest. She had instructed him to gather knowledge, to attempt to understand the origins of their Life-less world, as she had forgotten. His journey took him twelve days and twelve nights, and by the time it was over, he found himself ~~bettered~~ changed.

It was silent, at the Beginning.

'A Complete, Annotated History of Chasca, Including Relevant Translated Mythologies. Chapter: Scroll the First' by I. Nisomn, ex-acolyte of the Aonian Archives.

(Archivist's note: He has crossed out 'bettered' and replaced it with 'changed' in a second revision. The neutrality of this word interests us, and in our opinion, changes the meaning drastically. Nisomn himself was changing as he researched this, we think. For better or for worse, we do not know. Clearly, neither did he.)

Chapter Five

[planet: Gahraan] + **[location: The Lower Quarter]** +
[year: 6066]

Asha had never run so fast in her life.

The Sentinel's grating voice echoed in her ears. *If you do not do as I say, your mother will die.* She hadn't stuck around to hear what he had to say after that, she had just stared at him for a single agonising moment, realising that she might already be too late, that he might have had an accomplice waiting to take her mother, that this whole charade in the alleyway, the hologram and the story, his chilling directive, was likely just a distraction. Then she had run.

Her street was empty. Curfew was minutes away and she was the only one to be out so late, stupidly close to getting sanctioned.

Placing her hand on the touchpad by the doorway of the family unit she shared with her mother, she stepped over the threshold as the door slid open with a faint hiss, revealing the sparse insides.

"Hello?"

"Asha, I can explain," said a voice.

Asha yelled, half in shock, half relief. Her mother stood on the other side of the unit, hands clenched into nervous fists by her sides. Asha ran to her, throwing herself into her mother's chest, wrapping her arms around her, pressing her cheek into the cool skin of her mother's neck, breathing in.

"I—" Asha could barely speak. "I thought you'd be *dead*, I don't understand what's happening—that man, he said—"

"He told you, didn't he?" Her mother was shaking, shudders trembling through her.

"What?" Asha whispered. *No,* she thought. *No, no, no—*

"He told you about her. Your sister."

Asha stilled. She stepped back.

Iyanda was a wreck. Dark circles bruised her under-eyes. Her tight regulation bun was in disarray, locs falling out of it over her face. Usually, her mother was a calm, collected person. She didn't shake, as she did now, didn't wring her hands like a worried child, or look over her shoulder every few seconds in abject terror, like she was waiting for the end of the world to come crashing through her front door.

"Mama," the dread was back, crawling its way across her skin. "Please, what's happening?"

"Asha." Her mother's voice was quiet, her gaze trained on the floor. "You need to listen very carefully to what I am about to tell you."

"*Mama, I don't understand—*"

"You must!" Her mother finally looked at her. "You *must* understand. So, for once in your life, don't fight me. Just listen." Her voice sounded strange. Tinny, almost, and far away. Asha shook her head, trying to focus. Her head throbbed where the Sentinel had thrown her into the wall.

"The man who was here—what did he tell you?"

"That he was going to kill you! We should tell someone, the guards—they'll protect the interest of the empire and keep us safe. I know we shouldn't make ourselves stand out, but he threatened to kill you, Mama—"

70

"No guards." Iyanda's tone was final. "Asha, please, I need you to focus. What did he say?"

Asha realised she was still clutching the hologram in her sweaty palm. "This," she said. "He gave me this. And told me to find her, or he would kill you. He said she was the only one powerful enough to stop it. I don't know what."

Iyanda was looking at the hologram projector in a daze. She reached for it, hands trembling, and turned it around, looking for the on button. She pressed it.

Between them, a ghost surged into being, glowing gently in the dark of their room.

"Oh my god," Iyanda pressed her hand to her mouth with such force the skin went pale. "That's her?" She looked at Asha. There were tears in her eyes. "He gave you this?"

Asha nodded.

Wiping her eyes, Iyanda switched off the hologram. Silence filled the room. For a minute, neither of them spoke. *There's too much to say*, Asha thought.

How was this possible? How could she have a *sister*? A sister—if the Sentinel was to be believed—detained on *A'lkari*. The Emperor's stronghold. Nausea gripped her, just thinking that name.

"So, it's true?" Asha said finally. "I have a—a sister?"

Iyanda nodded.

"How?" Asha swallowed, desperately trying to hold it together so that she could understand. "Why didn't you tell me?"

This didn't feel real. It had always been her and Iyanda against the world, against everyone and everything in it that had tried to tear them down. In a not so small way, this felt like betrayal. The Sentinel's words echoed in her mind. *Raised in ignorance by a coward, kept in the dark, at the cost of . . .*

Of what?

Her mother was no coward, but the Sentinel had known things about Asha that no one else could know. Had known things about her mother that Asha herself didn't. Had spoken about Iyanda like they'd met before. Not only that. Like they knew each other. What did he know about her mother?

"When did this happen?" Asha asked, unsure about how to proceed, but desperate for information—anything that could help her make sense of this.

"Twenty-three years ago," her mother murmured. "It feels like a lifetime has passed since then."

Twenty-three years, Asha thought. She had so many questions. How did the Emperor get her? How did this alien, the Sentinel, know this about her mother, a human, when Asha didn't. How had she—

Hold on.

Twenty-three? Asha's logician brain snagged on that number. Twenty-three years ago . . .

She frowned, trying to find the flaw in the logic of it, the inconsistency that was ringing alarm bells softly in the back of her mind.

Asha's supposed sister was twenty-three years old. She had clearly been born after humanity's attempted settlement on Gahraan—her date of birth had to be sometime in 6043.

6043 . . .

Her heart dropped. She felt light-headed. *It couldn't be.*

Humanity had had two years of peace after landing. 6026 to 6028; enough time to terraform four spots in the desert of the planet's southern hemisphere, before Thracin had discovered the 'infestation'. He'd enforced a strict population cap and conscripted half of humanity into his army, leaving the other half to starve, until one day a construction force touched down in the red dust and started building huge concrete buildings in long rows. The warehouses.

Her mother's parents had both been conscripted, leaving Iyanda alone. She had been raised in the group creche for a few years until she was old enough to live by herself. Or so Asha had always been told. As for her father—that subject was as good as banned.

The population cap had ended in 6048, a solution to the workforce that had been dwindling for twenty years. The sibling – *sister* – she had become aware of a mere hour earlier had supposedly been born in 6043. She was twenty-three. But there were no twenty-three-year-olds on Gahraan. You were either over thirty-eight—born on the ship, or in the two peaceful years after settlement—or eighteen and under, born after the cap had ended.

It was impossible.

Either her mother had managed to conceal a pregnancy, the birth of a child, and then *an actual child* during the invasion . . . or the alien was right.

That girl is your mother's first daughter. The one she had before she arrived on Gahraan.

Asha and Iyanda stared at each other. She had no doubt her mother had seen the cogs turning in her mind, the realisation on her face. Iyanda went to speak, but hesitated, and Asha had to restrain herself from placing her hands over her own mother's mouth to silence whatever confirmation was coming, from saying *no, don't. I don't think I can take anymore.*

Then her mother spoke. "When I was brought to this planet, I was alone—" and re-arranged Asha's entire world in half a sentence, dissolving the fundamental truths of her reality in less time than it took to charge up a gun and shoot it, in a voice so quiet Asha had to strain to hear her do it, to unravel a lifetime of untruths, unspooling all of them in one pull, letting everything collapse, whilst Asha watched it all thunder down, raising clouds of dust that billowed into the sky, great and grey in the resulting silence.

"I was one of millions fleeing the Consortium and their fraudulent allegations—they were hunting for human slaves that they could call indentures, and I was caught at the wrong place at the wrong time."

"What do you mean 'when you were brought to'?" Asha's voice was a whisper. "I—I don't—you were born here. We were *all* born here."

Iyanda sighed, resting her head in her hands and taking a breath. "I come from a place far from here, where great jungles cover the planet instead of sand, and the sky is so blue, and there are no domes, and you can see all the moons and stars." Her voice was quiet. "I was raised by an entire village. My family were sentients of the gentlest kind, and I miss them every day. We—" She stopped. Swallowed. "We were free."

"The planet I grew up on doesn't have a name in our language. I—I don't even know what sector it was in. I was a foundling. I crashed onto the planet in some kind of craft—a life preservation unit, I think—just outside the village. The people who lived there took me in." She smiled faintly, "Raised me like their own until I was about sixteen. Then, one night the village was raided. A platoon of human Consortium soldiers, if you can believe that. They killed my family. They killed them, and I was—" She broke off. "I didn't do anything to stop it. The soldiers spared me. Maybe because I was human-looking, and it was a shock to them. I don't know. They slaughtered my family and let me live. Before I had you, I often wished I had died in that jungle.

"They forced me aboard their ship, and then on to another one, and another one, and another one, until I was so far from anything I had ever known that I couldn't even recognise the stars. I was horrified, and disorientated, and weak. But I managed to escape. I don't know how long I had been captive. Long enough to become very weak. The soldiers, they—" she broke off again, shaking her head. "The ship I had been on made an unscheduled stop for fuel at a busy space station. The soldiers allowed me up for fresh air. By this time, I had been pregnant, and given birth."

Asha clapped a hand over her mouth. "*Oh*—"

Her mother didn't stop. "I left the baby and ran for my life. I begged for someone to help me, but no one would. Then finally somebody asked me if I was human, and I thought, *is that what I am?* So, like a fool, I just said yes." She shook her head. "They snatched me off the street and brought me here."

"Mama . . ."

"Unspeakable things had been done to me." Her mother's eyes squeezed shut. "The thing about power, Ash, is that it corrupts. And those soldiers had been taunted with power like dogs with scraps of meat. They went crazy for any tiny bit they could get. And I was there, and I was defenceless." Iyanda winced, pressing her fingertips to the centre of her forehead, as though to ward off an oncoming headache. When she opened her eyes, they were wet with tears.

Revulsion and anger boiled—*writhed*—inside Asha, shock and disgust jockeying for first place in her heart. Suddenly her rock-solid convictions were gravel and sand. There was *so* much she didn't know.

"My life had been simple, happy, and suddenly it became this vile thing, the life that you've grown up knowing. The real world chewed me up and spat me out. It changed me. Made me mean so I could survive. I made some terrible mistakes. But it also meant that I ended up here, and I got you. And I wouldn't give you up for anything." She took a shaky breath. "I know what you're thinking. That I gave up on your sister. You're right, I did. At that time, your sister represented the worst of what had happened to me. I was young and unprepared, and I hadn't asked for any of it. So, when I had the chance . . ."

"You left her."

"I'm not proud of it, but I was even younger than you are now, Ash. What would you have done?"

Asha couldn't answer.

"I named her, you know. I had learned to speak Universal Standard, and I named her—" Iyanda stopped. When she continued, her voice was a whisper. "I named her Aziza because I liked the way the symbols looked, and I liked that it had symmetry. I thought, I'll give her a beautiful name, because that is all I can give her. I scratched it into the side of the box they had given me for her bed, and as I ran I told myself they'd let her keep it." She shook her head. "But I wouldn't be surprised if they gave her a number, just like they gave us, and let her name be lost, like I was lost." Iyanda looked her daughter in the eye. "I am no criminal, Asha. I simply did what I had to, to survive. You understand that, don't you?"

Asha squeezed her eyes shut, nodding. But it was too much. Too much had happened.

"I—" she started speaking before she knew what she was going to say "—I saw her."

"How?"

"The Sentinel—"

"Asha, you must be careful, he lies—"

"No, before. He didn't tell me. I *saw* her. In my mind. Like a memory, but . . . that's impossible. We've never met."

Her mother had gone very still. "Asha, what else did you see?"

"I saw someone walking towards me, through golden light. I

saw a planet imploding. I saw lightning, and . . . I saw her. My sister. Older than in the hologram. She looked thin, and . . . and sick." Asha watched her mother. Both had tears in their eyes. "She reached out for me. And he said . . . he said that if I didn't find her, he would kill you."

Iyanda pressed a hand over her mouth. "Oh, god." She looked like she might cry, and suddenly, Asha *saw* her: a small woman, scarily thin, dark circles under her eyes, hand clasped to her mouth to prevent any noise from escaping. Somehow, through the haze of her own confusion, through the lines on her mother's face, just for a *moment*, Asha saw a young woman, who had simply got older. A woman that time had happened to.

It was like a blow. She felt winded, like she'd fallen from a great height and landed on her back, all the breath punched out of her by gravity.

"Asha, we need to leave. If we stay here, he'll find us, and he'll drag us into it, and I won't let him use you, *I won't*. He told me, years ago, that he'd come for you when the time was right, and I tried to know when that was, so I'd be ready, but I was complacent. I let this place change me, let them make me into another stupid drone—" She was pulling their second uniforms out of the cubbies they kept them in, and throwing them on the bed. "Put this on, we'll need extra clothes, carrying them will slow us down—"

"Mama, I don't understand—"

"We're leaving."

"To go where?"

"Anywhere. We have to get out of here. I had to do this alone, for so long, I won't let you be alone. I'll go with you. I'll—*Ah!*" her mother yelled. Her hands flew up, clasping her forehead.

"Mama, are you okay?"

Asha," her mother's voice was frantic. "Asha, help me."

She turned.

A burning line was carving its way across the centre of her mother's forehead. It was a pale gold, throwing off light and a sizzling sound as it cauterised the flesh, a thin curl of smoke winding up to the ceiling.

Asha yelped, jumping back. The line abruptly changed direction, surging downwards at a sixty-degree angle towards her mother's eyebrow—

"*It burns—*"

There was nothing Asha could think to do. The line changed again, the same angle, upward to connect with the first line, where it sparked and then burned out. Leaving a perfect, upside-down equilateral triangle carved into the centre of her mother's brow, glowing with golden light.

Asha remembered the Sentinel's hand, his fingers brushing over her mother's brow.

"Asha. It's him." Her mother clasped her hands tightly. "He's taking me, I'm so sorry. I should have known he would."

Asha grasped her hands back, tears streaming down her face. "Don't leave me, please, don't leave me. I can't do this without you—"

"Darling, you can't lose yourself now." Iyanda was crying too. "I know this is hard, and I'm sorry. I never wanted this to happen. I never wanted it to find us—"

"*No—*"

A low ticking sound filled Asha's ears. She half expected more visions to come, but the only image that appeared in her mind's eye was the patchwork face of the thing that called itself *Sentinel,* his needle teeth glistening behind a smile.

A tiny circle seared itself into the centre of the triangle.

"Find your sister. Find out where we came from. That's the key." Asha felt her mother's hands loosen. She looked down.

They were crumbling to dust. "You don't have to do this the way he tells you. There is *always* a choice." Iyanda's body was disintegrating, the symbol on her brow shining brighter and brighter.

"Do *what* the way he tells me?"

"Asha, I love you, okay? Don't ever forget that." She was just a face now.

"No," Asha gasped, tears streaming down her face. "*I'll find you.* I won't let him hurt you. I'll find you, Mama, I'll find you—"

But her mother was already gone.

It helped, in the end, that she had never been allowed to own anything.

It meant there was nothing to carry except the projector, shoved down the waistband of her work trousers, and her modified tablet, clutched in one sweaty palm.

She'd lain on the ground for the better part of an hour, watching the seconds tick past on the tiny digital clock above the door, replaying her mother's words. Her mother's last words.

"She's not dead," she said out loud to herself, and tried to believe it.

Eventually, the logical part of her brain had screamed loudly enough to drown out the part shrivelled in fear and confusion.

You have to leave—now. If you want any hope of saving your mother, you need to go.

She'd pulled her tablet out from under her mattress and navigated to the folder labelled *Someday.*

Today, she thought, and had to sit down for a moment, her eyes screwed shut. *No. There's no time to panic. You have been preparing for this for years. You can do this in your sleep. You just never believed you'd actually ever* go through with *it*.

She just had to be brave, like her mama said.

Be brave, Asha.

She stood up and opened the door.

The Imperial Aeronautics Academy loomed in the darkness.

Set two miles or so away from the housing compounds, it was a long walk through red sand dunes. The dunes were not subject to surveillance—there was nothing valuable there, and if someone wandered out and died, the guards did not care, and the Emperor certainly didn't either.

She walked quickly, keeping her body low, moving from rock to rock, staying out of sight. She could see the road that led from the human settlement to the Academy, which was used to transport new parts from the factories, and supplies from the ships that landed on the Academy's runways to the warehouses. Those runways were Asha's way out, or rather the dome above them was—it was only part of the dome that opened automatically on motion sensors, as it was totally inaccessible to humans, and only really serviced the school. Not exactly a high security location.

Her route took her parallel to the road, which was a hundred or so metres away. Now she was close enough to see that there were lights on in the guardhouse at the end of it, right by the entrance to the school.

She crouched down behind a scrubby bush. This part of the plan was crucial, relying on her ability to hack into the Academy's systems unnoticed, and do something that was actually very simple: turn off a light.

At this hour, according to the timetables, the guards in the watch tower were the only official personnel in the Academy, besides people Asha could not account for, such as staff, or students.

She pulled out her tablet, took a deep, steadying breath, and got to work.

The Academy's systems were not well protected. Once, Asha had tried to get into the shipment database for the whole of Gahraan, the one that logged where the weapons they made went. She had planned it out for months in advance, testing it a million ways, until she was sure she had it right. Her hack had been detected within six seconds of the attempt. The Academy was a different story. The most interesting things kept on the school's system were the students' grades and timetables, as well as a backdoor route to the system that automated all the building's facilities. Air conditioning and filtering, shutters and ventilation. Lights.

Asha entered the final line of code and looked up.

The guard tower went dark.

Without hesitating, she took off, running across the dark road, and through the pedestrian gate.

She was inside.

Ducking through a doorway, she jogged down a deserted corridor, opening automated doors with her tablet as she went.

Part of her couldn't believe this was working. Part of her would have been surprised if it hadn't—she had spent years on this plan. A plan that should have been a pipedream, and now suddenly wasn't.

She'd even been to the Academy a few times. Never to break in, never to do anything other than connect to the Academy's closed system internet to download more heavily encrypted files. It had been an insane risk to take. One that always left her shivering with nerves when she made it back to her bed. But, just like the other illegal things Asha had done, getting away with it only made it easier to do again.

It was just that, lately, the risks had been getting bigger.

Almost like she'd known.

Those nights she'd sneaked out, knowing she was getting closer to the day her mother would pull back the curtain between them one morning to be met with every parent's worst nightmare. Nothing. A missing child in a world where missing children meant dead children, or taken children; spirited away to some distant mine in some distant quadrant.

Don't think about that, she told herself, repressing the mental image. *You have to focus. If you can't get this right, your mother dies.*

Asha felt the panic rise in her throat. For a brief second, she allowed herself to imagine the moment she broke out of the atmosphere. She'd have to slip into hyperspace as soon as she was able to avoid detection, but there would be a moment when she'd look behind her and see a rocky red planet, striped with white sand and wispy cloud cover, and know she was leaving it behind.

Someday, she'd always thought. But she'd never thought she would actually do it.

Heading towards the runway, she ran through the rest of the plan in her mind.

The first ever Academy class that Asha had taken—illegally, of course—was a year-long syllabus that guided its pupils through the preparation of an aircraft for flight, right to lift-off, to breaching the atmosphere and entering hyperspace. She completed it for the first time in just under one month, repeating the simulation every night, unable to stop, the concepts so easy to understand, and, when they weren't, so satisfying to solve.

It also, coincidentally, provided the perfect explanation of an escape route.

The instructor's voice echoed in her mind: *by the end of this class, you'd be able get off this planet in a rusty bucket, if that's what it came down to.*

Asha had taken it to heart. *If that's what it came down to.*

She had no chance at stealing the jets that most frequently used the runways, or even waiting until morning and stowing away in one. They were too closely monitored—locked in a secure hangar, underground. And far too small for Asha to get in and out unnoticed.

No, her target was in the workshop, a small building to the side of the runway. In it were three jets—banged up, ancient models used in the training videos to explain dashboard controls and emergency repairs.

By her estimation, it would take about three or four hours to make one flight-worthy.

Five hours later, Asha sank to the ground, feverish with exhaustion.

Her hands were throbbing, her knuckles sore, and her palms black with grease. But she was nearly finished. Wiping them on her trousers absentmindedly, she allowed herself a moment of pride, before wishing she had some water. Sweat dripped down her face. Her mouth tasted bitter and salty. She would have been finished by now, but she had been interrupted; the guards had taken it upon themselves to do a sweep of the school after the power outage. She had been underneath the jet, half inside the fuselage, when she'd heard their voices and footsteps echoing down the hall. There had been no time to turn off the light. She'd just tucked her legs up into the body of the plane and hung there, abdominal muscles screaming, arms turning to jelly, as the two men had pushed the door of the room open with a creak.

"Stupid kids," they had mumbled, before switching off the light.

Asha had hung there for another minute, convinced they were waiting in the dark for her to reveal herself. When she finally dropped, arms shaking with exertion, and peered out from under the jet, she had been alone. She could have cried in relief, but there was no time. So she'd picked up her tools and kept working.

Now, there was just one part she needed that she couldn't find on the bench, or in any of the drawers that lined the walls. She would have to risk a trip to the next room over.

Nodding to herself, she breathed in, and breathed out. *I just need one more part. I've got this.* And she moved to push the door.

Just before her hand touched it, it swung open from the other side.

Asha fell into the unexpectedly empty space, stumbling against the sudden nothingness, her knees cracking against the floor. She looked up, heart in her mouth.

A pair of students stood in front of her, their black and white cadet uniforms lined with badges on either shoulder. *Third years,* Asha thought. They must have been studying late, or they were here early. She wondered what time it was. She hadn't been keeping track.

"Who the fuck are you?" the one on the left said.

"I think it's *human,*" said the other.

"Oh my god. What is it doing here?"

"I can understand you," Asha said, who was used to being disparaged, but had never had anyone assume she couldn't understand basic speech.

The students jumped back. One of them—a girl, she thought,

though it was hard to tell, she didn't see aliens often—narrowed her pale eyes. "You're not supposed to be here." Her secondary eyelids shuttered across her eyes, wetting them. "Have you come to steal something? That's all you do, isn't it? And what's some tech to you, after you stole a planet?"

The other student laughed nervously. "We should call security . . ."

"No," said the girl. "If we get caught here, we'll be suspended, and we won't graduate. It's not worth it. Besides I think we should have some fun with our new friend." Asha started backing away. "I heard, that if you cut one, they bleed red dirt instead of blood." She reached over to the tool bench and picked up a small draughtsman's knife. "And imagine how crazy it would be if we could get a picture with a dead one."

Asha became keenly aware that she did not have a single thing on her person that could be used to defend herself besides her fists.

She put up her hands. "Please, I don't want any trouble, I'm leaving."

The girl ran at her.

Asha was reduced to her most basic component: instinct. She threw herself to the ground, crawling underneath the ship, and out the other side. Scooping up a wrench, she threw it at the girl, who gasped, as though she had thought Asha incapable of fighting back. The other cadet swore loudly, and started running towards her from the other side, but she hooked the tip of her boot under a low table and flipped it. The tools resting on it flew through the air. She heard a clang and another yell. Something must have hit them. Her mind careened past various options—hide, and hope the girl didn't find her? Double back when she had gone, get in to the aircraft and go—a straight shot forward down the hangar's internal runway, and then out and *up* through the tunnel that led to the surface? A bead of sweat rolled down her back. She spun three-hundred-and-sixty degrees, trying to find somewhere, *anywhere*, to hide, listening all the while for the girl, who was around her somewhere—

A booted foot crashed into Asha's back. She was thrown forward onto the upturned table. Her head smacked into the wood, turning her vision dark for a moment, and then there was a body on top of hers, pressing her down. Asha slammed her foot into the girl's knee joint. She heard a crack. The pressure vanished, and Asha spun around.

The girl screamed and slashed at her.

Asha ducked the first blow, and lashed out with her legs, hoping to worsen the knee injury, but the girl was shielding it. Asha's foot bounced off her shin, and she buckled slightly, but managed to stay standing, lashing out again with her knife. Asha barely dodged it, stumbling to the side, off balance. But before she could right herself, a fist smacked into her temple.

She *reeled*.

Pain bloomed from her cheek outwards, sinking into her brain. She tried to turn, to give an answering blow, but her legs wouldn't obey her, so she lurched forward, raising her hands to the alien girl's face, raking at her eyes, clawing down her cheeks. The girl was quicker, stronger, better fed, combat trained. Asha was used to quick brawls behind warehouses, settling childish scores, not fighting for her life. She was, however, unlike the girl, used to pain. She lashed out with her foot and didn't connect— and suddenly the girl was behind her. She turned, thinking that if she could just find something, a tool maybe, that maybe she could hit her—

But the girl had more hatred in her, and Asha didn't stand a chance.

The knife was cold then burning hot when it sank into her

side. The girl was too close, and she could smell blood. Black spots swam across her vision, she could see her arm rising again, felt the descent as the knife tore through her flesh a second time. The pain was at once immediate and distant, devastating and nebulous, but contained. She was reduced to the two jagged pieces of meat either side of the entry point; she was so far away from it she may as well have been dead.

Dimly, as if from underwater, an alarm began to wail.

The girl's head jerked upwards, eyes darting around frantically. She swore, looking down, as if realising for the first time what she had done—realising that Asha was a thing of flesh and blood, not a character in a video simulation—and then she *pulled the knife out of her stomach.*

Somewhere past the agony—past the slicing and burning and rupturing—she heard the girl's footsteps limping away.

And then she was gone.

And Asha was dying.

A woman of earth and char stepped from the hillside to give Adesola three gifts.

The first gift was material: You may use this to summon Sensit. This you must do soon. For you will need a trusted companion.

The second gift was knowledge: You may find Dandeyi. You must journey far from here to do so. You will know him from the crown whose spires rise from his head, you will know him from the moment you touch.

And the third gift was permission: You may call yourself Hero. This is a privilege, not a right, and one you must earn on your great journey, as you pursue what you have been instructed to pursue.

Bring back Life, instructed Mother. Save us all.

How will I know when the time is right? How will I know when to proclaim this world almost ended and set forth to find those who would save it? How will I know anything without a Mother of my own? – I. Nisomn

'A Complete, Annotated History of Chasca, Including Relevant Translated Mythologies. Chapter: Scroll the First' by I. Nisomn, ex-acolyte of the Aonian Archives.

(Archivist's note: In various places Nisomn has annotated the text. When we examine these annotations, it becomes harder to separate Nisomn the fugitive from the man we knew. Nisomn was a scholar, a refugee, a loner. Prone to moments of caustic humour and bouts of ever-darkening anger, he was, at his core, unpredictable. Often, he was terrifying, but more commonly, he was not. He was insane, we thought, with his talk of a prophecy. Now we are beginning to suspect we were wrong.)

Chapter Six

When Obi woke, it was to the temporary shock of another person lying in his bed.

He'd been dreaming—vividly.

Snatches of it came back to him . . . A great hall, columns soaring into the dark. Footsteps echoing loudly in the cavernous space. His own hands, covered in blood. And a child's voice . . . tinny and far away, whispering across the city, two words he couldn't remember.

He shook his head, disorientated for moment. Golden light danced behind his eyes. As he blinked it away, he realised he wasn't in his bed, he was in *George's*, and *that* was who the arm currently flung over his stomach belonged to. He relaxed. George lay on his front, sheets tangled around his waist, his back a mile of bare moonlit skin. His hair was sticking up in all directions and his mouth was slightly open. Obi felt a small thrill at the intimacy of it, of watching another person sleep, half-clothed, after—

He smiled. But it faded quickly. *One night.* What had he been thinking? They didn't have the kind of relationship that meant one night was an uncomplicated thing.

He scrubbed a hand across his face. He felt so restless. Maybe it was the dream—or maybe it was the fact that he was back where he had started, three long years ago.

In this room, the memories were so close. Another lifetime, almost visible in the dark, playing out just out of reach.

The first time Obi had left, he had been nineteen, and terrified. It had been a night just like this, creeping into the palace to visit George. He'd fixated on an insane idea about the two of them. He'd wanted to ask George to leave with him. To leave the palace and the royal life he despised behind and be . . . something. Something other than scared, and secret, and painfully undefined.

They'd argued (of course they had, it was possibly the worst idea Obi had ever had, and that was saying something)—Obi refusing to look to the future, George obsessed by it, of what it would demand from him, what it would shape him into.

Back then, Obi had never been able to understand why they couldn't just avoid the question of their future until it was here, and he'd said as much. But then George had looked him in the eye and replied: *There is no future for us. Do you not understand that, Obi? If you had anybody else*—George had looked so awful, so full of pain—*it terrifies me, that I am the only person you have.*

So, Obi had collected the fragments of his pride off the floor, and walked out—striding away from his problem, and the truth of it, and the deep hurt in his heart that let him know, unequivocally: everyone you love will discard you. He'd walked straight through the city at night, all the way to the house he had once lived in with his father, until he had disappeared. He'd gone to his father's room, and laid on his bed, and cried.

When he was done crying, he opened the box of Artefacts stowed under the bed, abandoned for a decade, and began to methodically stow them in his coat's myriad pockets. *These are all the places he's ever been. All the places he wanted to go.* A spark of hope. *Maybe he was going to use them to search the future for a cure. Maybe that's where he's gone . . . out into the world to find something he can use to help me,* he thought. *Well, now his Artefacts are mine, and I'm going to use them as a map. A map that might lead me to him, or the cure. Or both, if I'm lucky.*

He didn't think, *what if he doesn't want to be found?* Didn't think, *He left you at eight years old, and all this time you told yourself he loved you too much to abandon you in a city where no one else knew you existed, that something bad must have happened which meant he couldn't come back, but what if you're wrong?*

Instead, he picked an Artefact at random, a small ring made of rock, and thought: *I don't care if this kills me, I just want to be gone, gone from this vicious city, to somewhere new.*

The jump had been excruciating. He put two thousand years between him and George, and lost a rib in the process. And so, he had begun to search for his father, barely knowing where to start.

Three years later, in the cold, moonlit dark of the prince's room, Obi tried to decide if he'd done the right thing by coming back to England. Empty-handed, a miserable half-cyborg, convinced his father was dead.

Maybe there are no right or wrong actions, he thought. *Just the things people do, and the way others feel about it.*

A bird whistled shrilly outside. Wind gusted through trees. Obi was turning back over to try and get some more sleep before the sunrise when he heard the child's voice again, louder this time, like someone was standing by the bed, whispering in his ear.

Is anyone there?

He froze.

Gently, he moved George's arm from his stomach, swung his legs over the side of the bed, and stood, moving to the window. He pulled back the curtain and looked out. There was no one there. But still . . . he could hear the echo of that voice. *Is anyone there?.*

He froze. The child in his dream . . . it was coming back to him now. Brown skin, hair shaved close to her scalp. Wide eyes, her clothes . . .

He remembered the little boy from the bridge, whispering *men's trousers* in scandalised tones, and the royal news report, abandoned on a desk in the hallway—

The room from his dream swam up through his subconscious. That sense of emptiness, of a giant space. He knew that place. *The British Museum.*

Chills prickled down Obi's arm.

Before he knew what he was doing, he was struggling into his jeans, cramming his arms into his T-shirt and throwing on his coat. He had to know who this voice belonged to. Most likely it was a hoax. *But hoaxes don't call to you in the night or appear in your dreams. Hoaxes don't make you feel like someone is watching, even now, waiting for you to—*

Obi stopped, his fingertips on the door handle. What was he doing? Running away again?

No, not running, just investigating. He couldn't leave this be. If it was an Artefact, it was significant enough to be worth collecting. If it wasn't, he could put his mind at rest, and return. Either way, he wasn't going anywhere. He'd told George he was staying this time. And he planned to keep his word.

"Obi?" George said from behind him.

Obi jumped and turned around, heart in his mouth.

But George was still asleep. He mumbled something else, eyes firmly closed, and rolled over in bed. The beam of moonlight from the open window fell across his face. Obi watched him for a moment, looked at the soft rounded shape of his eyelids, the eyes that darted beneath them, and thought, *you're all I want. And I think I'm finally brave enough to stay and ask for it. To stay and see what it might cost to be happy.*

He would go and investigate this possible Artefact—if it was a good one, he'd steal it. If it was nothing, then his growing sense of unease would be alleviated, and he could rest easy, knowing that his dream was just a dream. The sun would rise, and he'd be back in bed, and George would wake with a shock at the hour, just like he always did, and Obi would climb out of the window, laughing, and they'd start this again, for real this time.

Somehow.

He nodded to himself, then pushed open the door, and slipped out.

The British Museum in 1812 was just a single building, a seventeenth-century mansion named Montagu House. Obi was crouched behind a hedge, looking down the wide path with narrowed eyes, trying to determine the patrol schedule of the two guards that comprised the museum's security, as well as wracking his brains, trying to remember the best way in. The building was three storeys tall, but Obi would not be visiting the upper levels; according to the canvas signs surrounding the building, the 'ghost' was displayed in a room in the left wing of the second floor.

It was a place Obi was familiar with, though he didn't like to think about it. As a kid, he'd come here once with his dad, on a night not too dissimilar to this one.

One night every year, they'd hit somewhere new, searching for Artefacts. It was the only time his father ever smiled—and this was the last place they'd ever gone. Obi had been ten years old, buzzing with excitement. His father had been in a better mood than usual, as they lay in the cold undergrowth of a hedge, just inside the gate of the Museum.

"Do you see the dogs, Obi?"

"Yes, Dad. They're really big . . ."

"Shh. Yes, they are. But they're dumb, and we're smart."

"And we have *magic*—that Father Time gave to us!"

His father had grinned. Obi remembered feeling so proud of himself. So big and grown up for making his dad smile. "We do. And tonight, we get to use it." His father held out a hand. "Come on, son, let's go."

Six months later, his father was gone.

The click of boot heels made him jump. *Shit*. He'd stopped paying attention. He looked sharply upwards but saw nothing.

Then, humming.

It was the guard—rounding the corner of the museum. And, if the other, softer set of footsteps were anything to go by, they had a dog.

Obi sprinted up the stairs at the front of the building that led to the entrance and tucked himself behind one of the stone columns, his back to the door. Squeezing his eyes shut, he willed the guard and his dog to keep walking.

The footsteps stopped.

Obi rolled his eyes. Of *course*, they did.

The dog was visible now, snuffling around the base of the stairs where Obi had stood only moments before. It was a bloodhound with black fur. Obi was glad to be able to keep his enemy in his sights, but if he could see the dog, it meant the dog could see him. It also meant its owner wasn't far behind. Obi just hoped that whoever they were didn't think to look upwards.

"Anyone there?" asked the guard, his tone brisk and unyielding.

Obi froze.

The dog whined, snuffling excitedly around the base of the steps.

No, no, no. Please, no.

The dog began to climb.

"Where you goin', dog?" said the guard softly. "Found something? If it's another bloody squirrel, I'll have your—"

Obi took a deep breath, then stepped into the moonlight. "Not a squirrel," he said. "Sorry."

Then he raised his left hand and shot the guard square in the forehead.

The tranquilizer dart was small but potent, glowing faintly blue as it emptied its contents into the guard's bloodstream. He dropped like a stone and began snoring quietly.

Obi looked at the dog. They locked eyes. The hound's mouth opened. Obi raised a menacing finger, widening his eyes.

"Don't you dare make me use—"

The dog *howled*, raising its head to the sky and alerting everyone within a couple miles' radius of their precise location.

He fired his last dart into the dog's haunch.

The howl petered off, and the dog slumped to the ground, peacefully asleep.

With much irritated grumbling, Obi hauled both dog and guard behind a pillar, and sent up a quick prayer to anyone who might be listening that they weren't discovered before he had got what he had come for.

Two pins found their way from his sleeves into the locks of the door. A few sharp, professional twists later, both bolts slid open.

The turn of the doorknob in his hand was satisfying, to say the least.

Stepping smartly over the threshold, Obi started his countdown. He had to be quick; the second guard would find his colleague unconscious at the patrol switch, which was in—he checked his watch—twenty-six minutes. Regardless, 'linger unnecessarily at a crime scene' wasn't exactly top of his to-do list. Turning left, he swiftly exited the long entrance corridor and entered the first room of curiosities. A few objects caught his eyes: a jewelled pin, a rusted dagger, a piece of broken pottery—each calling out to him faintly of times unfamiliar. It was painful, seeing all these Artefacts, knowing he was done with time-travelling. That he would never be able to use them—or any, ever again.

So why are you here? whispered his conscience. He ignored it. This was different—he wasn't going to run away again. He couldn't afford to—he'd been lucky so far, with what the Sickness had decided to take from him. And though it didn't strike every time, the risk wasn't worth it. He was staying in London. But there was something about this Artefact—if that's what it even was. A feeling, like dread, but more inevitable.

The stairs to the second floor were dark, clouds of dust rising with every footstep. With a thought, he lit up the palm of his prosthetic bright blue, dialling up the brightness until he was able to see the room at the top of the staircase. *Worth every penny*, Obi thought smugly.

The ghost was easy to find, big red arrows had been painted on wooden signs, advertising the exhibit. As Obi drew nearer, he noticed a faint yellow glow illuminating the space beyond the arch, seeping into the corridor, and flickering strangely, like firelight.

When he stepped into the room, he froze.

The child stood, flickering in and out of existence in the centre of the room. It was just as the ticket boy had said: beige trousers and a long-sleeved shirt hung on her thin frame. She was tiny, not any older than six or seven, with warm brown skin, a shaved head, and a look in her eyes that seemed to belong to someone older.

Slowly, Obi walked closer. The image was being projected

from a tiny black box that the exhibition curators had placed on the floor, probably believing it to be possessed. Briefly, he was surprised that the thing hadn't been handed off immediately to some archbishop upon discovery and destroyed with the swiftness of God's hand on earth, before he remembered there was arguably nothing that British museums liked more than holding on to things they had no business holding on to.

A symbol rotated slowly by her head. No, a seal, with writing on it that Obi had to concentrate very hard to read. It was so familiar . . .

His eyes widened. *Universal Standard.*

It was a language that rose to prominence in the 5500s A predominantly mercantile tongue, it bridged the gaps in understanding between people from different planets, and later, military personnel sent out by the governing body of the galaxy—which at that time would have been . . . Obi wracked his brains but couldn't remember. He'd only been that far once, and it had been a disaster. He'd lost his eye. But that was where he'd first heard the rumours of a cure being developed by a secretive, likely magical cult—a cure *all*. Something that would heal any wound, or illness, including, he could only hope, his sickness. Through whispers in the streets and gossip from the skyways, as well as a slew of predictions from nearly-almost-but-not-quite reputable sources, he'd narrowed its creation down to a fifty-year period in the early 61st century.

And the symbol rotating above the young girl's head said *Consortium Footage: 3C/QM/500/48.*

It was a date. The footage was from early in the year 6048. He didn't know who or what a Consortium was, but that year . . . this Artefact would take him further than he had ever been. *Maybe my father's there.* Mentally he slapped himself. *Forget your father. If he were alive he would have found you by now. You made enough of a racket in enough centuries to let him know. What about the cure? This could be it.*

No. He wasn't doing this. He was not going anywhere. He'd made a promise.

I should leave, he thought, circling the hologram. *Go back to George. I shouldn't be here.*

Something caught his eye.

On the far side of the box was a groove—no, three grooves, arranged in a triangle.

Obi's heart skipped a beat. *Calm down,* he thought desperately. *You're tired, you're just seeing what you want to see.*

But it was there. Undeniably. So small, he might have missed it entirely if he hadn't known to look: a tiny circle engraved at the triangle's heart.

The same symbol from the page his father had left him.

The symbol of the Order of Legends.

Without thinking, he picked the projector up.

For a split second, everything seemed fine. The hologram flickered and turned off, sensing the motion. The box sat small and innocent in the palm of his hand.

Distantly, he heard a ticking noise.

Bright golden light burst through the gaps in his fingers, nearly blinding him. Slamming his eyes shut, his secondary instincts began to take over, the power that coursed through him—the power that sensed time, rushing around everything like a river—sending out probes. The box was radiant with sentimental energy. Usually, he had to focus, still his mind, and then sift through the layers of it to find the source of it—the person who had cared about that thing, or used it, or made it, been buried with it, sometimes—so that he could hone in on them, and their time, and make the jump.

This Artefact was different.

Memories were filling his mind, recollections that didn't belong to him rushing towards him, filling him with a sharp, pricking hatred for a place he had never been or even dreamed of. The smell of sand and smoke clouded his nose. A bright, blue sky visible through translucent hexagons flickered above him and then winked out. Red sand stretched into the horizon. His back—and legs, shoulders, arms, wrists, neck, and knees—hurt. He saw a girl who looked like the child from the hologram, flesh and blood this time, and older, shouting at someone, tears streaming down her face.

The acrid burn of a desert planet curled around the back of his throat.

Was it . . . No. Surely not?

The electric hum of machinery and the smell of ozone-tinged destruction confirmed his suspicions. He glimpsed a statue and a temple, and felt a prayer rising in his throat. Tight cornrows pulled at his scalp.

He blinked, and the darkened museum filtered back into sight.

The projector glowed faintly golden, and then went dark.

He didn't realise what was happening until it was too late.

Obi felt the ground open up beneath him, felt the sky open up above him, felt reality bend and warp, turning on the axis of the box in his hand, pulling him away against his will. The museum around him began to dissolve.

He tried to drop the projector, certain that it was doing this—but his fingers wouldn't open.

The museum disappeared.

For a moment, he stood in darkness.

His last thought before he ceased to exist in that time and place was of a boy with chestnut hair and cool green eyes, a boy he'd made a promise to, who was now sleeping in a palace alone.

In the Now, Adesola took the thing Mother had given her and smashed it on the ground. In the Beginning, Sensit felt himself become untethered from time. As he re-appeared in the time he had been created in, he saw the face of his fellow Hero and wept for joy. It had been so long. Too long.

'A Complete, Annotated History of Chasca, Including Relevant Translated Mythologies. Chapter: Scroll the First' by I. Nisomn, ex-acolyte of the Aonian Archives.

(Archivist's note: We know that these myths constitute a sort of aetiology for the Chascan culture—they believed them to explain the beginnings of their civilisation, and thought this cycle—the creation of three heroes, and their meeting again and again across space and time, was fated. A simple prophecy, so engrained in the culture it had become a fact.)

Chapter Seven

[planet: Gahraan] + [location: beyond the dome] + [year: 6066]

Asha never thought she would die surrounded by spaceship parts.

She clutched her side, dimly aware that it was aching. Her hands came away slick and red.

She was bleeding out. She wasn't surprised. She wasn't sad or scared. She wasn't much of anything in that moment.

A soft, shimmering light caught her eye. Lying next to her was the hologram's projector. She'd put it down when she'd got to work. The tiny black box seemed to taunt her now, the closest thing she had to her mother was a flimsy projection of a sister she had never met, and now she would die on the floor of a workshop, on the planet her mother had said she had to escape.

Tears rolled down her cheeks. Through the blurriness of her vision, it almost looked like the projector was the source of the shimmering. It was sort of pretty, the golden glow radiating from it like a solar flare. The light brightened as she watched, blooming like a flower in the darkness of the deserted classroom.

Just beyond the glowing weapon, a shape flickered into being.

Asha blinked, her eyelids growing heavier by the second. She tried to sit up, to move even her fingers, but her body felt restrained by invisible ropes, her head weighing a thousand tons. The shape moving within the projector's flickering light slid sideways into the shadows and disappeared. Her mind registered belatedly that the shape had been a human—a boy in a long coat.

The box let out a flare of light, significantly larger than the previous one. Asha felt heat against her skin, like she was next to an open fire.

Hands closed around her upper arms, forcing her into a slumped sitting position. Pain lanced through her. Her instincts screamed at her to fight, to claw and scratch her way to freedom, and then to run. But her arms hung useless by her sides.

She forced her eyes open.

It was the boy in the long coat—his face panicked, eyes wide, the projector in his hand, growing steadily hotter and brighter by the second. Except, that wasn't *possible*. The projector was still sitting on the ground, melting a hole into the plastic floor.

Drowsily, she came to a solution so improbable she nearly laughed. The two black boxes were *identical*. From the size and shape, to that strange symbol carved into the side, like a geometric eye.

The boy cursed and dropped his box. When he stopped flapping his hands about long enough for Asha's tired eyes to focus, she saw one of them was shiny and burnt, angry blisters already forming from the heat. The other was—

Digging through the pockets of his coat, the boy grunted in frustration, swearing under his breath as he searched for something without success.

As if remembering he wasn't alone, he turned to Asha.

"Hey, hello?" he took three quick steps forward, then shook Asha's shoulders. "We need to leave, otherwise we're gonna die." When Asha didn't respond, the boy frowned harder, his eyes roaming over her body until they came to rest on her hands and the dark red blood slicking her fingers.

"Oh God." He grimaced. "Can you even hear me?"

Asha blinked once. Slowly. It was as close to a nod as she was going to get.

"I'll take that as a yes, then." He smiled grimly. "Listen, I'm not sure what's going on, but I think I created a—a paradox. I've arrived too early in your timeline. You haven't lost your—your hologram thingy yet . . . The same object can't exist twice in the same time and place without there being some kind of—" he gestured around for the right words "—cosmic retribution."

Asha was too far gone to talk, so she settled for blinking at him again.

"This has never happened before, I'm so sorry. I think there's going to be an explosion. A big one. I'm certain of it, actually, and if I don't figure out a way to stop it, we're both going to die. Us, and half this planet. *Boom*. Gone." His face fell. "God, I don't even know where to start . . ." He looked down at the box in his hand. "I could send this one back. I don't know if it will work. I've never done it before. My father, he could . . ." He screwed his eyes shut. "*There's no time*."

As if he had reached a decision, he went still, bringing up his other hand to cover the projector.

The boxes had grown brighter, their combined heat raising the temperature of the room to a nearly unbearable level.

Asha noticed that the boy was missing half an eyebrow. She closed her eyes, and must have momentarily lost consciousness, because when she opened them, she was moving. A hard bony surface dug into her ribs. The boy had put her on his shoulders.

Blearily, she gazed around. They were walking up the ramp into the ship. The boy set her down on the floor. The lights of the dashboard were a twinkling constellation. Asha had never been this close before.

"Do you know how to fly this thing?" the boy asked.

Desperation was unmistakable in his voice. "We need to get out of here."

"Press that," Asha mumbled. She pointed at a button under the dashboard, to the left of the pilot's seat. The boy pressed it. The engines began to groan, and after a moment, the craft began to taxi down the underground runway.

Asha looked ahead. She felt a fire roaring to life inside her, burning hotter than the pain of the stab wound. *I did this,* she thought. *A nothing human from a nowhere planet made this ship fly. And I'm going to take it so far from this place I'll never have to see it again.*

She could see the opening in the roof, the tunnel that would take them to the surface, to the stratosphere, and then . . . across the galaxy.

With a groan, she placed one hand on the joystick and pushed. With the other, she entered the equations she had been learning for years now, ready for this moment, the one she had never thought would come.

Asha launched them into the air.

The tunnel was dark.

And then, behind them, a bright orange light came billowing up, huge and so hot she saw white in the centre, black smoke blossoming skywards like a dark flower, slowly opening.

"The explosion," she heard the boy say. "I didn't stop it."

In the rear-view cams, she saw a boiling mass of burning debris surging towards them. Adrenaline crystallised her vision—her hands moved of their own accord, preparing them to enter hyperspace.

They cleared the tunnel, speeding towards the stars.

For a moment, she could see the four domes spread out beneath her, the human settlements glowing softly in the serene night.

Distantly, a noise echoed, like stone cracking.

Then, beneath her, and only a few miles away from the domes, the Academy exploded, and her vision was engulfed in flames.

Asha woke up slumped in a pilot's seat, shirt crusted in blood, looking out into the vast, black vacuum of space.

For a moment, she thought she was dreaming. Or dead.

She gazed outside, brain spinning, stomach churning at the hugeness of it, the way it stretched on for lightyears, all around, pricked with lights like distant beacons. Each of them a star, or a world. An uncountable number of people.

Sitting up was a struggle. She scanned the dashboard, checking off green lights, her anxiety lessening with each one.

Everything was in order.

The projector.

She froze, then felt around her waistband. It wasn't there. Something else was though—a rough patch of fabric, glued to her skin, hot to the touch, pinching at her flesh. A medipatch, sloppily applied, but doing the job. *The stab wound. Someone's patched me up.* Left alone for a week, she would be able to lift it and find only a scar. *But who—*

The boy.

She sat up with a jolt. The events of her escape returned to her in flashes. The students, the knife, the hologram projector glowing—

The Academy. She'd blown it up.

Pressing a hand to her mouth, she tried to calculate the radius of the blast. Would it have reached the housing compound?

Thracin.

Asha's hands shook. And where was her projector?

Placing her sweaty palms on the armrests of the chair, she heaved herself into a standing position. Stabbing pains shot up and down her leg, flaring from her ankle. She must have twisted that too. She didn't dare look—not at her ankle, and not under her patch. She couldn't; she would probably pass out, and she couldn't afford to pass out right now. What she needed was to find the stranger who had saved her life, and possibly kidnapped her.

"Hello," she called out, limping through the tiny archway that led to the cramped space of the ship's interior.

There was no reply.

Then Asha saw it: a foot, sticking out from behind two small metal barrels.

"*Hello*," she bellowed.

There was a grunt and then a *smack* as the owner of the foot sat upright and collided with the metal beam above his head. He swore, then crawled pitifully out of the gap in the wall where he'd been resting. He was human, Asha remembered with a jolt, as all six foot something of him stood up. Or at least he looked it.

"Hi," he said.

"Who are you?" she asked. "And where's my projector? The black box. You were holding it, what did you do with it?"

"Your projector? You're worried about a projector when you snatched me from my city, from my *time*, and brought me here against my will? Who does that? What are you, some kind of witch?" He seemed to get a little scared then, as though convincing himself of something in his panic. "You're not actually a witch, are you? One of the Magekind?"

"What are you even *saying*?" Asha was furious suddenly. *Who did this guy think he was?* She barely cared—he must have the projector. She needed it. It was the only clue the Sentinel had given her—the only piece of this insane puzzle that she could hold in her hands. "I'll ask you one more time. Where is my projector?"

But he wasn't listening. "I was just minding my business," he said, gesturing wildly, "exercising some—some professional, *intellectual* curiosity—and your 'projector' pulled me out of my century and into this one. Which is shit by the way. It's a shit century. I've got blood all over me, and I barely escaped an exploding building with my life. Now I'm stuck in space— *space*—with a child. At least my translator chip still bloody works—"

"Actually, I'm eighteen!"

"Oh, great!" He threw his hands up in the air. "That's perfect." Sitting down heavily on one of the barrels, he put his head in his hands. "Incredible." A few moments passed. "Your projector is gone. I sent it back. Well, I sent mine back. But mine was always yours. Probably managed to create a causal loop—that would explain the paradox and *that* would explain the explosion. Which would have destroyed your version of the projector. So, yeah, it's definitely gone."

"*Gone?*" An ice-cold chill ran through her. "No. It can't be. I—I need it."

"You saw that building blow up right? You called it the . . . Academy? Your projector did that. Well. I guess I did it. But not on purpose. I arrived too early in your timeline."

It was Asha's turn to sit down. The projector was the only thing she had that proved any of this was real. The only thing she had to remind her to keep going. The only image of her sister, Aziza. "Who are you?" she asked. "And how did you get it into the Academy? Were you . . . following me?" An awful thought struck her. "Did *he* send you? Are you with the—the Order of Legends?"

He froze. "How do you know that name?" Realisation dawned on his face. "It was your projector . . . but it had their symbol on it."

"It's not really mine," Asha said hastily. "It was given to me."

"By who?"

"A strange person. An alien." Fresh fear welled up in her just thinking about the encounter. "He—he threatened me. He took my mother. Told me he'd kill her if I didn't do what he said. Do you know who they are?"

"No," he replied, looking horrified. "I think my father did but . . ." he shrugged, looking defeated, as though the things his father knew were anybody's guess. "Is your mother alright?"

Asha opened her mouth to speak, but couldn't. Her eyes smarted. "I don't know."

"Oh, god." He replied, clearly taken aback. "I'm so sorry."

"That's why I was at the Academy. I needed a ship so I could leave and go find her. I have to find her."

"Hey," he said. "It's okay. I'm sure it will be okay."

"I don't need your pity." Even to her own ears her voice sounded weak. "I'm fine."

"It's okay if you're not. What just happened was awful—"

"*I'm fine.*"

"You're crying."

Asha heaved out a sob. "No, I'm not." She turned her face away, pressing the heels of her hands into her eyes. But in the darkness loomed the Sentinel's patchwork face, his hawklike stare, and that voice inside her mind, the one she knew, somehow, but did not recognise.

"Hey, kid," came a voice. "There's no need for that. Look, if you cry, I'll cry." She heard the boy approaching slowly and kneeling beside her. "What's your name?"

"Asha." Blood heated her face. He was talking to her like

she was a child. *You are a child,* she thought. *A child without her mother who just wants to go home.*

"Asha. Okay. I'm Obi." He patted her shoulder. "Um . . . there, there," he said, with as much effort as he could muster. "Look, I'm not thrilled to be here, either. I was—I was supposed to be done . . . travelling. I was supposed to stay put. And there was someone I hadn't seen for a very long time. We were going to try and make things work . . ." He trailed off. "I guess what I'm trying to say is, we've both lost something recently. You lost your mother, and I . . . I lost my second chance. But we're here now. So, we have to do what we can with what we've been given." He nudged her. "Or what we stole."

Asha looked at him out of the corner of her eye. He grimaced, and then stood and started patting his body all over, like he was searching for something in one of the pockets of his ridiculous floor-length, black-brown coat.

Looking around the tiny craft, he muttered, "I didn't lose anything this time. Why didn't I lose anything? Maybe because I didn't choose to leave. But what brought me here? And why can't I get back?"

"What are you talking about?" Asha asked, voice hoarse. He kept talking about time, *timelines*—

She remembered for the first time that he hadn't always been in the workshop—that he had appeared there, blinking his way into existence like a light, turning on.

"I'm talking about how I got here." His face was incredibly dynamic, Asha thought, even as a chill swept through her. Emotions moved easily across it. Frustration, confusion, regret. "There was a light," he murmured. "There's never a light. Usually, it feels like stepping off a cliff. It's a choice. This time, there was a bright golden light, and something reached up, out of the darkness beyond the cliff, and dragged me over."

"You fell off a cliff?"

"No." He looked at her, as though sizing her up. "I travelled here from a different time. Another century. I was in one place—I found your projector there. It shouldn't have been there. When I touched it, it brought me here, against my will."

"Another . . . century? That's insane." He must have hit his head. Gently, she said, "I'm not sure where you came from—"

"*When.*"

"—but the box was not a teleportation device."

"*I'm* the teleportation device," he said. "And in any case, it looks like I'm stuck here now. I can't go back."

"Is it because somebody is after you?" Asha said. "The government?"

"As far as your government is concerned, I don't exist. No, it's not that." He shook his head. "I'm really stuck here, in this time. I tried to go back, immediately, as soon as I realised I'd jumped without wanting to. But a golden light flashed all around me, and I found myself back in that classroom. It must be the sickness. Maybe it's reached a final stage, and it's taken my powers for good." He paused. "It seems like getting a cure is my only way back now."

"Back to where?" Asha narrowed her eyes. "I don't know if you understand what happened, but we escaped Gahraan. We can't go back there. And what do you need a cure for? Are you—are you sick?"

"Listen, I already told you. I'm not from around here."

"But you're human, aren't you? You look it."

"Thanks?" Obi looked vaguely offended. Asha narrowed her eyes further. "Well, I am human. But not completely. Not in the way you would think of it. What year is it anyway?"

"Excuse me?"

He looked at her, clearly irritated. "The year. What year is it?"

"Year 100."

"Of what?"

"Year 100 of the Hard Peace. The one hundredth year of the hundred worlds' mandatory induction into the Consortium." He looked confused. Asha did some quick maths. "In Old Pan-Galactic, it's the year six-thousand-and-sixty-six. How can you not know that?"

"Sixty-six?" He rubbed a hand over his jaw, looking as though he were calculating something in his head. "That's mad. The box said forty-eight," he was muttering. "Though, that probably increases my chances."

She thought back to what he'd said. *I travelled here from a different time. Another century.* He was either very, very confused or . . .

"Might as well make the trip worth it." He closed his eyes, as though trying to get a handle on his emotions. "God, I was so close to having what I wanted."

Asha recognised the hurt on his face. The frustration that came when your own life was taken out of your hands. And he'd mentioned something about being sick. Maybe he needed an ally just as much as she did.

"Look," she said. "I'm not one hundred per cent sure what your deal is, but I just need to get to A'lkari. Or somewhere close. Anywhere, really. Just—away from that planet we left, towards somewhere where I can get a better ship, or find someone to take me where I need to go." Obi gave her that look again, as though evaluating her. Asha continued, "If you can't go back to . . . wherever you came from, you could always travel with me," she said. "If you want. And I really should thank you for helping me with my wound—and—"

"And aiding and abetting a runaway in her mission to break out of a secure facility using stolen government property?"

They both laughed weakly, looking at the star-speckled darkness outside the windows.

"Yeah," she smiled. "Something like that."

Obi held out a hand. "Alright. When we reach civilisation, we can go our separate ways."

Asha looked at the proffered limb. His skin was a dark, rich brown. The muted wash of starlight played over his face—

Suddenly, she was stood back in that alleyway on Gahraan, sand whipping past her feet, a stranger staring into her eyes, visions assaulting her mind, like waves crashing onto a crumbling cliff face.

A hand, reaching out to her, and above it a young man, his dark skin an ocean of stars, reflecting the blue and purple and silver of the galaxy that hung in the darkness outside the window behind him.

"It's good to see you," she said to Obi, without ever deciding to say it. Without understanding why. She felt a feeling wash over her, like cool air; for the first time in her life, she was exactly where she was supposed to be.

For a moment they stared at each other, grey eyes meeting black-brown, and there was a word on the tip of Asha's tongue. A name. One she'd never heard, but half-remembered.

Then it was gone as soon as it had appeared, and they were strangers again, standing in a jet hurtling through space, so she took his hand and shook it, and her vision, just for a moment, was shot through with gold.

Sensit turned to Adesola and met her eyes.

"This journey will be incredibly hard," he said, simply. "Are you prepared and willing to do whatever we must?"

Adesola nodded. Then she said, "Are you?"

'A Complete, Annotated History of Chasca, Including Relevant Translated Mythologies. Chapter: Scroll the First' by I. Nisomn, ex-acolyte of the Aonian Archives.

Part Two

'Never does a story tell only a singular tale. Look closer. *Closer*. A story is a story of many, and the tale it will tell is one that spans ages.'

Ancient Chascan proverb. First recorded c. 3100.

Chapter Eight

[planet: error] + [location: error] + [year: error]

The old creature awoke in darkness.

Taking in the absolute dark of his surroundings, he thought bemusedly, *I am almost beyond memory. They have nearly forgotten me. And yet I wake. How?*

The answer came to him almost immediately. A vision of two hands, clasping together in the mortal realm. The golden light of the prophecy flashing like a portent, surrounding them, though they did not know it.

Oh, I see. It is starting again.

He stretched his limbs. His armour rattled, rusted with age, and the corrosive dark of the void. Old age had turned him ugly. All that time spent sleeping. Amassing power but not using it, absorbing the fallout from last time (not the *first* time, just the last time), had made him ancient and overgrown. His eyes were myriad, as were his tails, and tongues of flame, and black feathered wings.

No, he didn't like this. *I am a Hero*, he thought, remembering. *Not a monster.*

One of his tongues flicked out to the taste the air. The worldskin was so thin here. Like gossamer, easily torn. With enough will, he could walk through it, opening it just like a . . .

Door.

It appeared as he thought it, unfolding into a grand arch of brightness, suspended above him in the gloom where he lay like a corpse. As the door materialised, the laws of the void changed, and suddenly (though it hadn't moved) the door was not above him, but in front of him, and he was standing. The creature—*Hero, I am a Hero*—supposed that prophecies were, in a way, the final law. The axis upon which all other laws spun. Upon which all worlds spun—hurtling through space, fulfilling the ultimate prophecy: fate.

Fate had led him here, after all. Trapped him here. In this void, like a waiting room for re-incarnation.

He knew how this was supposed to go: the door appeared, he stepped through it, he found the poor doomed child upon the shoulders of whom an entire world had placed an unimaginable burden—*save us or die trying*—and he nurtured within them the flame that might help them become what he had been, long ago.

Hero.

The door was large, and cracked ajar. A sliver of starlight fell out. He supposed he *should* walk through it. Do what was expected of him, demanded of him by this loop, this damned circle called history, that told him who he was, and who he'd be, what he should fight for.

But there had been a feeling growing inside him ever since the last time, when his mortal counterpart had shrugged off the mantle and the title and expectations and forged a new path. It had doomed the whole planet . . . and yet.

It had also seeded an idea in this old creature's mind. An idea that said: *Heroes aren't meant to serve, they're meant to be worshipped. Heroes aren't the whimpering pawns of prophecy, the pathetic, powerless agents of fate. And if they are? Then I want no part in it. Not again.*

Reaching into the air, his fingers closed around a sword hilt. He drew his weapon from the sky like pulling it from a scabbard, light burning around the exit point, and then he took a breath, feeling for the soul of his mortal counterpart—the lucky individual he was supposed to be guiding to greatness.

It was . . . split.

His hand on the sword hilt faltered. *This was interesting.* A split soul generated huge amounts of power—crackling like electricity along the edge of it where it had torn. Uncontained.

It was what he'd been waiting for. Delivered to him like a gift. Enough power to break the cycle, to become something of his own. Something more than a mould-riddled puppet of the prophecy. He could use this power to create something of his own. A place he could rule where his word was law, not the law of some prophecy. Some words written on stone a thousand years ago at the dawn of a world that was over now.

A world that was dead.

It was decided. In one great slash, he brought his sword down through the air, and split the skin of the world. The gash was ugly and violent. The worldskin shivered in the breeze that blew through—a breeze that smelled of river water and coal smoke. Like rain and history and a place that could be home.

As he stepped through the tear in the fabric that separated worlds, his armour stitched itself back together. In one shining wrist guard, he saw his face: the brown skin, rich and warm, the amber-golden eyes, gleaming like a lynx's. And the russet auburn of his hair, as muddily red as the rich clay he'd been born from. Lightly curling wisps of it blew past his chin, and on the breeze was the scent of cool water.

Belatedly, he thought of his siblings—the shield-bearer and the crown-wearer—and cast his eye back towards the void in search of them. But they were already gone, making ready to meet the little heroes they had been bound to by the prophecy.

The last one left. What an honour. Yes, he thought, as he stepped into rain. *This time, the honour is all mine.*

Chapter Nine

[planet: error] + [location: error] + [year: error]

Alarick Amadi had always despised royalty of any kind. He did not believe any one person should wield so much power over so many other people simply because they had been born into it. Perhaps this was because he had been born into absolutely nothing and harboured no small amount of resentment because of this. Someone had once called him a 'self-made man' but this was not true. Alarick had not had a hand in his own making; that had been someone else's doing entirely.

He resented that, too.

The London night he now walked briskly through was cool, laced with a chill that rasped under doorways and whispered between the cracks in windows. Shivering, he pulled a lighter and a pack of cigarettes from his pocket, then remembered that neither had been invented yet and put both items back. A few streets and howling gusts later, he decided he did not care, and lit up. Leaning against a wall, he pulled smoke into his lungs and allowed himself to admit that he was, in fact, exhausted.

Thinking about why he was here, probably suffering from hypothermia and frostbite, and breathing in all kinds of poison from the factory smog that hung over London, he scowled. Alarick was proud of his scowl, the carefully cultivated thing that it was. His predicament—for want of a better word—all boiled down to one thing, essentially; his complete and utter inability to resist a pretty face. Although, he thought, to call his late wife 'pretty' was a gross injustice. Also, he had been in love. That had to count for something.

Now he had a son who he hadn't seen in ten years. A son who was sick with a legendary virus. A son who was in incredibly grave danger.

Alarick had been sitting in a bar, staring at the bottom of his cup, three hundred years away from 1812 when he had felt it.

The rip. Tearing through the fabric of spacetime.

And then—

A visitor. The clash of ancient armour on a cobbled street, and someone, or *something*, stepping through.

An intruder to the timeline. Alarick had felt Time pause, for a moment, and consider.

Imagine a boulder, dropped from a height so great it is like a visitor from another world, crashing into the middle of a river so powerful that it has run through the same gorge for a thousand years, uninterrupted. This is a river that carved its own path through a mountain, that split the earth and rushed in; a pebble dropped into it would make no difference, large rocks might make a splash, but ultimately, they sink and are eroded by the rushing stream of the river—by Time. But this boulder is mountain-sized, and dense with a compound not native to the world that this stream runs through. It is an anomaly.

Now imagine the water meeting this rock. The moment it collides with its dark alien surface and races upwards, displaced. Heaving and groaning around the rock, *warping*, the scream of white foam and clear water, the currents confused, the silt churned up from the bottom, and beneath the tossing water, the things surfacing that should have stayed buried.

The river is not weak. It is strong and it adapts, and so, it splits.

And buried corpses peel from the riverbed, dancing in the stream.

Alarick felt all this, heart beating faster, as the quiet music of the shitty bar seemed to fade into nothing. An intruder to the timeline, reforming it with their presence alone.

I'm not going back there, had been his first thought. *Not my city anymore, not my problem.*

But, as Alarick's hands gripped the sticky edge of the bar, all he could think of was another lifetime, and the woman in his arms, limp, dead. The way he had reached out with his power, in all of his grief, and wrenched backwards the hands of time—

A split in the timeline. Just like before. I vowed, never again—

He wrenched his thoughts away from the memory, but his heart thudded louder still. *No*, he couldn't let that happen again—wouldn't let it happen again.

But this split, this anomaly, had nothing to do with him. Surely, he could walk away? Slip into another century and hope his own heart didn't hold him accountable.

If only it hadn't been for the boy.

Obi can't leave the city. I was there for his Anchoring—I saw the effects of the sickness. If he jumps, he risks dying. He'd have to be crazy to even consider it. He must still be in London.

Shit. He needs my help. Really needs it. This time.

The whole city did, and Alarick knew it. Knew that something awful had fallen through the skin of the world, and he had felt it for a reason; the great creature called London was calling in a debt.

You watched the timeline split years ago, and fixed it. You're the only person who can save this city—the only person who knows how.

He also knew that Obi wouldn't want to see him. That he wouldn't care his father hadn't left on purpose, only that he hadn't come back. And all because he couldn't face a son who was sick because of him.

You're a coward, Alarick. He drained the last of the alien alcohol, grimacing at the taste. *Yeah. Yeah, I know. But there's nothing I can do. He'll never forgive me.*

Unless.

Unless he did go back.

An idea had formed in his mind, spurred by a decade's worth of guilt, the drink, and one image; his son, looking at him with pride in his eyes, like he used to when he was younger, when Alarick could still impress him with cheap tricks, and take him to the museum.

If I go back, and investigate the breach, find the intruder and eliminate them, I can reverse the split in London's timeline. I can save Obi's life, and *the city he's Anchored to. He'd* have *to speak to me. Maybe we could even work together. I would have the chance to explain . . . everything. About his mother. And why I left.*

And if, after all that, Obi couldn't find it in his heart to forgive him then . . . well, he never would, and Alarick could leave again at least knowing that he had tried.

And you can visit her grave, he thought. *Leave flowers. Peonies, her favourite.*

For a moment, he had wondered how he'd got there—light-years away from the city he'd trapped his son in by not raising him right, not teaching him what he should have. Away from the city where his wife was buried; so far from the bones of his life's greatest love.

He had put his cup down, settled up with the barkeeper, and left.

The jump had been seamless, like falling through clear water, so the first breath of cool, smog-thick London air was like a punch to the gut.

The first thing he had to do was find Obi. It would be easy enough—he could feel the familiar energy of his soul from a mile away.

He closed his eyes, concentrating.

A building at the city's centre. Near to the river. *Westminster.*

As long as he wasn't hiding somewhere in Parliament or in the royal bloody residences, this shouldn't be too hard.

Chapter Ten

[planet: Earth] + [location: London] + [year: 1812]

George felt tired all the way to his bones; taking on so much responsibility for directing the proceedings of the war had begun to take its toll. He hadn't been sleeping. Hadn't been eating properly. Hadn't had the time.

He sunk to the bathroom floor, sliding down the wall until he was collapsed on the cool tiles. He had sought refuge in the starkness of the room's white walls after a particularly gruesome night terror, and now found himself wondering how it was possible, or *fair* that he could feel so sorry for himself for losing sleep in the luxury of a palace over the hardship of *doing his job*, when men were laying down their lives against Napoleon across the Channel.

He closed his eyes. Lately he felt as though his life had become a constant grasp for more time, more sleep, more answers. A desperate clutch at less responsibility and less of the crushing loneliness that seemed to hang over him like a weight. Although, if he had asked any of his advisors about a cure for loneliness, they would have simply pointed to the calendar, and the date that loomed closer.

He opened his eyes, blinking slowly in the dim light. Then he looked down at his hand.

The ring was simple. A band of gold inlaid with a small

diamond. A far more extravagant one was being worn by a girl six months his senior. Her name was Gisela. She lived in Braunschweig, Germany, and he'd been told—*assured*—that she was lovely. They had exchanged letters. Well, she had written to him and George's clerk had written back. In her letters, she called him Augustine.

They were to be married in the spring.

He twisted the ring on his finger. Remembered the frantic dash to get it off when Obi's presence in the entrance hall had been announced. Shame burned on his face.

It was highly unusual for him to even be wearing one, but Gisela had apparently insisted on it. He didn't care enough to refuse. Hadn't thought Obi would ever be back to see it.

His life was slowly being taken from his hands, but he supposed he had been a fool for thinking it had been his to control in the first place.

Suddenly, he was furious, and sobbing—the kind of uncontrollable crying that appears out of nowhere. Tears spilled over his palms and through his fingers, where they dug into the bags under his eyes.

His ring was cold where it touched his cheek. With a shout, he pulled it off and flung it to the other side of the room. It bounced off the wall and skittered across the tiles to land on the floor at his feet.

Dear God, he thought. *I wish this would stop. I wish I could go back to being fifteen. I wish I was still the boy who wore his heart on his sleeve. The boy who was courageous and stupid and brave. I wish I was the same soul I once was. I wish I could forget. I wish all of this would* stop. *I wish*—

I wish.

He didn't think he wished to *die*, he just didn't want to live as himself anymore.

Wiping his face on his sleeve, he stood and faced himself in the mirror. His eyes were bloodshot, cheeks blotchy, his hair dishevelled. Angry red crescents peppered the skin under his eyes. George saw a man he did not recognise.

He blinked, and the box with the soul fragment was in his hand.

He did not remember making the conscious decision to leave the bathroom, cross the hall, and open the cabinet where he kept the box, but he had, and now that it rested in his palm, heavy with promises and the knowledge of what was inside, he realised he faced a decision.

He could keep the box. Bury it at the back of the cabinet amidst old clothes and faded papers and children's toys. It would be out of sight, but nowhere near out of mind. If he kept it, he was actively holding on to the past, to the boy who had left him. Again.

If he threw it away, who knew what would happen?

Who knew what would happen to Obi?

He nearly questioned if he cared, but George had never been able to lie to himself like Obi could.

His hands shook.

Fumbling, he placed the box on the bed and dug a small glass bottle out of his pocket. He held it up to the light. A reddish-brown liquid filled the bottle. Apparently, it was enough for three doses. The royal physician had prescribed it for his migraines and nightmares and had told him he was welcome to as much as he needed. It also helped with the tremors he had developed lately.

Unscrewing the cap, he tried to convince himself that there was no shame in taking the drug. It soothed him, helped him to feel as though there was hope for his situation. It also made him feel more . . . whole. Lately, he had felt as though he were being pulled in two different directions. It was completely illogical, and made little to no sense, but he felt almost at war with himself.

The laudanum did much more than soothe him, though.

George knew what opium was, knew of the men and women who had fallen prey to its charms and now lolled, decaying and debauched, on the filthy floors of the hazy, smoke-filled dens that infested the city. He knew that the drug was responsible for the near euphoric state he was left in after a dose or two—or three—of the medicine.

He brought the bottle to his mouth and tipped the whole thing down his throat. Nearly gagging on the sharp, bitter taste, he pressed the back of his hand against his mouth, grimacing.

The effect was almost instantaneous. His head cleared; his limbs felt lighter. The quality of the light in the room changed a little. It was less harsh, less blinding.

He returned his attention to the box that now lay on his bed. His vision seemed more focused, more lucid. He noticed that the colours of the box were now inversed. The box itself was silver, the lock was black. George blinked, and they switched back. Shaking his head, he grabbed the box with steady fingers. Dizziness threatened to overwhelm, so he sat down on the bed. The world tilted again, so he lay down, curled up on top of the duvet, clutching the box in his hands. He pressed a sharp edge to his cheek momentarily, revelling a little in the pain.

I miss you, he thought. *Why did you leave without saying goodbye?*

But what else had he expected?

He fell into sleep quickly, like stepping off a cliff edge into warm, dark water—the laudanum like stones around his feet.

A strange feeling near dawn woke him briefly. He thought he must have heard something—or seen it through the soft black of his closed eyelids. But the wakeful feeling didn't last, and he quickly fell back to sleep.

If he'd stayed awake, he might have walked to the curtained window, to pull back the curtains. He might have seen—past the drizzle spattering softly against the glass—a bright flash like lightning, in the air above the British Museum, just over a half hour's walk north-east.

He might have returned to bed only after looking out the window, feeling confused, but tired, and so finally turning over to sleep, only to stare in horror as the shining surface of the grand standing mirror in the room's darkest corner began to wobble. No, ripple. The entire surface moving like a liquid, rather than glass.

No one can say what he might have done when a hand clawed through the mirror's surface and grabbed the wooden edge, hauling a head after it, and a torso, and finally two legs. The intruder unfurled like a black, metallic flag—dark armour protesting softly at the movement, brown skin turned to deepening lilac in the moonlight, auburn hair casting shadows over eyes that glinted amber, like a large cat's.

Perhaps, if George had been awake to protect the box he had fallen asleep holding, the next few years of his life might have gone very differently.

But he was not.

So, when the intruder went silently—preternaturally quietly—towards the bed, to lift the box slowly from where it lay by George's lolling palm, the prince could not defend himself, or the thing he had been sworn to protect. He could only keep sleeping, whistling slightly on the exhale, oblivious to the fact the box containing a portion of Obi's soul was no longer in his possession.

The ancient Hero tucked the box out of sight, took one last glance at the young man on the bed, and shook his head. *Too easy. This one is not meant for greatness, only to accompany it, and become invisible in its shadow.*

The Hero tapped the rusted point of his sword to the glass of the mirror, causing it to ripple once again, before stepping through the surface like it was only mist, or a normal doorway. Within seconds he was gone. No trace of him remained, but a line in the carpet, dug by the corroded point of a very old sword.

For a moment, all was as it had been before.

George slept on as rain spattered against the windowpane, the bottle of laudanum glinting dully in the moonlight. The whole of London was asleep, or wanting to be. The night outside the house as quiet as death.

Then Alarick Amadi walked through the door.

Or tried to. He slammed into a wall of power. The impact was so shocking, he was hurled back into his own mind, senses burning, while something watched him from the shadows of it, a thing with blood-red eyes. He had never felt anything like that in his life.

A deathly pale, phantom hand curled around his consciousness, wrapping skeletal fingers around his brain.

Alarick yelled, gathering his strength, trying to summon enough willpower to expel the intruder. To separate his thoughts from the probing, violent hand now snatching at his defences—

And then it was gone, just as swiftly as it had arrived.

His vision cleared slowly, the static clarifying, until the room was visible once more. He swayed on his feet, shivering. It had been so long since anyone had brushed aside his defences so easily—he had believed they were nigh on impenetrable. His palms itched.

The remnants of magic in the room beyond the door were electric. His fingertips felt fuzzy, his skin charged. Magic like this was rare. One did not simply happen upon it. Or at least, he never had—and he'd been everywhere. He'd spent time in so many centuries over the years, son in tow for some of it, and never experienced anything like this. Never on this scale. It was not of this world, that much he was certain of.

There were very few things that could wield so much power. None of them good.

London, he thought, was proving to be far more difficult than initially predicted.

Alarick slipped over the threshold into the prince's chambers. Reaching out with his mind, honing in on that sense that allowed him to pinpoint the energy rolling off Obi's soul in waves.

It was gone. His son was nowhere to be seen.

He scowled, swearing under his breath, before stepping further into the room. It was huge, the second in a network of rooms that he thought belonged to the Prince of Wales, or maybe his son. Had Obi just left? Why couldn't he feel his soul's energy anymore—

There was someone on the bed. Previously obscured by the mound of covers and assorted pillows, a face was visible now, as Alarick moved around the room, pale in the grey-blue light, brown hair falling across the pillow in disarray.

He remembered suddenly, something Qala had said a good few years ago. They had arranged to meet in a dive bar on an outlying planet, for old time's sake. *He is quite . . . taken with one of the royal sons. A prince, known to be rebellious, considered by many unfit for his title. I believe he has entrusted him with the care and protection of his soul fragment.*

Alarick had nodded and smiled and said, 'Oh, really?', because it would have been rude to say, 'Don't talk to me about the kid.'

But he had immediately banished the new information from his mind, to assuage the guilt.

It came back now, in full force.

He had been tracking Obi's fragment, not the boy himself. *For fuck's sake.*

He was stood over the Prince now, looking down on him. He was good enough looking. Normal face, normal . . . hair. Alarick recalled what he knew about the royal line after 1812, which wasn't much. This was King Augustine, he'd come to power later in life, outlive all his siblings, but never have children. The line would pass to his cousin, who would, if he remembered rightly, be Queen Victoria. Lord knew what Obi was doing getting involved with a royal, but that was the funny thing about love, wasn't it? Or at the very least, infatuation. It led you astray. *And brings only unhappiness,* Alarick thought grimly. *He'll learn.*

Beneath him, the prince—*George,* wasn't it?—stirred. And then, to Alarick's horror (it was far too early in the morning to be conversing with anyone, let alone the other half of his son's . . . entanglement) opened his eyes.

They stared at each other for a moment—Alarick, tall and dark, short beard shot through with grey, George, pale and confused, blinking rapidly as though attempting to dispel a hallucination.

"Who in God's name are you?" the prince slurred.

"Your worst nightmare," Alarick said. Which was funny, but the boy turned deathly pale and looked almost like he was about to cry. "Jesus Christ, I'm kidding. That was a joke."

George stilled suddenly, the atmosphere in the room intensifying in seconds. His mouth fell open, as though he had seen a ghost.

". . . Obi?"

"Obi? *What?* No. Is that—please tell me you're joking?"

George looked startled, then relieved. "Sorry, I simply thought that perhaps you were him from . . . the future? I apologise, that sounds insane, but I—I don't." He pulled his shirt up over his shoulders and got out of bed, blinking slowly. Toying with something by his bedframe, he said, "Well, if you're not him, then who are you?"

Alarick scoffed, *if he hasn't figured it out by now—*

A scraping sound echoed, and suddenly George was out of bed and standing up, the cold, razor-sharp point of a sword digging into Alarick's neck.

"Alarick." The boy's eyes were remarkably lucid. Piercing, almost. It was incredibly unnerving.

"Yeah, that's me."

"Why are you here?" The tone of his voice had changed. It was cold, impersonal. No trace of inebriation lingered. *Clever.*

"Thought I'd do some sightseeing, take a river cruise, maybe *check up on my son—*"

"He thinks you are dead. Did you know that?" The sword dug in harder. "I did not see him for three years, because he ran away, to the future, chasing you. To find you. He's more metal than man now, you selfish bastard. He sacrificed so much of himself because he thought finding you would help him to understand himself. To understand where he came from. But all it gained him in the end was pain." Alarick felt a warm trickle of blood leak down his neck. *Alright, this has gone far enough.*

He flicked his fingers. The sword disappeared—thrown forward a couple of hundred years in time. George inhaled sharply. Alarick smiled and said, "Don't move."

George threw a punch that connected squarely with the underside of Alarick's jaw.

His head snapped back. Dull, throbbing pain spreading fast. Alarick staggered. *Well, that was unexpected.*

They held each other's gazes, both unwilling to look away, to betray any sign of weakness—

"Oh good *God*!" George exclaimed, flapping his hand around. "That was *so painful*! How are you not unconscious? Or at least somewhat concussed?"

Alarick wiped the blood from under his nose and smiled. "You kept your thumb inside your fist, didn't you?"

"I think it may be broken." The boy sounded half strangled.

"What kind of father doesn't teach his son to box properly?"

"My father is the *ruler of this country*."

"I don't see your point."

George huffed. "You still haven't answered my question."

May as well be blunt. "Look here, you little shit, I'm here to see Obi. I need to warn him of something. And tell him to take better care of the part of his soul that he left with you."

Geroge looked disbelieving. "Well, I'm sorry to tell you, but Obi is not here."

"What?"

"You just missed him, I'm afraid. He was here last month." A strange, painful look came over his face. "It was just two weeks ago that he came to . . . er, to visit, I suppose."

Shit, Alarick thought. Then, he had an idea. *Ah! Not shit.* If Obi was gone, he could use his absence to his advantage. "When is he coming back?" he asked the boy.

"I could not say," George replied, rather tersely. "He did not care to inform me."

"Eeesh," Alarick said. "Aren't you supposed to be his boyfriend or something?"

The kid went so violently red that Alarick seriously thought he might have to perform some kind of manoeuvre to get his heart going.

"Okay," he said. "Moving on . . . I have decided to stay here, indefinitely. I'll handle the situation, deal with whatever it is that's going on in this trouble-magnet of a city, and then when Obi returns—he has to, it's his Anchoring Place—I'll be here, saved soul in hand, having saved the day. And then maybe he'll let go of his grudge and forgive me." He nodded, satisfied, talking more to himself than the prince.

But the boy's eyes had narrowed when Alarick mentioned 'the situation'. And when he mentioned Obi's forgiveness they turned to dark slivers of green.

"Forgive you?" George's voice was quiet. "You think that is all it will take? You, gliding in here like some kind of hero, and he is just supposed to take your absence from his entire life in his stride and *forgive you*? And what 'situation'?"

"Son," Alarick said. "I didn't ask for your opinion, nor do I care for anything that a British prince has to say about forgiveness. So, if you don't mind, just get me that box with his soul fragment in it so that I can protect it properly, and I'll be on my way."

George's eyes widened. "The box," he breathed. Turning swiftly around he stared at the bed. "Where . . . ?" He strode forward, messing with the bedclothes. "It was here." He ran to a glass-fronted cabinet by the far wall, his face falling at the sight of empty shelves,

"Well, where is it now?" Alarick growled.

"No, no, no!" George said, ignoring him. His voice was strangled. "This cannot be—"

"Son," Alarick said, voice changing from vaguely intimidating to 'I *will* fuck you the fuck up' in a few octaves. "*Where is the goddamn box?*"

George turned back around, face pale. "It's gone."

Chapter Eleven

[planet: none] + [location: free space] + [year: 6066]

"If you're really a time-traveller," said Asha sceptically, glancing at Obi where he sat in the passenger seat, "explain how it works."

They were sitting in the cockpit, Obi skittish and fidgety, Asha guiding the ship as they jumped through public hyperspace tunnels, leading them further and further away from Gahraan. It was surreal, to watch the darkness glide by, the distant nebulae, the million stars and their hundred worlds, blue-green glow of interstellar clouds and the hyperspace tunnels that connected them, blinking in and out of existence.

They'd been talking for a while. After she'd made the connection between him and the boy she had seen in her vision, she'd almost fainted. It was eerie now, knowing that she had seen something before it had happened. And, of course, there was that feeling. Like she'd known Obi for years. Longer. She wanted to find out who he was, to understand why she'd seen him. To gauge whether or not he was a threat.

Reluctantly, she'd told him about Aziza—not her mother's story, but a halting description of events that explained why she had to get to A'lkari, and in return he'd spun a rambling tale that sounded like something out of a story. A father who had left him. A punishing, mythical illness. A prince, waiting for him all alone in a castle, and of course, the way he could apparently *jump through time.* He seemed quick to offer information about his life, but not about himself. Things that had happened to him, but not the way he had lived them. And sometimes, under the near frantic energy and quick grins, she thought he actually looked quite sad.

"Yeah, okay, um," Obi said, breaking her train of thought. "Well, all I have to go on is a page from a book that I . . . found in my pocket." He shook his head. "In the footnotes of that page there's a very brief explanation. I'll read it to you." He rummaged around in an inside pocket, producing a yellowing piece of paper. Clearing his throat, he read, "'*The colloquial usage of 'Guide' was first coined by young recruits of the Order, unable to pronounce the archaic name of 'Arïcoaryuŋ'. The term derived from the most credible theory to date on how the Arïcoaryuŋ are able to gather the energy to jump such vast distances and over the span of so many years. This theory states that a 'Guide' harnesses the sentimental value of an object and utilises that powerful energy to return or 'guide' the object to a certain time and place; often the time and place where it was valued most by a sentient lifeform.*'"

Asha pursed her lips, frowning. Any other day, she would have laughed herself to tears. But maybe he was telling the truth. He didn't seem crazy. And if he was a time-traveller, maybe that explained why she'd seen him before she'd ever met him.

Then something at the bottom of the page caught her eye. Next to an unreadable string of text was a symbol. The same one on the projector. The same one that etched itself onto her mother's face before she disappeared.

The Sentinel's face flashed in front of her eyes. *You will call me Sentinel*, he'd said. *Sentinel of the Order of Legends.* It was their symbol. Asha froze. Distantly she heard Obi talking, but a rushing noise had filled her ears and her heart was slamming into her chest. *No.* She had to stay calm. What had Obi said before? His father knew about The Order of Legends but that he himself knew nothing—

"Are you alright?"

"Yes! Sorry." She had to get herself under control. "What were you saying? You're one of them? A guide?"

Obi nodded, looking suspicious. "I just said that. Are you sure you're okay?"

Asha nodded vigorously, over-playing nonchalance while her mind raced. *He said he hadn't been sent by the Sentinel, but what if he'd lied. Of course he would lie. What if he was here to kill her? Or to ensure she followed orders—*

No, said the rational part of her brain. If he had been, he would have never shown her that. It would have given everything away. Best to stay calm and keep a keen eye on him. He might seem trustworthy, but she had to remember there was only one person she could trust now in this whole galaxy—herself. And if he did know something, but was keeping it from her, maybe she could get it out of him later.

Keeping her voice level, she asked, "So, you can just pick up any object that someone owned, and then—*just by touching it*—you can alter, I don't know, matter itself or—or the fabric of the universe, or *physics,* as we know it, anyway—and travel through time and space?" She narrowed her eyes. "There are *so* many reasons why that should not work." Obi looked vaguely affronted. She pushed further. "And even if it somehow *was* possible . . . what if more than one person owned something? What then? And how do you ever touch anything without being pulled into another time? And *since when* was 'sentimental energy' even a credible, convertible, or viable energy source? What if—"

"You're a curious one, aren't you?"

Asha shrugged.

"I can only use objects which were *really* valued by someone at some point. There has to be enough sentimental energy to power a jump. Your projector, for example. How did you feel about it?"

Despite her suspicions, the mere mention of the projector sent a pang of loss through Asha's chest, tinged with embarrassment. It must have shown on her face, because Obi smiled knowingly.

"Exactly. You were invested in it; it was directly connected to your dreams, your aspirations, your hopes, and fears. It was drenched in sentimental value, and therefore, sentimental energy."

"Okay," she paused. "But what if all of this hadn't happened? What if I had grown up and kept it. Given it to my . . . uh, my daughter? And she loved it for an entirely different reason, but she still loved it and was emotionally attached to it? What then? Who would it, you know—" she gestured vaguely "—*guide* you to?"

"Ah," Obi said. "Well, that's the fun part, I guess. I get to choose." He shrugged. "I get a feeling for all the different people who have owned something, and how they felt about it, and where and when they lived, and then—" he shrugged again "—I just choose."

Asha sat up straighter. He could choose? What if there was a way that he could guide them to Iyanda? The shirt Asha was wearing—it had been her mother's once. What if he could use it to help Asha get her mother back?

She tried to keep her face neutral. Though seeing that he carried something associated with the Order of Legends had raised her suspicions, he seemed nice enough. But if he thought she was trying to use him, that could change. She eyed the scar on his face, a long one that flicked up from his jaw, through his eyebrow, narrowly missing his eye. He could fight.

Keeping her voice meek, and her eyes focussed firmly ahead, she wondered aloud, "So you could do it right now? Go somewhere? If you had the right object?"

Out of the corner of her eye she saw him grimace.

"Well," Obi said. "Not really. The sickness I told you about—I'm still sick. And, unlike before, I care enough about my life not to risk it all on one jump. I have someone waiting for me. Someone I—uh, care for. Dearly. Who I must return to. So I can't, or I'd—" he broke off.

After a moment's silence he pulled back the long sleeve of his dark coat.

"I can handle this," he said, waving his metal arm. "And this." He tapped his eye.

"Really, that too? Well, it looks great. I can't even tell."

Obi laughed. It sounded genuine. Everything about him sounded genuine. "Two ribs, a molar . . . one of my toes too . . . That was weird." He shrugged. "But if I went anywhere now—well, it could be my heart next. A lung. I've been so lucky, in the past. But luck doesn't last forever."

Asha sunk back into her chair, defeated. He couldn't help her—why would he risk his life for a girl—a child—he'd just met. She was on her own. Just like she always would be.

She realised she'd been silent for a few moments, so she asked the most obvious question. "If you can't go back without risking your life . . . what are you going to do?"

Obi sighed, shaking his head. "There are rumours of a group called the Magekind. They experiment with medical magic. I think they work for the Emperor. They're the only ones who have a hope of ever curing me. I will seek them out and ask the price. Hopefully it is one I can pay. The cure is my only way home."

The Magekind. Asha nodded. "They exist. I saw them once or twice, when I was younger. Sometimes they would come to Gahraan. Take some kids, some adults. To experiment on, is what everyone always said." When she was younger, older children fashioned the scientists into wizards dressed in white, who snatched naughty children from their beds and took them to the Emperor to be eaten as a punishment for disobedience.

Obi nodded grimly. "Then I have to find them. I'll get the cure, just like I always wanted, and I'll go home. Again."

"I'm sorry," she murmured. "I'm sorry I brought you here. I don't know how I did it, or why. Or if it even was me. But I'm sorry you're so far from home."

"It's alright." Obi said softly.

She felt for him. They hadn't got off to the best of starts, but he had dragged her onto the ship and away from danger, patched up her wound, comforted her, and told her a story that sounded a lot like the truth. That meant something.

They lapsed into a comfortable silence, Asha gently steering, Obi fidgeting with a loose thread on his T-shirt.

"I've never met my sister," Asha said, after a while. She had conveniently left this part out before, but after Obi had told her about his painful life, she felt oddly compelled to share a little of hers. Obi looked up, confused. "My sister," she added in a quiet voice. "I've never even seen her face." She paused. "Well, I have, but it was a hologram. She was much younger in it than she would be now."

Next to her, Obi looked intrigued. "The projector—the hologram of the girl. That was your sister?"

Asha looked at him warily. "How did you know what was on the projector?"

"I saw it, back in London, in my time. Before I brought it back here. I heard her voice in my head . . . she asked '*Is anyone there?*'."

"Yeah, that's what she was saying in the recording—"

"No. I heard it. In my head. Like she was speaking directly into my brain."

Asha stared at him. *I should tell him,* she thought. *That I saw him in my vision. But I just don't know if I can trust him.* It felt like crucial information. She didn't know why, but it did. *But he heard your sister's voice,* she thought. *And he mentioned a golden light, just like the one you saw when the Sentinel came for you. Maybe he could be an ally.*

She opened her mouth—

The shrill sound of a klaxon pierced the still air.

Asha jumped to her feet.

"What the hell was that?" Obi asked, his voice low.

Adrenaline shot through her body as she slipped through the hatchway to the cockpit, her fleet sliding over the too-polished floor.

"Asha—"

"Hold on," she snapped, "I know what I'm doing." She did not know what she was doing, but she needed silence. Desperately, she scanned the control panel for a tell-tale red light, or rapidly decreasing pressure gauge. Everything seemed to be in order, but still the klaxon screeched, high and keening, grating on her frazzled nerves, driving her towards panic. Then the sound changed slightly, flattening to become a series of unending beeps.

"Well, that's not ominous at all," Obi whispered.

She didn't bother to reply.

Please no. No, no, no, no, no. Asha's hands flew over the system's interface keyboard. The alarm shut off without warning. *Did I fix it?* She thought.

But the flat, even voice of an AI replaced it. "Unidentified craft," it intoned.

Asha's heart jumped into her mouth.

"Please identify yourself."

Asha turned to face Obi. "It's the government," she said, her voice a strangled whisper. "It's a Consortium ship." Her throat was closing up. "How the hell did our sensors miss this? I can't see it. It's not even showing up on the radar!"

"They must be cloaked," Obi said.

Asha squeezed her eyes shut. Of *course* they were. What in Thracin's name were they supposed to do now?

"Obi, we're dead."

"We could get lucky? Maybe we can talk ourselves out of it and—"

"We're human. They won't listen."

Abruptly, a shadow fell across their faces, blotting out the light from the stars around them as the ship dropped its cloaking shields.

Looking up and out of the window, Asha steeled herself for the inevitable sight of a two-man government issue patrol ship—small, with a knife-sharp nose and heavy thrusters on each side. Manoeuvrable. Nimble. Easy to coast above residential streets.

What she really saw was far worse.

The hull of the biggest ship she had ever seen in her life eased into view, dwarfing their miniature craft. She could barely process its magnitude.

"That looks like a cargo ship. Why is a cargo ship asking us for identification? Why do they care?" asked Obi, incredulous.

Asha jumped as photons streamed from a groove in the dashboard. They swirled upwards, forming a slightly transparent screen that glowed with a soft, blue luminescence. A simple message blinked into existence on its surface.

"What do they mean, *prepare to be boarded?*" croaked Obi.

With a groan, their entire ship lurched sideways, the interior filling with a sickly purple light. The artificial gravity shut off without a sound, and suddenly they were weightless. Asha's tangled curly hair floated around her face like seaweed. Obi reached out a hand and snatched up his coat as it floated past, random objects beginning to drift out of the pockets.

Asha was finding it harder and harder to breathe. The horribly bright purple light and the subsequent loss of gravity could mean only one thing.

"Tractor beam," she said. Her heart was thudding a frantic rhythm in her chest. She'd seen this happen sometimes, to random humans, plucked from their meagre lives and taken Thracin knows where for Thracin knows what.

"They're taking us into the hold. They must know this ship is stolen—" She took a deep breath. "Do you see those symbols on the starboard side? I've read about them. The first one means whatever it's carrying is organic. Plants or livestock . . ." She squinted. "The next symbol—I don't know. It's similar to the symbol for danger, or caution, but see how it's linked to the third symbol?" She took another breath. The air was thinning. "That's what they put on autonomous AIs. It's the symbol for sentient life. Combine 'danger' and 'sentience' and you get . . ." Her voice trailed off, breaths heavy in the silence. "I think—" she paused for just a moment before steeling herself for what was to come "—I think its cargo is *criminals*. It's a prison ship."

"You can't be s—"

"Obi, I think we're being arrested."

An adventure is never easy. Perhaps if it were, it would be called something else.

'A Complete, Annotated History of Chasca, Including Relevant Translated Mythologies. Chapter: Scroll the Second' by I. Nisomn, ex-acolyte of the Aonian Archives.

Chapter Twelve

[planet: none] + [location: free space] + [year: 6066]

"This is bullshit," Obi said. "And that's putting it mildly."

Asha nodded in agreement. Tipping her chin back, she rested her head on the concrete wall, shutting her eyes tightly against the fluorescent glow of the overhead lights.

They had been playing prisoner for two days already, and Asha was going out of her mind.

After they had been hauled from their stolen aircraft—Obi cursing and kicking, Asha silent and nauseous—the Consortium soldiers had shoved them into decontamination cylinders, and then into cells. Each one housed two people, and they were arranged in blocks of four. The other six occupants of their small quadrangle had been arrested on the other end of a hyperspace tunnel, leaving a space station that was a known site of black-market trading—its remote location meaning it was hardly ever raided by the Consortium. They called it 'the NIS', and had told Asha and Obi multiple times that if they had met them outside the prison, they'd have kidnapped them, taken them to the NIS and sold them as slaves, or prostitutes, or even wall decorations, for a price that made Asha's eyes water. She vowed to never set foot in the place.

"We need to get out of here," Obi was saying for the hundredth time, clearly as miserable as Asha felt. "You're our girl

146

with the plans, what are you thinking?"

Asha squinted at him. "Girl with the plans?"

"I'm working on it. Come on. If you can break out of that awful prison planet you used to live on, you can break us out of here. How'd you do it?"

"I had years to plan that. I had a tablet, so I could hack into government databases to get flight school textfiles for, you know, learning theory, and also to download simvids of different manoeuvres and flight patterns—those were how I learned to fly. I had to steal a ship. I don't have any of those things here."

"When you talk about 'back home'," Obi said curiously, "what was it really like?"

Asha shrugged. "Bad."

"A woman of few words, I see."

"I'd just rather not talk about it." A pause. "Sorry. Look—"

Sharp footsteps sounded outside their cell—a contingent of guards moving quickly. They both sprang to their feet.

"What—" Obi started.

The cell door slid open, spilling bright white light and four guards into the cramped space.

Asha and Obi cringed backwards, but the guards advanced, blaster rifles slung over their shoulders.

Two of them grabbed Asha, slamming handcuffs over her wrists before she had a chance to protest. They pinned her arms to her side and shoved her forwards, marching her into the corridor.

"Asha!" Obi cried. "Hold on, I'll get you out, I'll—*get off me*—just hold on! I won't let them *mmph!*"

She threw one last look over her shoulder to see Obi kneeling on the ground, handcuffed, a muzzle over his face, eyes wild, the glowing tip of a blaster digging into his temple. The guards forced her face forward, clawed fingers digging into her jaw.

Asha stumbled, her ankle twisting, bright pain flaring up her calf. She cried out, and the guard to her left snarled, "*Silence, prisoner,*" in a voice Asha immediately recognised as robotic. The guards were androids.

They rounded the corner, tearing her away from Obi's shouts and into a featureless corridor.

She held her breath, squeezing her eyes shut, straining to hear past the metallic footsteps, listening for the sound of a gun blast, for the dull thud of a body hitting the floor—for the universe to announce: *you are alone. Again.* But they turned another corner, a door sliding shut behind them, and the sound of his resistance faded to nothing.

The guards kept up a relentless march through the maze of hallways, until they pushed her through a door that required retinal scanning to bypass, and then shoved her to her knees in an octagonal room with drains in the floor and every kind of weapon imaginable on the walls.

Asha was struck with the nauseating certainty that they were going to kill her. She could already see it. One of them would take a gleaming axe from the shelf and swing it in a wild arc, slicing through her arteries and her spine, severing her head from her body. Her blood would slide down the drains in a river of crimson and her corpse would be efficiently disposed of in the large black container in the corner marked 'For incineration', never to be buried, never to be mourned.

One of the guard-droids kicked her in her ribs. She felt newly sealed skin split open like a wet paper bag. The pain took her breath away, blunt and stabbing. She doubled over but did not cry out—her hands shook with fury in their restraints.

Three of the droids left the room. The one who had kicked her stayed, before moving to the wall and reaching for a small pistol.

"No," she groaned. "No please."

But the droid did not listen.

There was nothing she could do, no way out, no plan, nothing. Except—

Oh.

She remembered red sand whipping past her feet, the blank visor of a guard, and words, fighting their way up her throat, shoved down at the last minute. *Sedition.*

"Emperor Thracin is a tyrant and a maniac who does not deserve the throne any more than I do."

The robot turned.

There were certain behaviours a civilian could exhibit that demanded immediate punishment. Seditious writings and speech were high up on this list, and the punishment for such things was simple: starvation. Droids were programmed to dock ration points for most infractions, the number of points docked corresponding to the severity of the transgression. If Asha had been at home, her daily rations would have been docked by seventy-five per cent.

But she wasn't at home, anymore.

"Sedition will be punished. Divine Might is Divine Right. Divine Might is Divine Right. Divine Might is Divine—"

The droid's eyes turned blue as it attempted to process her misdemeanour and failed. Her face would not be featured on census records this far out into imperial space, just her number, which she'd refused to give. Humans were perishable goods and were classed as such, and they were undoubtedly too far from the closed system of Gahraanian satellites that stored human records for it to access those. Its mouth opened. "Request denied. Seeking alternate route. Do not m—"

Asha lunged forward, swinging her cuffed wrists to smash into the droid's skull. The metal of the cuffs slammed against the grinding metal mandible plates of the droid's face. Pain exploded down her arms, her knuckles throbbing. She gritted her teeth and swung again, and again, and again, until the droid went down, still frozen as it tried to process her punishment without success. By the time she was done, she could barely see through the tears streaming down her cheeks. The red smeared across the droid's white mask matched the bloody mess of her hands.

"Soldier?" she said, but it came out in a whisper. She cleared her throat. "Soldier?"

No reply. No alarms were blaring, either. No cold, artificial voice reprimanded her over the speakers. There were no footsteps outside, no angry soldiers shouting commands.

Her breath trickled out of her, slowly at first and then all at once. She could have wept more. Could have lain her head down on the floor and cried until she fell asleep. But there wasn't *time*.

Obi, she thought. *I have to find him.*

She scrambled to the section of the wall where the bladed weapons hung and slid the razor-sharp blade of a dagger under the panels of her handcuffs. It sprang open, the cuffs releasing. Still no alarms. Her eyes widened, disbelieving, as the silence continued. Then, a roar of noise jolted her back to reality. Her first thought was that she had been discovered and that the chorus of voices belonged to a squadron of guards, but as she listened, she realised that the noise was almost . . . jubilant. Feet stamping, and harsh laughter. She could also hear screams of agony and howls of pain. She hurried to the door on the far side of the room, and looked out of the small, circular window set into the top.

A cavernous room stretched out beyond. Row upon row of sentients were crammed into the space, all of them somehow wild-looking—face pieces whirring and hungry for blood. At the centre was a ring—a fighting ring—where two figures brawled. They were locked together, all but leaning on each other. Half of a curved, serrated sword lay forgotten, next to a blaster rifle that had been cut in half and was still smoking. A hologram flashed above the ring, numbers flickering on it. A timer. Asha could scarcely believe her eyes. The pair in the ring had been fighting for just over twelve hours.

The weapons around the walls of the room she'd been taken to now made sense. She was being prepped to go into the ring. She checked the doors she'd been brought through—they required access codes to open, and the previous set had a retinal scanner—neither of which would work for her. She eyed the broken android.

Her only way out was through the ring.

Surveying the weapons on the walls, she went straight for the guns. There was a decent selection, but the grips were all wrong, none of them suited to human anatomy, and none of them quite deadly enough, none of them intended to help the bearer win too easily.

Yet.

The thing about Consortium manufactured weaponry was that it was so easily modified. Just like the android had been familiar, so were all the weapons. All the parts were compatible with one another as they were all made by the same three companies. Companies that outsourced large amounts of their manual labour to the factories on Gahraan. *Yay for weapons assembly day,* she thought grimly, before grabbing a solid looking blaster and a smaller, more precision focused pistol, and getting to work.

Taking apart the guns was child's play and tinkering with the extended burst heat-ray setting on another gun until it was hot enough to melt metal was a fun little challenge, but welding the two guns together in such a way that she could grip, stun, and shoot-to-kill was a little bit harder. Her hands shook slightly as she worked.

The job was done in just under seven minutes. Eight, if you counted the time it took for her to breathe, swallow, and remind herself there were no quotas to fill today, maybe ever again, that Gahraan was just a point of light in a vast galaxy, and that she was going to *escape*. Again.

She was still wearing the prison garb. Somewhat reluctantly, she made her way towards the black container labelled 'For Incineration'. Maybe there would be something in there she could use . . . She flung it open.

No way. It was a pile of clothes. Mostly ripped and bloodied prison jumpsuits she didn't want to examine too closely. But there, amongst the paper-thin material, was Obi's long coat. She yanked it out, and her standard issue beige factory uniform and white undershirt was underneath it. As much as she hated the sight of it, her uniform was durable, made of a strong canvas-like material that would protect her skin from scrapes. Quickly, she struggled out of the jumpsuit, pulling on the familiar clothes, and shrugging Obi's coat around her shoulders. It was heavy—the pockets clinking and rattling with who knew what—but it would provide extra armour against whatever awaited her past that door.

The doors. She had seen retinal scanning points by some of them.

Hesitantly she turned back to the android guard. Propped up the head with her foot, she leaned over it, snatching up one of the thin pieces of metal she had stripped from the outer plating of the gun. She slipped it into the android's eye socket and with a shove, popped the whole thing out, trailing wires. Grimacing, she shoved it into the breast pocket of Obi's coat before snatching up her new gun, and bracing herself by the exit.

It made sense that the door to the ring wouldn't have any security—there was only one real way out. And, as it slid open, she was hit by the crowing of the commentators and the screams of the crowds. The air was hot and muggy—a shock after the cool, antiseptic scented air of the prison, but just as foreign, just as unsettling—swamping her with its iron tang. One of the figures in the ring landed an explosive punch, throwing their opponent onto their back. The crowd hushed, straining forward in anticipation of a killing blow. The figure picked up the broken sword, turning back to the fighter that sprawled limply on the ground.

"Do it!" someone screamed.

The fighter smiled. Blood dripped from a ruby-red mouth, broken teeth curving upwards in jagged spires.

They shook their head, and then, before anyone could stop them, turned the sword onto themselves and fell onto the blade.

A gasp rippled through the audience, followed by groans of disappointment.

Asha stood stock-still. All she could see was the wet end of the blade protruding from a broken back.

Her vision tunnelled, focusing on the facts; this was her fate if she did not escape, and to someone who placed survival above nearly everything else, that simply could not compute. Until now, this whole experience had been terrifying, but in the way a nightmare is terrifying after waking. This was the moment Asha's terror ceased to exist somewhere outside of her and instead took root in her heart.

She did not make the conscious decision to run, but it was what she did. Sprinting along the rows of spectators, she weaved past hulking, muscled bodies and ducked outstretched arms, while frantically scanning the perimeter for an exit. Sweat stung the cuts on her hands. Her breath was coming in short, painful heaves when she finally saw it: an *open door*. She barrelled towards it, feet pounding along the ground. Then she stopped short, nearly tripping.

Two guards were dragging a figure through the door and towards the tunnel that led to the ring. The prisoner was putting up a fight, kicking and writhing, but his hands were bound and his feet tied together. It took four guard-droids to hold him down, cut his bindings, and shove him into the tunnel, but they did it. The door closed behind him without a sound.

The last Asha saw of Obi's face were his grey eyes, white in the darkness, and his mouth, shouting protests she could not hear.

Their adventure did not start well. Mother had warned them not to stray from each other's sides, but Sensit did not listen, and ran forward into the mist, eager to slay the fabled beast that guarded the mountain pass they sought to cross. Adesola snatched at the air in front of her, but he was gone, slipping away into the fog like the cold breath of a phantom.

All she could do was follow and listen for his screams.

'A Complete, Annotated History of Chasca, Including Relevant Translated Mythologies. Chapter: Scroll the Second' by I. Nisomn, ex-acolyte of the Aonian Archives.

Chapter Thirteen

George sat on his bed in disgrace, Alarick on the other side of the room, pacing back and forth.

"I think I know what took it. The soul," Alarick said, turning to George. "And there's no way you could have stopped it from happening, so you can stop looking like a kicked puppy."

George felt sick to his stomach. "But the palace is guarded," he said, more to himself than Alarick, who, for many reasons (but principally for the way he had abandoned Obi), he did not like. "I—I cannot comprehend how this could have happened—"

"There's a monster," Alarick said, not seeming to care for a thing George had to say. "In your city."

George narrowed his eyes. "Pardon me?"

"I felt . . . something ugly, something *evil*, in this room, before I entered it."

"Before you *broke in*—"

"And before that, I felt a presence . . ." Alarick gestured around, as though trying to find the right words. "Step through. Like, oh, I don't know, Lucifer, let's say. In fact, let's say something fell from the sky, like an angel pushed from heaven, but not . . . holy. This thing is pure evil. And it's looking for power, that much I can guess. Things like this always are. And the fragment of Obi's soul that he left here was emitting power like a beacon."

"*'Things like this?'*" George didn't understand what Alarick was saying. "What power?" He shook his head. "I'm sorry, I don't—"

Alarick waved a hand, dismissing him. "I'm sure you've realised by now that there are things in this world that exist outside the realm of the ordinary?"

George nodded, though he was still at a loss. But he'd had practice at this—conjuring a semblance of competence and understanding when other people looked at him like they expected him to comment on the matter at hand. He did it every day.

"Like Obi," he said, slowly. "He lives with half a soul inside his body. He walks through time like it's air."

"Yes." Alarick nodded. "Just like Obi." He smiled in a way that made the hair stand up on the back of George's neck. "Just like me." He considered George for a moment. "You're alright, you know. You believe in souls because you've seen them, and you believe in magic because you know my son and you've seen what he does, and now you know me—have met me—and you've not passed away in a dead faint at the ridiculousness at all of this . . . so I think you might be good. Or good enough." He narrowed his eyes, and George felt naked for a moment, like Alarick's stare had pierced through his clothing and his blank, guarded expression, and seen the whimpering, fleshy thing that cowered inside him, and was scared of what was happening, because it did not understand.

"And you feel you owe a debt to this country," Alarick continued, voice soft, "because when you were pushed out into this world, and given a name, that name called you *king of it.*"

"I don't understand—"

"Help me," Alarick's voice was gruff, his posture stiff. George could tell immediately that *help* and *me* weren't two words he combined often. "Help me get my son's soul back. Please."

"Why me?"

"Oh. You know." He smiled, toothy, just like Obi did, with those perfect white teeth. "Desperate times."

He had no reason to trust Alarick. But there was a feeling in his chest, a rising excitement and fear, and something like awe, and the feeling was so close to the way he felt when Obi was around that—

"Yes," George heard himself saying. "Yes, of course I'll help. What do you need? An accomplice? I can do that, I'll find a way—"

"No, no, god, no. Nothing like that." Alarick grimaced. "I need a royal seal of approval. Or your backing—to investigate. I'm going to stop this creature and recover my son's soul, but I can't do it from a jail cell. So, I will have to be allowed to . . . operate outside the law. I will also need your word that you will refrain from getting any grand ideas about heroism or interfering with my investigation, as your fate as ruler is incredibly sensitive to the timeline split. If something happened to you, it could change the world forever in ways we can't even begin to understand."

"If I were to die, do you mean? It could, in a sense, alter or influence future events?"

Alarick nodded. "The arrival of this creature . . . it has already set something in motion, a split in the timeline." He closed his eyes wearily. "It has compromised the . . . structural integrity of this world." George got the sense that Alarick was translating for him, like his French tutor, or his Latin *magister*. Thinking in one language and speaking in another. "There are two possible shapes the future ahead of us might take, two pathways we might go down, depending on how we handle this breach of our world's skin. The one that already awaits us—normal life, all the woes and joys of a timeline marching forward as it is supposed to. Or, one of chaos, a deviant path that I cannot see the shape of. Whose destination none of us can foretell." Alarick smiled, but there was little humour in it. "Believe me, given the choice, I would let you and your line perish. In fact, the day this whole damned palace burns to the ground with the leeches that live in it still inside, preferably screaming, I will clap for joy and probably perform a celebratory dance. But I'd rather take the future I know over the future I don't. So, I guess you'll have to stay."

George swallowed. The stuff about the timelines was nearly nonsense to him, though the anti-monarchist and frankly treasonous sentiment glared plain as day. But the royal seal Alarick had mentioned was something he could surely obtain. "Alright," he said. "I will arrange your impunity. But you have to let me help you. Really help you. I want to be by your side."

Alarick groaned. "This can't be happening," he muttered.

"This is my mistake. Obi trusted me, and I ruined everything. I have to try and atone for it."

"Listen, kid. This isn't about atonement. Frankly, we don't have the time. You want to atone? Go to confession. What I'm talking about, tracking a powerful creature from another dimension, killing it maybe, isn't the kind of thing you do to feel better about yourself. It's the kind of thing you do if you maybe want to *die*, or if you have no other choice."

George glared at him, determination etched on his face.

"Why should you care, anyway?" he said viciously. "You left him before, what's so different now?"

Alarick stared at him. "Obi needs to know that I care."

"I'm not certain that you heard me before, but you should know that he looked for you."

"Excuse me?"

"Obi told me that he went . . . into the future to find you. He travelled through time to try and locate you. But he couldn't."

Very deliberately, George thought, Alarick's face became totally unreadable. He seemed to struggle for something to say. After a moment, he said through gritted teeth, "But he's sick."

"I don't believe he cared about that. He just wanted to have someone." George shrugged. "A family."

There was silence. A long silence, in which George started to think he'd said something very wrong.

Finally, Alarick said, "If you want to come with me, get a gun, as I will not care if you die, and will make no effort to prevent it."

Then, without a change in expression, he walked out.

George was pulling on his jacket with plans to go and see the armoury about a gun, when someone knocked sharply on the door.

"Your Royal Highness?" It was Alastair, his grandfather's butler. Which meant—

"Your grandfather wishes to speak with you," said the man-servant. "He says it is of the upmost importance, and that you must come at once, Sir."

George doubted Alarick would wait for him if he were late.

"Alright, Alastair, tell him I will arrive shortly."

"Sir, I—"

George sighed. "I suppose he told you that you were to accompany me right away?"

"I am afraid so, Your Royal Highness."

George muffled a groan and stood up. Swiping a hand quickly through his hair, he shrugged on his jacket and sash, then opened the door.

"Very good, Sir," said Alastair, and his tone was apologetic.

Grandfather must be in one of his moods. They happened occasionally—he would shake off the madness for a moment, remember George, his son's only heir, existed, and call him in, mostly to dispense useless and often shocking advice on how to run an empire that no longer existed in the same way it had when he had been a boy.

He followed Alastair down the corridor that led to his father's room, servants bowing and curtseying as he passed. He smiled at each of them, but it was forced. This meeting was bound to be excruciating, and he already wished it to be over.

When they arrived at the royal chambers Alastair smiled weakly at him and then knocked.

"Good luck, Sir," he said, and all but ran back the way they had come.

Coward, George thought. *But I'm no better.* He smiled tightly at the oaken door.

"Enter," said his grandfather, so he did.

The wind blew George's hair into his eyes as he stepped onto the balcony where the king stood. One of the old man's thin hands gripped the jewelled top of a cane, the other grasped the marble of the balcony, vice-like. The sun was setting.

"Grandfather."

The old monarch did not turn around. Whether it was a show of indifference, or a hint at his deteriorating physical condition, George did not know, nor did he care. Neither of them spoke. A garden of manicured hedges spread out before them, a fountain gurgling pleasantly at their centre. And beyond that, London.

"This is my legacy," George's dying grandfather said abruptly into the silence, sweeping one withered hand in an arc over the city. "This is what I leave you to protect."

Whatever George had been expecting, it had not been this.

He felt his heart should be racing, but instead it beat with a slow, thudding inevitability, as though a grandfather clock hung, resolute and foreboding, inside the cavern of his chest.

"We were an empire, once," said the old man, his eyes downcast. "It is all gone now. My fault. If I could just—the colonies, *America*—I fear . . ." His shoulders slumped. He pointed to the streets spread out in the distance.

London sprawled before them like a monarch on a throne of steel, always reaching and growing and crawling with desperate life. Factories billowed black smoke into the sunset, and George was reminded that while the city was now fuelled by coal and supported by iron girders, it hadn't always been. Not in his grandfather's day.

"All of this—" the king gestured "—is in your hands." He blinked. "*Your* hands." And then, "I was barely a man, too, when they gave me this country." As if from those words George would gain some innate knowledge about his grandfather's own childhood, about the pain and posturing that came with coming of age at court nearly a century ago . . . About his grandfather's own father—the man he had inherited the crown from—the battles he had led and lost, conquering countries he had no right to; the blood spilled and pride stripped away, and how he had had a country already and that *Hanover* was the blood that ran in his veins, not *England*. How he had taught him to rule as if Britannia was only powerful if she too was sprawled on a throne, the rest of the world crushed and squeezed for resources, then discarded, held in place beneath one iron-clad boot.

Words welled up inside George as though a different person was speaking through him.

"We kings may be victims of circumstance, grandfather," George said, "but we are never truly victims. We do not suffer, not really. Not like our people do, not like our soldiers do on the Spanish Peninsula, or our children who scrape out a life in the factories and the workhouses. Not like the people in—in the empire, who we forced our rule and violence upon for no reason except monetary gain—"

His grandfather held up his hand—white skin withered and crusted with rings. Immediately, George stopped speaking. (Immediately, he was ashamed; he was seven, he was twelve, he was sixteen, and he—*God*, he had hated this man, this relic, just as much back then as he did now. *Well*, said the voice in his head—the one that sounded like Obi. *Don't just cry about it. Do something.*)

He opened his mouth.

"*Do not speak,*" said the King. Anger was turning his face red, the blood engorging veins that jumped in his forehead and neck like thick worms. Despite his age, George's heartbeat quickened. "*Monetary gain?*" his grandfather roared. Spit flecked his lips. "Have you learned nothing from your studies, from your education on our great country? There is an *order* to this world, and it must—" he slammed the flat palm of his hand against the marble railing with a dull *smack* "—be kept! It is not about the money. It has never been about the money. It is about submission and dominance. Racial superiority, and a firm hand."

George shook his head, so furious he felt a dull roaring in his ears. "Who are *you*—merely a man—to claim dominion, and superiority, over other men? Why must they submit to you? Are they not men, too?"

His grandfather's watery eyes darted across George's face, his mouth moving minutely, as though reaching for the precise words he needed to communicate the severity of his disgust and disappointment, to gather up all the ways George had failed his vision for the family and the country, time and time again, to recount down to the pennies and the seconds all the money and time he had wasted trying to make his worthless grandson ready for something he clearly never would be: a crown.

"Who am I?" his grandfather breathed. "I am the king. And you are the heir to my throne, and my empire. Your grievances against the work we have been mandated to carry out by God are shameful. *They shame me.* I would not be surprised if it was this knowledge that were killing me, as you have made no further attempts since any of our last quarrels on the subject of your uselessness to reform your discipline or your mastery over yourself *or of others.*" His grandfather's voice was quieter now, but it shook with emotion. "At the very least I can find comfort in the knowledge that you are soon to be wed, and might have the opportunity to practice exercising this mastery over a willing subject." His grandfather's hands were claws over his cane, his voice disbelieving. "How dare you question my dominion? My superiority? The position we claim over others rests on our *civilisation*, and our *breeding*, and our *sovereignty*. It is the hand of God in everything we do."

But I don't believe in God, George thought wildly. *And I never wanted the throne, never mind the fact that the mere thought of it has become repulsive to me now, the poison of it plain as day.*

"Every day, I am reminded that out of my sons it should have been Frederick, or even William, and not your father to be born first. His line is too weak, it is plain to see. Where he succumbed to drink and the shame of hedonism, you have succumbed to increasingly shameful ideologies. You have always been like this, since boyhood." George stared resolutely out over the gardens, face blank. "Even any one of your aunts would have made a better job of it. At least they do what they're supposed to. New babies every year for the last five."

George had nothing to say to that.

They passed a quarter of an hour standing there in the

resultant silence, looking out over the sterile green of the garden as it fell into dusk.

When it was finally dark, his grandfather spoke again, his knuckles white on the jewelled handle of his cane, and George knew what was coming.

"Soon I will be dead. And your useless father will be king. And then it will be you."

George nodded.

"I would not care," The king turned to him. "If it were anyone else. But you are so keenly a disappointment to me. To even think of that crown resting upon your head feels like a betrayal to this country."

"And yet," George replied, voice calm, though the anger that burned inside him was two decades old by now. "It will. And there is precisely nothing you can do to stop it."

He turned his back on his grandfather and walked to the door. He had more pressing things to deal with than one old man's dying despair at the decline of a world that should have died long ago.

The people of his city needed his help. He could not waste another second doing anything else.

Chapter Fourteen

[planet: none] + [location: free space] + [year: 6066]

Obi had been bound, gagged, and—he was fairly certain—mildly concussed, then shoved roughly out of a door and into a tunnel, and now he was here.

A dark room, floor shining with water, a mirrored sheen that reflected the dim strip lights flickering on the ceiling. His shadow stretched across the floor, all the way to the outline of what looked like a door set into the wall at the far end of the narrow, rectangular space.

In the brief time he'd had control of his faculties on the way here he'd glimpsed a fighting ring, its dirt floor stained with blood. A corpse, impaled, eyes open. He'd seen a thankless victor waiting to be re-imprisoned, and a crowd shouting for total annihilation. He was fairly confident he knew what was on the other side of the door, and he'd heard the click of the lock as the guards had left him here. To what? Prepare? They hadn't even given him a weapon. Everything hurt. God, he was so disorientated.

Outside the dark room, he could hear the shouts building to a crescendo, rising and rising and—

The door was rising, too, incrementally, the red light spilling brightly into the lightless tunnel like bright blood into dark water, crawling towards Obi's feet. The crowd's cheers reached peak volume and then surpassed it, and Obi felt like he was drowning, so he took a breath, but the air tasted like blood.

He wasn't a fighter, had never been a fighter. Running was what he was good at, running and getting away. Obi was an eel, not a lion, slippery and fast, but no teeth, defenceless. He had to find a way to hide, to—

He flattened himself against the wall, out of the light. Praying he was invisible to anyone in the crowd, he brought his hands up in front of his face, focused on the place where his forefingers touched, and used it as a point on which to centre his power.

As his fingertips sparked, he brought them closer towards his face, until heat warmed the bridge of his nose. Pinching the skin under his eyes, he tested it for give. Then he began to peel his face off.

A web of sentimental energy caught between his pinched fingers like a gossamer silk. Slowly, he pulled it away from his face, neck, chest, and legs, and then released it, to let it stand on its own. The silky energy rippled, filling out, and turning dark, until a person stood before him, a phantom version of himself, constructed from his own recollection.

The phantom's scar was bigger than in real life, he was certain, its stature a little shorter, more stooped, the eyes far paler, grey as snow, rather than the slate colour they were in real life. The frown lines were deeper cut than they had any right to be. The scars left by the acne of his younger years had to be exaggerated, courtesy of his own insecurities, but it was still painful to see.

The phantom raised an eyebrow (the only one it had), jerking its head towards the opening door, and the arena beyond.

"Yeah," Obi said, grimacing a little. "Sorry about that."

A roar split the air, and the door cranked upwards, disappearing into the ceiling. From his position in the shadows, he watched his opponent stumble out of the door on the opposite side of the arena. The phantom version of himself—the memory—stepped out too, blinking into the light and the thunderous screams of the crowd, looking perfectly corporeal, *thank god*. He heaved a sigh of relief.

It was now or never.

He slipped around the edge of the open door, praying fervently that all eyes were locked on the fight. Back pressed to the wall, he shuffled to the side, and hooked a leg over the low wall separating the audience from the fight. These seats were relatively empty, as the best seats were midway up, and on the long edge of the oval. He jumped over.

Then the other person staggering out into the arena, wrenched a sword from the compact dirt of the floor, and swung it in a glittering arc.

The blade sliced straight through the phantom.

The crowd surged to its feet, ready for the bright spill of blood.

The phantom re-formed on the other side of the blow.

Silence.

"Oh, fuck—"

The crowd went crazy, protesting the rigged fight. The guards looked around confused.

One of them stared straight at him. Obi watched the realisation dawn on his face—

"Obi!"

He whipped his head towards the stands above him, certain he had heard his name.

BANG.

A shot slammed into the wall next to his head. He looked up to see the guard levelling his blaster rifle at him from the landing of a flight of stairs above. Obi swore and went to duck, but someone was frantically waving their arms in his direction . . .

Asha?

Obi gaped as she came barrelling down the stairs behind the guard, hesitating only for a moment before slamming into him and pushing him over the stair railing with her shoulder. He fell in a heap at Obi's feet, groaning. Asha craned over the railing, her mouth hanging open in horror, as though she couldn't quite believe what she'd done. Obi realised belatedly that she was somehow wearing his coat, and grasping a gun in one hand.

They both looked back at the guard, lying still on the ground, his leg bent at a horrific angle.

"I'm gonna be sick," Obi mumbled.

Asha put her foot up on the railing and hoisted herself up and over, then lowered herself gingerly down until she was dangling from it with both hands. With a squeak, she let go, coat billowing. Just as she hit the floor, two guards appeared at the top of the staircase, rifles primed to shoot. Obi grabbed Asha by the arm and yanked her forward.

"I hope you have a plan, because I'm fresh out."

"Don't worry," she said, picking up the pace. "Just follow me."

In the cave of the great beast, Sensit raised his sword and brought it down seven times; one for each of the thing's heads. But for every snarling maw he dispatched, three more grew to replace it. He hacked and sliced, scything and sawing his way through pound after pound of serpentine flesh.

"How can I defeat you?" Sensit asked after many hours, the clay of him dripping with blood and spattered with viscous gore.

"Stop trying," replied the beast's thousand heads. They looked down at him from above, eyes glinting like so many stars. "It is impossible."

But Adesola had stopped to read the words engraved on the stone of the great mountain, and she spoke them aloud, commanding the creature to bow its head and let them pass.

Sensit looked at her in wonder when the creature obeyed. She merely looked at him and said, "I will save you from anything, even if it costs me my life." Sensit heard the warning that remained unspoken: do not lead me to death through folly and pride. *He bowed his head. "We walk together, or not at all."*

"Together," she repeated, "or not at all."

'A Complete, Annotated History of Chasca, Including Relevant Translated Mythologies. Chapter: Scroll the Second' by I. Nisomn, ex-acolyte of the Aonian Archives.

Chapter Fifteen

[planet: none] + [location: free space] + [year: 6066]

When the guards had dragged Asha through the corridors on her way to the ring, she had felt a rumble in her feet that was as familiar as her heartbeat; that beautiful sound of an engine starting.

Now, she was retracing her steps, heading for a place she had only ever dreamed of entering; an honest-to-Thracin *hangar* housing space-worthy craft. Her feet thudded against the ground as she ran, Obi not far behind her.

"How do you know where we're going?" Obi gasped. "There are so . . . so many stairs. I know we're technically running down them, but I think I'm about to pass out."

"It shouldn't be much further. Just—"

There it was. The distant rumble, but not so distant this time. And no longer under their feet. She stopped abruptly in front of a large door and pulled from her pocket the black eyeball she had ripped from the android's socket before entering the arena, holding it up to the retinal scanner. It trailed wires that slapped wetly against her hand. Vaguely she wondered what the fluid was.

Obi let out an incredibly undignified screech and pointed at the eye.

"Is that a—Asha, is that a—*is that what I think it is?*"

She shrugged and shoved it back into her pocket. "I took the other one too. Might be useful."

Then the door hissed open and they were standing in a room containing a fleet of spacecraft so high-tech it almost brought tears to Asha's eyes.

She ran over to the nearest jet—a slick little beauty of a plane—two seats with room at the back for supplies, fully equipped to jump through star gates and enter hyperspace, fitted with two compact laser cannons mounted under the cockpit and on the nose. She reached out a hand and laid it on the sleek, monochrome surface. There was something different about the way the metal had been treated. She bent down, trying to catch the light on its surface . . .

"Asha, we need to go!" Obi said.

"*One second.*"

Translucent hexagonal panels coated the outside of the craft. *Oh.* She'd imagined this was possible. Read the theory. But hadn't thought she would see these in her lifetime and now—

"Asha, would you hurry up? I can hear footsteps!"

She shook her head mutely. "Advanced optic cloaking."

Obi raised his eyebrows.

"Like this cargo ship, only more elegant. They can cloak their ships using the latest optic tech, rendering them invisible to the naked eye. It's been done before, but no one has ever managed to construct panels that will fool the eye of almost any species. If I'm right—"

"Hey!" shouted a gruff voice. "What are you doing?"

Asha's heart stopped. A guard was running towards them, blaster out, headpiece crackling with voices. Back up must already be on its way.

"Obi, quickly!"

She decompressed the entrance hatch and jumped in, hauling

Obi after her. The hatch closed with a hiss. She wrapped her fingers around the joystick.

A laser bounced off the side of the craft, sparks ricocheting onto the ground.

And then they were off.

The plane shot into the air like a bullet. Asha steered them towards the door of the hangar. They had to get out, they had to—

"Oh my god, the doors."

They were closed. Of course, they were closed. And now the ship would crash into them in *seconds* unless . . .

Asha had no other choice. She opened fire. The control panel by the exit shorted out and exploded. The red locking lights turned off and the door began to slide *open*, but they were nearly on top of it, and it still wasn't wide enough for them to slip through. At this rate, they would lose both wings and most of the fuselage, the gap was so thin.

"*Hold on*," she yelled.

Asha yanked the joystick violently to the left. The craft flipped, turning vertically on its side.

They slipped through the gap—*just*—and out into the night.

Stars rushed towards them—the darkness infinite and cold, the space in front of them so huge and vast that it defied true perception. Asha's hands fumbled at the controls, her throat felt choked with fear, and the only thoughts in her head were screaming, *this isn't anything like the simvids, this is real life, and oh god, I've only ever watched other people do this* virtually—*what the hell was I thinking*—

She jerked the controls, trying to right the jet, but over-compensated. They swung around, veering off course. A charge of pure light cannoned past them, trailing heat and imminent death. *They were being fired on.* Obi yelled, then clamped a hand over his mouth, eyes wide. The blast had missed them by metres.

Asha's hands were shaking as she urged the craft forward, willing herself to press on the controls more gently this time, still trying to think, to form any coherent thought besides *OHMY-GODFUCK*, as they accelerated into the cold dark, faster and faster, until they trembled on the edge of a speed faster than light. Another bolt of energy slammed past them, except this one *grazed the wing*, and sent them spinning, tumbling through the black, over and over. Her hands slid over the controls, sweaty and trembling. She couldn't *think*, she could barely breathe, and she was so aware of the hundreds of simulations she'd seen, similar to this one, that had ended with a blank screen and a fail mark and a little pixel animation of a jet exploding into a thousand fiery pieces.

"*Asha*—" Obi said helplessly, as she managed to wrench them around, pushing them forward, and she realised he was gesturing to a thin trail of smoke streaming from the wing that had been hit.

Her heart jumped into her mouth, and maybe it was the adrenaline, or something in Obi's terrified voice that did it, but suddenly a snippet of an overheard conversation rose up out of the reservoirs of her recent memory, fully formed. She latched onto it, and opened the onboard map, searching frantically for the name she'd overheard in the cells.

It was nowhere to be found. It had sounded like a transport hub, so surely it would be accounted for on the map. Unless it was too far away for the small jet to reach—

Then she saw it—a port symbol. And underneath it: *The Nautikos Interstellar Station*.

The NIS.

With one hand, she *slammed* the button that would tip them over the precipice into hyperspace, and with the other, she entered a sequence of equations she had learned from simvids on Gahraan that would, with any luck, see them through hyperspace, and out the other side, depositing them somewhere the Consortium would have a very hard time finding them. Her fingers were a blur; her breath came in sharp gusts.

They shot forward.

Asha fought to breathe—

The jet vanished into a blur as the stars around them stretched, and they were flung into the brightest dark she had ever seen.

Sensit called for Adesola, peering through the mist of the marshes where he had left her.

She returned his call, and when he found her, he was startled to see her sitting astride a flying demon. She had captured one of the enemy, and bent its will to hers.

Adesola offered a hand to her companion. Sensit accepted, swinging upwards to sit beside her on the broad back of their new friend.

Hidden wings unfurled and caught the breeze.

Soon they were flying.

'A Complete, Annotated History of Chasca, Including Relevant Translated Mythologies. Chapter: Scroll the Second' by I. Nisomn, ex-acolyte of the Aonian Archives.

Chapter Sixteen

[planet: Earth] + [location: London] + [year: 1812]

The ship's wooden floors were slick with damp and crusted with sea salt, coils of rope sitting like pale snakes in the damp, dark corners. For the past few weeks, Alarick and George had been following a trail of whisperings and rumours; of miracles, of strange sightings in the city. George remembered one woman's account very distinctly. A baby, stillborn and blue, had been laid in its casket, dressed in the clothes it should have worn to its christening. The mother beside it, weeping into the folds of its lacy gown. Then, in the small hours of the morning, a cry. The baby bawling with the strength of an infant at full health. The mother had awoken at once, just in time, she had said, to see the pale hand of an angel brush the baby's brow. Her baby had been blessed by God Himself, she had whispered reverently, clutching the infant to her chest as though it were made of solid gold.

If it was a miracle, why did it feel so unholy?

If any of it were even true.

George's neck prickled, his eyes darting around. The whole thing made him feel sick with anxiety, whilst simultaneously granting him a sense of purpose that felt rather dangerously like the most tangible thing in his life right now. A mandate stuck firm in his mind amidst the roiling sea of self-loathing in which dark shapes cruised for victims. His impending marriage, his country, his father; they all threatened to swallow him whole. This mission was like a grounding weight, a lodestone in the dark.

Save Obi's soul. Save the city.

It didn't matter that this increasingly felt like an impossible task. Didn't matter that they had been searching for nearly a month since that night Alarick had first appeared, chasing rumours. Didn't matter that since that night George had felt *watched* in a way he could not describe. Observed. Like an insect in a microscope slide, trapped between one piece of glass and another. Exposed and unable to escape.

Tonight, their search had led them to the docks, where a whole boatload of sailors had been hauling gunpowder the day before. One of them had lit a pipe too close to the cargo and a spark had set the whole boat ablaze still tethered to the pier. Everyone aboard should have died, and they had, albeit briefly. The next day, the same sailors had reported for work, seaweed still hanging limply from their work clothes, smiles gaunt and inhuman. Their families were overjoyed, of course. But other people whispered, called them the 'Skeleton Crew' like something out of an old wives' tale. At first, George had been hesitant to investigate. It sounded so eerie, so unnatural and strange, but Alarick had insisted, and George was going out of his mind at the palace, and so he'd come along.

Something crunched under Alarick's boot, splintering like dry wood.

They both looked down.

It was a bone. Clean of flesh and any sinew, so white it almost glowed, and now cracked cleanly in half, shards of it littering the floor around the breakage.

"Ergh," said George.

A creaking to the left had them both turning sharply, trying to make out the source of the noise. It could have been the sound of the old boat's sodden timbers settling in the water, but it didn't sound like that. It sounded deliberate.

"Who's there?" Alarick called. "Show yourself."

George watched as he eased a hand inside his coat and brought out a pistol, its barrel a dull gold in the light slanting through the floorboards above them. They waited for a reply.

Two minutes, then five.

Nothing.

George turned to Alarick, "You don't suppose we should—"

A thud.

They both tensed, eyes peering around in the gloom, trying to see every corner at once.

Alarick jerked his head. "Quickly, get back-to-back."

Another thud, followed by a low scraping sound.

"Should we not—"

Thud. Scrape. Slide.

George flung himself across the room, pressing his back to Alarick's. He drew his sword out of its sheath, its familiar leather grip moulding to his hand. The steel sung as it left its scabbard, a battle cry, a call to war. A throwing down of the gauntlet.

Thud. Scrape. Slide.

Groan.

George inhaled sharply. "What was that?" he hissed.

"I don't know," came the reply. "I have my suspicions. I dearly hope they are wrong."

The next thud, when it came, was far louder and far closer than it had been before.

There was another groan, low and guttural, like a wounded animal. Instantly, George was reminded of a childhood horse, one he had lost, wounded in a hunt. The animal had misjudged a jump over a fence and caught its leg on one of the pointed stakes protruding from the top, impaling its thigh. The squealing roar it had released still made George sick to his stomach thinking about it, and now, as he heard the low, agonised groaning of whatever thing it was keeping them company on the boat, he could not help but remember. They'd put the horse out of its misery, but George had wept for days. He had a feeling he would not mourn the death of whatever creature lurked here, in the shadows. The thing groaned again, almost screaming.

"*Help me.*"

Then it dragged itself into the light.

It was a child. A boy of about seven or eight, clawing his way across the floor. He could not stand because he had no legs. They were mangled past the point of recognition, and even George, who had never seen such an injury in his life, could recognise the effects of blunt trauma. This boy had been crushed by something a thousand times heavier than him, a mast, or a joist, perhaps, and it had turned his legs to a bloody pulp.

The child looked at them, groaning in that low, keening way, his eyes wide and fearful, skin pale and tinged blue.

Not a miracle. Not an angel. Something else entirely.

"*Help*," the boy groaned again. "Please—"

Alarick had moved from behind George to standing next to him. They were the same height, but George had never felt more diminished in his life. The boy's teeth were chattering, his eyelashes webbed together still, as though he were wet. In fact, all his clothes were soaking, his hair plastered to his forehead.

"It . . . It h—hurts," he mumbled. "It hurts so much."

Alarick sighed. "This is what happens when you disrupt the natural order," he said. "Things slip through the cracks and are loathe to return."

"You don't mean—"

"Yes."

The boy wailed, and the sound flew like an arrow to George's heart, piercing it. Guilt bubbled inside him. This boy was a subject of his. It was his duty to protect his subjects, and he had failed. Miserably.

George felt his hands begin to shake. *No*, he thought desperately. *Not now, please, not now.*

The boy had not looked away from them, staring with wide, glassy eyes. The reality of what he was was undeniable. The blue lips, the blackened fingertips, the mangled legs and pale, pale skin. The distended bloatedness of him.

This poor boy had died, *drowned*, and had been brought back from death, but only partially. He had slipped through the cracks of this *creature's* supposed miracle and landed badly on the other side. He was not meant to be, and it showed.

"What are we to do?" George asked.

Alarick was still. "I think we ought to put him out of his misery."

There was a pause in which George steeled himself.

"Go, then," Alarick said. "Wait outside."

George looked at him sharply. "I may not—"

"I can see your hands shaking." Alarick's stare was blank and unyielding. "Go and take your medicine before you become such a liability I am forced to dispatch you, too."

Heat flared in George's cheeks. "You have no right to talk to me in that way."

Alarick shrugged, and flicked the safety catch off his pistol.

George looked at him searchingly for a few moments, trying to find Obi in his gaze. The compassion and the warmth. The morality and the love of good.

He found none. It didn't shock him.

By the time he was outside, his hands were trembling violently, sending jarring shudders up his arms. He could barely grasp the bottle of laudanum without dropping it, and uncorking it took several moments, but he did it. The bitter taste in his mouth had barely faded when Alarick joined him on the dock, the sound of a gunshot still ringing. Neither of them spoke.

The river water lapped feebly at the shore of the Thames, shingle sliding over smooth rock run through with greyish sand and blue-tinged silt. The water was black as night, glittering as fiercely as the city it divided. George breathed in its damp and earthy river smell and exhaled any certainties he had once held about the future. Even tomorrow was no longer guaranteed. Not with a creature prowling the streets, and a wrathful yet unknowable time-traveller as his only hope for salvation.

He looked to the sky, and its boundless stars.

Where are you? He wanted to shout. *I need you. Come home.*

Chapter Seventeen

**[planet: none] + [location: Nautikos Interstellar Station] +
[year: 6066]**

The Nautikos Interstellar Station appeared out of the darkness in front of them, looking from a distance, Asha thought, like a decent-sized moon.

After escaping from the prison ship—she still couldn't believe that sentence applied to her—she had put them into hyperspace. The whole ordeal had taken a lot out of her, and the journey was long, but she hadn't been able to sleep, and now they were barely half an hour away from the NIS, so rest was out of the question.

Next to her, Obi was passed out with his mouth open. *Gross,* Asha thought fondly. Then she caught herself—they weren't friends. Just allies. And with the NIS looming in front of them—a transport hub where they could both hopefully find passage to the places they were seeking—maybe they would be strangers again sooner than she had thought.

Asha urged the jet forward, locking the sensors onto the station, and trying to get an understanding of its scale. It glittered all over with lights, and was roughly spherical in shape, though an odd object protruded from it—landing pads, perhaps.

It was only a few minutes later that she saw what it really was.

At first, her brain supplied the word *ecumenopolis,* but that was incorrect. The lights all over the surface weren't cities, or one planet-wide city. They were objects in their own right: entire space stations, satellites, docking equipment, shuttles, and whole ships that had docked one day and never left were all half swallowed in the chaos, fused together over time.

A million lights blinked on and off, channels of traffic drawing thicker lines of brightness over its surface.

The skyways.

Ships drifted to and from the station's surface like ants scuttling in neat rows across the black dirt of space.

It shouldn't have existed. It was incredible.

Asha swiped over the display in front of her, opening the jet's docking interface, and searching for a connection—a vendor selling a space, perhaps. Or, depending on the organisational acumen of the criminals said to run this place—free docking garages. They had found a small package of hard currency in the jet's compartment, along with a comms device and a medikit. Emergency supplies for a Consortium pilot. Obi had smashed the comms device to avoid it being used to track them. And Asha had taken the jet offline shortly after entering hyperspace. With any luck, they were untraceable. But Asha didn't want to leave that to chance. They would dock the jet, dump it, and find another ride out of here as soon as possible.

She looked at Obi's exhausted face out of the corner of her eye. *Assuming we decide to stick together, that is.*

A connection pinged up onto the windshield display. A vendor selling a short-term docking space for about half of the currency they had. She clicked *accept*. They needed to get out of the ship as soon as possible. Once they were in the chaos of that port city suspended in space, they'd be as good as invisible.

Asha took a deep breath, and guided the jet towards the docking station.

They disembarked on the fourth floor of a huge, ancient craft that had somehow been cut in half, forming a layered structure, in which vendors had constructed makeshift buildings—in many cases simply attaching awnings to the walls, supported at the front-facing end on two poles that formed a kind of entranceway. Thankfully, the docking space she had chosen was large enough to land in with her limited experience, and the vendor made no fuss about storing a craft that was clearly stolen.

"How'd you come by something like this?" he asked, running one slimy hand over the exterior. He seemed to resemble some kind of amphibian creature—with large, wet-looking eyes and hairless blue-grey skin. "Two humans like you?"

She narrowed her eyes. She'd seen his longing look. Likely at the cloaking panels she'd noticed earlier. "Why? Would you be interested in taking it off our hands?"

"Hmph," came the muttered reply. "Stole it most likely." Then, louder, "I'll do you five-fifty."

Asha shook her head. "A jet like that is worth five thousand and fifty at least."

"Not without ownership certificates and certainly not with all that damage." He pointed one slimy, webbed hand at the charred patch on the wing. Asha scowled. Any decent mechanic could fix that in a few hours.

"Nine hundred," she said.

"Four-fifty."

"A thousand."

Obi interjected, "Do either of you understand how this is supposed to work—"

"Seven-fifty," Asha said, ignoring him. "And that's my lowest offer."

The vendor glared at her. She glared back. She'd gone through hell to get that ship. And she'd flown it well. No way was this creep taking it off her for any less than seven hundred. That was three-fifty each for her and Obi. Surely enough to buy them both passage to where they needed to go. If only the jet had been capable of travelling the entire distance to A'lkari—but it was too small, the fuel costs would have been astronomical. They needed this money.

After a long few seconds of silence, the vendor nodded, complaining under his breath whilst he opened a drawer under his counter, and withdrew seven-hundred-and-fifty digits worth of hard currency, the small round chips disappearing into Asha's pocket as soon as he handed them over.

"Good to do business with you. Now get out of my shop."

The NIS was just as strange a place as the prisoner had described. Shanty towns crowded round the base of ancient satellites that had become entangled in the giant structure beneath their feet, a hundred years ago or more. Asha saw a shop trading from the burned-out husk of an imperial transport craft, whilst someone else napped under its broken-off wing.

Taller structures rose up occasionally, with giant screens flickering on their sides. Asha stood watching a broadcast for a few moments. A warning scrolled down the screen, advising on the disruptions to fuel supply lines due to a disaster on a planet called San. The broadcast made it sound like the entire planet had somehow been destroyed, but surely that wasn't possible?

"We need to find a way off this place," Obi muttered. "Offer free labour in exchange for room, board, and passage to somewhere else. Or see if the money from the sale of the ship is enough to get us two beds on a transport heading to Xesca, or Endlian—any of the planets near A'lkari."

Asha turned to look at him. "Us?"

Obi nodded. "There's no sense in us splitting up now. If we can get close to A'lkari, and I can see you safely on your way, then I can take my time, ask around a bit, see if anyone knows anything about the Magekind, and how they might be contacted." He looked around shiftily—Asha could tell the place made him nervous. She understood—it felt like a thousand eyes were watching them wherever they went.

"So we get out of here as soon as we can, and decide what to do after we get back to civilisation?" she muttered.

Obi nodded. "I'm game if you are."

Asha would have been lying if she said she didn't feel relieved. After all they had been through, to say goodbye here would have felt like being abandoned.

They had to keep a low profile, so they stuck to the back streets. Asha glimpsed a bustling market through the alleys that led to the main thoroughfare. There seemed to be stalls for everything at the port. Tonics for feathers and fur sat next to scrubs for scales and talons and beaks. A shop that traded exclusively in what looked like mud seemed to be very popular with the amphibious-looking species the vendor had likely belonged to, whose three-webbed fingers and large, wet-looking eyes reminded Asha of an old Earthern animal she had once seen a picture of. The patrons blinked moistly at her and then Obi, skin rippling and shifting in colour from a dark, earthy green to a colder, more hostile blue. *Stay away.* She flushed and lowered her eyes. They stood out here, among the bustle and the colours, the shadows and the grime—two humans, unaccompanied and seemingly unarmed. They might as well have painted targets on their backs.

They hurried on. Obi providing a whispered, merry commentary of the goods. He was in suspiciously good spirits. Probably just happy to be back in a place he could walk freely. They even stopped by a shopfront selling hot boxes of a steamed grain, topped with strips of charred meat, fresh vegetables and a spicy sauce. Asha, who had lived most of her life on nutrient paste squeezed out of a tube, barely knew where to start. Everything was so different, so new . . . but there was a feeling bubbling up through the panic, that felt a lot like joy. When she finished her food—licking the cardboard of the box, and the utensils—she realised that her face hurt from chewing and smiling. That her chest felt warm, and her stomach full. Obi passed her a bottle, and the water in it tasted like fruit.

It took two hours of walking through winding back alleys to reach the docking stations. They'd asked a shopkeeper where they might find people willing to take passengers who worked in exchange for room and board, and they'd been directed here, to the sunny bustle of Dock 12-K, where ships pulled in with smooth regularity, disgorging their wide-eyed passengers and jaded crew members into the madness of the port. But a warning had come with the directions. *Good luck finding anyone who'll take you two. Paying customers are having a hard enough time finding a ride after the disaster on San. A few of our regular freighters were docked when the planet was destroyed, so we're operating at less than half capacity. Not to mention the price of fuel means that tickets are at a premium. So, like I said. Good luck to you.*

"Let's just ask someone," Asha had said. "The worst thing they can say is no."

A few hours later, they had learned that the worst thing someone could say was not, in fact, no. Asha had also learned that if she and Obi wanted to board a ship, the owner would have to be certified to transport 'live goods', and also take out insurance on them, or risk paying heavy fines if the craft was stopped and searched. Any captain who wanted to turn a profit on a voyage through ticketed passengers would laugh in the face of two people without any money, whose mere presence on the ship would discourage any self-respecting traveller from setting foot on it. Someone had even begun to speculate if they might recoup some lost profits by turning Asha and Obi in to the government in return for a reward.

Now the sun was going down, sinking past the artificial horizon and the high-rise buildings—descending ships like boxy birds gliding down to rest.

"Please," Asha was saying to the captain of the most recently docked ship, "we won't cause you any trouble, you won't even realise we're there. We'll help with cleaning, cooking, anything—just give us a room and a meal once a day and take us to Port Xesca. We can't offer you anything else but—"

"You must be mad," sneered the ship's captain. "Who let you loose from the pens, anyway?"

Asha closed her eyes. This was clearly futile, but she had to try. "I know that it would be unconventional—"

"Unconventional?" He bellowed a laugh, as if Asha had actually told a decent joke. "It would be career suicide. Now get off my deck!"

They got off his deck.

Obi squeezed her arm. "Hey, it's alright. We'll find somewhere to stay and try again tomorrow. Someone will take us."

Asha didn't reply. She was exhausted. Tired and hungry. Upset. She trudged over to a low wall and sat down, ignoring the dirty looks from people nearby. Groaning, she put her head in her hands. "What was I thinking?" she mumbled. "I—"

"Hey!" called a voice.

For a moment, the person who had spoken was obscured

by the crowds. Then they parted, and a young man appeared, dressed in the rough-looking black trousers and white shirt of what seemed to be the unofficial uniform for deckhands around here.

Gold flashed across Asha's vision, blinding. She blinked it away, confused. *Light reflecting off a window, maybe.*

The first thing she noticed was his skin. Once, as a child, she had found the remains of a sandsparrow's nest, half covered in scarlet sand. Nestled among the fragile ruin of the sticks and collected fibres was a half-crumbled eggshell that gleamed like a precious gem. Its cool green might have passed for sun dappled foliage. She'd tried to pick it up but it fell to pieces as soon as she'd touched it, the thin, almost turquoise shell disappearing into the sand. His skin was the same colour. And his features . . . two eyes, a crooked nose, a nicely shaped mouth. He looked almost human.

As Asha watched, eyes narrowed, he waved and smiled, revealing straight white teeth enclosed on either side by longer canines that curved inward slightly, turning his grin slightly dangerous. His eyes were dark, and his hair was dark, too, a mess of black that fell into his eyes, and down his neck a little, curling around the sides—

Asha's heart stopped. Two short horns jutted from his brow, tapering to blunt points about a handspan from where they grew seamlessly out of the skin of his forehead, and immediately, *immediately*, Asha was back on Gahraan, cowering in the red dirt of the street as she looked into the Sentinel's eyes and saw the future.

Two horns curving from their head towards a sky split by lightning. A rush of something that feels wild and old, and out of her hands.

You. Asha thought. *You, you, you.*

He stared back at her for just a moment, and there was something in his eyes, something like recognition—

"Hi," Obi said, standing up and moving in front of Asha protectively, blocking her view. Their eye contact broke and she slumped, feeling somewhat disconnected from a circuit, unplugged from a power source. "Everything alright?" Obi asked. His posture was wary, waiting for the young sailor to tell them to get lost.

But he didn't. Instead, he nodded his head at the ships. "Sorry about that. They're a bunch of sell-outs. You make more money these days if you abandon common decency and embrace the Emperor's values instead." He shrugged. "I heard that you needed a place to stay?"

Asha stood too. "We do. We have money, we're not asking for favours."

He shrugged. "Even if you were, there're ways to earn your keep. How much you got?"

Asha told him.

"That's fine. More than enough for both of you. Someone should have taken you by now." The slightly serrated canines were revealed when he spoke—larger than they should have been, and sharp-looking enough to draw blood. "Though I guess everyone is more wary these days, especially after what happened to San."

San. The planet that had been destroyed. She was suddenly suspicious—what if this was all an elaborate set up constructed to eventually get them to denounce the government so they could be arrested for dissent? "Who are you anyway?" she asked.

"My name's Xavior. I work on that ship right over there. Deckhand." He pointed at a beaten-up looking freighter and waved at one of the crew members. They waved back.

The boy's smile widened as he watched them take it in, sharp teeth glinting in the fading evening light. "So, two humans on the NIS. A little far from home, no?"

Asha narrowed her eyes. "And what about it?"

"Well, I'm assuming they didn't let you leave Gahraan for a holiday. What are you running from?"

"We're not running from anything."

Not quite a lie, but not true, either.

"Don't worry," Xavior said, his easy smile never leaving his face. "You can tell me, I won't judge."

Asha narrowed her eyes even further.

Obi raised one and a half eyebrows at her. *Stay cool.* "We aren't in the habit of explaining our movements to strangers. Anyway, it's complicated, and I'm sure you have better things to be doing than listening to the life stories of two random strangers."

"I don't have anywhere to be."

Asha looked pointedly at Obi.

"Oh, cool, well I, uh . . . " he trailed off.

Xavior tilted his head, looking intensely sceptical.

"We're siblings," Asha blurted out. "Travelling to Xesca. You know, the trading outpost near A'lkari—"

"Yeah, I know where Xesca is."

"Okay. And do you happen to know of anyone currently travelling there? Or stopping on the way?" She paused. "Anyone who will transport live goods without insurance?"

Xavior looked at her, raising an eyebrow. "You shouldn't do that."

"What?"

"Talk about yourself the same way they do. Or you'll start to believe it."

"How inspirational, Xavior." Asha smiled insincerely. "You should write that down."

He had the good grace to seem embarrassed, and changed tack. "Look, I think I can help you."

Asha and Obi exchanged glances.

"Really?"

"That ship I work on—the *Stayanax*—we're due to leave tomorrow and could always use an extra pair of hands. Xesca's on our route for obvious reasons, so . . ." He shrugged. "I mean, I can't promise you a ride, but I can introduce you to our captain, Isi. She's never been a massive 'rule' follower, so." He put that in air quotations, shrugging as he did so, even though Asha was pretty sure he was talking about Imperial Law. She raised an eyebrow. "So, it won't be a problem that you two aren't technically citizens," he continued. "Anyway, work is work as long as you don't break anything valuable or get too many fingerprints on the windows, right?"

Obi looked at Asha like, *please say yes to the kind stranger, we need his help, remember?*

So, she nodded. "Okay. Yeah, thank you."

Xavior smiled. "Not a problem."

"Maybe this Isi will like us so much she'll let us stay for free," Asha said.

Xavior threw his head back and laughed, and Asha was struck all of a sudden by the structure of the bones in his face, and how they worked so *well* together.

"I never got your names," he said, laughter lingering on his face.

"I'm Asha," she shook his hand. The material of his gloves felt rough against her skin. That golden light seemed for a moment to diffuse through the air, like a solar flare, or the light of the setting sun—

"Obi." The boys shook hands, and the light glared brighter, so she put up her hand to shade her eyes, but it didn't really help.

Then it was gone, well before she realised where she had seen it before, and Xavior was walking away, towards the ship called *Stayanax*, and the next chapter of their journey.

"Come by in half an hour. I'll introduce you to Isi and we'll see about getting you that lift to Xesca. Until then—" his voice was nearly drowned out by the shouts of the surrounding crowd, "—don't be late."

The great beast set them down a continent away, alighting in a clearing in a forest. This new land appeared at first to be barren of monstrosities, and they were one land mass closer to their companion than they had been before. But, as they journeyed further through its spectral forests, the demons soon came out to play.

'A Complete, Annotated History of Chasca, Including Relevant Translated Mythologies. Chapter: Scroll the Second' by I. Nisomn, ex-acolyte of the Aonian Archives.

Chapter Eighteen

[planet: Earth] + [location: London] + [year: 1812]

Indisputably, Alarick Amadi had been born gifted. It was true that he was a Guide, and that he could harness the sentimental energy an object possessed and use that energy to facilitate jumps of cosmic proportions through millennia and across lightyears. But fortunately—or unfortunately, it really depended on who you asked—he had another gift.

When Alarick Amadi was born, his name had not yet been Alarick Amadi.

His name had been nothing, and he had been no one, but it would not remain that way for long. When he was two years old, his parents had died of radiation poisoning on the charred and abandoned husk of planet Earth—fundamentalists who believed someone had to pay the price for the slow murder of the planet and so had rejected the opportunity to escape. He had survived, as he was no longer human like they were. This had nothing to do with his parents, and everything to do with him—or, at least, the *him* that he would one day become. The energy that fuels the creation of time-travellers works in mysterious ways, and it is for this reason that Guides are *made* and not *born*.

The soul of the sentient has to be *right*.

When Alarick was thirteen and the last of the people left on the shell of the planet that had once housed the human race were either dead or at death's door, he had entered his

Anchoring. He had no one to help him bind his energy to any time or place or object and so, by all rights and laws and beliefs, he should have died, and he did.

Briefly.

Alarick's heart stopped beating, his soul was ripped and shredded past the point of recognition as his body ceased to exist on the physical plane of reality that it had before.

Then.

Then, he woke up in a field of snow ringed by craggy black rock, feeling whole and safe and *awake* for the first time in his life. This should not have happened, but he had no way of knowing this. The sentient who had observed his quiet and instantaneous arrival, however, did.

Smiling, the Sentinel of the Order of Legends walked over to Alarick's prone form and helped him stand. The Sentinel was unlike anything or anyone Alarick had ever seen, as he had no knowledge of life on other planets besides the decaying one he heralded from. He was scared but didn't show it. He thought that he might be dreaming, but he had learned somewhere that the human brain couldn't construct faces in dreams it hadn't seen in real life, and he knew he had never seen a face as savage and as haunted as this one. He did not consider the idea that perhaps he simply wasn't human.

"Oh," said the Sentinel, towering over Alarick. "Hello."

Alarick did not reply. The Sentinel smiled. "I saw a face just like yours, child, in the prophecy pool of an oracle when I asked it to show me my future. And now you are here, delivered to me . . . " A pause. "But you do not *feel* like a Hero—"

(*Ain't that the truth*, Alarick thought, to mask the hurt.)

"—nor do you feel selfless enough for sacrifice." The Sentinel tapped his chin, a cruel smile spreading across his face. "I think the prophecy is *meddling*."

Alarick spat a frozen twig out of his mouth. *This guy is fucking nuts.*

"Do you know what you are?" asked the Sentinel.

"Some kind of freak, I think."

"Hm." The Sentinel considered him. "And have you a family?"

Alarick blinked, a thousand emotions swelling inside him. "No," he said. "Not anymore."

"Would you like one?"

Now, he lay in the ruins of the cottage he had tried to raise a child in, sprawled on his old and rotting mattress, about to play god.

His left hand rested in a clump of dandelions that had sprung out of the floorboards, his right flung over his face to block the light that shone through a hole in the thatch of the roof. He blew out a long sigh, his breath stirring dust motes into a dance.

As Alarick's body lifted—feet dangling drowsily above the mattress, eyelids fluttering, white light shining out intermittently whenever the lids raised—one of his shoes fell off. Then, all the light vanished from the room. Alarick hypothesised that this was a preventative measure written into the magic he performed that was supposed to prevent any intrusion into a moment that was the closest thing he ever got to feeling holy, but deep down he suspected that maybe his power preferred the darkness because arcane things nearly always did.

He reached out his hands, closing them slowly to fists, as though pulling on chains with every finger.

Here was the thing about Time: it was everywhere, in everything, concurrently. Nothing had not happened yet; there was nothing yet to happen. And tangled up in it, for a good long while yet, were people and their things; roads and rivers of energy, flowing from the past, to the present, and most importantly, into the future. All Alarick had to do was find one, grab hold, and let it take him wherever it went. Some might have called it a kind of future-telling, or divination. He preferred to think of it as communion. Time was his church, and he, nothing but a man, asking from it whatever it might be gracious enough to give.

Lying there, he gathered his thoughts and intentions, and focussed on what exactly it was that he wanted to find out. Then, he turned to Time, knelt at the river's edge and asked it: *On this path, what happens next? What lies downriver?*

Behind his closed eyelids, a world began to take shape. The history of humanity unfolding and unfurling like the leaves of a blooming flower, until Alarick was suspended miles above a city where factories billowed thick smoke into the sky, and boats chugged sluggishly across the river that bisected it. He could feel the years and minutes and seconds flowing slower like they were tears sliding down his face, so he held up one hand, and they stopped.

The answer to his question spread out before him.

Quiet.

The whole city was . . . silent. Eerie and still as a ghost town. The usual hubs of noise and chatter, commerce, and movement nowhere to be found; the boats on the river did not move, and not even the birds made noise. It was like coming upon a great beast, asleep in the wilderness, its breath barely discernible, hidden in a shadow.

How?

At first, Alarick was confused. Casting his gaze from Elephant and Castle to The Regent's Park, stillness and silence stretched as far as the eye could see.

What is this?

A section of sky opened underneath his hands, as he pulled it and stepped through it, manipulating the fabric of the world in such a way that meant he was deposited inside the saloon of an ale-house that faced the river. It was the first location he had thought of when he had silently requested the world show him a busy place.

The ale-house was full of people, eating and drinking and talking . . . but not moving. They were all as still as a picture in a frame.

This was the silence he had noticed.

Alarick moved among the frozen people and wondered what had done this to them—because it certainly hadn't been him. A man's flagon of beer sloshed over the rim of the glass, the cloudy droplets glittering in mid-air like hard gems, unmoving. A woman's glove hovered between the hand it had fallen from and the ground, the silk shimmering dully in the low light. These people were frozen in time.

Show me more.

He rose above the buildings, wind buffeting at the hem of his coat. The Mall stretched out on either side of him, St James's Park and the river behind him. He turned in a circle, eyes narrowed, trying to find a hint of movement—

An image sliced through his skull like a hot knife through butter—

Darkness, a twisted body, too many limbs, eyes of fire, curled up on chequered marble, twitching in pain. A wet tongue flickering out to lick its festering wounds, a whimper. And, there, on the ground, shining in the moonlight streaming in from the domed roof, a bloody sword with a crystal blade—

"Oh no," said a voice, soft and dangerous, from behind him. "You weren't supposed to see me like that."

Chills erupted down Alarick's neck. Slowly, he turned, his hands already reaching into his pocket for his revolver.

There was a man in front of him. *Or, rather,* Alarick thought, *something expending a lot of energy in order to look like a man.*

It, or *he* stood, just like Alarick did, on nothing, a hundred metres above street-level. His flesh was the sickly grey pallor that became of brown skin after it had not seen sun for many years. Wind moved his auburn hair in limp tendrils that brushed his harsh jaw. He wore a black suit, strangely modern. With a black shirt and tie. On his lapel a pin glimmered—a little silver thing, in the shape of a sword.

"Hello, strange traveller." The man's voice betrayed his age. It was old, and awful. Empty as a starless sky at night, and just as dark. "I don't recall you seeking permission to come here. To arrive without a sacrifice into a future where I rule."

"Sacrifices are for gods," Alarick replied. "Not interlopers. Now, why don't you tell me who you are, and what you want, and maybe we can come to an agreement."

For some reason, the creature smiled at that. "You're right," he said. "Sacrifices are meant for gods. Just like souls are for humans, swords are for heroes, and trinkets are for travellers."

Alarick narrowed his eyes. *This thing knows what I am.* But he could recognise when he was being baited, so he didn't reply to that. Instead, he said, "Why the resurrections? They big fans of necromancy in the world you come from?"

The creature laughed. "No, no. Nothing like that."

"Then what?"

"If I told you, it would ruin the surprise. And I do love surprises."

Alarick resisted the urge to shoot the creature in front of him out of pure frustration.

"Oh, no need to look so enraged. As you said earlier, there

is an agreement to be had between us. And I think I can get you to come around." One clawed, armoured hand waved, and suddenly, the box with the soul fragment was sitting in the creature's palm. "If I offer you this."

Alarick did not move.

"If you want it back, you can have it. In exchange for one thing." The creature moved forward, gliding through the air like a wraith. "The rest of it. Where is the rest of it?"

Alarick kept his face blank. *He must be talking about Obi. He must have gleaned certain information from the soul but not all—he knows we use Artefacts to time travel. Likely knows I am Obi's father, and knows that the soul is split. He must need the whole thing—the entire soul.* And then the obvious question occurred to him: *What does he need a soul for?*

Alarick chose his next words carefully. "The rest of it is else-where. But that is the least of your concerns." If what the demon wanted was Obi, then it would be impossible to ever reach an agreement. He would not trade his son, or his son's location, for half of said son's soul in a box. Really, it was not a choice—he would have to take it.

Quick as lightning, Alarick stepped forward—but not into the space in front of him. Manipulating the world he had cre-ated, he folded the fabric of it, and stepped through, appearing behind the creature as though he had teleported there whilst withdrawing his revolver from his pocket and placing the barrel firmly against with the back of the demon's head. He slipped his finger around the trigger.

"This is my city," he whispered in its ear, voice no more than a growl. "I don't know which world it is you came from, or why you chose this one to invade, but you are not welcome here. Give me back that box, and leave this place, and we will have nothing further to discuss. Stay, and keep it, and I promise you—you will not see a summer here. You will not survive past the month's end."

The creature ignored him. "I see. You sought out this future, as you thought within it you might find the path to my destruction. This is an impossible task, and you will fail. I have fought worse foes than you, and I was not beaten." It was as though he could not feel the gun pressing into his head. *Couldn't feel it, or did not care.* Not for the first time that evening a dread chill ran through Alarick's blood. "I am the shadows that bind you to your past, and the violence that breathes within you. I am your fear and your doubt, and the contaminated, corrupted blood that runs through the veins of your child. The corruption you put there."

Alarick's past didn't have shadows, as there wasn't enough light to differentiate them from the darkness in the first place. Therefore, he wasn't so much bound by shadows to his past, as ruled by them in his present. The creature had meant to scare him—but Alarick looked upon his worst fear every time he stared into a mirror.

"You look like him, you know," the creature said suddenly, in a different tone. "Like the one I saw in my dream, when I slumbered between worlds, and waited. But you can't be him, can you? You are no Hero."

"*Jesus Christ,*" Alarick replied, sick suddenly of this whole conversation, of strange, evil people who entered his life and immediately tried to tell him what he wasn't. "I don't have time for this," he said. And shot the creature in the head.

Darkness.

The whole world flickered out—pitch black and cold, and for single moment, Alarick saw before him a creature of unimaginable horror—

And then the gun was being wrenched out of his hand by

an armoured claw, and the monster he had just tried to kill was crumpling it into scrap metal between his fists. The bullet hole in his head closed before Alarick's eyes, and the creature's face was thunder and his eyes were gold fire, and his voice was full of ancient fury.

"Alarick Amadi, you should not have come here. You need to leave before I make you."

Sometimes, just before Alarick touched an Artefact, he got a feeling—a terrible feeling, like all of his animal instincts screaming at once: run. The creature standing in front of him now gave him that feeling.

Quietly, quickly, he reached out with his power, following the threads of time that eddied around the thing in front of him, spiralling strangely, kaleidoscopic and wrong. Part of it was the timeline—it was investigating him, too, like a body sends white blood cells to destroy an invader, the timeline warped around him, trying to erode his impact, to fit him into history with minimal deviation from the set path. And it was failing. Hence the imminent split.

But there was something else—a pattern in the current of time that Alarick had never seen before. Like a repetition, or a glitch, stretched out behind him.

And then there was the golden light.

It swirled around the creature, flowing through his body like blood.

Alarick pushed further.

It couldn't be—

He only realised that perhaps he had gone too far when the demon's eyes flickered almost imperceptibly and grew brighter; lightning flashing with the thunder of his expression. Then he lifted an armoured hand above his head and, before Alarick's eyes, began to draw something down through the air, something that shone, splitting the sky in a narrow line as it came through into this world.

"I am older than this planet," the creature said, his muscles straining with the effort. "I have lived three lives now, and remember the way it felt to die every time."

Alarick could see what he was holding now—his hand was wrapped around a golden sword hilt. And still he kept wrenching the weapon out of the air, pulling it through the skin of this world, as though from a scabbard.

"I measure the passage of time in the fall of empires and the death of civilizations. I have come to this place, this place where I was supposed to find my successor, and have instead decided to succeed myself. To become ruler of a city whose citizens exist to serve me, as I once served others. The scales must tip eventually, and now I have enough power to ensure they come swinging my way. I am a Hero; victory is my destiny. What is yours?"

Then he pulled the rest of the weapon free from wherever he had summoned it, and thrust the blade through Alarick's chest.

Dimly, Alarick heard the demon laughing. The sound slid under his skin, burrowing into his cells, consuming him with an agony that burned like fire.

He looked down at his chest. The sword had passed through it, completely.

He realised why: the sword was not a true weapon, just an imitation of one. A phantom.

He heard one last thing before the blackness swallowed him, and it was a threat he would remember for the rest of his life. The voice of the creature rang out in the silence, so foreboding that even the thing that ruled the grey chasm between worlds opened its eyes.

"This may be your kingdom, but you are *not* king."

Chapter Nineteen

[planet: none] + [location: Nautikos Interstellar Station] + [year: 6066]

"Xavior," Isi said. "I thought I told you not to bring in any more strays."

It was a quarter past eleven. Obi and Asha were standing at dock 12K, in front of the ship called *Stayanax* and its reptilian captain, Isi.

Xavior stood behind her grinning, eyebrows raised and shamelessly bashful, "You said you were being worked to the bone only yesterday, so I simply thought it would help take a load off, that's all."

"Hmph," Isi replied, narrowing her eyes at them. She was striking, no doubt about it—red scales glittering and polished, yellow markings under her umber eyes lending her gaze an air of intensity Obi was beginning to suspect was more than skin deep. Two compact little guns sat in hip holsters, plasma storage chambers glowing faintly in the dim light. Her shirt was white and simple, her boots brown and tipped with metal. All the better to kick heads in with, Obi assumed. She seemed like that kind of lady.

"Can you clean?" she asked.

"Uh, yes, ma'am." Obi replied.

Asha nodded.

"*Are* you clean? Because I don't mind drinking—honestly, I'll probably join you—but drugs are a hard no."

They both nodded quickly.

"Can you do basic arithmetic? Flight paths and trajectory and such?"

"Erm . . ." Obi said.

But Asha nodded again, and then she said, "But I'm better at fractalics. I've also memorised every base component there is for hyperspace equations and can use them in immensely pressured environments."

Obi blinked, then remembered the scramble into the stolen jet, Asha's hands trembling over a numerical keyboard, the yank of a joystick and the stars stretching. Well, she wasn't lying.

Isi paused at this information. "Lower or higher fractalics?"

"Both."

"Hm." Her tongue flickered out absentmindedly, tasting the air. "Consortium trained, I assume?"

"*No, ma'am,*" Asha replied, taking her cues from Obi, it seemed. "Self-taught, but I—I'm good, promise. And I want to learn."

Isi considered Asha, her face unreadable.

"You gonna get the hell out of my way when I ask?"

"*Yes,*" she replied.

Obi nodded his agreement, too.

Isi made them squirm for half a minute more before nodding. "Alright then. Welcome aboard our ship, *Stayanax.* You better not fuck this up, 'cause I *will* be holding Xavior accountable for said fuck-ups. That being said—" she turned to Xavior, "—you will show them the ropes, and you will make sure they are earning their keep. If I catch even a *hint* of any slacking or begin to suspect that my orders are not being followed *to the letter*, I will eject you from the airlock."

"Understood, ma'am."

"It's 'Captain' now, suds, and don't you forget it."

She turned, walking towards the gangplank, waving her hand over her shoulder. "Give them Scuttle's old room, Xavior. Thracin knows he doesn't need it now."

"Suds?" Obi asked, as she disappeared into the ship.

"That's what she calls our newest recruits. Because you'll be doing all the scrubbing? It sounds stupid until you get about four days in and you realise you've barely seen anything but suds sliding across metal flooring in days—makes you feel like you're going crazy." He sighed. "Can't say that I miss it."

Obi was beginning to wonder if this was a good idea, so he looked at Asha. She seemed to be visibly relaxing as Xavior spoke, shoulder slumping out of her usual tension-filled posture, permanent frown disappearing. *Oh*, he thought, realizing why. *How sad.* Because it was painfully clear why she seemed so soothed by the idea of working and cleaning for two and half straight weeks with what sounded like minimal reprieve. Why Isi's sharp tone and profanity and commandeering attitude hadn't fazed her in the slightest. It was what she was used to.

Obi thought back over the past few days. Maybe Asha's permanent frown and quick temper were less signs of her constant anger—though he did not dispute that this was very real—and more signs of her constant bewilderment and a deep-founded confusion at the strange new world she now found herself in. She had mentioned schedules and rations and guards that weren't afraid to use a stun baton for minor infractions; she was either scared or not scared enough back home. This ship represented the most ordered, structured environment she had encountered since leaving Gahraan. *And*, he thought, *if Isi's threats are serious, then her life depends on her direct usefulness and the efficiency of her contributions to the ship. On her ability to follow orders.*

Distantly, Obi realised Xavior was speaking.

"—and you guys get Scuttle's room because . . . because—"

"He's dead, isn't he?" Asha asked. "You're giving us a dead person's room."

"Well . . . I wouldn't say *dead* so much as . . ." He screwed up his face—*hm*, Obi thought, *great bone structure*— "As . . . permanently out of commission."

Asha raised an eyebrow.

"Okay, fine, he is dead. Scuttle died. Isi killed him—not that I was supposed to tell you that."

"*Isi killed him?*" Obi said. "What did he *do?*"

"Well, I don't actually know, but Hannei told Chef who heard from someone on the bridge crew that he used the wrong polish on her boots and she just shot him."

"That cannot be true."

Xavior shrugged. "You never know, with her."

"So, she's a psychopath then."

"Hey," Xavior said. "Only I'm allowed to call her that. Listen, she might seem . . . slightly unhinged, but she's a good person. In all seriousness I would be dead without her, and so would most of the crew. Trust her."

Obi eyed him sceptically. Asha said nothing.

"Anyway, I'll give you the grand tour in the morning, make introductions, et cetera, and then you can get to work. But for now, rest. How does that sound?"

"Perfect."

Asha looked at Obi and smiled. Maybe they would be okay after all.

Scuttle's room was homey, yet utilitarian; two bunks stacked on top of each other, opposite two mismatched, yet cosy looking armchairs. For light, there was only an old, flickering plasma lamp that Obi had decided to call 'charmingly antiquated' instead of 'a dangerous chemical hazard'. A threadbare rug was tossed across the metal floor, almost like an afterthought. Empty shelves lined the walls. It was to be home for the next two and a half weeks.

Obi flopped onto the lower bunk and stared at the bottom of the one on top. Someone had scratched a message into the thin metal. *Kick here for a slap.*

Asha had gone to find some clothes to sleep in, but she'd been gone almost half an hour. Likely being chatted up by that Xavior boy. Obi smiled. Poor kid was in for the shock of his life.

Finally, there was a knock on the door.

"Yeah?"

It was Asha. She was in pyjamas—socked feet and pale pink love heart-dotted clothing so incongruous with the scowl on her face that Obi barked out a laugh before he could stop himself. The scowl intensified.

"It's not that bad," he said, sitting up.

Asha stalked into the room. "Isi said it was all they had." She looked pained. "There are *bows*."

"Adorable."

She rolled her eyes and sat at the bottom of Obi's thin bunk, leaning on the wall.

"It's so weird, being in space," she said. "I'm so used to . . . to two feet on the ground, stars *above* my head, not . . . pressing in on every side. It's unsettling."

"You get used to it," Obi replied. "I've been on my fair share of long-haulers and it can be fun. Depends on the crew mainly, but Isi seemed cool, if intimidating, and Xavior seems solid, if strangely casual about murder. We just have to pull our weight and we'll be fine. Anyway—" he poked her with his foot "—we have each other. Can't be that bad."

"Thanks, Obi," she replied, scratching her scalp absentmindedly. She'd undone her braids and washed her hair, scraping it up into a puff on the top of her head. Wispy curls escaped, backlit by the warm lamplight to give her a haloed look. *An angry angel in kid's pyjamas*, Obi thought, *a teenager too busy running from the law to comb her hair.*

Asha grimaced under his gaze, mistaking his expression for judgement. "I know it's not practical, but my mother usually braids it," she said. "She was going to redo it the night I left. Now it's messy but I don't want to braid it again because . . ." She sighed. "It wouldn't be the same."

"Oh, Asha—"

"Also, I'm terrible at it," she confessed. "Can't get my parts straight at the back." She shuffled her feet. "Would you . . . could you do it?"

Obi looked at her and felt something like heartbreak.

"It's fine. You don't have to. I'm sure I can manage."

"No!" He waved a hand. "Of course I'll do it. But I've never done it on anyone besides myself, so keep your expectations low."

Asha grinned, her shyness forgotten. "Aw, is that what you say to your boyfriend, too?"

"Oh my god," Obi groaned. "Firstly, why are you like this? And secondly, *he's not my boyfriend I told you that like seven times.*"

She grinned, looking far too pleased with herself, and Obi saw a different, distant version of their lives pan out—one where they'd been cousins, or siblings even, and she had asked him to redo her braids quickly before she wrapped it up and went to sleep.

He sat down on the lowest bunk and pointed to the floor. "Come on then."

Folding herself down, she shuffled back, until her spine was pressed against the bed frame, and Obi's knees bracketed her shoulders.

Pulling his afro comb from an inner pocket, he gently untied the strip of fabric gathering her small, damp ringlets together, and began parting her hair, sliding the thin needles along her freshly scrubbed scalp. There was a loving mathematics to it—in the precise lines of each part, the gathering of three damp, ever-replenishing sections and their overlapping language—a promise of protection. The very last time his father had ever done this for him, he had murmured gruffly, *this hair will not break; you will not break; you are beautiful,* and told Obi, *your mother used to say that. To me. When she would—*

But he hadn't been able to finish, and had instead stood up abruptly, knocking over a chair. He had locked himself in his bedroom for three days, and on the third day, Obi knocked on the door, before pushing it open to find an empty room. His father had gone.

"It takes me so long to do this myself," Asha murmured, jolting him out of the past. "I tried, in the shower, but it was so bad, Obi. You don't even want to know."

He laughed, gathering the middle section and splitting it in three. "Well, my dad used to say that it's harder to do yourself because you're not actually supposed to do it alone." He struggled to remember his father's exact words, but he remembered the shape of them. "It's like ... a ritual that requires other people, that *wants* for other people. But not just anyone—people you trust. For a community."

Asha considered that in silence. Obi wondered what she heard when he said 'community'.

"Thank you," she said after a while.

"It's fine, I told you, it's really no problem." He was nearly done now, braiding the last of three rows, Asha's thick hair shiny with the remnants of the black castor oil he kept in the same pocket as his comb. The tiny bottle's thick brown glass was still miraculously intact, even after all the coat had been through these past days.

"No, I mean . . . for everything." She paused. "You don't have to say anything to this, but I—I've never had a friend like you before. Back home—" She broke off. "There was never any time to be normal." Her voice sounded so horribly small. "And that was, well, it was *fine*, but now that I know what it's like to laugh without being scared of someone hearing . . . it makes me so sad that I used to—" She swallowed, hard. "That that used to be my life." In the reflection on the glass, Obi saw her close her eyes. "And I know we're each doing something really dangerous. Something so dangerous we might not survive it, but we've made it this far together, against *so many* odds, that I can't help but think we were meant to meet one another, and that we were meant to help each other, or something." She shrugged. "I don't know." A tired smile touched her voice. "Maybe I'm just so tired I've become delusional."

Obi was quiet as he finished the last of the cornrows, tying them off at the midway point like Asha had, and combing through the hair she liked to leave free, twisting the tight ringlets around his finger to give them definition.

"Well," he said, finally, trying to remember the last time anyone had ever spoken to him so openly, expecting nothing in return. "I am also so tired that I'm bordering on delusional, but I don't think you're crazy, and I would like to thank you, too. For everything. I think we've got a decent chance at pulling this off, but I doubt I would be so certain if it weren't for you." He patted the top of her head. "All done."

Asha shuffled around, smiling. Putting her hands under her chin, she smiled sweetly. "How do I look?"

"Surprisingly innocent," Obi replied. "It's horrifying, please stop."

"Never," she said, then she got up and ducked out of the room, running to the bathroom. The door clicked shut behind her.

Obi flopped onto his back. Asha was undoubtedly hard to pin down, hard to get a read on, but it felt good to be in her confidence. He had never had a friend who wasn't George before, so it was strange to think that this short-tempered, impulsively reckless and obscurely kind individual would be the one to buck the trend and capture his heart.

Friendship.

It was a strange and unfamiliar feeling, one that had filtered slowly through his consciousness over the past few days to settle tentatively in his good graces.

He smiled. There were certainly worse things.

It wasn't until later that evening that Obi began to suspect he was being watched. He was on his way to the bathroom for covert face-mask application purposes when he knew for certain there were eyes on him. The back of his neck prickled as he walked down the shadowy hallway outside his room, the lights flickering on dimly as he passed them. The bathroom door slid soundlessly open as he stood in front of it, to reveal a shabbily tiled room filled with the expected amenities. The lights flickered on, the watched feeling persisted. Obi turned to look in the mirror, his own reflection looked back. He closed his eyes, trying to control his breathing. It was completely irrational to think there was anyone here besides himself. Unless Asha was playing tricks. Which he sincerely doubted. Eyes still closed, he splashed water over his face, the warmth of it was comforting. Perhaps he was being paranoid for no reason.

He opened his eyes.

Needle-sharp teeth grinned back at him, a bare scalp glinted, decorated with a spiky tattoo, its spires circling her head like a crown. The cowl of a cloak bunched around a thin neck, bright eyes roamed over his face, taking it in.

"Oh, for god's *sake*," he whispered angrily, "leave me *alone*."

The woman in front of him shook her head. "Not a chance. I have been searching for you for years. Then you turn up in the Order's time and I'm supposed to ignore it? What are you doing here?"

Obi glared. "You knew my father, not me." He moved away from her, towards the door. "And he hated the Order of Legends more than anything. I told you before and I'll tell you again—I want nothing to do with your creepy sect, and nothing you can offer me will change my mind."

"The Order could be your home if you let it—"

"*I have a home.*" It took everything he had not to yell in her face. "I had a home. I was right there." He shook his head, staring at her. The last time he had seen Qala, he had been nine years old, nearly ten. He had still lived with his father.

She was one of the more regular visitors. Alarick seemed to respect her—and like her—as though she were his much older sister. They'd stayed up late, taking up the cramped kitchen of their tiny house. Obi had been on his way to bed when he'd heard their hushed tones.

"Will you ever tell him about the Sentinel's theory?" her voice was soft. The clink of glasses sounded in the background. "About why you came here in the first place? About who he might become?"

Alarick was silent. When he eventually spoke, his voice was firm and cold. "It's not him. He's just a kid."

"But he won't always be. I would have thought you'd understand how time worked by now."

"It's not him, Qala."

"We each have our own destinies, Amadi. You can protect Obi from his, or you can teach him. His Anchoring will start soon. You should bring him to the Order. We'll teach him, shelter him. Prepare him for when the time comes."

Something slammed onto the table. Alarick's hand, most likely, or his glass. "Nothing is coming, Qala. You will not take my boy like you took me."

"Alarick, I—"

"But if you're right, and the prophecy is coming for him, then you have to protect him, if I can't. You have to, or—"

A floorboard creaked under Obi's foot. Alarick swore softly, before getting out of his chair. Obi had run back to his tiny bedroom, heart pounding. Throwing himself onto the bed in time to hear the door slam.

Now, Obi thought, as he stood in the bathroom of a spaceship halfway through a quest whose end point was the centre of the galaxy, he at least had a decent skin care routine.

Seeing Qala again after all these years was disconcerting to say the least.

"I've come to tell you something," she said slowly. "As a courtesy. And to ask you a question—as a matter of urgency."

Obi nodded. Better to get this over with.

"I know where your father is," she said.

Obi saw white. His heart clenched. This couldn't— There was no way that— *He was dead.* Obi was sure of it.

"My father died," he said. "Otherwise, he would have come back for me." He was shaking. "Or I would have found him."

"Oh, Obi—"

"Where?"

"I'm sorry—"

"*Where?*"

Qala's voice was even. "London."

"*Qala*—"

"February. 1812."

Obi closed his eyes. His heart was hammering, punching at his ribs. So, Alarick Amadi lived. He lived and still apparently had enough of a hold on his powers to go back to where he had left his son. Maybe he had gone looking for Obi. Could it really be that he was trying to find him after all these years?

He opened his eyes. "And what is your question?"

"Will you come with me to the Order of Legends?" Qala asked. "It's where you belong." Her voice was soft but persistent. "Obi, there's something starting, out there in the universe. All around us. Something is coming."

Obi could barely concentrate on what she was saying, still reeling from the knowledge that his father was alive. But something in her tone made him focus.

"Something's coming? What?"

"I can't say. I've already said too much."

"You haven't said anything?!"

She looked around, shiftily. "If you come to the Order, we can tell you. We can help you . . . prepare."

"Prepare for what?" Exasperation was making him angry. "And even if I wanted to—which I don't—I can't. I have to help my friend. She has no one. I was like that once—all alone in the world. And I tried to fix it for myself by risking my life for a man who had abandoned me. I can't get home. I've ruined everything with the only person who has ever cared for me."

"What if the Order could give you that back?"

"Give what back?"

"Your way home," she said. "A cure."

Obi froze. "Excuse me?"

"A few years ago, we received a communication that used

214

your father's old codename. It was the first tip off we'd had that he was alive since he disappeared. It didn't tell us anything about his whereabouts—only that he'd travelled to 6027 to tell us something."

"What did it say?"

Qala cleared her throat. "*Boy is sick. Arm is gone. Help me, please.*" She shrugged. "We knew what had happened immediately—somehow his son, you, had contracted the sickness. What we didn't know was that your father was no longer caring for you. By the time we had successfully synthesised the cure, and tracked you both down to London, neither of you were there. We've been chasing you for years now, Obi. But you move too fast through time. I could never keep up. Then you turned up here." A strange look passed over her face. "Like fate was finally stepping in."

Obi kept his voice level. "You're telling me there's a cure?" he took a deep, ragged breath. "There's a cure because my father knew I was sick, but was too much of a coward to face it? To come and help me himself? So he ran to the people he despised, rather than talk to me, and begged them to fix his own mistakes?"

"Obi—"

Obi felt hot anger surging up in him. "And now you—knowing I need it, but only offering it to me if I give in to your demands."

"I'm sorry, Obi, but it's not up to me. The Sentinel . . . it's his plan. But it's for your own good, you just don't understand that yet. And what other options do you have? You were going to go the Magekind, weren't you? The Emperor's magicians. You were going to ask them to cure you in exchange for your powers."

Obi looked away from her, humiliated. "I didn't think I had any other choice."

"They're owned by *Thracin*, Obi. He controls them. They could have turned you in, captured you, imprisoned you indefinitely—"

"And how is the Order any different?"

Qala went quiet, studying him. "You remind me of your mother when you get like this. Running headlong into situations without a plan and landing squarely on your feet anyway. If luck could be inherited, I'd say you'd won the genetic lottery, never mind the fact Alarick never had any."

Obi looked downwards. He wanted to say, "Don't talk about my mother." But glimpses of the woman who'd birthed him were so few and far between it would have felt like robbing himself.

Qala reached out and touched his shoulder. "The Order isn't your enemy, Obi. The Sentinel made mistakes with your father, but we've learned from them. And, if you ever want to get back to London, you need us. You might as well hear what we have to say." She withdrew something from her cloak and pressed it into his hands. It was a small stone, nondescript but for the symbol on it: a triangle with a circle in its centre. The symbol of the Order of Legends. The same symbol that had been on the projector that had led him here in the first place. "When you decide, pay us a visit. You can use this like an Artefact. It will guide you to us."

He looked at her. She was a ghost from his past, tied to him by the string of fate, looped around his neck by his father. He could take up her offer right now. Go to the Order, hear what they had to say and then take the cure. But what if they wanted to own him, like they'd owned his father? Obi knew Alarick had still woken from nightmares years after he'd managed to leave them. What had they made him do? And why did they want Obi? To carry on his father's work? He had no idea. And, hanging over the choice was his friendship with Asha. The rude, funny, angry, genius girl, all alone in the galaxy, on a suicide mission to save her sister and her mother. How could he leave her now? How could he betray her fragile trust like that?

He shook his head at Qala. "I need time to think."

She nodded. "Alright. Three weeks, by your Earthern calendar. That's the best I can offer."

"Fine," he muttered, and stepped past her, walking out of the bathroom.

By the time he had turned back to ask how she had even found him, she was gone.

As they journeyed through the new land, they told each other stories to keep the shadows at bay.

'A Complete, Annotated History of Chasca, Including Relevant Translated Mythologies. Chapter: Scroll the Second' by I. Nisomn, ex-acolyte of the Aonian Archives.

Chapter Twenty

[planet: none] + [location: free space] + [year: 6066]

In the end, the *Stayanax* set sail with little fanfare, engines rumbling to life beneath Asha's hands and knees as she scrubbed scuff marks from the second-floor corridor.

She had to take a moment—her eyes squeezed shut, heart thudding, hand grasping the sponge so hard that her fingernails dug into her palm—because while her feet were planted firmly on the ground, she felt so free she might have been weightless. She tried to catch Obi's eye from the other end of the corridor, but he was absorbed in his work. He'd been quieter lately, more closed off. *Probably planning his next moves for when we reach Xesca,* Asha thought dejectedly. *Without me.* She shook her head. That was two weeks away. Until then they had one last mission together: adjust to life on board the ship. Outside the window, she could see the dark, pinpricked expanse of space, the NIS growing smaller and smaller in the distance.

They'd made it this far. Her heart grew light with the knowledge that the next step on their journey awaited them, growing closer, somewhere out amongst the limitless stars.

I'll save you both, she thought, picturing her mother's face, and the little girl from the hologram. *I don't know how, but I will. And now I'm closer than ever.*

The first day was hard, but the tough work was comforting,

and it was nothing she wasn't used to. The day after that was even harder, on account of the newly-aching muscles, but, as she settled into the space-hauler lifestyle, she found there was indeed a rhythm to it.

Wake early (at the sound of the ship's alarm, not with the sun—*there is no sun, remember?*), grab breakfast to eat on the go, say thank you to Doctor Hannei for brewing such lovely tea, try not to burn your mouth on said tea, but also try to finish it before arriving in the common area where chores were posted every morning.

Chores: scrubbing, scrubbing, *scrubbing*, but also transcribing memos, and some basic coding work for Asha. They might be asked to fold laundry or assist the mechtechs with basic repairs (Asha secretly felt proud every time she managed to surprise them with her knowledge) or count stock and input it into the system that calculated possible revenue. But Asha's favourite way to fill chore slots was with the ship's chef, a large sentient named Ossock whose grey, leathery skin always smelled of spices, and whose six arms, and huge smile apparently reminded Obi of 'that cool cat-bus from Totoro', whatever that meant. He was incredibly kind and didn't ask much from her in the way of conversation. His voice was deep, but quiet, with a lovely accent that, unsurprisingly, Asha had never heard before. Sometimes he talked about the family he had left behind on his home planet, Dau, and how much he missed them and their rickety, sprawling old house that perched on stilts above the mudflats outside the city. He explained their customs to Asha and told her what it was like before Thracin's occupation, told her about the food cart he had carried on his back for years until he had saved enough money to open his own restaurant. When Asha wondered aloud what it would be like to live in a world where you were allowed to benefit directly from your own labour, she saw pity in Ossock's eyes that she barely understood.

Lunch was a loud and busy affair that Asha learned to bear quickly and learned to like not long after that. She sat with Obi on one side, and, increasingly as the days passed, with Xavior on the other. Xavior; quick to smile and even quicker to laugh, irritable when tired, insufferable when hungry, outspoken and—to Asha, at least—shockingly liberal. The sun at the centre of any room. He was trouble—she'd figured that out after barely a day had gone by—always playing tricks and teasing someone or taking your words and twisting them inside out until you were red-faced and he was laughing. *Always*, he was laughing. Asha had never met someone so good-humoured—and fine, maybe she liked him a little bit, and no, she wasn't particularly sorry.

In the evenings they ate, and then dispersed: to their rooms, to the bridge, to the common area. Often, Obi, Xavior, and Asha congregated there, lounging on couches and playing card games or vidsims—Asha always won the flightsims ('Night-Wing Destroyer 3: Pilot Assassin' was her favourite), while Obi lamented the lack of something called 'we tennis' which was apparently *awesome*—laughing and messing around until Isi told them to shut up and go to sleep.

Usually, that meant that Asha would go back to the room she shared with Obi and stay up late into the night, working on an assortment of new tech, just to keep her edge. There was a smartwatch that she had found in the electrical refuse pile, fixed, and linked up to extra navigation satellites, as well as the web. There was also an old broken gun that she was trying to strip down to its most basic elements, with the aim of fitting it all inside a slim band that would close around her wrist and re-assemble itself on command. She had a prototype, but it was barely functional. The challenge was all of the fun though, and for the first time, she could work on her projects without flinching at the slightest noise or resorting to stealing parts. It felt fake, like she was living in a dream. But then she'd see Isi display rare affection towards Xavior and it made her think of her own mother, all alone somewhere with the Sentinel, and the illusion was shattered.

I will find you, Mama, I swear it. And if I don't, I'll die trying, because there's nothing for me, if you're not here. Nothing. I'd be so lost.

She also thought of Aziza. Her sister. The best friend she'd never had. Sometimes she found herself wishing that she could talk to her, tell her every insane thing that had happened in the past few days. *Are you okay?* She found herself thinking. *I hope you're okay, wherever you are. You don't know it yet, but I'm coming to get you. To take you away from these people.*

Sometimes she even let herself imagine the moment they met. But thinking of these things was incredibly painful, so she kept as busy as possible, throwing herself into the routine of the ship, and planning with Obi what they'd do when they reached port.

It was almost enough.

One evening, they were all lying on their backs on the scratchy carpet, making obscene shapes on the ceiling out of their hands and an old, flickering holoset, when Ossock lumbered past. Seeing the cook out of the kitchen was a rare sight. They all sat up.

"Quickly," he said, all of his arms waving. "There's a whole school of them!"

Xavior's eyes lit up immediately. "Oh! Come on guys, you'll *love* this."

They followed his lead, running down the corridor towards the ship's bridge. The filters that covered the ship's large, forward-facing windows had been turned transparent.

The sight beyond was . . .

Well.

An eye blinked at them from beyond the window, pupil huge and iris semi-luminous, set into what looked like a cliff-face, until the eye blinked slowly and the rock around it *moved*, and Asha realised that a vast creature swam—flew?—beside them on the other side of the glass.

"It's calving season," Ossock said in his quiet, matter-of-fact way. "Look."

A smaller creature darted forward, small fins flapping, strange weedy plants flowing from its skin to cloud the air.

They all walked closer to the glass, pressing their hands against it to peer out, eyes wide.

"Getting a bit close," cautioned one of the pilots. "We'll pull back."

The ship veered slightly away from the eye, circling back to get a better vantage point, and stay out of the range of errant tailfins.

"They look like . . . whales," Obi whispered. "Do they—is that . . . are there plants growing on them?"

"Yes," replied Ossock. "These creatures are capable of supporting entire ecosystems on their backs. They are a vital part of the interplanetary biosphere, but they are dying out."

"*No*," Asha said, her own vehemence surprising her. "Why?"

"Why do you think, child? Why does anything die out before its time now?"

"Thracin," Xavior muttered.

Ossock nodded. "Our esteemed Emperor enjoys free labour far too much—as I am sure you are well aware—and these proud creatures represent to him the equivalent of a freighter ship without the need for fuel. A transport service not requiring captain, crew or pilot. It is . . . barbaric, but I am no longer surprised by barbarism. Not even when it comes cloaked under the guise of efficacy meant to serve a greater civilisation, and especially not after what I have heard from my family in the middle belt."

Asha looked at him, confused. "What have you heard from them?"

"It's the weapon, right?" came Xavior's voice. Asha turned to him and was surprised to see real anger marring the usual sanguinity of his expression. "They're saying the Emperor has built a planet-destroying weapon."

There was a stunned silence.

"No one knows for certain," Ossock said. "There's no great beam of light before the destruction. He gives no warning—no orbiting ships blot the sun from the sky and drop bombs powerful enough to cause such ruin." His large, round face was more solemn than Asha had ever seen it. "It is as though the planet turns on itself—natural disasters destroy the surface, activating at impossible rates. Planetary rotation speeds accelerate, electrical storms trigger hurricanes, and mega-tsunamis wipe out entire continents. I have heard of a planet named Hadar that was once a stunning metropolis, now plunged into an ice-age that will last a millennium. They say it was hit by an asteroid that appeared to change its own course, as though wrenched out of its usual orbit by some unseen force." He waved the arms on one side of his body in a gesture Asha had learnt meant frustration. "But there is not enough proof that we may lay the blame on the Emperor's shoulders. It is only thought to be him, as all the targeted planets have been sites of rebellion and unrest."

"Rebellion?" Asha repeated. "There are people who—who stand up to him?"

Ossock sighed. "There are people who try."

Asha watched the whale creatures swimming through space outside for hours after the others had left, thinking about planets spinning impossibly faster, and once-great cities covered in ice.

Small asteroids crumbled on contact with the slow sweep of the huge beasts' tails, the greenery on their backs swaying slightly with each movement. It was hard to gain a sense of proportion when looking out into the vastness of space. In the evening, as they finally drew away from the melancholy creatures, Asha could almost trick herself into thinking that they were the same size as the palm-sized fish that swum in the shallows of the oases during summer. All too soon they were gone, specks in the distance made indistinguishable by the surrounding stars.

Later, much later, she would recall the following days as just a series of images, of moving pictures: Xavior, leaning on a mop and grinning at her with his sharp teeth, Obi laughing at a joke she had made, a running gag they had about something she couldn't even remember, like it was the funniest thing in the world. The scratchy feeling of her duvet on her chin, drinking hot tea with honey stirred into it and wanting to cry at the taste, it was so good. The way her blood seemed to buzz when Xavior looked at her a certain way, the feeling of his gaze on her making her feel more stupid than she knew was possible, more alive than she'd ever been in her whole life. Doors that locked, bathrooms without cameras. Group meals, and in-jokes and Obi chasing her down the hall in a towel after she and Xavior stole his clothes from outside the shower. Those days, she often thought, were surely counted amongst the best days of her whole life.

It was on the ninth day that everything changed.

"Ninth days are for resting," Xavior explained to Obi and Asha as they walked to breakfast. "Or, at least they are for normal people. Isi, you have gathered by now I'm sure, is not normal. Also, she has so little regard for her minions—that's us—that she practically has to be read our rights at the end of every week to ensure that she actually lets us off the hook. So, we work from breakfast until lunch, and then: freedom!"

Asha nodded. Free time was fun—she had learned that over her first few days on *Stayanax*, having not really been overly familiar with the concept before. But a whole half day? Surely there weren't enough leisure activities to fill *seven hours*?

"What . . . would we do?" she asked.

Xavior grinned, canines flashing, eyebrows like black daggers. *Trouble*, she thought, again.

"What wouldn't we?"

It was one of the best days of Asha's life, in the end. Dimly, she realised this could be deemed pathetic, but she was too happy to care.

They were gathered in the common room after dinner, when it happened. Someone had brought out something called *punch*, which was fruity, with bubbles, and had acquired a strange after-taste shortly into the night. Asha's head felt weird, and someone else had strung up twinkling coloured lights, which were pretty and also . . . moving? Or maybe that was just her.

They were also playing music, which had made Asha jump the first time the speakers had turned on—crackling with static until someone gave them a good kick and sound jumped out, quite unlike anything she had ever heard. Yes, people sang on Gahraan, tapping out rhythms on scuffed knees and clapping softly, but that was always whispered and half-frantic and nothing at all like this. Obi looked a little sad when she mentioned this, but he always looked a little sad, even though he tried so valiantly to hide it. *Brave boy.*

He didn't look too sad now, though, as he twirled her around to the music. Both of them were laughing uproariously at her energetic attempt to copy a dance he was trying to teach her that had no name in the Universal Dialect, but that she could almost say in the original English: *lin-di-hop*.

"You two look like you're having fun."

It was Xavior, looking highly amused and sipping punch from a very large mug that had '*galaxy's best chef!*' written on it in bold letters.

"Ossock's going to kill you when he sees you took his cup," Asha laughed.

"Ossock couldn't kill a bug. I'm not worried."

"Maybe you should be. He knows it was you rummaging through the snack cupboard last night."

Xavior shook his head serenely. "Whoever that was should be ashamed. I hope he catches them. They sound like a real menace."

Asha smiled. "Menace is the least of it—he's ugly, too."

Xavior rolled his eyes, but he was smiling as well. "You look nice, by the way."

She squinted back at him. "I look the same as I always do."

Xavior sighed.

"I'm going to get more punch," said Obi.

They watched him leave, but he didn't get even halfway across the room before he was stopped by Ossock, who began gesturing around as though he had lost something. They watched in confusion, until he mimed drinking and then shrugged—an interesting thing to watch someone with six arms do—and Asha felt Xavior freeze beside her.

"Ah, shit."

She snorted. "Told you so."

"Shit, *shit*. I need an alibi," he looked frantically around the room before his eyes landed back on her. "Dance with me?"

Asha blinked. "Okay." *Wait, what?*

"Great, wait here."

226

He ran over to a side table, distributed the large volume of punch between three other unattended cups, before hiding Ossock's mug behind a large vase of synthetic flowers. Asha glanced towards Obi. He was a terrible liar, and so it was only a matter of time before he gave them away. She saw his eyes dart nervously in their direction—

"Can I put my hands on your waist?"

She turned around. Xavior stared back, looking sheepish.

"I guess . . ."

"You guess?"

"Yes, fine."

His hands settled above her hips. She put hers on his shoulders. Gently he steered her through an uncomplicated set of steps that she soon got the hang of.

"Not bad."

She shrugged. It was nice, the soft lights and lively music, Xavior's hands firm on her waist, crew members chatting amongst themselves in all corners of the room. Over Xavior's shoulder she could see Isi watching them all from the doorway, a fond look on her usually serious face.

"You know," said Xavior, pulling her attention back, "I've been thinking—"

"You'll want to be careful doing that," she murmured, but stopped smiling when she saw the look on his face.

"—and I'm beginning to suspect that you and Obi are lying to us."

Asha didn't react, which was probably what gave her away.

"I'm right, aren't I?" Leaning closer, he lowered his voice. "What's wrong? Don't you trust me?" She could hear the smile in his voice.

"It's not about trust." She replied a little crossly, startled by the closeness, the feeling of his body heat against her. "You're the one who picked up two runaway humans on the NIS anyway. Anything we said was to protect ourselves. You would have done the same thing."

Xavior retreated. "You're right," he said. "But you need to tell me the truth at some point. Sooner rather than later. I need to know you aren't putting us all in danger."

The music swung low, and he dipped her. The room spun, lights drawing lines in the air. Grabbing on tight to Xavior's shoulders to steady herself, she replied through clenched teeth, "I don't *need* to do anything. But I will tell you because I—"

Because I like you, she wanted to say. *Because I want you to like me. Because I love being here and being part of this, and I couldn't stand to be alienated again. Because I'm tired of keeping secrets.*

"Because it's the right thing to do," she finished weakly.

"Hm."

They stood up and kept dancing. Asha forced herself to breathe evenly. Technically, the only thing she and Obi had lied about was their destination and being siblings. It had felt right at the time—they hadn't known how he'd react to the idea of aiding and abetting two runaway humans on a highly illegal prison break. But now . . .

"Just remember that you asked for it," she said.

Xavior tilted his head in obvious curiosity. "Well, it'd better be good after that little warning. Oh, stop frowning, I'm only joking. Partly."

Caught up in their conversation—and her own frustration—Asha forgot to double-step. Xavior stood on her foot just as she tried to rectify the mistake, and the resulting yank pushed them both off-balance and into a heap on the floor.

"*Ow.*"

The other crew members clapped and laughed good-naturedly, which took the edge off the embarrassment, and suggested

Xavior had survived the fall intact. A sopping wet patch of carpet by her hand told her that her punch couldn't claim the same.

"Your fault," Xavior said, sitting up and rubbing his head. "That was one hundred per cent your fault."

"Except I'm pretty sure *you* were the one who stepped on *my* foot."

Xavior stood, offering his hand. She rolled her eyes at him and knocked it away to stand by herself.

That was when it happened.

Touch was an interesting thing to Asha, who had only ever been touched with any measure of kindness by her mother. Other touches had been violent, or predatory. Horrifying and painful. Slaps and kicks and pinches. She had been groped by guards, pushed around by other workers. Once, she'd been tazed. So, she was used to feeling strange these days, skittish and electric, occasionally sick, when touched by other people—the brush of palms, a hand resting on her shoulder. A hug.

Tactility, she knew, was the capability of a person to feel or be touched; the degree of a sentient's responsiveness to stimuli that interacted with that capability; a language everyone spoke that lent itself just as easily to violence as it did to love. Everyday magic. But also, in this case, magic of the not so everyday kind.

As Asha's scarred, brown knuckles touched Xavior's smooth, pale green palm, she *felt* in more ways than one. On a minute level there was skin on skin; the rough spiral of fingerprints, grooves like valleys, translucent keratinocytes brushing up against each other—tectonics on a microscopic plane—body heat, a faint clamminess. On another level, an entirely unexplainable, inexplicable level—a level that spanned ages, though neither of them knew it—there was: *wind on her skin, ash in the air, a leather strap over one arm and a jagged crystalline object in front of her face refracting the sun, blood on its shining edges—*

Asha gasped and staggered, barely aware of Xavior rushing forward to help her until his hands were a breath away from her skin—

"*Don't touch me,*" she bit out, moving backwards across the floor. "Don't, I—"

Xavior took a step back, his eyes wide. "Are you alright?"

"I don't—" Asha shook her head—which was pounding suddenly—and squeezed her eyes shut. "Did you feel that?"

Xavior shook his head slowly, looking mystified. "Feel what?" His fingers twisted nervously in the hem of his shirt. "Do you want me to get Doctor Hannei?"

Asha shook her head. "No, I . . ." she started, but trailed off. "My head hurts."

Xavior looked slightly relieved. "Oh yeah. That'll be the punch." He gestured towards the sleeping quarters. "Would you like to go lie down? I could walk you to your room?"

Asha nodded.

He offered his arm, but she eyed it warily until he dropped it. Their elbows brushed as they made their way through the small crowd, and Asha flinched, but nothing happened. They were both wearing long sleeves, though, so maybe . . .

"I'm sorry," he said, when they reached the quiet stretch corridor outside of her room. "If I did anything that made you uncomfortable. I was sort of joking when I said you and Obi need to come clean. I get it—everyone has a past. That's your business. I was only curious."

She looked at him in confusion, his face was uncharacteristically serious. "No, it's—it's nothing. It's okay. I want you to know. I don't know why. But I do."

He didn't reply. Just looked at her like she was looking at him, and so the moment stretched on without breaking, silent and expectant of something Asha couldn't quite identify. Maybe it was that that loosened her inhibitions. Maybe it was whatever Xavior had put in the stupid punch.

"I saw something," she whispered. "When I touched you."

For some reason, this made Xavior duck his head. "What did you see?" he whispered back, and *good*, she thought, *he recognises that this is to be a secret. Not sure why, but it does* feel *like a secret thing.*

"A shield, I think. Made of crystal. Dripping blood. There was smoke, too. I felt . . . a breeze on my face." She stopped walking, but the hallway kept moving. *Thracin*, she felt strange. "Have you ever felt a breeze?"

Xavior laughed and nodded. "Yeah, Asha. I have been outside you know."

She blew lightly on his face, which was suddenly so funny she started laughing until she couldn't stop, then she nearly stopped, but she looked at his expression—so *confused*—and dissolved into giggles again. "Silly spacer boy grew up in a vacuum. Bet he's never even seen a cloud."

Xavior's face changed so abruptly at this that Asha stopped laughing instantly.

"Xavior?"

He smiled strangely, shaking his head. "Forgot you didn't know."

"Know what?"

His head tilted. He was considering her. Asha had never felt so acutely considered before. "Sometimes," he said, "I feel like I've known you for a fair while longer than I actually have. I assume you know things. It's incredibly unsettling. I would say that I recognise you . . . but that can't be true." He studied her face. "I didn't grow up in a vacuum, Asha. I know what a breeze is. I had a planet, but I can't go back there. Had a mother, too, once, but she was killed, and I was locked away, and after that—" He stopped, eyes distant. "Well, I don't remember. Not a second of it. From the ages of seven to eleven, by the Old Pan-Galactic measure. Half a decade blank, and now I'm *here*, eight years of new memories and two pseudo-families later, and I barely even know who I am . . . *Shit*, that punch." His words were running together slightly. Closing his eyes, he took a firm step backwards.

Asha didn't quite understand, but she *wanted* to.

"Xav, I—"

"I think I'm going to head to bed, now," he said. "I'll find you tomorrow."

"Not if I find you first," she said lamely, out of habit, but she wanted to say more, she just . . . didn't know how.

"Night," she called out, belatedly, inadequately. But he had turned a corner, and was gone.

Often, as they walked through the ghostly forest, Adesola felt Dandeyi calling to her. She could barely remember their face, so long it had been since she'd seen it. So long had it been since they'd embraced. Nevertheless, the voice of her distant Hero-in-arms called to her, a world away.

"I await you, my love. One day we will meet again."

'A Complete, Annotated History of Chasca, Including Relevant Translated Mythologies. Chapter: Scroll the Second' by I. Nisomn, ex-acolyte of the Aonian Archives.

(Archivist's note: This idea of remote telepathy may simply be metaphor, but it reminds us of some of your more nonsensical ramblings. About blood calling to blood through the ages. About prophecies and the cyclical nature of history, and three heroes living among us who might, someday soon, attempt to save the world. I had not been aware that our world needed saving, but the war of unification is in its final throes now, and that cruel general Thracin grows more big-headed by the day.)

Chapter Twenty-One

[planet: none] + [location: free space] + [year: 6066]

Asha woke the next day to the low wail of the morning alarm and a headache so fierce she thought her head might actually explode.

Obi groaned into wakefulness in the bunk beneath her.

"*No*," he whimpered. "Please, no. I can't."

Asha had never agreed with anything more in her life.

Gingerly, she swung her legs over the side of her bunk to climb down the ladder, head throbbing, mouth dry. Stumbling into the bathroom, she turned on the tap and bent to drink, tepid water spattering her face and neck.

By the time she made it to breakfast—a grumbling, ashen-faced Obi in tow—she felt very vaguely more alive. A cup of tea helped to soothe her throat and calm her headache, and, one full stomach later, she felt a little further away from 'corpse-like' and a little closer to 'human'.

Xavior, she noticed, was nowhere to be seen.

"Pass that thing," Obi said, gesturing in a way that could only be described as floppily.

"The water jug?"

"Hhng."

The rest of the day passed in a blur, from which Xavior was conspicuously absent. And worst of all, try as she might, Asha could only remember strange fragments from their evening. She remembered, *I'm beginning to suspect that you and Obi are lying to us,* and the resulting promise to tell the truth. She also remembered Xavior looking uncharacteristically sad, and something that *must* have been a dream, but had felt incredibly real. *A shining piece of crystal, edged in gold . . .* she shook her head, frustrated. Maybe he was still mad at her. She resolved to find him and ask.

He wasn't at dinner, and when Obi asked Isi where he was, she just told him to mind his own business, so there wasn't any help to be found there. Then Obi turned in early, and so Asha found she had some time to herself.

It took her just under an hour to search the ship from top to bottom and come up empty. Maybe Xavior was in his room. *Fine.* She wasn't going to harass him.

Making her way back towards the upper decks, she barely registered the footsteps approaching from the other direction, until she smacked firmly into someone and—*flames on her skin, a baby's shriek, the hiss of a sword from a scabbard*—then she was sprawled on her back, blinking up into fluorescent overhead lights.

"*Ow!*" said Xavior, rubbing his chin.

She groaned, sprawled on the floor. Her head was throbbing again—it felt like someone had taken an axe to the back of her skull. Just like last night when—

She sat bolt upright. Because she *remembered now* what had happened the previous night—the thing she had thought was a dream, but she now realised hadn't been. She hauled herself to her feet and jabbed an angry finger in Xavior's face.

"*What did you do to me?*" she snarled.

Xavior scrambled backward. "Nothing!" His eyes were wide. "What are you talking about?!"

"Last night," she said. "You told me you put alcohol in the punch, but was there something else? Is that why you're avoiding me?"

Xavior's eyes got wider. "What? *No*. I would never do that!" He peered at her, looking worried. "Are you feeling alright?"

"If I felt alright, would I be stood here, *asking if you put hallucinogens in my punch?*"

"No," he said. Then, "Wait, hallucinogens? Have you been—" he looked around, lowering his voice "—seeing things?"

Asha looked away. This couldn't be happening. It would have been better if he wasn't so frightfully earnest. She wasn't used to people being worried about her. It made the whole thing immeasurably worse. "I don't know!" she shouted. "I don't know anything! I just feel like I'm going crazy—like there's something in my head that shouldn't be there, and I don't want to be losing my mind, but I'm so stressed all the time that I think, oh god, *maybe I might be*, and it's all just too much, it's so *much*, and I just want a break!" She was breathing quite hard, stunned at the force of her own feelings. But that was just how she felt—how she'd felt for days now, like she was going crazy—like all of this couldn't actually be happening to *her*.

"Asha . . . " Xavior said.

"I don't want sympathy," she looked back at him, glaring. "I want answers. And the only thing any of my *'hallucinations'* have in common is you, *so start talking.*"

Xavior couldn't have looked more confused if he'd tried. His mouth was open, as though he wanted to say something—anything—but he was at a genuine loss as to what he could offer her that might make her feel better. "I'm so sorry," he said. "I—I don't have any." He looked around and scowled at something behind her. Asha turned. One of the crew members had a panel open in the wall, and was very obviously listening to their conversation instead of fixing the plumbing.

Xavior leaned forward. "Look, why don't you come to my room, and explain what it is you've been seeing? Maybe we can figure it out, together."

Asha searched his face. She found nothing but sincerity. "Fine."

Xavior's bedroom was smaller than the double bunked one she shared with Obi, but where theirs was bare-walled and sparsely furnished, Xavior's was undeniably lived in. Two pairs of shoes were lined up under the window, posters were tacked up on the walls—bands she'd heard him talk about, and movies. It felt strangely intimate, to see the place where he slept, the place where he was alone. She was arrested, suddenly, by the fact that there was a stack of comic books on his bedside table, and a single sock peeking out from under his bed. She thought something ridiculous and incoherent like, '*Wow, sock,*' and then realised what she was doing and wrenched her gaze back to Xavior and the problem at hand, before she could be struck down by the force of her own embarrassment.

"It started last night," she said quickly. "When we were—when we fell. Maybe I hit my head . . . " She trailed off, unsure.

"What did you see?" Xavior asked gently. "Maybe that will help us to understand."

Casting her mind back, she winced at the strangeness of the memory. It felt painful in her mind, like a bruise in the flesh of her recollection. She pressed on it, and it ached.

She closed her eyes. "It's like I'm in someone else's body, looking out from different eyes. Whoever it is—whoever I am—they're not here, they're somewhere . . . *different*. There's grass." She breathed in, and it was like a doorway opened in her mind, tender around the edges. "There's smoke," she murmured, "and ash falling, and I'm carrying something made of crystal." She could feel the solid weight of Xavior's hand on her arm. "There's a baby crying, but that's different, that's later—*ow!*" She gasped, and opened her eyes, Xavior had stepped forward in concern. She could feel his breath on her forehead.

A warrior, striding across a dying landscape, glowing pieces of ash raining down around them.

"Dandeyi," she whispered.

Immediately, a migraine split the back of her skull like she'd been struck. She stumbled backwards, bumping into the wall. She was blind, her vision starry. Hands outstretched, she fumbled for the wall, and found it, grappling her way to the floor.

A voice echoed through her mind. *Nearly, little one. Come and meet me.*

She knew that voice—it was the same one that had spoken in her mind when she'd seen the future in the Sentinel's gaze. The voice from Gahraan that had said, *you took your time. Is it starting again?*

She screamed.

"Asha!" Xavior was next to her in an instant.

"Don't touch me," she gasped, and he sprang back. Something was clicking into place—but how could that be possible?

"I think it only happens when you touch me," she said, then registered what she had said, and how ridiculous it sounded. "Oh my god, I am losing my mind."

"No, you're not—don't say that. It's going to be okay." Xavior trailed off, clearly just as confused and worried as she was. He looked—to Asha's horror—like he wanted to hug her or something, but he kept his distance.

"If I'm not losing my senses, then what is wrong with me?"

THE PRINCIPLE OF MOMENTS

She closed her eyes. Maybe she had been knocked out by a guard during the Anniversary celebrations on Gahraan and this was all the vivid dreaming of her comatose mind. Maybe she was really dead and everything she had seen the past few days had all happened inside the space of a second as her dying brain released its final chemicals. She opened her eyes and looked at Xavior. "I . . ."

"Maybe you're not losing your mind . . ." he shrugged. "Maybe it's being woken up."

"What are you talking about?"

He sat back down, next to her but not touching. "It's hard to explain, so of course there are sceptics, and it differs from culture to culture . . ."

"Just say it."

"A gift. It sounds like a gift. A manipulation of energy."

"I don't—can't do that," she said, exasperated. It sounded like Obi's gift, when he tapped into sentimental magic. But she'd *know* if she had that kind of power, wouldn't she?

"Maybe not before now. I mean, it's a rare trait only exhibited by a few species—the ability to tap into whatever energy it is that threads through the galaxy like a web, connecting everyone. So the chances are slim. But if you really are seeing things . . ."

Asha nearly said, *Xavior, that is impossible.* But then a small voice in her head interrupted. *Back on Gahraan you saw the future like it was a memory. You met a time-traveller and now, whenever you touch Xavior's skin, the visions get worse. Would it really be impossible?*

"It's the only explanation I can think of," Xavior said.

"How do you know any of this?"

Xavior looked like he was in two minds. Then he said, "When I was a kid, a few of the people I grew up around could do

239

strange things. I mean, *I* can do strange things—or, used to be able to. Not anymore. Not after . . . *well.*"

Asha looked at him sharply. "You? Does this have something to do with . . . with what you said last night, about not knowing what you are? About the years that were taken from you?"

He screwed up his face, reticent, and stayed that way for long enough that Asha was about to let the whole thing drop, but then he said, "I didn't always look like this," and her words died in her throat. "Where I come from—*came from,*" he continued, "about a third of the population was gifted in some small way. They used to say it was because of our ancestors, whose planet we left a few generations before mine. My mother had an affinity for water, my aunt could speak any language—" his shoulders slumped "—I could change my appearance at will."

Asha drew in a breath.

"One day, the Consortium came for us, as they came for so many. They were looking for something. I don't know what. They took a few of us, though I don't think they found it. After that—nothing. There are . . . flashes of memory. I know I was tampered with. Experimented on, chemically and . . . magically. It was the Magekind who did it. They altered my power. I—" He broke off. "When they decided they were done with me, they dropped me on a planet called Aonia, the home of the Diplomats' Guild—it's neutral territory there. I was half-mad, half-delirious, and hadn't seen light in *years* . . . The people who helped me there said I should try to change myself, to see if I still could, I guess. But my power was all wrong. Corrupted. If I change my appearance I can't change it back, anymore."

"Oh. *Oh.*"

He smiled ruefully. "Yeah, *oh.* That was pretty much my reaction when I realised I'd never get my real face back. I barely remember what I used to look like, though, and it was never fixed, so . . . yeah."

"I'm so sorry," she said. "I'm so sorry that happened to you."

Xavior shrugged and looked at his hands. "Look," he said, steering the conversation back around to Asha's problems, "why don't we just—" he offered his hands to her, palm up "—see what's going on, together." He shrugged. "Maybe there's a message in it. Maybe if you engage with the visions willingly, they'll make sense, or be different."

A message, she thought. *Come on, Asha. Be brave.*

She looked at his palms, pale green, and crossed with lines. Each with four fingers and a thumb. She sighed.

"Alright," she said grimly, "here goes nothing," and she took his hands in hers.

Smoke on the air, sun glaring off water—

The body that had housed her was thousands of years and hundreds of thousands of lightyears away, but her essence, her very core, was touching down in a field of billowing reeds and wildflowers.

"Asha," said a voice, faint and indistinct.

As though through a semi-opaque mist, she felt Xavior's hand shift in hers, to let go. She gripped his wrist, trapping his skin against hers. She had to see this, she had to *understand*—

She felt an arm under her knees, and a soft pillow beneath her head as she was laid down.

I trust him, she thought.

The voice said her name again, but this time it was different. This time is sounded like—

Adesola . . .

Whispered on the wind.

A jagged skyline reared up before her, voluminous clouds filling the vast expanse of blue with downy pink. She stood at the top of a tree-filled ravine. In front of her, twin rivers ran side by side, glittering gold in the midday sun but never touching. Her palace stood proudly on the hill, turrets piercing the clouds, its drawbridge flung open. She felt as though she knew all of it intimately: every leaf and rock and jewelled droplet of water.

Except—no.

That palace wasn't *hers*. She lived in a sterile cube. Her name was . . . her name was . . .

"Your name is Asha Akindele; your name is Adesola Hero," came a voice again, deep and commanding. She spun around, trying to source it, and came face to face with a dark-skinned, strikingly muscular woman whose hair curled out from her head like a desert cat's mane, shining and glorious, buffeted by the breeze.

A shield made of crystal and edged in gold was strapped to her arm. It was shaped like two diamonds over-lapping, and Asha had never seen it before in this lifetime, but she remembered it.

"Blood of my blood," the woman said, "heart of my heart. I am so proud of you." Her voice rumbled, like thunder lived in her throat. She reached out a hand and brushed her palm over Asha's cheek. Then she said, "You have come so far, since I first awakened in you. Since the prophecy called out to me and my warriors-in-arms and told us: *I have come. Pick up your weapons. It is starting again.*"

Asha couldn't tear her eyes away from this woman—her rippling muscles, the painful, beautiful radiance of her face. And the shield, jagged and golden-edged, splitting the sunshine into its component parts and scattering them on the ground—red, orange, yellow, green, blue.

"I know you," Asha said.

The woman nodded, smiling gently. "You were me." Reaching out, she enveloped one of Asha's hands in hers, scarred fingers pulling Asha forward. "Come. I will show you."

Asha blinked, uncomprehending, and suddenly she was looking out over an enormous crowd, thousands of faces turned upwards to face her, reverent and rapturous.

Adesola stood behind her. "Look," she motioned for Asha to look in the reflection of the great glass window opposite her.

She wore a gown of pale pink silk, a headdress of the same material wrapped around her curls. And her face . . . Arched eyebrows sat above large, dark eyes and a broad, elegant nose. Eyes so brown they appeared a glossy black stared back at her, lashes curled and lids tinted with a dark pigment. Her full mouth was pursed in concentration, the shape of it terribly familiar, like looking at the feature of a loved one.

"You stand in the body of your ancestor," Adesola said. "The last queen of the planet Chasca. Her name is Tiwa Akoni, and today she ascends the throne, and receives her royal power."

I look like my mother, she thought. *And me. I still look a little like me.*

Asha's left arm felt heavy. She looked down. The glittering shield rested above one hand. She held a gleaming sword in the other. An old man stood in front of her, a glowing crystal set into his forehead, the gem shining brighter as he chanted on and on in a language Asha had never heard before.

Asha answered in the same language, nodding her head, and vowing, vowing, *vowing*.

She looked out over the sea of Chascans as the final object of the holy trifecta was placed on her head.

Sword.

Shield.

Crown.

A column of light consumed her, blasting through the oculus set into the roof and channelling down hundreds of glass funnels lined with mirrors to light the flame that would burn until her reign ended. The flame blazed magnificently at the opposite end of the cavernous hall, smokeless and pure, writhing and *alive*. A feeling blossomed within her—one that sent roots of power through her feet, racing down into the core of the planet, speaking with it, learning it.

"The planet grants you its highest gift," the priest intoned. "Every ruling generation, this gift is bestowed upon one of your line. The power to mould the earth, to call on the ground beneath your feet, to shape the stuff of this world in a way beyond even our wildest imaginings. It is a gift and a curse. You will be the first of our planet's defence at the advent of the prophecy. But if you die, the gift dies with you."

"Do you feel it?" Adesola's voice whispered in her ear. "With a wave of your hands you could send an earthquake through this city, flatten it, then build a new one from the ruins, all in a single day. One of your children will have this power, and one of hers . . . and so on, until the end of the Chascan line."

A dish of soil was laid in front of her. She looked at it. Without even having to move, she could feel it—each of the atoms that held it together, and the energy that hummed in the space between. She raised a hand; the soil drifted skywards. Asha smiled.

Thunderous applause rained down upon her, and the trifecta of objects warmed against her skin, as she started to realise that this vision, this shared recollection she was being permitted to inhabit, was not a dream, or a hallucination. It was the answer to a question she had not yet asked.

Who am I?

Her mother's words, spoken what felt like a lifetime ago, resurfaced in her mind: *Find your sister. Find out where we came from. That's the key.*

She stepped off the dais, and the world spun with her as its axis.

Asha fell into a bed. Opposite her, a man removed his crown, before lying next to her, holding her face. Tiwa's face.

"The uprisings have spread. The North is overrun with rebels and the South has closed the bridges, sealing themselves off. We are doing everything we can but every day a thousand more troops defect. I fear the sun is setting on our line. The monarchy may very well end with us, my dear," her husband whispered. "Everything we have worked for will be lost if we do not act soon."

"Perhaps that is life," Tiwa whispered back. "Perhaps we are merely the ones chosen to usher in a new age. Heroes of a sort, ourselves, just like the Three of old. The kind who make way for the everyman to become ruler of himself."

Her husband shook his head, exhaustion clear in every line of his face. "I wish it were only that. But there has been news, from one of the outer provinces."

Tiwa sat up, her nightgown rustling against the sheets as she turned to face her husband. "News?'

He nodded. "A boy arrived at the palace yesterday. A tiny thing, not yet eighteen. Ran through the conflict, through towns burned to the ground by insurgents, and fell at the feet of the palace guards, his only possessions the clothes he wore on his back." Her husband sighed, and somehow, Tiwa knew what was coming. "He begged an audience with me."

"On what grounds?"

"On the grounds that he had seen the face of Blessed Adesola in his dreams, walked in her body, wielded her weapon."

'But there are hundreds who claim the same, year in, year out—"

"He knew the prophecy."

Tiwa's blood ran cold.

"Recited it, word for word. Exactly how it was written, carved into stone, a thousand years ago. It's the calling. He has been called."

As King and Queen of Chasca, they were the only ones alive who knew the prophecy in full. Tiwa settled back into the pillows. A dread feeling was descending over her, Asha could feel it in the quickening of her heart, the cold sweat beading on her forehead. But there was another feeling as well. An acknowledgement of inevitability, a seeking of inner strength. *I will be tested. I must rise to the task.* She was struck by a deep, deep sympathy for the boy. So young. Too young. Perhaps it meant the prophecy would not come to fruition for many more years yet—it was simply contracting around the new age it would usher into their world, preparing for its labour.

She looked up at the mural on their ceiling. The fated lovers, Adesola and Dandeyi, embracing, strong arms intertwined, a mosaic river of golden light swirling all around them, their long, blue-black hair melting into the night sky above them. The legends foretold that they would love each other in every life. *Beauty and tragedy once again go hand in hand,* she thought. *The circles of history wind ever tighter. One day they will close. But today is not that day.*

She closed her eyes, and the darkness of the royal bedroom was swallowed by the light of a tense cabinet room full of people. The king was seated in front of them, making a speech. "Hard times are ahead. Desperate times are ahead. It is for this reason that we must be united against all calamity, that we must stand strong against all which would make us weak, and stay vigilant: if the Heroes are awakening, so is the prophecy. Remember the old lore. We walk through the hallowed halls of history now, and it shakes one's courage to think of it—of all that is foretold we must endure. But we are prepared. We have always been prepared."

Behind him sat three youths. Two young men and a woman. The boys were both dark-haired, one brown-skinned with short, curly hair, the other mid-toned with hair as dark as a raven's wing that fell to his shoulders. The girl was also brown-skinned, with strawberry-blonde hair cropped close to her head.

Tiwa's heart sank for them, even as she rejoiced for her planet. The Second Prophecy foretold its destruction. But in those three young Heroes, she saw the chance for their salvation.

The world around Asha blurred—time passing—and then it was a decade later, and Tiwa was kneeling in the prayer room that housed the holy trifecta of objects.

The planet beneath her feet cried out in pain—it was dying. The war had ravaged its surface, each line of the Second Prophecy coming to pass like a blow from the executioner's axe. And it would have been alright, if only it weren't for the Hero that had abandoned them all. The paler boy with the dark hair. Choosing pride over service, choosing himself over the heroism that came in serving one's people. He was the sword-hero. Sensit's counterpart. Tiwa had always thought there to be something strange behind his eyes. A cold intelligence.

But it didn't matter now. They'd lost.

She'd come here, to this sacred place, to do the only thing she could to secure a semblance of a future for her people—the ones she herself had sworn to serve, but had failed to.

Her stomach was huge beneath her dress—swollen with the life of her child. A child whose father was dead and whose planet was doomed. The child for whom she would claw from the universe a better future.

Before her was the altar that held the crown, sword, and shield, with its engravings of the three doorways, and the scenes from the founding myth of their planet.

In her hands, she held the words of the Third Prophecy, ripped from a book, stolen from a library that was rubble now.

She began to read.

By the end of the first line, the sword in front of her was ablaze with light. Her heart froze in her chest. She kept reading. Then the shield was shining, and finally, the crown.

She would send them out into the galaxy, three beacons for three Heroes.

One last chance to save the hundred worlds, if they were up to the task.

The words on the paper were burnished gold in the crimson spill of the setting sun.

In the reddening light,
A queen surrenders her fight,
Three weapons are sent to the skies,
To be found when the time becomes right.
To begin, the tyrant's weapon must die;
The task ahead needs three knights.

Trial the first sees spires of ice,
An allegiance is forged in desperate times.
The second a mountain, an unpayable price,
Where wills shall be tested—a battle fought thrice.
Trial the third, is trial the last,
And will reveal all the secrets hid by the past.

Two warring futures, like blades clashing, sing,
The old Hero must choose, or lose everything.

248

A guide taken home. A godling. A ring.
The Kingdom-less crowns himself, unworthy king.

And in the end, when the dust has turned golden,
Conqueror meets conquered, and the last piece is stolen.
A knight rises up, but falls and is broken.
To doom, or to glory?
The choice is the chosen's.

She called upon the power that resided within the trifecta and stepped into the resulting column of blazing light. The release of energy flattened much of the surrounding countryside and simultaneously set a prophecy in motion.

Asha felt the energy channelling itself through Tiwa's body, using her as a conduit for destruction on a scale that her mind could barely comprehend.

An entire planet destroyed. The trifecta vanished. Sword, shield, and crown flung out of the atmosphere and into the nothingness of space to begin the arduous task of waiting. Waiting to be found, or destroyed or forgotten, perhaps.

The column of light disappeared. Tiwa fell to the floor, unconscious, pulling Asha into the darkness. Just before it became absolute, Asha felt the scene change again.

When the light returned, Asha was giving birth.

Agony. Anguish. Determination. These were the things she felt, as though all of her being had been distilled into those three qualities and then reduced over time until only the pain was left.

"*Get it out of me,*" Tiwa screamed, and Asha threw her head back and *pushed.*

When she regained consciousness, the palace was burning, and a child, wet with blood and fluid, lay at her feet. Flames licked along the bases of the marble columns that ringed the room, melting rare jewels from their fastenings and scorching marble with their searing heat.

Tiwa forced herself to stand, cradling her child in her arms, whispering professions of love for the daughter who wouldn't even remember her face.

Asha staggered into the cavernous atrium, supporting the child's head with her arms and trying to ignore the way it felt like she had been torn in half.

She muttered a word, and then reached out a hand. A ship built itself out of the earth and its minerals, taking its fuel from the planet, and its design from an insect. An inner chamber that would preserve a single life long enough to see. Tiwa opened the hatch. The inside had been specially crafted for this purpose—to secure her legacy, and the legacy of her people.

"Let her sleep in peace," she prayed. "Let her sleep until there comes a time when she may wake and be safe."

Then, using the last of her strength, she lifted the child into the ship and closed the hatch.

The ship took off into the night, and like a captain that goes down with her ship, she did not seek escape. She knew her place was with her people, even if that place was the afterlife.

The last thing Asha saw before the roof of the palace collapsed were three comets trailing fire, blazing bright as diamonds against the night's black sky.

I have seen them. The Heroes. In a dream, sent to me by fate. I looked upon their young faces, and I felt such sorrow, but also such hope. I was so jubilant in my discovery that I told it to the young girl who cleans my study—I grabbed her and shook her for joy! She did not understand, and ran off, as they all do. Nobody umderstands, so I

will record it here, where someone else might find some value in it.

In my dream, I watched three Heroes step from a column of white fire, pale fire, into a strange room. A room like one found on space-faring craft, I think. But one unlike any I have ever seen. Too modern. I think they will not be born for many years, that it was a craft from the future . . . I wonder . . . I wonder if the Third Prophecy will happen all at once; if it will be cataclysmic. Perhaps not. Perhaps its slow machinations already grind under the feet of our great universe, and we are already nearing the tyranny that our chosen three must lose so much to overcome. Yes, lose. One cannot read a prophecy such as this and not read loss in every word of its sorrowful scripture.

I wish our Heroes all the best, and can only hope that when the time comes, I may pass on my knowledge in the most effective way possible: face to face. Yes—until the prophecy makes itself known, I have realised, I cannot die.

Transcript of a late-night voice recording of I. Nisomn, found in his study after his unannounced departure from the Guild.

Chapter Twenty-Two

[planet: Earth] + [location: London] + [year: 1812]

"If I may offer my opinion, we should—"

"—the soldiers are tiring, Your Highness. They're hungry, lethargic—"

"—Bonaparte is relentless in his attacks. He forces his men to march forward at high speeds, covering vast swathes of land in mere months in an attempt to catch us unawares—"

"—the situation is dire, but there is hope. There are talks of a Seventh Coalition—"

George couldn't take it anymore.

"All of you leave," he said. "At once. *Get out.*"

Silence was his only response.

George stood, straight-backed and rigid until the last man had left the room. Then he collapsed onto a chair and sunk down until his back lay on the seat and his legs were sprawled out under the table.

He swore a filthy sailor's curse before groaning loudly and sliding fully onto the floor.

"I cannot do this anymore," he grumbled to the empty room. "I refuse. On—on the grounds that is *bad* for my *constitution.*"

He sighed. He could make dramatic excuses until the bloody cows came home, he knew this—did it all the time actually, to cover up (brattiness is easier to accept in a prince than weakness, and oh, *God* was everything he did these days calculated? Had everything he had ever done, possibly, been added up just like arithmetic?). But it wouldn't change the fact that the crux of the matter was his exhaustion. He had not known it was possible to be this tired. His courtiers and generals thought him insufferably lazy and indolent, but the reason behind his crippling lethargy— the reason he kept entirely to himself—was the double life he was forced to live. By day, he was the Regent's heir, engaged to a German princess who deserved so much more than he was able—or willing—to give. By night he hunted a creature through the streets of London with a time-traveller of extraordinary ability by his side. He hid bruises under high collars and slid scraped palms into silk gloves every morning whilst trying to imagine what his father would say if he attempted to explain it all away: "Sorry I fell asleep at the council meeting earlier, it's only that I retired at four in the morning after spending an entire evening lying on top of a brothel in an attempt to pin down the location of the creature who has stolen Obi's soul, but despite spending every night trying to find him I haven't even laid eyes on him yet." He would smile then, and say, "No father! I have never touched hallucinogenic drugs in my life."

And, despite what he would tell his father, were he asked, he downed laudanum by the bottle in an attempt to stay sane, to repress the memories and the night terrors and the shaking, and felt the drug sinking its claws into him a little more with every single dose.

"You alright down there?"

George started, sitting up so quickly that he smashed the bridge of his nose onto the rim of the table.

"*Argh*," he groaned, pressing the back of his hand gingerly to split skin. "What in god's good name do you want?"

Alarick ducked his head, looking semi-apologetic.

"Sorry about that, didn't mean to startle you—"

"Well, you did. How did you even get in here?"

"None of your business. Anyway, I've got news."

"Oh?" George dragged himself out from under the table and sat down heavily on the chair. "It had better be good. I am not in the mood for . . . shenanigans."

"Heh," Alarick said. "*Shenanigans.*"

"Oh, just spit it out will you."

"I know why he's raising people from the dead," Alarick said, and smiled. "I know why he targets the children and babies, the mass-deaths caused by accidents. Why he shows himself to his targets instead of stealing at night, taking what he needs, and leaving. It's because he's not taking anything. Not yet. He's playing a long game, genuinely helping people . . . in order to help himself. He's a hero, doing what heroes do best: creating a myth. Gathering secrecy and spinning magic around himself like a web. A web of power in which he will trap us all. In which he will wrap the city, until every last one of us is caught." He shrugged. "I hope that doesn't qualify as shenanigans, Your Highness."

George looked at him. Then he reached into his pocket and withdrew his emergency dose of laudanum before tipping it back and drinking it in one swallow. Much better.

"I think the creature is trying to become . . . something like what you might call a god.' Alarick repeated, his voice was quiet, but firm. *He only said 'I think' for my benefit,* George realised. He cast around for a response and came up with nothing. Alarick forged ahead. "In my experience, the power of a god, or of a thing masquerading as such, comes largely from belief. If no one believes in their existence . . . *do* they exist? How can they? The people in your city, the ones crushed under the foot of your desperate strivings towards progress, the needy, the dying—that is where he will get his power. Where he has already started to get it."

George groped around for the right words, the one to show he understood, and had a plan, and that he would fix this, somehow, if it was the last thing he did. But Alarick's gruff voice spoke again, chilling George to the bone.

"I can sense him. On the periphery of my power." He paused for a moment trying to find the right words. "Time moves around him differently. He—" A pause. "He moves through time differently. Not in a line, or down a road. But . . . in circles. Circles that keep going and going into the future, and far, far back into the past."

"How?" George asked, though he scarcely understood what he was asking. "Why?"

Alarick's voice was quiet. "I believe he has lived before. In a world with different rules, perhaps, than this one. The world where he was a hero. The world that bred this contempt in him." Not for the first time, George saw an unidentifiable emotion cross Alarick's face. Worry, or anger, or both. "And I believe that he and my son are connected, somehow." George felt his heart stop. Alarick shook his head, lost in thought. "I don't understand it. Unless the prophecy—No. Not him. Not yet." He looked back at George, his jaw set. "We need to find out what his intentions are with Obi's soul. The longer this creature has it, the worse the risk—" He cut himself off. "We must find him. Put an end to this sick game he's playing, laughing at us from the shadows while we chase rumours around our own damned city." He paused, frowning, before looking up sharply. "Unless. What if . . . what if we've been looking at this the wrong way?"

"The wrong way?" George managed to say, though his mind was still stuck on what Alarick had said. *I believe that he and my son are connected, somehow.*

Alarick nodded. "He's already proven that he is too powerful to be caught, or even observed when he doesn't want to be. But he likes a game. To taunt and play with people. Bend the rules of life and death like we're all just his pieces on a board." George remembered the young boy, seawater mixing with the blood running down his face. He thought of Obi's stolen soul, locked in its box. *A very maudlin game, with very fragile pieces.* His chest felt tight. He wondered what Obi would have done in the face of this. There was a pounding in his head.

"What are you saying?"

"We've been entertaining him for too long. Running around like scared children, desperate and not making any effort to hide it. Likely fuelling his power through our own dogged belief in his existence. So, for a week, we will do nothing."

George opened his mouth to protest, but Alarick silenced him with a look.

"We don't speak his name, we don't think of his face. We don't speak to each other about him—in fact you will not contact me at all. To all intents and purposes, we forget he exists. By week's end he will show himself, I'm sure of it. If what he says is true, and he was a hero once, then he won't take well to being ignored. He will find us. He won't be able to resist."

The walls of the ballroom were spinning. The orchestra had struck up a lively tune that had all the eligible bachelors of London's aristocracy grabbing girls in frothy dresses by their waists and spinning them in giddy circles.

George watched the dancers from an alcove on the mezzanine, nursing a flute of champagne and the beginnings of a headache. He should really be down there enjoying himself. This was his party, after all. He just . . . He couldn't help but think that the next time he set foot in a ballroom with the intent to dance the night away, to forget the outside world for a single evening . . . would be on his wedding day. The day that would include vows and kisses and the exchange of rings, and promises doomed to be broken, and that would, inevitably, give way to the night.

He sighed and took another sip of champagne. The taste was cloying, sweet, and suddenly disgusting. He put the glass down and went to fetch some water.

A pair of girls were whispering at the top of the stairs.

"—they say he has eyes as gold as guineas, and he revives people from beyond the grave—"

George withdrew sharply, pressing himself behind a nearby column and straining his ears above the din of the ballroom.

"—surely that's just common people talking?" said the blonde. George rolled his eyes. "It sounds just the right kind of scandalous to capture their attentions so completely . . ."

"No, no," the brunette interjected. "Just last week Elizabeth Miller—you know, Charles' cousin with the *masses* of red hair? Died of smallpox."

"Oh yes, I heard about that . . . such a pity, I—"

"But wait! I saw her just last week outside Sotheby's at the Exeter Exchange chatting up Henry Beaulieu—absolutely *shameless* of course, you know Liz. So *of course* I got as close as possible, and overheard her telling him that she had been saved by some kind of angel. 'The Angel,' she called him. She said he had appeared to her in a circle of light, dressed as a knight of old, and whispered right in her ear that he was saving her for when the world is made anew! I've even heard that they're putting up a little church for him at the corner of Iffley Road. Though I heard that from Samantha so it likely isn't true."

The girls laughed and linked arms, walking down the stairs and out of earshot.

George's stomach dropped. So, not only had the rumours of the creature's power made it to the upper echelons of society— crawling closer and closer to the ears of his father—the belief in this thing was garnering such attention that a *church* would soon be erected in his honour.

Alarick's words echoed awfully in his mind: *The power of a god, or of a thing masquerading as such, comes largely from belief. The people in your city . . . that is where he will get his power.*

George had watched fads spring from less—a type of waistline on a gown, a way of passing love notes—he'd even started a few himself. And in those cases, all that was needed was a single appearance by a person with influence, a mention in a society paper, and whispers would race through the gossip channels of London like a flame down the wick of a bomb. *A church?* If the rumours had made it all the way to the aristocracy . . . George felt sick to his stomach at the thought of all that power flowing towards their enemy, strengthening him. And even worse—what would happen when people figured out these so-called miracles were nothing more then re-animated corpses walking the streets of the city?

A cool, marble banister appeared under his hand—he must've stumbled and caught it. He felt bleary and unreal, spread too thin, like gauze pulled in so many directions you could see each individual strand and the gaps between them. His life was too much water and not enough wine; a second's worth of time to fill a minute's gaping silence; stitches pulled too early from a wound, near-healed but not quite. His mouth felt dry. He needed a drink.

But, as he cast his eyes around for a waiter, he caught a glimpse of the impossible.

A dark, elegant hand reaching for the slim neck of a wine bottle, a strong profile, a sharp jaw, piercingly grey eyes offset by strikingly dark skin. A vision in a black suit—white teeth, sharp grin, smiling, smiling—

The glass dropped from his hand.

"Obi," George whispered. But he had disappeared, swallowed by the crowd.

George ran, skidding down the grand staircase, barely avoiding the other partygoers, and stepping on more than a few coat-tails. He slowed as he reached the dancefloor, peering through the crowds for a sign, for anything—

There. Walking towards the balcony.

"Excuse me! If I could just—My apologies, if you don't mind—" With as much grace as he could muster, George pushed his way through a crowd that seemed alarmingly intent on sucking him back inside and finally made it to the balcony doors. He opened them an inch and slipped outside.

The wind was cold, howling at the altitude, immediately chilling him through his clothes. Music from the ballroom carried softly out into the night, only to be snatched away by the wind.

The balcony was empty. George caught the sound of violins and a melancholy piano, indicating a slow dance that he was more than happy to be absent for. He could see a couple walking towards the fountain in the gardens of the park, their chaperone following at a respectable twenty paces. He looked up at the sky and sighed. Of course Obi wasn't here. What was he? Stupid?

No, his conscience supplied, *just inebriated.* God, he wanted to—

"Hello," said a voice.

George turned to his left, startled, hopeful.

He froze.

A young man who looked to be around his age, but who

George knew for a fact was not, was leaning against the marble balustrade of the building. His auburn hair was loose, falling in waves to his chin, silky strands of it lifted by the breeze to brush his chin and mouth. His suit was black, as was his shirt and tie. The brown of his skin had a lifeless undertone, grey slightly, like meat left too long out of the cold. Gusts of frigid air rolled off him like fog, dropping the temperature on the balcony, freezing the water in the atmosphere, making it cold and dry and near-impossible to breath. The back of George's neck prickled. He clamped his jaw shut to stop his teeth chattering.

"You," he said, voice hoarse and heart pounding. *Alarick was right, he's found us.* "What do you want?"

The man standing in front of him—the creature haunting his city, the monster stalking his citizens, the god-thing that had stolen Obi's soul *right out of his hands*—turned his head to the side, smiling slowly. *Like a snake,* George thought. *A snake in a man's skin.*

"I have come to find common ground with you, Your Highness," he said, dipping his head in a mocking bow. "To talk, if you are willing?"

George's heartbeat tripled in speed inside the space of a second, which he had not thought possible as it was already close to beating its way out of his chest. "I'm nothing like you, demon," he said. "The only common ground between us is the thing you took from me."

His adversary nodded thoughtfully. "I'm not so sure. I wonder if we have more in common than you think." He stretched a hand out over the marble of the balcony's edge and looked out across the gardens, into the night. "Princes and Heroes, both of us born only so that one day we might die and, in doing so, herald something new. The next generation of lambs for the slaughter. The newest crop of youths, put up on pedestals so high that their falling is inevitable."

George narrowed his eyes. "Is that what you think you are? A hero? You're a thief. And a necromancer. A demon."

"A demon! Now that is one I have not heard before. Though I suppose if this is the life I have now chosen for myself, I ought to get used to it." Gold eyes met his. "And though heroism does not preclude thievery, I am no thief. The soul is yours to take back at whichever time you so desire." He smiled. "For a price."

"No price. That box belongs to someone who I—someone I care greatly for—"

"The one you see in your dreams, the one you call out for in the dark of night. The one you think of when you look at the stars." The demon's voice was quiet. "The traveller, wreathed in golden light. The one the mirrors show me. The one who speaks to me, though he does not know it."

George's frown deepened. "I don't—"

"Don't deny it," that startling gaze was back, locked onto George like a target. "I can feel it. I can feel everything about you when I'm holding this. You and this soul. You're connected. Destined."

And suddenly the box was right there. Hovering in his palm, the lid ajar, blinding light spilling through the gap.

Later, George would not be able to say what came over him.

He simply saw the box, and lunged.

The demon laughed, and side-stepped, inhumanly fast, blurring as he did so, and appearing on the other side of the balcony. George's outstretched hand closed around nothing. He wheeled around just in time to see the box disappear once again.

"I won't play your games," he said, breathing hard. "I won't be baited by you."

The demon's smile grew wider. "Bit late for that, no?"

"What do you want from us?" George asked, almost yelling. "The people that you're bringing back from beyond the grave . . . why? What purpose does it serve?"

He flicked his fingers in dismissal. "What purpose? Mine. I need worship to bolster my power, and I'm very good at garnering it from the dead."

So Alarick had been right.

"But they're no longer dead."

"Not now, but they were. Then I stood over their graves and whispered my name and told them to build me monuments and temples and to pray to me in those temples and, after they clawed their way out of ditches or through six feet of dirt, they did."

"They call you the Angel."

Sensit nodded.

"We already have a god in this country."

"Your god is ancient. He sleeps, lying blind, preferring not to bear witness to the perversities committed in his name. Besides, how do you know he did not send me to test you?"

George was silent.

Sensit waved a hand. "This is immaterial. By the summer solstice the city will be mine. And I will have the rest of this soul, whether it is given willingly, or not."

"No one in this city will ever give you anything willingly."

"A shame . . ." The demon paused. "As I might need someone to keep me company. Someone to rule by my side." His golden eyes were bright, his voice was low and smooth as velvet. "Would you like that?"

George momentarily forgot how to breathe.

"Are you propositioning me?" he asked, disbelieving and completely bewildered. "I already told you, no. Why on earth—"

"Because I do. Because I want you." His eyes, like ichor spilled over purest marble, looked suddenly obscene. "Because I feel as though I know you. As though a part of me already did, before we met. The man in that dream. The one you love. I think it is him—I think I am him. I feel what he feels, but I can't—"

"*Don't talk about him.*" George's voice was quiet, but rising. Discussing all the things he cared the most about with a creature sent from hell. From another world. "Don't say his name." He couldn't stand this. But he needed to find out as much information from this creature as he could, and then, so help him, he would kill it. "Why this city? What do you *want?*"

"I know what you're really asking." The demon leaned forward, spreading his hands in understanding. Like they were co-conspirators. "*Why you?* Correct? *Why now?*" He nodded again, the picture of pleasantness, and George wanted to wrap his hands around the man's throat and tear him apart. "It's always the same story with people like you. A Hero knows that questions such as those are not even worth the breath it took to ask them. It doesn't matter why you, or why now, or why here—only that it *is* you, right here, right now." He smiled faintly. "So, you put your head down, keep your guard up, and give it everything you've got. Even your life, if that's what it takes. Or your sanity."

George's voice was firm. "You cannot come here, with your nonsensical ramblings, talking and talking in an attempt to confuse me. I will not be swayed. That soul was left in my care, and I will get it back." A jolt of adrenaline ran through him. This man might have been a monster, but monsters could be slain. He wrapped his fingers around his ceremonial sword, where it had lain, sheathed and forgotten at his waist, and drew it. Moonlight sparked off the blade, a long slash of silver shining in the air between them. "Now are you willing to bargain, or shall I run you through and be done with it?"

"So, there is something to you, after all," the demon said. "This could be fun." Then he closed the gap between them, seeming to glide past the outstretched length of George's blade, before lifting two perfect, marble-white fingers and pressing them to George's mouth.

Cold.

Impossible cold. Fractals of ice burying their way under his skin, leaching the warmth from his bones, consuming it. The clatter of his sword hitting the floor was like shattering glass. He jerked, gasping, and one of the god's fingers slipped inside his mouth. George ripped himself away, shivering, jaw aching, throwing himself across the balcony to safety on the other side.

Or rather, he tried to do that. Tried with all his might to move, to lift even a single finger, to yell, or scream, to somehow exercise his ability to control his own body. But he couldn't. *He's cast a spell on me,* George thought, panicking. *He's going to eat me alive.*

"Much better," the demon whispered. "I think I like you better like this. Helpless. It's humbling." He arched an eyebrow and grinned slowly—a predator watching his prey struggle against the canines already piercing its velveteen throat. "Where I'm from," he said, voice low in his throat, "the princes used to pour libations of scarlet wine and golden honey in my name, and kiss the stone faces of my statues with open mouths when they thought no one was looking. And an attempt on my life was met with a death sentence." He removed his finger from George's mouth, sliding it against his teeth, his lower lip.

He had a predator's grace, George thought distantly. Long athletic limbs and wild eyes. An arctic wolf. A snow leopard.

"How terribly illicit," George replied, deadpan, finding suddenly that he could speak.

"Ah, I got distracted. No, no, no. No more talking from you.

264

It's my turn. You will answer when spoken to." The demon began to walk around him, as though viewing him from all angles, like a battle prize, or a piece of meat.

"I need something from you. Something I'm willing to trade for this box, and its contents. The old man didn't know, and was foolish enough to try and hurt me when I offered him a fair deal." George thought of the haunted look on Alarick's face when he had asked about the encounter, about the jagged, ugly scar, right over his heart. "I don't think you will be so foolish," the demon said. "Now, tell me, where is the other half of this soul?"

The same thing he asked Alarick. George shook his head. "Nobody knows. He could be anywhere on the globe. He could be in a time that hasn't yet passed."

"You both lie. *I can feel it.* Yes, there is a fragment of the soul in the future, but there is another here, in this city. And every time I track it down, it leads me here, to this palace." The god snarled. "He must have hidden it with you—"

CRACK.

A gunshot fired from somewhere to George's left, and a chunk of the balcony blasted to pieces, marble scattering across the floors, a sliver of it slicing into George's cheek.

The bright pain awoke him. He became aware suddenly, as though rising from a waking dream, that he could move. Shoving the demon away, he scrambled to the other side of the balcony.

"George!" roared a voice from a few metres away.

George and the demon both turned, and there was Alarick, standing on the next balcony over, coat billowing in the wind, smoke rising from the barrel of his gun.

"Get the box!"

George threw himself at the demon. They crashed into each other, hot muscle meeting flesh as cold as stone, and somehow, he heard the clash of armour, invisible but there, and then he was being pushed with the strength of a hundred men—away, away, away. He crashed into the balcony's edge, and heard it crack, distantly. His head swam, he could barely open his eyes.

Another gunshot. Another. More marble scattering across the floor, into the night. Alarick swearing.

Then, a blurring shape walking towards him. Upwards, a silhouette against the yellow light spilling from the French doors that led back to the ballroom.

The demon walked towards him—there were two, three, four of him as George's vision shifted in and out of focus. Then a foot, crunching down on his hand, breaking it. A crack racing through the marble under his palm, connecting with the crack dug out of the floor by a stray bullet. George felt the corner of the balcony that he lay on jolt, and then dislodge from the rest. Stone crumbled and fell, crashing to the ground fifteen feet below. George fell, his ribs smacking into the rough stone edge of the broken balcony. And then he stopped falling and stunning pain lanced through his arm, his shoulder socket screaming, and his hand cracking further, as the demon ground his foot into it.

George hung from the side of the balcony, suspended only by his hand, crushed to a pulp, and his broken wrist, held in place under a heeled boot.

"You think you have won this time, but you are wrong," came a voice like splintered glass. "I have seen the future, I know what comes to pass. Enjoy your life while you are still able to live it, princeling. I will be back for you, and next time, you won't survive. *My name is Sensit.* Do not forget it."

Then the boot was gone, and so was the ancient warrior, and George's broken hand was sliding down the rough edge of the jagged stone, as he fell almost in slow motion, a thick red trail of blood smearing in its wake.

When he hit the ground, he did not feel it.

Warm covers lay over his body—a suffocating deadweight. Every single limb ached dully, his head throbbing. He groaned, and even that felt like fire scorching down his throat.

"Water," he whispered. "Please."

There was a rustle of skirts, the trickle of liquid, and then a cool glass of water was pressed into his outstretched hand. He could barely grasp it, but there were hands slipping under his back, pushing him gently into a sitting position, and then bringing the glass to his mouth. With immense effort he lifted his eyelids and blearily took in the scene before him.

He was in his bedroom, which he recognised immediately. The light outside was low, early evening perhaps, candles burning dimly in all the corners of the room.

Then, he remembered. Gunshots. Alarick. And the warrior, *Sensit*, demanding George give himself another fragment of Obi's soul. A fragment that didn't exist.

"Darling?" said a voice. "How do you feel?"

George froze.

Floral perfume, soft lilting 'r's, smooth hands, round nails, the muted shine of a tiara.

"Mother?"

Queen Caroline blinked slowly. "Yes, my dear?"

George stared at her in disbelief. He hadn't spoken to his mother in months. Part of it was guilt and a kind of awkwardness—after his father's affair, his mother had been accused of taking lovers and having illegitimate children. To this day, George had never brought it up, never wanted to know if it was true. He had denied all rumours on her behalf, and pretended not to have read the articles calling into question the circumstances surrounding his birth, and claim to the throne. George also knew he reminded his mother of his father, and hated that they looked alike. The last time they had spoken she had talked about moving to Italy. It did not make sense to him, her being here.

"Is everything quite alright, George?" she asked.

"Yes, mother, I'm fine."

She frowned, worried. "Well, I am not too sure about that!" Her hand came up to brush the bandages over his head, and his eyes throbbed. "You fell three storeys, my love. The court physician says God Himself must have had a hand healing your broken bones, but that you may have scarring where something hit your head." George grimaced. "He says it is a miracle you survived, and that it is because God loves this family, and that you have served Him so well, that you are here and not in Heaven." She hugged him, and he was forced to clench his jaw in an attempt not to wince or cry out. The pain in his arms was enough to take his breath away, and for a brief second, he was falling again, chunks of marble battering him, *burying him*—

It had all become so real so quickly. The dead boy, talking to them, seawater in his hair. Mangled, bloodless legs, dragging behind him. Then the party . . . the false joy of seeing Obi the crowd, only to realise it was *him*—

"Have you seen any of your cousins lately, George?" his mother's voice jolted him back to reality. "They miss you, you know."

He didn't have time to think about his cousins! He wanted to sit up and shake his mother, tell her there was a creature of unfathomable power resurrecting dead bodies all over the city. But it hurt to breathe, let alone sit up, and she would only have worried for him, and called the doctor. So instead he said, "No mother. But when I am better I shall write to them."

They fell silent, the soft patter of rain outside the windows echoing dimly inside the large room. Glass bottles full of syrupy cordials the physician had prescribed to treat him glowed in the low light, the colour of blackberries or purple wine. George looked at his mother. The candlelight softened her edges, the narcotics blurring her face into its base components. Kind brown eyes, so much more vacant than they had been before. Full lips downturned. Frown lines, and greying hair, and the circlet of gold on her brow.

A queen and a mother and a woman and a sacrifice, of sorts, he thought.

She gave her life to this family.

He had never spoken to his mother about his father's affairs, and certainly not about her own. He doubted he ever would. It wasn't because he did not care. Far from it. It was because he did not know how.

"I think I shall sleep now, Mother. You do not—If you have other duties you must attend to, do not allow me to keep you here."

His mother cooed at him, brushing her ring-laden fingers through his hair.

"I will stay until you are well, and until Princess Gisela arrives. The physician has assured me you will be upright and walking by the date we set." She smiled at him. "Not long now, my love. Not long now."

George's heart clenched.

"Mother, what—what is today's date?"

"It is the sixth day of April, darling."

"The sixth . . . the sixth! But the wedding is—"

"On the eighth, dearest, yes. I'm afraid there is no way to postpone it. I had hoped, due to your condition, but it would seem . . ." She trailed off. "Your grandfather was most keen for you to be wed as soon as possible." She spread her hands in apology. "There is nothing to be done."

George stared at her, willing with all his might that the horror he felt internally would not show in his expression.

"I see," he forced out. "I see."

His mother looked sad. "My little prince," she said. "All grown up."

George smiled tightly at her as he twisted the lid off the bottle of laudanum he had spied on his dressing table and tipped it down his throat. He had fallen from a balcony, and lost a fight with a demon who had stolen Obi's soul, and was resurrecting the dead for his own personal army of worshippers. Was it awful that all of this paled in comparison to the threat of being wed?

Even as he wondered this, the laudanum was coursing through his blood, relaxing his muscles as the familiar euphoria swept over him. Elation and a quiet, consuming rapture flooding his senses. He sighed, sinking further into the pillows. This was better. Much better. He hadn't realised quite how sad he'd felt before.

Sleep reached out its arms for him, and he welcomed the embrace, falling into unconsciousness with a blank smile on his face and a muffled struggle in his heart.

Two days later, he was standing shakily at the altar, the notion of sobriety but a distant memory, staring dazedly into the wide, watery eyes of his wife-to-be.

Obi, I'm sorry. I have no other choice.

Besides, he wouldn't remember it in the morning.

Chapter Twenty-Three

[planet: none] + [location: Space Port Xesca] + [year: 6066]

They reached Port Xesca during the night of the fourteenth day, so when Obi woke, the view out of his window was of a bustling port and a dusky red sunrise rather than the endless black of space.

He and Asha had packed the night before, so they chatted as they dressed. She seemed less involved with their conversations than usual, like she wasn't listening, or her mind was pre-occupied with something else. He'd seen less and less of her as the journey had continued and she'd begun spending more time with Xavior. At first he'd felt jealous—*my friend, not yours*—but he'd soon reprimanded himself. *How old are you, twelve?* Besides, anyone with an ounce of common sense could see that *something* was going on. And he'd never seen her look so . . . well, happy was the wrong word, she barely ever looked happy. It was a kind of charged excitement. It lit up the tension between the two of them and echoed in the whispers that passed between their bent heads in the corridor. Even the significant and mystifying eye contact they would make at the dinner table made Obi wonder what kind of mystery they were solving together in their minds. Though he supposed that falling for someone was like that: an adventure for just the two of you. New paths and new dangers, and a strange new companion who you caught yourself feeling like you'd known for years.

The disembarking alarm sounded, jolting them out of their comfortable silence.

"Shall we?" Obi said, nodding his head at the door.

"Yeah," Asha replied, but her voice sounded small.

She doesn't want to leave, he thought, his heart sinking. *The bubble of safety just popped.*

"Asha . . ." he said. But he barely knew what to say. "Asha, it—"

"Don't," she said, cutting him off, not unkindly. "It's okay. Whatever happens, it was worth it. For this." She paused looking away from him. "A room of my own—well, a room of *our* own. Food. Proper food. *Friends.*" Her head dropped further, as though she were trying to hide her expression from him. "I feel lucky. And I know it's wrong that I feel that—that I should know all of this is a—a right, something I'm entitled to by virtue of being alive. That's what Ossock says, anyway. But, Thracin, it doesn't feel like that. It's never felt like that. And I knew it couldn't last forever, but sometimes I hope it would." She wiped at her eyes.

"Come here." Obi pulled her in for a hug, squeezing her until she laughed and told him to stop. "Let's go."

Xavior was waiting for them, as was Ossock—brown paper bags spotted with grease in two of his hands.

Asha ran towards them, shoving Xavior out of the way before throwing her arms around Ossock's middle and hugging him tight.

Isi was nowhere to be seen, but Obi assumed she would show eventually. *Probably crying in her office at the thought of our departure.*

Obi hung back as Asha said her goodbyes, before bidding

his own. It was harder than he'd thought it would be, to think of leaving everyone. When the chef handed them each a bag heavy with sugar-dusted, pan-fried dumplings, he found himself strangely overcome. He would miss this crew, motley as they were.

Xavior was trying unsuccessfully to beg the last dumpling from Asha—*"Just a lick?" "Ew, no!"*—when they heard the entrance hatch open.

"Who—" Xavior started, but was cut off by a snarling voice. "Where are the units?"

Obi's skin broke out in gooseflesh so quickly it was almost painful, instinct screaming danger in his ear like an air raid siren. That word *units* conjured memories that smelled like blood and tasted like ownership and . . . *and didn't belong to him.* He looked at Asha—her head had snapped forward towards the source of the voice, and she was radiating so much fear and anger that he could feel it in the air like humidity. He had never seen her so distressed.

"*No*—" she started to say, but it was too late.

Three amphibian-looking sentients walked up the *Stayanax's* gangplank and into the bridge, guns slung low on their hips and over their shoulders, knives strapped to their arms over their rough clothing, teeth razor-sharp and glinting.

"Isi?" said Xavior slowly. "What's going on?"

She stepped out of a shadow by the door to the captain's quarters. Possibly she had been there the whole time.

"I'm sorry," she said. "When they heard we had . . . illegals on board it was either sell them out or—or give up my license." Her shoulders slumped, her eyes were pleading. "And I *can't*. Not after I fought so hard to get here."

Xavior's face drained of colour, his mouth hanging open. Obi's heart jackhammered. Beside him, Asha was shaking. Trembling with anger, but also, Obi sensed sickly, fighting the urge to throw up. Sweat prickled on his back.

"Not too bad," the tallest of the slavers was saying, eyeing up Obi and Asha like carcasses strung up at the butcher's shop. "Not too bad at all. It will be a pleasure to take 'em off your hands, Captain."

He strolled towards Asha, eyes calculating.

Isi nodded blankly. Obi wanted to *strangle* her. Beside him, Asha twitched. The slaver was inches from her and, as Obi watched, he ran one of his slimy looking fingers down her middle braid.

Asha growled, then froze, realizing exactly what it was she had done. The slaver smiled, then clapped a hand over her mouth.

"None of that," he said. "But you'll learn soon enough." He kept his hand in place, moving to stand behind her.

Obi's hands convulsed into fists. *God,* he wanted to reach for his power and pull on it, unleashing chaos like pulling the pin of a grenade. But Asha and Xavior were unarmed, with guns pointed at them, any sudden movements could cause their deaths. He had to choose his moment carefully.

"A three-piece set will fetch a hefty price," the thug on the right was saying. "That one on the left . . . Are they, erm, meant to be green?"

Xavior froze.

"*No.*" Isi's face switched from controlled blankness to violent desperation in seconds. "Not him. You can't have him. He's—he's not like them, he's one of us!" Obi saw her hand jerk towards her holsters. *Go on,* he thought. *Do it. Let's see if we can tell what 'one of us' looks like when our blood's mixing all over your precious little scrubbed clean floor.*

"Oh yeah?" said the slaver with the eyepatches. "He got his papers?"

"Well, no, but *look at him*, for Thracin's sake, can't you tell?"

The slaver shrugged. "Looks the same to me. Besides, no one'll be able to tell the difference, when it comes down to it. Might even rack up the price and see if anyone's dumb enough to bite."

The last member of their gang looked at Isi, eyes narrowed, voice low and menacing, "Say, *Captain*, where's that license you were talking about?"

Isi's eyes closed. Obi felt a vicious surge of satisfaction that could have belonged to Asha or himself.

"Isi," Xavior said, voice hollow. "It's alright."

"Damn right, it's alright," said the first slaver, his claw still covering half of Asha's mouth. "Better get going. Hopefully the skyway won't be too congested, Thracin bless us."

"*Thracin bless us*," echoed the two other slavers.

Obi heard Asha suck in a muffled breath. Then she dipped slightly beside him, as though she had almost collapsed, before righting herself. Sweat poured from her forehead as though she was concentrating very hard, or perhaps, restraining herself—*oh*. Realization struck him.

She had been about to kneel.

His stomach lurched sickeningly, and he stopped caring about consequences and outcome and the idea that they might die *right now*, stopped caring about exactly whose anger it was that he was feeling, about whose fear was sending violent shudders down his spine. Because their fear—the three of them, Obi, Asha and Xavior's—was collective in that moment, roaring in a perfect trinity.

Obi's palms *burned*. He began gathering his power to him, feeling out the ribbons of time and memory that drifted around all of them, visible for a moment if he looked hazily into the middle distance. He was getting ready to pull on them, when the slaver nearest them said, "Alright, we'll take them," pulled out his baton, and shocked Asha in the stomach. She went down. Obi was stunned, immobile—and then he was reaching, pulling power towards him like a thousand ropes, ready to lash out, to blow the ship to pieces *if that's what it took*. But he had forgotten the other slaver.

Something cracked against his spine, sizzling with electricity. Everything went black.

Obi came to lying on his back against a cold surface, his head resting against something much softer and warmer. Voices murmured above him. Asha's voice rasping and upset, Xavior's steady and low, but strained with worry.

"A'lkari?" that was Xavior's voice. "You're going to A'lkari. And Obi knows about this? He's encouraging this?"

Obi felt movement—Asha nodding. He realised his head was lying on her lap. His spine ached, the pain radiating into his ribs. His abdominal muscles were cramping from the force of the baton's shock. *How long ago had it been?* Not too long, he didn't feel stiff—he was still loose with pain and the remnants of adrenaline released during the confrontation. But still, he couldn't move—couldn't even open his eyes. Asha and Xavior must have recovered faster.

"Xav, I know—"

"No. You don't know," he said quietly. "*I* don't even know and I spent five years there. The Magekind took everything from me. They'll take it all from you, too. It's not safe." He sounded more serious than Obi had ever heard him. "You'll die. If you make a single mistake, you will die. Your chances of making it out alive are slim to none."

"But you know why we have to."

She must have told him about our plan, Obi realised. He knew they'd been getting closer, but he'd been so wrapped up in his own problems since Qala had offered him her ultimatum that he hadn't realised. He did know Asha had spent a night in his room. He had assumed it was for . . . obvious reasons—she'd gone completely silent when he asked, and mumbled something about *getting to know one another.* But maybe they really had just been talking. *She must have told him about how she escaped,* Obi thought. *About what she's doing out here, who she's looking for, but left out her destination. But she's told him now. She trusts him. Good. She'll need someone by her side when I leave to get the cure.*

"Asha," Xavior said. "We should talk about the other night, there's something I need to tell you."

"About what I saw? Xavior, I—"

"No," his voice was uncharacteristically serious. "About what *I* saw." A pause. "You told me there was a woman in your dream, a warrior who led you through a kind of story . . . a vision of the past. Well, I've had a dream, every single night since then, and I didn't think it was related . . . didn't think much of it really. Until last night."

Asha's voice was a whisper. "What was the dream about?"

"I was walking through a wasteland. Ash was falling from the sky, like there'd been a—a fire. I saw my reflection in a pool of blood, but it wasn't me. It was someone else. A warrior with long dark hair and golden eyes. And they were . . ." He shook his head, as though he was about to say something stupid. "They were wearing a crown."

"What changed?"

"Before, the dreams always ended when I heard someone say my name. But last night was different. Last night, when I heard my name, I turned around. And I saw who was calling me." He paused. "Asha it was you. Or her." He sounded confused. "For

277

someone reason . . . I couldn't tell the difference. She walked towards me, through the smoke and fog, and . . . when she didn't look like you, she looked just how you'd described. Tall, beautiful, golden-eyed. With a shield on her back, catching the light."

Xavior's words cut through the daze of Obi's pounding head and aching muscles. He had no idea what they were talking about, but something about it seemed unbearably familiar. As though he had had the same dream, but forgotten it. He moved a little, and his headache screamed at him. "Ow," he mumbled. He would ask them about it later. Now, there were more pressing matters at hand.

"Where are we?" he rasped. His throat felt raw, like all the skin had been stripped from the inside.

"Obi!" Asha said, she touched his cheek gently. "Good, you're awake, I was worried." Cradling Obi's head, she slipped her folded jacket gently underneath it. "Don't try and move," she said. "It's not worth it for the first few minutes." Obi cracked open an eye and was treated to the sight of Asha's chin, scraped, bloody, and bruised on one side from where her face must've hit the floor after being stunned. She sighed. "We're trapped. They've taken us to some kind of local jail, holding us until they can transport us to . . ." She shrugged, clearly furious. "Wherever they want."

Obi groaned. "Prison? Again? I feel like we're doing something wrong here."

Asha exhaled a tiny laugh, but her hand on his face was trembling slightly, and from the hoarseness in her voice, he could tell she'd been shouting, or sobbing. *You're looking after me,* he thought, *but who's looking after you?*

Fighting nausea, Obi hauled himself into a sitting position, dragging himself to sit next to her, his back against the cold stone wall. Tear tracks showed clearly through the dust her face had accumulated during their kidnapping, but they were blurred slightly. He could imagine her wiping them savagely away even as more fell, desperate not to look weak, but hurled so violently back into the past she thought she had left behind that she couldn't help it.

"We got a plan?"

Next to him, Asha trembled with rage. "The plan is, I'm going to find that sorry excuse for a captain," she said, "make her regret even thinking about selling us out."

"She'll get what's coming to her," Xavior said. "Those slavers will, too. If there's any justice in this universe, I swear they'll pay the price."

"No," she said quietly. "No, they *won't*." Her eyes were red-rimmed and fierce, brimming with a fury so deep and visceral that Obi almost flinched away. "Didn't anyone tell you? It's going to be us. *Us.* We'll be the victims—the ones paying the price—because when the *thing* in charge of this mess decided that some people were only worth anything bent over an assembly line—killing themselves to arm the empire, to keep the empire comfortable and warm and fed—the loser of every fight, every wrongdoing, every betrayal, every *wrong look* became decided in advance." Tension was described in every line of her body—shoulders bunched, forehead furrowed, eyebrows dark and outrage thunderous. "But of course, a loser is different to a victim, as one of those things assumes the object's suffering, and I have never *suffered*." Her voice, smothered in sarcasm, was growing louder by the minute. "No, I get to work all day, and sleep in a nice little cube, and drink my meals out of efficient little plastic bags." She looked disgusted. "And, of course, one of those things assumes the object's ability to inspire sympathy and I have never been worthy of *anything* like *that*. Sympathy? No! I'm not to be pitied. *I should be grateful.*" She was blinking hard, spitting the words onto the stone-tiled ground, expelling them. She breathed harshly into the quiet of the cell for a few moments, and when she spoke again, her voice was quieter. "To be a loser, you have to have started the fight equally. The fight had to be *fair.* But he had everything, and we had nothing, and all we wanted was a home." Her voice was nearly breaking. "To be a loser assumes parity, assumes *equality*, and I have never been equal to anything that doesn't come with a fucking price tag attached."

Obi closed his eyes. "I'm so sorry," he said into the deafening silence.

"So am I," she replied. "But I am not beaten."

He opened his eyes. Next to her, Xavior was looking at her in quiet awe, obviously feeling like an idiot about what he had said. *Good*, Obi thought, though he knew he had meant well. Asha had been pressing her eyelids with the tips of her fingers, eyes closed, mouth a grim line. Now she looked up. "I will never be beaten. Not while my mother and my sister are counting on me. I can't. I *can't.*" Her voice broke on the last word, but they both pretended not to hear it. *She needs to believe she has more left to give*, Obi thought, and suddenly saw himself in her face—felt the weight of the arm he had nearly killed himself to acquire hanging heavy at his side. *Eighteen.* It felt like decades ago.

"You'll find them, Asha," Xavior murmured. "We'll get you out of here."

Obi nodded his agreement.

"Well, as soon as we do, I'm going to find a way to make sure we never get locked up anywhere ever again. I'll build something, I'm sure I could find a way to jam the energy fields if I had the time—"

She was cut off by a sound that echoed through the cell. They all jerked their heads towards the corridor that lay beyond the impenetrable energy field. Footsteps, coming from outside. Suddenly, prison guards were rounding the corner, dragging a small, limp body between them. They pushed the body through the energy field—the person collapsed on the floor, sprawled on their face.

They let out a low grown, pulling themselves into a sitting position, short limbs flexing with muscle. In the low light, Obi could only make out a bulky cloak, and some kind of helmet, perhaps, strapped to their head like a plate. Their eyes were tiny chips of yellow, hidden behind the helmet's visor.

Obi looked at the others—they shrugged, looking wary. He turned back to the small figure sitting by the bars, gently massaging their leg.

"Hello?" he called out softly.

Their new cellmate grunted in reply, before unstrapping something on the back of their head. The mask-like visor fell away, and the bright chips of yellow light resolved themselves into two giant circular eyes, glowing softly in the dimness like an owl's. The helmet was not a helmet, Obi saw now, but a pointed ridge of bone that extended over their face and ears like a wide-brimmed hat.

"Hello," they replied, peering at the three of them. "Some riot, huh? My name's Sab. What did you get done for?"

"Um," said Xavior. 'Riot?'

Sab narrowed their eyes. "Because of the nursery." Their small cellmate was clearly suspicious they hadn't heard of it. "Off-worlders, are you?"

"Yes," Asha said. At the same time Xavior mumbled, "Not exactly."

Sab peered at them. "Oh my!" came their surprised cry. "You're human, aren't you?" Clambering to their feet, they stepped forward for a closer look. "Holding you here temporarily, are they?" Obi saw Asha nod. "How extraordinary. Poor things. You know there is a small movement to free your kind, and all others that the Emperor indentures, chaining poor people inside his impossible contracts." Obi saw Asha go still. "Anyway, that explains why you wouldn't know about the riot!" Sab exclaimed, pulling their cloak tighter about their small frame and settling back down onto the floor. "Well, it happens sometimes, but not in a while, and not on this scale. The people here have been unhappy for years, demonstrating on and off. But then last week some of the Emperor's agents stormed a business—they hadn't complied with the newest tithe. Privately run essential services were exempt until last quarter, but I suppose his Excellence has to pay for his latest warship somehow." They sighed again.

Asha, Obi, and Xavior all exchanged glances. Asha looked shocked—it was likely, Obi realised, that she'd never heard a soul alive speak about the Emperor like that.

Sab continued, taking the silence as a prompt. "The business was a nursery. The soldiers set the whole place on fire. Killed three children—called it an accident of course, but witnesses said otherwise." A weary shrug. "Unrest was building, so they brought in some troops. But then some bright young person decided to hijack a Consortium jet and shoot the statue of the Emperor off the side of the biggest temple in the port. Half the wall went with it, and, of course, when people looked out and saw who was firing on them, they thought it was the government."

"Has that happened before?" Asha asked, disbelieving. "Surely they knew it must have been hijacked?"

Sab shook their head. "The Consortium has never been afraid to remind people who's in charge. They'll bomb a city flat to prove a point. And of course—" they let out the longest sigh yet "—they have their weapon."

The planet destroyer. Obi remembered the sadness in Ossock's face as he'd explained it to them.

"He's a monster," Asha said.

Sab shrugged. "I don't know what he is."

They had the beginnings of a dubious and slightly pathetic plan for escape laid out when it happened.

A soldier on patrol was walking past their cell, gun raised, carrying out the same checks he had each quarter hour. They were all in their agreed positions—Asha and Xavior pressed to the walls, one on either side, waiting on Obi's attempt to summon an apparition that could trick the guard into opening the cell door. He wasn't sure if it would work—if he would be able to concentrate past the migraine that felt like it was splitting his skull open after that electric jolt—but he had to try. He couldn't be the one to let them down.

"Ready?" he whispered.

"Ready," came the replies, Sab included.

Then the soldier's comms unit crackled to life at his hip, and he froze, his hand faltering at the panel by the gate. Fumbling with the device, he lifted it to his mouth and said, "Excuse me, can you confirm that is evacuation level *five?*" before looking stunned, nodding curtly, and running back down the hall, his quick, frantic footsteps retreating into an echo.

"What," Xavior asked, voice low, "was *that?*"

At the same time, Asha murmured, "Evacuation?"

Obi let his hands drop to his side. "Great. Now what?"

Asha got up, peering outside the cell, trying to make out the source of a vague sound that had started at the end of the corridor, and seemed to be growing closer. She reached a hand towards the energy barrier as though to touch it, and an alarm blared to life.

WAAOOOOW! WAAOOOOW!

Asha leaped backwards, staring at her hand and then back at the gate.

"What—" said Obi.

But before he could finish, a contingent of about twelve Consortium soldiers ran past the cell. It looked like the entire staff of the small prison, all of them hurrying towards something.

Or away, Obi thought.

"Quickly!" one of them said. "There's not time—"

An automated voice boomed out over the speakers. "EVACUATE. EVACUATE. THIS IS AN EVACUATION WARNING, LEVEL FIVE. TIME REMAINING UNTIL DESTRUCTION: THIRTY MINUTES. PLEASE FOLLOW DESIGNATED ROUTES."

They all looked at each other in shock.

Xavior broke the silence, running to the barrier, and shouting into the corridor. "*Hey! You can't just leave us here!*" he slammed the heel of his hand into the barrier, cursing at it. But the soldiers didn't even show signs that they had heard, let alone that they might turn around and help. Under the sound of the blaring alarm, their footsteps soon faded into nothing. Xavior lifted his hand slowly up to the barrier, pressing his hand against it. "We *can't* be stuck in here," he said quietly. "No way." He turned back to face them. "We have to get out. If it's not safe for them, it's definitely not safe for us. Whatever's coming . . ."

Behind him, the lights on the barrier between them and the corridor flickered once, and died.

"*Um,*" Obi said.

Then, like something out of a nightmare, the lights at the far end of the corridor began to turn off.

Darkness crawled towards them in echoing *clangs*, travelling down the hall, bay by bay, the alarm still wailing through the now-deserted jail.

In the darkness, the energy barrier that sealed them in shone for a moment, in bright, plasmatic blue.

Obi saw Asha's terrified face, carved out in shadows and the sapphire gleam of the light.

Then the barrier disappeared.

The darkness was total and absolute. It occurred to Obi that while the barrier had been keeping them from the rest of the jail, it had also been keeping the rest of the jail from *them*.

Something ran past their cell—swift and shadowy, feet thumping on the ground. They all flinched back—Obi swallowed a strangled scream. The cell opposite theirs had been the only one they could see into, but it had been empty. A sick feeling settled over him as he realised that didn't guarantee all the cells in the facility were. In fact, they definitely weren't. And now all the doors were open.

A low wail echoed from some distant corridor beyond the darkness. A chittering sound stuttered out in reply.

Adrenaline shot through Obi's bloodstream. He felt like a livewire, exposed.

Sab's eyes provided the only source of light, until Obi turned on the torch in his palm. Their small cellmate stood fluidly, surprisingly lithe, and went to the edge of the cell. Slowly, they extended a stubby hand past the place where the barrier had been. Obi flinched, waiting for it flicker back on, for Sab to be thrown back. But nothing happened. Sab stepped out into the eerie hallway. "The whole facility is like this," came Sab's voice from the darkened corridor.

"Why?" asked Asha, her voice urgent.

Sab shrugged. "I didn't see any occupied cells in this wing

when I was brought in, but I didn't get a good look. Whatever is going on in here, you can be certain we aren't alone."

"It must be evacuation procedure," Asha said, and Obi could practically see the cogs turning furiously in her head. "But surely they would transfer us to a different facility?" She frowned, looking out into the dark, red-lit hallway. "What is it that they're running from? What is 'level five'?"

Sab turned back to them, yellow eyes luminescent in the dark. They murmured simply, "It's a good question, but I don't plan on sticking around long enough to find out," and pulled their strange visor up over their face. With a nod, they slipped away, black clothes blurring into the shadows as they disappeared down the darkening left corridor.

"Okay," Obi murmured, then turned to the others. "That was weird, but they're right." He pointed to the darkened corridor. "If we want a chance at esc—"

"THIS IS AN EVACUATION WARNING, LEVEL FIVE. TIME REMAINING UNTIL DESTRUCTION: TWENTY-SEVEN MINUTES. PLEASE FOLLOW DESIGNATED ROUTES."

Asha was muttering to herself—probably calculating something—a deep frown etched into her forehead. "Okay," she said. "We were all unconscious until we woke up in the cell, so I think we should go the same way as Sab—it's our best bet. And we've got time. Almost half an hour to get out, before . . ." She trailed off. "Whatever it is that's about to happen."

Obi could barely make out her face in the dark, the white beam of light emanating from the torch in his palm providing the only illumination. But she looked determined. Scared, but ready to face it.

"If we can find a ship, I can at least get us off the ground. Jets are no use though, I need something space-worthy. Something that can get us somewhere else. There should be a hangar nearby, we just need a map to it."

"Maybe there will be some signs we can follow," Xavior murmured.

"Yeah, because there will definitely be *exit signs* in a prison," Asha whispered back.

"Hey! That's not what I *meant*—"

Something slammed into the wall next to them. At first, Obi was too stunned by the force with which the wall—now lacerated with scratches—had been impacted, that he didn't move.

There was a sound like wings beating, and in the beam of his torch light something writhed on the ground in front of them, hissing in pain from the collision with the wall.

A solid, scaled body. Flashing, intelligent eyes. Leathery wings and thin arms curled protectively around an injured abdomen, leaking shining blood onto the dark floor.

"Get back," Obi yelled, but he was too late. The alien struck, eyes wild with pain and fear, lashing out with a clawed hand, and all Obi could do was—

Xavior screamed.

At the last moment, he'd run towards their attacker, trying to draw its attention away from Obi and Asha. It's clawed wing slashed him across the chest.

Obi saw blood splatter the wall.

The alien gave a harsh cry and half-flew, half-slithered away down the corridor.

"No!" Asha yelled, running towards Xavior. He was on his knees, clutching the left side of his chest and moaning in pain. Obi ran forward, grabbing Xavior's good arm and throwing it over his shoulder.

"We don't have time to stop, Asha," he said. "Get the other side of his arm, we have to go."

Xavior nodded limply in agreement. His breathing was harsh but even. Obi hoped the wound was only surface deep.

Carrying their injured friend between them, Asha and Obi stepped out into the corridor.

There were noises in the dark—Obi thought he heard some-body laugh, a low chittering sound that seemed to come from far too close by. They pressed together as they limped through the facility, Asha desperately scanning the darkness ahead, Obi fighting to keep Xavior upright, and take most of his weight so Asha wouldn't have to. Xavior's jaw was clenched shut, sweat beading on his forehead. They just needed to get to a ship. It would have first aid on board, and then they could—they could—

Obi's boot hit something. It scraped noisily across the floor, with a sound like nails on metal. They all jumped. His heart thudded against his ribcage as he swung the torch's beam wildly—

"Hold on . . . " Asha mumbled, bending down to retrieve something just outside the beam's perimeter.

It was an assault rifle, standard Consortium issue, and it had just been left there, lying on the floor in the murky dark.

The hairs on the back of Obi's neck stood up. Shivers pricked down his arms.

Something is very, very wrong here. Whatever we thought it could have been—the riots, a training exercise . . . it's something worse.

Asha's frown deepened as she looped the gun around her shoulder via its cross-body strap. Obi shone his palm ahead of them. None of them dared looked outside the beam as they walked further towards what they could only hope was the exit—though there were occasional red emergency lights set into the walls, placed at long intervals from each other. It felt like walking deep under the surface of a scarlet sea.

Then, just ahead: a door, spilling flickering blue electric glare into the corridor.

They sped up.

It was a control room, swivelling chairs left in disarray, paperwork abandoned half completed, snack wrappers strewn across the desks. *They left in a hurry.*

A wall of weaponry hung at the back, but it was mostly stripped clean. The only thing left were a few black, military issue knives.

It was strange enough that the door had been left wide open, but the screens stopped them in their tracks.

Each one displayed the same message, normal programming paused underneath.

EVACUATE, EVACUATE, EVACUATE.

"*Come in—!*" said a voice, crackling against static. They all jumped, whirling around. The noise had come from their left—Obi shone the light wildly in its vague direction.

"—to Facility Seven. Facility Seven do you read me? Evacuation orders were *delayed*—destruction is—" the voice cut out abruptly, replaced by static. It was a comms unit—a handheld one. It must have been left by someone as they evacuated. It crackled, hissing garbled words against the floor. Asha bent and picked it up, holding it close to her ear. The voice cut back in. "I repeat, planetary cleansing is imminent. The window for viable departure from 90-67X is rapidly decreasing due to severe atmospheric disturbances—" Another burst of static. Then, "—unviable. I repeat, five minutes until departure is unviable." The static cut back in, fading slowly to nothing.

They all stood paralysed with shock. Xavior sat down heavily on a chair, grasping his arm, pale and sweat, head lolling. Obi's heart was thudding, his mind racing down lines of logic, trying to believe that he hadn't just heard what he'd heard.

Asha brought her hand up slowly to her mouth. Her face was doing something terrifying. "*Planetary cleansing?*" she hissed. "Is that— is that *the weapon?*" She cast a desperate glance towards the screens, but their message remained the same.

EVACUATE.

"They're going to blow us up," she said. "In ten minutes, this planet will be . . ." She trailed off, and understanding flooded through Obi like a tidal wave.

No, he thought, *no, no, no*—

"We have to get out of here, *now!*" she shrieked, turning fully to face the myriad screens in front of them, her hands already reaching for the keyboard. They were a blur as she pulled up blueprints of the facility, accessed camera feeds, and squinted at them furiously. "There," she breathed, pointing at one of the screens in front of them. It was a grainy aerial shot of a building two kilometres away. "There's a bay of emergency craft. It's two buildings over, we can make it there, but we have to go now—we might be able to—to unlock one of them and get out." She turned to them, eyes wild, sweat shining on her forehead, and Obi looked to the screen, and the map on it, and realised that they were all about to die, pulverised in the immediate aftermath of whatever happened when someone killed a planet.

"That bay is *two kilometres away*—"

"THIS IS AN EVACUATION WARNING, LEVEL FIVE. TIME REMAINING UNTIL DESTRUCTION: TWENTY-FIVE MINUTES. PLEASE FOLLOW DES- IGNATED ROUTES."

Obi did the maths. They had just under five minutes. "*Fuck.*" He thought briefly about jumping. This felt different to the prison ship. This felt imminent, like they really could die at the end of that countdown, crushed by the agonal gasps of a collapsing planet. He'd never get the cure, never see George again, never find out what really happened to his father. Never get older than he was in this moment, which, *Christ*, wasn't very old at all.

All because he'd stayed.

"Wait," said Xavior. He looked pale and sweaty under the harsh blue lights. "I have an emergency contact. I—I think I can get out us out of here."

"What are you waiting for then?" Asha hissed.

Xavior gulped. "It's complicated, I'll—I'll explain later. But right now we need to get my communications chip."

"Where is it?"

He tapped his shoulder. "In here."

Obi felt faint. "We need to cut it out of you?"

Xavior nodded. "It's the only way. It was put in there for emergencies, so I could never lose it." He seemed stunned at the words coming out of his mouth.

Who is it, Obi thought, *that you would be reluctant to ask for help from, even if the alternative was certain death?*

Xavior clenched his fists. "This is the only way we can survive." Stalking over to the wall, he grabbed a knife from it, hands shaking. He gave it Asha. "You do it."

She took it from him, her eyes darting from Obi to Xavior to the screens and back again, and Obi knew she was trying, just like he was, to formulate any other solution that would see them out of this alive, and coming up empty.

"I could go back," Obi said, barely believing what he was saying. "If either of you have anything from onboard the *Styanax*, I could go back in time and warn myself. I don't know what would happen if I met myself in the past, but I'm willing to risk it. We would know Isi was going to sell us out, we'd be prepared—"

"No," Asha said firmly. "Your illness. You could die. It's not worth it. We can fix this here." She squeezed her eyes shut. "And if we can't then you have to jump." When she opened her eyes they were wet with tears. "You can't die here, Obi."

"Asha." Xavior's hair was stuck to his forehead with sweat. "Hurry up. Just do it."

She opened her mouth, forehead twisted with reluctance, but then the speakers blared out a new message. It seemed the facilities systems had rectified their earlier mistake: "CLEANSING WILL COMMENCE IN 100, 99, 98—"

Obi saw Xavior's skin slide open against the downswing of the knife. There was dull emerald-coloured flesh, a tiny scar, a tapering line of pale jade, then: white fat, before the blood welled up, green and bright.

"Can you see it?" Xavior groaned.

"I see it—"

Xavior gripped his arm below the cut, squeezing it. More blood dribbled out, soaking Asha's hands. Obi wanted to turn away, but his attention was caught by the look on Asha's face—she faltered slightly, her eyes unfocused. For a moment, her irises appeared to flash gold. *God, the panic is messing with my head.*

"—97, 96, 95—"

Asha shook her head, as though jolting herself back into the moment, before plunging her thumb and forefinger into his arm and easing out the chip. It was a flat device about the size of her thumbnail. Xavior wobbled on his feet, so Obi darted forward, grabbing one of his arms and hauling it over his neck.

"*Here,*" Xavior said, motioning for the chip. Asha gave it to him, but he almost dropped it, the blood and his wound making him clumsy. For a second Obi thought he would pass out from the pain and leave them, stranded, but then his thumb gained purchase through the gore, and he flicked a tiny switch on the device's side.

White light blossomed.

Xavior threw the device on the floor. It slid, trailing wet green against the black, and then: a shape, the size of a very tall person, drawn in bright white, phased into being above it.

The chip slid to a stop, and a figure came into focus, flickering slightly, shining like a miracle.

"*Tecmessa*," Xavior cried out, hair hanging limply over his forehead. "Help me, please."

The sentient, who appeared to be talking to someone past the hologram, turned around. Her hand made an aborted motion, as though she had wanted to press it to her mouth in shock, but thought better of it. She was very tall and very slender, angular limbs draped in a heavy-looking robe, tied at the waist with a simple sash. A third eye blinked from the middle of her forehead.

Recognition bloomed in Asha's mind.

"Xavior?" The sentient looked stunned. "Is it really you?" Belatedly, she seemed to notice Obi propping him up, and Asha standing on his other side, hands stained with blood. "*What's going on?*"

"No time," he said. "We need a rescue."

She seemed to snap into a different mind frame, all business. "Coordinates?"

Asha glanced at her watch—the one Obi had seen her modifying on the *Stayanax*—and told her.

"Alright," she said. "We can swing that—we're close enough. God, just about. Get to the roof—there are stairs—" she peered at her screen "—outside to the left." The woman was typing furiously, the keyboard just out of sight. "*Go.*"

And so they went. Asha scooped up Xavior's other arm and flung it over her neck, keeping his wrist in a death grip. Obi looked at her and nodded. They ran, sprinting past cells with

their horribly open doors, and the dim glow of the red emergency lights, veering left as soon as they could, and running up
the stairs that twisted higher and higher, until they saw a door,
flung open and juddering in the wind. Rain howled into the
corridor, soaking the stone.

They burst onto the roof.

Everything was dark. Then the biggest fork of lightning Obi
had ever seen split the sky, branching off like an ancient tree
and shedding a horrible light on what remained of the city, just
past the rooftops of the facility. Rain hissed from the sky and
hailstones as big as fists slammed into the ground, smashing
stone balconies to bricks and caving in the various domed
cupolas that dotted the horizon. Gale-force winds blew through
the buildings, shattered glass littered the floor, and there were
storm clouds above them, so big and dark the sky had become
nothing but a roiling mass of shadow. He felt like he was standing under the waves of a great sea, looking up at the storm-struck
surface.

And worst of all, the roof was *empty*—no sign of a rescue.

Next to him, Xavior stooped, leaning heavily on Obi. He
turned to tell Asha to help him pull the other boy up—

But she was gone.

"*Where's Asha?*" Obi shouted above the storm. "Did she fall?
Did you see?" His heart was in his throat, he was trying to turn
back, to go and find her, but Xavior was a limp weight at his
side, eyes closed, breathing shallow. He was bleeding from two
places now.

And then, across the courtyard, a beam of light descended
from the storm to form the woman from the control room.
She held out her hand, shouting something they couldn't hear.

Obi stood still. The noise of the storm seemed to fade into
the background, everything going slow and impossible, as he

realised that he was alone with an unconscious Xavior, and Asha was nowhere to be seen.

The woman grew more solid, beckoning to him. Her movements were frantic, she was looking at the sky. *He had to go.* If he went looking for Asha, they'd all die. But if they left, limping towards the light, then she would be done for. Maybe he could leave Xavior here and run back inside. But Xavior wasn't even *awake*, so how was he supposed to—

Footsteps, clanging on metal.

Asha appeared out of the doorway, running and screaming at him, the tiny comms unit clutched in her fist, something that looked like an entire computer on her back. She was pointing at the lady in the light with her outstretched hand, her eyes wild with fear as she careened past them, grabbing hold of Obi's shirt and pulling him forward.

On the horizon, a lightning fork struck a building, blowing debris into the air.

Obi felt like he was running through syrup, with everything slowed down and sped up all at once.

All he could hear was the thrash of the rain on the stones and his own ragged groans as he struggled on, Xavior's body slipping out of his grasp with every step.

They were five paces away, Asha's legs driving into the ground, her hand banded around his upper arm like a vice, tugging him forward.

Three—he stumbled, righting himself with a hand against the ground, pushing up—

Two—

A distant boom sounded, and the earth shook.

Obi and Asha reached out their hands, straining towards the woman's outstretched palm—

And then, nothing.

And then, *light*.

Loyalty is the quality that held our Heroes together through the hardship, I think. Loyalty borne of love for each other and not out of personal gain. They would be tested so many times before they could even begin to think of victory that if they had not been able to count on one other, all their efforts would have been wasted.

Excerpt from the abandoned notebooks of I. Nisomn, found in his study after his unannounced departure from the Guild.

Chapter Twenty-Four

[planet: Earth] + [location: London] + [year: 1812]

George was dreaming. He knew it was a dream because his hands were still, and his mind wholly his own. These things did not happen simultaneously anymore. Hadn't in nearly half a year.

The dream grew solid around him. His steady hands were cold—*freezing*—and wet with snow. It was flurrying around him, purple in the moonlit night. He was on his balcony, the gardens spread out before him. But immediately below him, lying prone on the steps of the palace, there was a body.

The snow around the body was pristine. No footprints, no sign of a struggle, no blood. Everything was silent. He could barely even hear himself breathe.

"Who the hell are you?" he half-whispered.

Then the body contorted, back arching violently, mouth falling open in a silent scream, and, impossibly, spilling from the open mouth, came a blinding white light.

Oh, George thought, inside the dream. *Oh, dear god, not this.*

The light lit up the body. It was a boy, his eyes shot wide open—grey irises like pale rings, pinprick pupils like twin bulls-eyes—before his mouth began working noiselessly, as though he had been muted. Then, a choked-out plea—*help*—and George was gripped by something visceral: he would have rather died than deny him.

George turned around and sprinted out of his room.

The corridor unfolded before him, as though the dream could barely keep up with his intention. He raced down the carpeted hallway before barrelling down the staircase and out the front door. He skidded to a stop at the top of the steps, snow falling thickly around him. The boy was lying still, but, as George watched, he curled in on himself, supporting his head with his right arm. His left sleeve whipped in the wind, flapping oddly. There was no arm there to obstruct it.

George walked down the steps, coming to a crouch by the shivering boy, who looked to be about his age. Without thinking, he reached out his hand, brushing snow off his brow, his fingers making wet lines of melted ice on the boy's dark skin.

"Who *are* you?" he whispered again.

The boy's eyes flew open.

"Help me," he groaned. "I don't know what—I don't what's happening to me—"

His spine arched again, cutting off his windpipe. Then the white light left his eyes and began racing down his neck as though it was in his *blood*.

George stared in disbelief. Was this a miracle or—or the devil's work, perhaps?

It was when the light reached the boy's heart and *pulsed* that George first formed the idea that he might be in over his head. The light pulsed again, and then separated from the boy's body, passing through his clothes in a brilliant white orb. His glowing chest strained upward, upward, upward—

And then, like a marionette with his strings cut, he slumped to the ground, leaving the orb suspended in mid-air. It shone like the sun. It was the most beautiful thing George had ever seen. He thought it might be the boy's soul.

The boy reached upwards, clumsily swiping at the light, trying to catch it.

The orb was floating higher in the air now, wisps of it snagging on the wind and disintegrating—dissipating into nothing.

"Q—Quickly," Obi rasped. "You have to keep . . . keep it safe. You—" He broke off, groaning. "You have to promise me. P—Promise me you'll keep it safe." Then his eyes had slid shut, and he had fallen unconscious.

The orb still hung in front of George, as though baiting him into action. He needed a box, or a container. There was one in the entrance hall. Faster than he had ever run in his life, he threw himself back up the steps, running down the hallway to the atrium with the snuffbox on the mantlepiece. Grabbing it, he ran back outside. The boy was eerily still, and the orb was nearly too bright to look at, but he brought the box towards it, and captured it inside. There were no flames, no holy fire. He had half expected to hear the voice of God himself, or Lucifer, or to watch as an angel descended from the heavens to take the boy away. But all was still, and all was quiet.

Softly, the dream's edges began to blur. It hurt to look at, so George closed his eyes.

When he opened them, it was summer.

Obi lay in front of him, in full health, grinning in the sun-dappled shade that filtered through the great oak at the far end of the gardens.

"Someone's going to see us," George said, but he was grinning, too.

They were lying face to face, propped up on their elbows, their bodies pointing in opposite directions, two books between them.

The summer of 1805.

He'd been fifteen, then, Obi already sixteen that February, and they must've been there for hours already.

Obi would be gone that December; George was already in love.

"I know," Obi said. He didn't sound bothered. He never really did, though. "I wanted to see you."

The George who knew this was a dream wanted to groan and roll his eyes. The George who didn't blushed furiously, and rolled away to hide it, sitting up.

It was at this moment that the part of George who was not living this moment but observing it, noticed the decay at the edge of his vision. Tendrils of darkness were crawling into the room, leaking from the walls and the light fixtures, crawling their way under the door, seeping into the carpet like wet rot.

"George?" Obi asked. "Are you alright?"

But George was looking around wildly, trying to locate the source of the encroaching shadow.

The tendrils were moving quickly, as though blown by the wind, whipping themselves into a tornado that ripped leaves from the oak and toppled a mossy marble statue.

"George?" Obi's voice sounded far away. "I'm sorry, I—"

George turned to look at him, but he was gone.

"No," he whispered. "No, no, *no*—"

The whirlpool of darkness split down the middle and a person stepped out. No, George realised, his heart plummeting. Not a person. *Him*.

"What do you want?"

Sensit's face was troubled. "I want to understand you."

"How? By invading my most private memories and . . . and *decaying* them?"

Sensit ignored him. Walking closer, he peered at George as though he were a small animal ready for dissection. As though trying to read the words George thought inside his head.

"I wonder what form my messenger took, when I told it to

make you come to me, that night, on the balcony." Sensit turned back to George. He looked so human. So flesh and blood. Solid and real.

Killable, said a small, hard voice in George's mind.

"It was him, wasn't it?" A strange look passed across Sensit's face. If George hadn't been so wholly convinced of his evil nature, he might have called it sadness, or longing. His whole demeanour seemed to change—at first, he had stalked into George's dream like the predator animal he was—cold, and calculating. Now, at the mention of Obi, he looked at George with wide eyes, like a child lost in a strange place. As though merely thinking of Obi had unlocked a strange vault of his memory. "Him. Who—who is he? The traveller wreathed in gold." He shook his head erratically, looking at George with wide eyes. "I see his face in mirrored surfaces. Feel his heart beating in my chest. I have seen through his eyes. A great darkness—*No!*" he growled. "No, no—"

Then, for a just a moment, the skin of the demon rippled and George saw—

A mouth, full of teeth, wide open in a silent scream. One wing, dripping gold blood, the black feathers raised and torn in patches. A blur of lashing tails. And all around, sunken into the skin, covering the face, the mouth, running along the spine, burning in the air, were *eyes*. They blinked red-gold, like the last light of a thousand dying suns, and stared at George with a cosmic hunger, like they had looked right through to the heart of him, and wished for nothing else but to devour what they'd seen.

Then the man was back, a tall, lean figure in a pitch-black suit, staggering on the uncertain edges of the dream, his sharply handsome face twisted into a knot of consternation. "Not now, not again—" He was panting slightly, as though in pain. "I came here to escape, but it has me—the prophecy has me—*no*—"

It was as though he had forgotten George entirely, forgotten where he was and why he'd come there. His suit shimmered and changed, melting into rusted black armour—clawed gauntlets clutched at the air. George saw an empty scabbard swinging at his hip.

Demon, was the only coherent thought to make it through the voices inside George's mind begging him to run. *Warrior from hell.*

Sensit turned to look at him. His eyes were haunted, ancient. "It's you," he growled. "It's always been you. And I was too blind to see it, too stupid to understand. If I am to succeed here, I need you to join me." He looked at George with a terrible hunger.

Somewhere past the mind-numbing fear, George found his voice. "I would sooner end my own life than aid you in any way. Whatever you need, you will not get from me willingly."

But what's stopping you from taking it? From taking me? George thought, sure that in the next few moments Sensit would turn back into that nightmare creature, lunge and devour him, killing him inside a dream, and dragging his soul away to gnaw on under an abandoned building somewhere. But then the sure voice of logic pierced the panic, and half a puzzle piece, long missing, slotted into place.

On the balcony, Sensit had said, *by the summer solstice the city will be mine. And I will have what I want, whether it is given willingly, or not.*

A lifetime of fairy tales flashed through his mind—witches who needed willing subjects to make their magic stronger. Sorcerers who seduced young women and men, only to kill them and use their organs for witchcraft.

"Am I—" George faltered, unsure. "Am I the other half of what you want?" No reply. Sensit's face was oddly blank. *He hadn't realised what he'd been saying. And now I've figured it out.*

Almost. "That's the problem, isn't it?" George asked, and despite himself—despite everything—he could have laughed. "Whatever you need from me, it has to be given willingly. I have to want to. Well, *I don't.*"

Sensit surged forward, his calm demeanour falling like a mask, and shattering on the floor.

"*I know you have it.*" His voice was three voices, an old chorus, and in it George heard one that sounded like the voice of the man he loved.

Sensit reached out to squeeze his hands around George's throat, but George ducked, hurling himself away, to the other side of the room. But two of Sensit's fingers had grazed his neck and the flesh burned where he'd made contact. George ignored the pain, raising his hands. He would fight the monster himself if he had to.

"Get away from me," he said, voice trembling. "Get out of my head."

That smile again, curved like a scimitar and twice as deadly. "This is *your* dream," Sensit said, stalking closer. "Why don't you make me?"

George heaved in a breath, and woke up.

The darkness of his room was a welcome reprieve from the blinding red-gold of Sensit's eyes. His hands were shaking worse than they ever had before and his neck ached. He stumbled out of bed, sweeping his hand across his bedside table in a desperate effort to locate his medicine. A vase of tulips crashed to the floor, deafening in the silence. His teeth chattered. *Why was he so cold?* His fingers grasped the bottle and ripped the lid off. The laudanum was bitter as ever, but he was used to it by now.

As the tremors slowed, he stood, walking shakily towards the adjoining bathroom. He lit a candle on the way, and pushed open the door, setting the small flame down on the side of the sink. He looked into the mirror.

Two bright, purple-red bruises were pressed into his neck. Oval shaped and angry, just above his pulse point. He resolved not to look at them. Pressing his forehead into the mirror, he exhaled weakly, his breath clouding the cool glass.

"George?" said a quiet voice. "Are you alright?"

He flinched. *Gisela.* He turned around. "Did I wake you?"

"The vase," she said, gesturing back into the room. "It was very loud."

Her German accent was especially noticeable when she was tired.

"Apologies, I was . . . ah, dreaming."

"*Albtraum?*"

"*Ja.* A nightmare." He stroked her hair, wilting a little inside at how brotherly they both knew the gesture to be, and smiled encouragingly at her. "*Das gute an Albträumen ist, dass sie nicht wahr sind.*"

She nodded, appeased, and likely soothed a little by the familiar language. He resolved to speak it more often. She turned to go, but stopped. Looking at his neck. Her face crumpled. *The bruises,* he realised. *She must think—*

Gisela swallowed and stepped closer. "You do not touch me, because there is someone else?" her voice was small. "I am your wife. Anything you want. Take it."

George felt sick. She didn't deserve any of this. He had wanted her to be comfortable, and happy. Not this, never *this*. How did he ruin every good thing?

"There is no one else," he said firmly. "Only you."

She shook her head and turned to go. Pausing by the door, she fumbled with something at the side of her nightgown. A string. She pulled it, and the entire thing fell away, revealing miles of bare, milk-white skin. On reflex, George looked away.

"Am I so horrific to you?" she whispered. "Can you not stand the sight of me?"

"Gisela, no, I—"

But she had moved beyond the light of the bathroom and shut the door behind her.

The good thing about nightmares, he'd said, *is that they are not real.*

His neck pulsed in memory of the two frozen fingertips that had pressed there.

If only that were true.

"The summer solstice?" Alarick asked, pacing up and down the chilly flagstones of the palace's basement. "That's barely two months away! Why didn't you tell me before?!"

"I'm sorry, I must have forgotten to send up some smoke signals for you during my wedding ceremony. Or would sign language over the archbishop's head have been preferable?" George closed his eyes. "Sorry. I suppose what I really mean is, what do we do?" He felt so out of control. "Bring in the army?"

"And have the whole city thrown into fear and chaos? Generate even more negative emotions he can feed off?" Alarick shook his head. "No. We have to ensure that we control more variables than him, that we gain a monopoly over the city in some way that is outside of his realm of power."

"But how?" George asked. "He is a *warrior from another world.* We are nothing compared to that. Humans limited by our mortal frailty and inherent ordinariness. Ephemeral. Powerless."

"You forget I am not human," Alarick said, "and far from ordinary." His eyes were dark, his brow furrowed. "He's not a god yet, and this is my city. The city I raised my son in. The city that harboured me when I thought all was lost and gave me a home and hope and something else to love that couldn't be taken from me as easily as a life."

George was silent, startled. He had seen Obi in that frown. Had heard him in the conviction of Alarick's tone.

"We aren't so different, you know. Him and I . . . I was never a hero, but I served people with my power, too. He's been driven mad. Mad for his freedom, to have control over others in the way he never had control over himself." He shook his head. "But to be honest, I don't care what he wants, or what he does, or whatever sad fucking story he tells himself every night about his childhood. Don't bring that shit to my city."

"So what do we do?" George said again. Then an idea came to him. "You're a time-traveller," he said. Alarick stared him, as if to say, *yeah, and?* "What if you turned back time?" George said. "Went back to before all of this started, and killed him, just as he was arriving in the city—you could go up behind him and run him right through—"

Alarick cut him off. "Don't talk about things you don't understand. You can't just turn back time. I tried it once, when my wife—" Alarick stopped. "It's not worth it. Time can't be re-wound. It's just not possible." He trailed off, stopping mid-pace, eyes widening in comprehension. George imagined for a second that he was receiving a prophecy sent from some benevolent god to help them, just like the heroes of old, but Alarick's next words killed that idea where it stood.

"I never told you what I saw in the future, did I?"

"No."

Alarick smoothed a hand over his forehead, rubbing at his dark eyes as though he could dislodge whatever it was he had seen. "London was quiet," he said finally. "So quiet, and the people . . . The people were frozen."

George wasn't sure he'd heard correctly. "The people were frozen?"

"Yes." Alarick replied. "Frozen in time."

"*How?*"

Alarick held up a hand. "Shut up, I'm trying to think."

George watched him, dread sinking in his stomach. A future where everyone in the city was frozen in time . . . It seemed like something out of a fairy tale. Everyone sleeping until the gallant outsider woke the prince with a kiss . . . Or the princess, rather. George shook his head, mourning the last of his sanity. Perhaps this was all one long hallucination. He wondered if he wanted it to be.

Alarick frowned in confusion. "But when I looked into the future and saw London frozen in time, the summer solstice hadn't happened yet . . . I only went forward by a single month. And the solstice is still two months away." He muttered something to himself, counting on his fingers. "Why would Sensit freeze the city before the solstice if that's when he gets what he wants? I'm assuming the power of the solstice will be enough to amplify the power contained in the fragment of Obi's soul, allowing him to raise all the dead in the city. Enough to overpower us all, and take London for himself."

George was beginning to understand Alarick's confusion. "But if Sensit didn't freeze the city . . . then who did?"

Alarick finally looked at him, comprehension dawning on his face. "I think we did." Then, "And I think I know how to do it."

"You do? How?"

Alarick paused, consternation twisting his features into something like a frown. In the end he sighed, grabbed his hat, and started walking towards the door.

"It's really better if I show you."

Chapter Twenty-Five

[planet: none] + [location: free space] + [year: 6066]

Asha stood in the atrium of a giant space cruiser, dripping dirty rainwater from the end of the world onto its shining floor. She held up her hand in time to see the last inches of her fingertips re-assembling themselves. Her body felt like it was buzzing—an echoing hum dissipating from her cells into the air.

Teleported.

In an instant, she recalled theories of soul manipulation, the ethical and moral dilemmas of rearranging the particles of a person.

My friends. She looked around. Obi was passed out on the floor, chest heaving, with Xavior sprawled over him, bleeding onto his leg.

"Help!" she shouted, stumbling over to them both. "Please, he's hurt. *Somebody help us.*" Dropping to her knees, she pressed her hands to his stomach. Blood pumped sluggishly around her hands—his shirt was soaked through with it. She looked to Obi. His face was serene where he lay, his breathing evening out. But who knew if his mind was alright, if it had survived the teleportation intact—

"What *happened* to you all?" asked a voice, and the woman from the projection was striding forward, red skirts billowing. She dropped to her knees by Xavior, waving over a team of similarly robed sentients. But before they could grab him and bear him away on their spotless stretcher, he sat up, swaying slightly and clutching at his chest, mumbling.

"*Help*—" he said, eyes darting around. "*Quickly, someone*—oh. We didn't die?" Then, with quiet disbelief, "We didn't die." His eyes closed, and his head tipped forward, hair falling over his forehead, horns curving gently upwards.

Asha's heart was in her mouth just looking at him. But he seemed okay. For now.

She went to Obi, shaking his shoulder. His eyes flew open with a start, glowing with a white light. She stumbled back, terrified, but then the light vanished, and he pushed himself onto all fours, heaving onto the floor.

Asha felt feverish. Like her skin had been chilled, but her blood was boiling. Her hands shook violently—her teeth chattered. The comms unit was clutched in her hand, its edge cutting into her palm, while an entire motherboard was strapped to her back, trailing wires. She knew she'd put them all in terrible danger, but she hadn't been able to walk away from that tech. If she managed to boost the signal from the comms unit she could listen in to private Consortium channels. And the motherboard contained compatible technology—she could build things with it that might get them into a secure base, or behind enemy lines without questioning. She had to do it for her sister. Any advantage she could get, she would take—she had to—or her mother would be killed.

She hugged herself, but her hands were stained with bright green blood, and it smeared all over her arms. Horror welled up in her just looking at it. There had been a moment, in the prison, when she'd seen Xavior get hit . . . She'd thought he'd been killed. *He's okay*, she reminded herself, looking at the two boys on the floor, both of them sitting now. *They're both okay.*

The woman from the hologram on the rooftop had stood up and was now staring at Asha—worry described in every line of her face. But there was another emotion. Something close to disbelief, but different.

Her face . . . Pale purple skin, finely wrinkled with age, sat over high cheekbones, above which, three deep set eyes blinked in confusion. Asha felt her heart beat faster. *I've seen you before,* she thought. *You're going to say something to me—*

"'Three people in a beam of white light . . .'" the woman murmured, seemingly to herself. "Three heroes appearing in a column of pale fire. Just how Ishoal said it would be, all those years ago, when I was a girl."

Ishoal, Asha thought. It was the name from her vision. Spoken by this woman, just like she'd known it would be. The world seemed to go quiet. The woman's face blurred. The room tilted. And somewhere, in the background of her awareness, Asha heard the rhythmic ticking of a clock.

She walked over to the window. Obi called her name but she barely heard him.

Outside the glass was Xesca, orange seas glimpsed in patches through the swirling white of its atmosphere, a line of molten red splitting the north hemisphere from the south.

The planet looked just like it had when she'd seen it weeks ago, staring into the Sentinel's eyes.

She pressed a hand to her mouth. "Is there a bathroom?" she mumbled. The woman looked at her with a mixture of concern, and fascination, before pointing down a narrow hallway.

Asha ran.

In the small room, she braced her hands over the sink, leaning her forehead against the cool surface of the mirror. Her whole body ached. She couldn't put too much weight on her left leg, or bright slicing pain would shoot through her hip. Vaguely, she remembered twisting it when she ran back for the computer.

Smears of green blood stained the sink under her grimy hands, and her nails were ripped and broken where she'd torn the computer apart, trying to salvage something from that place before—

She dug her fingernails into the cold, hard surface of the sink, feeling them bend. For a moment, she thought she might burst into tears, or cry out with the force of all the inarticulable frustration she could feel roiling inside her like an approaching storm.

There's nothing shameful about being angry, her mother used to say to her, *or even about being afraid. Not everyone can just take it, what it is to walk through this life as we do, and not be furious. And no one can be brave all the time. That's just a fact.*

She saw green flesh under her hands, the knife slippery with blood.

She saw a planet, eerily still in the vacuum, dead and broken, suddenly made into a mass grave, all those people *dead*, and she thought about how she missed her mother so much she'd been waking up in the night more and more recently with wet eyes and a feeling in her sternum like she'd been stabbed there, multiple times, with a serrated blade. How she had been dreaming of Aziza, always as a little girl, turning to look at her with the pain of a grown woman in her eyes. *Is anyone there?* Nausea rose in her throat.

This was all too much.

And that woman out there . . . Asha had seen her in the vision. And Xesca too. *She'd seen the planet die weeks before it had even happened.* What did that mean? So far, the vision had shown her Obi, who she could trust. And Xavior, who had helped them. Though he had also inadvertently led them into danger on board the *Stayanax.* Was it supposed to be a guiding force? Could she trust the vision, if it had only come to her thanks to the Sentinel?

She remembered her mother's words. *You must be careful, he lies.*

"Mama," she whispered, "I miss you. I miss you so much and I don't know if I'm strong enough to keep going. I hate this. I hate it. I'm so scared. I want to find Aziza and save you, to bring us all back together, to find a place where we can be safe, I do, *I do*, but I don't know if I *can*." The last word was a choked whisper.

No. She pressed her head more firmly against the glass. *You don't get to have a breakdown, not yet. Not now.*

Breathing in through her nose, she pulled herself upright, staring at the girl in the mirror—at her messy braids and the scalp between them, at the dull look in her eyes, and the washed-out brown of her skin under the fluorescent lights.

"You don't have time for this," she said, voice hoarse, her eyes red and stinging. "You can cry when it's *over*."

Then she turned around, motioned for the door to slide smoothly open, and stepped back into the hall.

By the time Asha rejoined the group, a bandaged-up Xavior was being interrogated by Tecmessa, and a dark-haired boy who looked a little younger than them had come up to join in. He looked human—startlingly so, amongst the variant chaos of the sentients on board—with straight dark hair and pale brown skin. He also looked quite young—fifteen maybe.

"Xavior," the woman said, and looked like she was losing patience. "What happened?"

"Probably something illegal," snapped the dark-haired boy. He looked furious.

Xavior wouldn't meet the woman's eye. He looked like he was experiencing his worst nightmare and had lost all hope that he would ever wake up from it. "Well, we were in a prison—"

"I told you! Definitely something illegal," the boy crowed, narrowing his eyes. "Where have you *been*?"

"*Koshiro*," the woman admonished, though she looked expectantly at Xavior like she too wanted to know where he'd been.

Xavior wilted under their gazes. "It's hard to explain."

Obi was looking blearily back and forth between the three of them. "Am I hallucinating," he whispered to Asha, "or do they all kind of look . . . similar?"

Xavior had struggled to his feet and was now being lectured by Koshiro, who was a head shorter than him. Asha squinted at them. *No*, she thought. *They don't look similar* . . . but there was something about them, when viewed as a whole, that seemed similar. Certain mannerisms, turns of phrase.

"*No way*," she murmured as a thought struck her. She recalled their conversation on the *Stayanax*. About how he was taken in by a family on Aonia.

"Xavior, is this your family?" she asked. "What happened?"

"You were only supposed to be away for six months," Koshiro said to Xavior, clearly hurt. "It's been two years. We—we thought you had died."

Obi raised his eyebrows.

Asha decided she would not be asking anymore questions.

By leaving, Xavior must have really hurt Koshiro. His eyes looked a little wet. "You said we were brothers," the younger boy said. "But you didn't even send a *message*."

"Shiro, I—"

"Koshiro. To you, my name is Koshiro."

". . . Koshiro, I'm sorry." Xavior had never looked so earnest. "I couldn't send messages because I had to lie about who I was and where I'd come from, and it would have been suspicious. Also, I may have lost my portable—you know, the one with all your contact information on it—in a pirate raid."

"You were attacked by *pirates*?"

"Actually, I *was* the p—"

"*Xavior*," interjected Tecmessa. "Another word out of your mouth and you'll be cleaning grease out of the kitchen vents for a month."

Koshiro and Xavior whirled around.

"You *can't* be serious?" Koshiro said.

Tecmessa levelled her stern gaze on him. "Unless you want to join him, you'll watch your tone. Poor communication skills or not, he is your brother by oath if not by blood and you must honour your word. And we rescued them from Port Xesca." Koshiro looked taken aback. "They just about escaped with their lives."

"Thank you, Tecmessa," Xavior said quietly.

"You all look half dead," she murmured. "Food. That's what you need. Come on. You can introduce us to your friends over the evening meal. Maybe explain to me what in the world you were doing in a jail cell on a planet marked for destruction. That way, we can all get acquainted." She looked at the nosy crew members ringing the atrium's perimeter. "Without an audience." The fabric of her trousers swished as she walked back towards the large doorway on the other side of the hall.

Koshiro glared at Xavior—who smiled weakly in response—and stomped after her. Xavior threw an apologetic look over his shoulder and ran to catch up, leaving Asha and Obi alone.

"Do you have any idea what just happened?" asked Asha.

"No," Obi replied. "No, I do not." Then he turned to her, grabbing her arm. "Asha, what you did back there—"

"We should follow them," she said, cutting him off. The last thing she wanted was for Obi to be disappointed in her. She couldn't bear it if he tried to lecture her right now.

Not waiting to see what he said, she pulled her arm out of his grasp, and went after the others.

Over a meal of crisp breads and thinly cut meats, accompanied by a thick, spiced drink that quenched Asha's thirst and drained some of the tension from her limbs, Tecmessa had laid out their situation. The ship, and all its occupants, belonged to the Diplomats' Guild—an order of scholars and Archivists, researchers and philosophers, who prized the pursuit of knowledge above everything, and had been granted diplomatic immunity in all quadrants by Thracin himself. Apparently, they received funding from the Consortium to ensure that Thracin's reign was documented with perfect clarity. But it was a strained relationship. The Diplomats were teachers, scientists, and historians who recognised and worshipped, almost, the objectivity of fact. They often came to a head with legates of the Consortium who preferred certain narratives over others. According to Tecmessa, their base planet was Aonia, where they congregated in an ancient palace—the last relic of a lost civilisation. Its ruins covered thousands of kilometres, but the palace was at its northern pole, half sunken into snow, but habitable.

While Tecmessa spoke, Asha tried not to look overly interested, playing the part of the grateful, shell-shocked human who'd never been outside an eco-dome. It wasn't hard. But despite her anxiety and exhaustion, her mind was racing.

Who was Ishoal? From what Tecmessa had said, it had sounded like he'd predicted them coming here. To the Diplomats' Guild. Tecmessa described it as a repository of knowledge as big as a palace . . . an entire guild of teachers and historians who could be tricked into divulging information. And the relationship they maintained with the Consortium likely meant private, secret documents were kept somewhere that Asha might be able to break into. Hadn't she seen a book in her vision? Perhaps it was on Aonia. Perhaps it would help lead her to her sister. Perhaps it would help her find this mysterious Ishoal.

Perhaps, perhaps. She was painfully aware that as of now, sitting at this table, surrounded by strangers, she had no plan, no way forward that might lead her successfully to her sister, and then to her mother.

The Guild was a glimmer of hope. She had to get onto that planet.

She sneaked a look at Obi and Xavior. Obi was quiet too, barely listening, clearly lost in thought. *Probably deciding if he's going to leave. Go his own way,* Asha thought with a pang of hurt.

Xavior was hunched over, pushing his food around his plate whilst the boy named Koshiro glared at him, and Tecmessa resumed her lecturing.

From what Asha could gather, Xavior had been taken to Aonia after his ordeal with the Magekind and found a parent in Tecmessa and a brother in her adopted son, Koshiro. The way Tecmessa told it, a small ship had descended into the depths of the ruin, and a person in robes of billowing white had stepped out, Xavior standing blank-eyed behind them. The person had left; Xavior had remained. And Tecmessa had stepped forward to rehabilitate him, because she had the space, and the relevant medical training, and an adopted son who had always wanted an older brother.

Because of this, Tecmessa explained, Xavior could claim guest status at the Guild, as he had two willing sponsors (Asha thought Koshiro looked less than willing, but she suspected all he needed was several sincere apologies and time to change that). Asha and Obi could not claim the same. Sponsors, Tecmessa explained, had to have known their sponsored candidate for a common galactic year before their sponsorship was valid. Therefore, they were refugees, seeking asylum. It did not occur to Asha at the time to ask how they, as non-citizens, even qualified for this right. When she did later, she began to look at Tecmessa in a different light.

"There will be a test," Tecmessa was saying. "Before you are allowed to set foot on Aonia. Knowledge is the Most Important Thing to us, and so we must be sure our priorities align. I would usually recommend sleep before attempting it, but there's no time. We make planetfall in three hours."

"A test?" Asha said. "What kind of test?"

"A simulation," Koshiro replied, stepping forward. "It will require you to make a decision. We can't tell you anything more."

"Thanks," Asha said drily, before Obi could stop her. "Really reassuring."

"How do we . . . simulate?" Obi asked, looking very sceptical.

"I'm guessing in *that*," Asha said wearily, pointing to a complex looking chair in the middle of the room.

Restraints curved over the arms and legs, white and geometric. Over the headrest, a jointed metal arm held what looked like a superior version of the virtual flight simulation headpieces Asha had often glimpsed through classroom windows on Gahraan.

Some of the old bitterness resurfaced strangely, right there in that spaceship, a hundred thousand light years from home and all the inadequacies it had revealed in her.

"You will sit," said Tecmessa, gesturing to the chair. "You will close your eyes—or not. The examination doesn't much care for consent; knowledge must be known, after all, and does not discriminate by willingness."

317

"The key is not to fight it," Koshiro said.

I'm too tired to fight, Asha thought. *And what else can I do? Ask for a ship, and take off if they give me one, with no clue what to do next, or where to go? The nearest transport hub for half a quadrant's just been blown up by the Emperor's mysterious weapon, and I would probably have to leave Obi, who looks relieved just to have been offered somewhere to rest his head for the night.*

So, she could run, again, or, she could sit down in the chair, run the simulation, and go with these people. Regroup. If they really were the keepers of the galaxy's knowledge like Xavior said, then this might be her best chance to learn something about the Emperor and his stronghold. About how someone might go about breaking into it.

Leaving now would be foolish—her mother and sister wouldn't be saved by a reckless child running into danger without a plan. The resources of the Diplomats' Guild could help her build that plan—whether they gave her permission to use them or not.

Out of the corner of her eye she saw Obi raise an eyebrow at her hesitation. She made up her mind.

Stepping forward, she walked down the stairs towards the chair, before sitting in it and placing her arms and legs in the loose loops of metal that snapped shut when Tecmessa looked sternly at them.

"Lie back."

Asha let her neck go slack, resting it on the headrest behind her. It was surprisingly comfortable. The headpiece descended under Tecmessa's guiding gaze, all utilitarian wires and strange geometric shapes that looked to Asha how calculating fractalics *felt*—complicated, but graceful and incredibly satisfying when viewed as a whole. She realised dimly that Koshiro was chanting and that she could hear the headpiece humming because it was now on her head, and that her eyes were closing, which was funny because the last time her eyelids had been this heavy had been the night before Isi had betrayed them and changed everything, which was what had led her here in the *first place*. She didn't think much else before the darkness took her, and, as her head flopped to the side, the last thing she saw was Koshiro's strange expression and the way he was looking at someone past her, like something precious that he'd lost and given up on had been returned to him.

Asha opened her eyes and saw a forest. She had never seen a forest before, only heard about them in stories.

Trees, impossibly tall and broad and alive, soared upwards to the sky, their branches as wide as main streets, leaves bigger than Asha herself. Sunlight filtered through to the ground, everything golden and quiet. So quiet it hurt.

Then she was thrown off her feet by a shockwave so deafening and destructive it levelled the forest around her. The crackling smell of ozone filled her nose and mouth. Swiping at her eyes to clear the dust and black spots, she gazed around, stunned. There was a newly formed crater a few metres to her left, something glimmering darkly at the bottom. Asha scrambled to her feet, picking her way past scorched branches and blasted earth to look cautiously over the side.

It was hard to make out at first. A screwed-up sheet of metal, here. A crumpled wing, there. Cracked glass, a smoking engine. Light panels leaking luminous plasma.

Then she saw the child.

The infant was strapped inside a cryogenics unit, unlike any other Asha had ever seen. It didn't have any of the usual hall-marks of a fully functioning commercial unit. It looked more like a piece of tech pulled straight from some non-engineer's head. It was the concept of a cryogenics chamber; frosted glass, a blurry face, coffin sized and *cold*, without any of the substance;

no energy source or generator was visible, no hydraulic stabilizer legs either, and she couldn't make out the light source that lit the unit from within, it didn't *look* like plasma—

There was a hiss. Steam billowed from the chamber. When it cleared, the child's eyes had opened, and time was skipping, *tripping* forward. Asha inhaled—

Five seconds became two, become one. An hour folded itself inside that second and shrank to make room for a week. A month halved and then pleated, collapsing the years into crinkles. A decade concertinaed into a memory, and Asha saw it all.

The child was discovered the next day by the local inhabitants of the planet. Creatures the size of transport cars covered in short white fur. They surrounded the crater and pulled open the door of the cryogenics chamber. Time blurred and shifted, and suddenly there was no crater, and the cryogenics chamber was a rusted shell of metal, and a young girl was running through the clearing. The lush green grass brushed her brown knees, and strange red flowers were clutched in her hand. One of the creatures burst out of the trees, howling and chittering, loping towards the girl. As Asha watched, the creature grew, its fur growing longer, legs lengthening and torso broadening. When she looked back at the girl, she saw that she had grown, too. She looked to be around eleven or twelve, her hair was curly and wild as a cloud, and her eyes were full of laughter. She ran back across the clearing, towards the creature who had grown up with her, and buried her face in its fur. The scene skipped and jumped, the sky darkening rapidly, and then blazing with stars. Somewhere in the trees, a fire glowed. Asha walked towards it, the crackling getting louder and louder until she realised it wasn't the popping of wood, but the sound of a community in harmony. The village was small, centred around a massive bonfire. Asha saw the girl and her friend—both older now—dancing around the flames.

The creatures watching cooed in delight, stamping their feet and whistling through their small mouths. Daylight broke, suddenly. Then a year had passed, and half of another sped by, too, and then everything slowed, and Asha was standing in the middle of a warzone.

The jungle was burning. Fighter jets zipped through the canopy above, weaving through the trees and dropping wave after wave of incendiary bombs on the village. Strangled screams and gunfire assaulted Asha's ears, smoke, ash and debris clogged the air, forcing her to pull her shirt over her mouth in an attempt to breathe without choking. The girl was being dragged away from one of the huts by a pair of uniformed soldiers. *The Consortium.* Which meant this must be . . . the Great War. One of the creatures, fur streaked with grime and dust, stumbled out of the hut. Rearing up on two legs, it swatted at the soldiers, huge paws swiping viciously at their visors.

Bang!

The creature slumped to the ground, muddy red blood leaking from a charred wound. The soldier's gun smoked. The girl screamed, a feral, inhuman scream, and thrust up her hands. A pillar of earth erupted from the ground, soaring upwards and smashing into one of the jets. Engine fuel ignited—a deafening sound splitting the sky as the girl crumpled suddenly to the floor, spasming, to reveal a soldier behind her, a baton crackling with electricity gripped in his white knuckled hand.

Then the scene folded in on itself, the burning night rearranging itself into day; the charred and smoking forest rearranging itself into the aftermath of a massacre.

The village was empty. Hulking shapes littered the ground. *Corpses.* The girl was nowhere to be seen.

Very suddenly, violently, almost, it occurred to Asha that she had been told this story *and* its prequel before. In a small one-roomed apartment, in her mother's voice, and then in a vision not dissimilar to this one, in a spaceship not a half a week ago, as she clutched onto Xavior's hand.

I don't know which planet I was born on, but I do know where I was raised, her mother had said. *I had a family who loved me, but they were taken from me.*

Bright images flashed through her mind; *a castle, a crown, holy fire. A shield, a baby's hand, a sword. A cryogenics chamber conjured with words alone.*

As her vision cleared, the world before her ground to a halt.

Smoke hung immobile in the air. The clouds stopped their furious scudding across the sky. Leaves loosened from trees stilled suddenly, floating in the air. Across the clearing, a woman watched her. Tall, dark-skinned and muscular, she stood silent and proud among the leaves, a statue wrought in obsidian. She held Asha's gaze for a few heart-stopping moments, before turning and walking away into the trees. On her back a shield flashed, bright and crystalline in the sun. Asha remembered a hilltop, and a view of a castle. *Our strength is in our understanding,* the woman had said, before. *Soon you will understand.*

Then the woman was gone, and so was the forest, and a voice was crawling its way up Asha's spine to whisper in her hear.

"Your name is Asha Akindele," it hissed. "You are eighteen years old, but you feel older, in your soul. There is something gathering around you and your company, something that you do not understand. But it has waited. Waited for a very long time."

Not one voice, Asha realised, but hundreds. All speaking in perfect harmony.

They said, "We are the forgers of peace. The harbingers of harmony."

They said, "We accept only truths. We thrive on Knowledge."

They said, "Knowledge is the Most Important Thing."

Then, there was a pause, and Asha hadn't known until that moment that quiet could *swell*. Could burst in a crescendo and expose true silence. Quiet in its purest form.

They said, "Everything you have just witnessed is true. We have granted you this knowledge as we believe it is yours to have."

Asha's heart stuttered in her chest. Xavior had mentioned a test. How could she be sure they were telling the truth? To present themselves as so dedicated to pure knowledge and fact, only to be lying to her at the same time seemed the perfect double bluff.

But there was something in the voices that made her doubt that. They practically shook with reverence. She simply *believed* them.

What does this mean? She wanted to shout. *What does it all mean?*

Oh, for god's sake, she thought, suddenly furious—with herself, with her mother, with universe. *You know what this means. You've known what this means for a while now, and you've been nothing but a coward about it. Stop hiding.*

"My mother isn't human."

And neither am I. Not fully.

The voices hummed their approval.

They said, "Asha Akindele, do you choose to remember what you have seen? Do you choose to claim the knowledge that is your right, and will be your power, your light in the shadow of ignorance?"

"Yes," she felt like she was going to cry. "I choose to remember."

They could try and wipe her mind with medicine, extract her memories with a scalpel and a torch; this was not the kind of thing you forgot.

My mother isn't human. And neither am I. Not fully.
"Well chosen," said the voices. "Welcome to Aonia."

The one to wield the shield must be afraid—we can only protect others if we truly fear what will happen if we fail.

'A Complete, Annotated History of Chasca, Including Relevant Translated Mythologies. Chapter: This Author's Informed Predictions' by I. Nisomn, ex-acolyte of the Aonian Archives.

(Archivist's note: Do you mean to imply, with these *informed predictions*, that the heroes of your legend will be made anew in our modern age? And that they will inherit the weapons of old? If so, where are they now? Do they have any idea of their greatness? How will they find out? It is . . . inconceivable. If we had not known you, we would dismiss this implication as the ramblings of a mad man. That is not to say you were not mad—you were. But only because you invariably saw that shining truth at the heart of things; a burden impossible to bear without the loss of at least a little sanity.)

Chapter Twenty-Six

[planet: none] + [location: free space] + [year: 6066]

Obi opened his eyes and saw a simpler time. It was snowing.

London was flung out beneath him, glittering and dark, the Thames winding a liquid silver path through the tangled metropolis.

He was sitting on top of St Paul's Cathedral. The corrugated turquoise metal of the dome curved away beneath him, a strong wind lifting the collar of his coat, biting and chilling and lung-aching and *home*. Tears stung in his eyes from the cold.

He wondered what year it was. The instinct was muscle memory.

Taking a deep, painfully cold breath, he pried his fingers from the railing he was clutching and let gravity pull him off the side of the dome. As he fell, the night was reduced to a blur of darkness and yellow lights, water glistening off cobbles, reflecting the stars.

He used his prosthetic arm to brace his fall, which wasn't very far—just onto the roof of the main cathedral hall—and rolled into a crouch. The eaves of the cathedral were sturdy, and he had done this countless times before. Grabbing onto the overhang of the roof, he hung for a single second, then dropped quietly past one storey of columns, their Corinthian flourishes threatening to snag on his coat. He took a moment to breathe and then he did it again, the floor meeting his feet with a muffled thud. Peering forward into the gloom, Obi smiled. The clandestine quality of the light here was the kind that lit his dreams more often than not.

London at night was a gorgeous, insidious thing. He hadn't forgotten.

Why was he here, though?

The thought slipped from his mind like smoke through his bare hands, trickling away on the breeze.

To see George, of course.

The thought didn't feel like his own, but it sounded like his. Dismissing a vague feeling of unease, he started walking.

A newspaper blustered its way towards him, caught on a gust of wind. He stopped it with his foot and picked it up. Shaking his head, he checked the newspaper's date: 10th April, 1812.

The headline stopped his heart in his chest, squeezed the air from his lungs.

PRINCE AUGUSTINE MARRIED TO GERMAN PRINCESS: GISELA OF BRUNSWICK, 8th APRIL.

He felt as though he were falling, plummeting from the edge of something jagged and into a dark and tossing sea. The paper slipped from his grasp.

Obi cursed, then swung the now blinkered direction of his thoughts violently onto the idea of Carlton House, and then to the door of George's rooms. He focused all of his will and want on that place and then he stepped forward.

When he put his foot down, he was exactly where he wanted to be. (This was not something he could normally do. He didn't question the sheer impossibility of it. *He was here to see George.*)

The door to George's rooms swung open.

Déjà vu was a rare occurrence in Obi's life, but he felt it fully then.

Wide, green eyes met his, and Obi swore his heart nearly stopped. But then he looked down at the hand that was clutching the doorframe from the inside and saw a ring, and suddenly the illusion was shattered. This wasn't a jubilant reunion. This was . . .

Well, he didn't know what this was.

George looked tired. He held his back straight, and his shoulders squared, but the dark smudges under his eyes and the tightness by his mouth betrayed him.

"Is it true?" Obi asked.

George looked so empty and absent that Obi could barely stand to look at him. Could barely stand to look away.

"I didn't have a choice." His voice was vacant.

I'm losing him, Obi thought.

"I was spectacularly drunk for it, if it's any consolation." The corners of his mouth turned down. "I'm sorry."

Obi felt light-headed.

George was mumbling to himself, "I don't want to wake up again without you. I don't want *him* to show up again and ruin everything. The way he talks, I—I can't keep . . . I don't know how long I can keep this up for." He looked down at his hands.

"Who's *him*? Wake up? What do you—oh." Obi looked around and saw the fuzzy edges of a dream. The words written on the document next to him were nonsensical, the paintings merely vague swathes of colour, and the view beyond the window dusky, uncertain twilight, when he was sure it had been the middle of the night when he'd arrived. He exhaled slowly. "This isn't real?"

"No," George replied. "Of course not. You're here. How could that be real?"

Obi felt that like a blow to his chest. He wanted to hug George to him, draw him closer and lose himself in the daze of being with him, of being close and warm with him. But a sinister voice said: *Look at him, he is destroyed. Do you really think you would make it better? Your own father didn't even love you enough to stay, and you want step back into this person's life, ruin a marriage? Maybe you two work better like this—confined to dreams.*

Obi walked away.

He watched George stumble over to his bed, muttering to himself, running his hands through wild hair, and felt guilt sinking in his stomach like a stone. Then he watched George pick up a small bottle and shake it, cursing in frustration when he saw that it was empty.

"George," Obi said, unease sweeping over him. "What is that?"

George looked up blearily. "It's medicine." Then angrily, "I don't know why you would care."

Obi walked over to him, easing the bottle gently from his shivering hands. He read the label. "George, this is an opiate." Obi fought to keep his voice calm. "Why are you taking this?"

"Because I am insane," George replied calmly. "Because I am plagued by dreams just like this one, that endeavour only to make a mockery of my most secret reflections." He leaned back, lying down on the bed, his hair a wash of darkness against the white. "I lie in this bed, next to my *wife*, and all that can be found in my mind are visions of you." His eyes were closed, squeezed shut. "If I am to be truly honest, it's been that way since I was a boy, and I don't know what that makes me. Hellbound, perhaps." He gave a low, brittle laugh—it sounded to Obi like the noise a person might make when they'd been trained out of crying at a very young age. "But I honestly think that might be the least of it." He still wouldn't open his eyes. "Where do kings go when they die? Because it can't be Heaven—that much I know."

"George, I—"

"I miss you," George said. He sounded delirious. Obi looked at the empty bottle by the bed and couldn't stand it. George held up a hand, as if to pre-empt Obi's objection. "Just let me say it. I miss you. I am half of myself without you here, and I wish—" He broke off. "I wish to know your heart, because at times I am so certain it feels as mine does. And I know that you are . . . reticent. And I understand that, and I think you have always known that I would be satisfied with stolen moments with you for the rest of my life, if they were all we might have . . . but only if I did not so adamantly believe you were deserving of much more than that. Of more than me, and what I can offer you." He sighed, opening his eyes, and staring at Obi with such a resigned, open longing that Obi felt like maybe he should draw the curtains. "So, I'll make do with dreams," George said, "and leave the loving of you to those who might do it properly."

Obi looked at the floor. He felt light-headed with George's confession, though part of him knew George had been confessing to him a little more every time he'd looked at him when they were younger—that maybe the expression George wore was so often unreadable because Obi had forgotten the language people used to say *I love you*, without actually saying it. . . . because then what?

Then it might mean that George actually cares for me, Obi thought. *Deeply. Which means that inevitably, he will leave.*

"You do know my heart," Obi said, helplessly. "I think maybe you're the only person who ever has." He didn't say, *who ever will*, because that would have been tragic. But it also would have been true.

George's eyes widened, and he stood up, walking slowly closer. "What are you saying?"

"I don't know," Obi said, and realised he was terrified. He didn't know how to do this, how to be honest about what he felt. "I just wanted you to *know*. That's all."

Then George was nodding, and slipping a hand behind his neck, and kissing him, and Obi thought maybe the gentle pressure of George's chest against his own was nearly enough to heal his heart.

The last time they'd been together like this, it had been fast and rough, George looking down at Obi from the dresser like he wanted to be put in his place. This kiss was nothing like that. It was a slow joining, the gentle, hot movement of George's mouth on his was like the rolling fall of magma from the lip of a volcano, rushing, hardening to rock and breaking open on its own forward momentum. George's mouth opened, their tongues sliding against each other, and for a few, glorious seconds, Obi couldn't think. He slid a hand under George's shirt, moved it down the small of his back, grabbing gently, pressing him closer, so that they each might feel all of the other. George's hand tightened on Obi's neck, and then he was pulling him forward, as he stumbled back, knees hitting the edge of the bed. They collapsed on top of each other, and George drew his leg up, pressing his knee against Obi's hip.

They broke apart, breathing harshly into the dim light. George brushed a hand over Obi's cheek. "I don't want to wake up."

"I'll come back," Obi whispered. "I'll do whatever it takes to get back to you." He bent forward to press their foreheads together. The cold press of George's wedding band seared into his neck. He ignored it.

George's voice was rueful, disbelieving. "I will see you soon, then."

Obi nodded. "See you soon."

Bending down to kiss him again, Obi squeezed his eyes shut.

When he opened them, he was nowhere, and he was alone. His face was flushed. His heart was racing.

The simulation.

"Obi Amadi, *Arícoaryuŋ*," said a voice, "You are barely twenty-one years old, and yet you have seen the centuries turn more times than you can count." Voices rang out in the silence. He felt the pulse of their words in the soles of his feet, in the palms of his hands. "Your heart wishes for so many things that even we cannot untangle them. You want to be selfless and strong, kind and brave. You wish to be worthy of love, you wish to be cured. All of these things are true, and yet the truest thing is this: you are afraid."

Obi bowed his head.

They said, "We are the forgers of peace. The harbingers of harmony."

They said, "We accept only truths. We thrive on Knowledge."

They said, "Knowledge is the Most Important Thing."

Then they were silent. Obi remembered; *green eyes, brown hair, a smile like the sun. A heavy heart, a golden crown—*

They said, "Everything you have just witnessed is true. We have granted you this knowledge as we believe it is yours to have."

A ring.

Obi had known it was true. He didn't know how he possibly could have known this, but he believed in intuition, especially when it came to George and the way he believed their souls had been one, once.

"Obi Amadi, do you choose to remember what you have seen? Do you choose to claim the knowledge that is your right, and will be your power, your light in the shadow of ignorance?"

He thought of George's solid warmth and the way his own almost-confession had felt to say out loud.

In the end, it wasn't much of a choice at all.

"Well chosen," said the voices. "Welcome to Aonia."

A note to my future self in this moment of clarity: all you have written is true and all you have written is important, but it is incomplete. The circle is half finished—this story has not ended, yet. But it cannot be completed at the Guild, it is too concerned with tradition. Innovation dies here, and so I must leave, find a new place. Found something new. An Order, I think. Dedicated to the fulfilment of the prophecy—to the saving of the hundred worlds.

A note, barely legible, taken from the margins of the journal of I. Nisomn. Found in his study after his unannounced departure from the Guild.

Chapter Twenty-Seven

When Asha opened her eyes, she found herself alone. She was in a small, cold room, lying on a narrow bed with her back to the wall. The room seemed to be half-cave, the walls bumpy and marked, as though the room had been carved out of the rock one chip at a time. A strange, faintly luminescent moss grew in one of the corners. She could hear wind whistling somewhere outside, and a draught blew through the room, terribly cold, chilling her skin.

Where am I? Her heartbeat was rising, pattering against her rib cage like a frightened bird. She closed her eyes, willing it to slow down. She didn't have time to panic. It didn't matter that she had no memory of waking from the simulation, or being transported to this room. That was where she was now, and she would just have to stand up and deal with it—

The door opened. Asha jumped, snatching the only thing in the room she could lift: the sheet from the bed. Maybe she could use it like a garrotte wire, or throw it in their face and run—

Tecmessa walked through the door. When she saw the sheet clenched in Asha's trembling fists, she raised an eyebrow. "And what on earth are you planning to do with that?"

Asha threw it back on the bed.

"Come with me."

333

Asha hesitated for a moment, unsure. But then she saw her mother's face in her mind's eye, and remembered why she was here. Her instincts whispered in her ear: *Trust no one. If you're smart, you'll use anything you can find in this place to help you understand your visions, and to find your mother. When you have that, you can get out of this place as soon as you can.*

"Well?" Tecmessa said, nodding to the door. Asha lowered her head, and followed the older woman, leaving the room quickly behind them in the twisting maze of corridors.

It was was freezing cold—Asha's breath came in mist, ghosting in front of her. The walls were black rock, glistening with frozen moisture, and interspersed at random intervals with jagged panels of a kind of burnished glass. It looked like they had been mirrors, once, and Asha could still make out a blurry, ghostly version of her reflection in the tarnished surfaces. Goosebumps raised the flesh of her arm, her teeth chattering. Tecmessa silently pulled a robe from inside her cloak and handed it to her. Gratefully, Asha tugged it on.

The small gesture of kindness gave her the courage to speak. "Where are you taking me?" she asked, drawing the hood up around her ears.

Tecmessa did not respond. Instead, she pushed open a grating stone door and showed Asha the end of the world.

An icy wasteland spread out before them—clouds drifted beneath the ledge where they stood, reflecting the pale purple of an early dawn sky. Mountains rose on either side, soaring into the sky like the tombstones of giants—their glassy black rock and jagged edges puncturing the horizon. Beyond the mountains, Asha could just make out an icy tundra, painted in swathes of purple and coldest blue, frost flashing pale green in the thin sunlight.

They were standing on the side of a mountain—the Guild

building with its black rock walls must have been carved out of the mountain's interior. A sickly claustrophobic feeling gripped Asha just thinking about it. All that rock just sitting on top of them.

Tecmessa nodded her head at something beneath them. From between the clouds, a narrow stone bridge emerged, stretching across the gorge in front of them. It was so thin and covered in snow that it had blended into its surroundings and Asha hadn't noticed it. It looked about wide enough for one person, or a party walking single file.

She looked at Tecmessa with wide eyes, waiting for her to reveal the real way to reach the other side of the gorge, but she was already making her way down the narrow set of stairs cut into the mountain that led to the bridge.

The thin shelf of stone glittered with ice.

With a wince, Asha followed her.

"You are being given a chance of freedom," Tecmessa said finally, when she caught up. Her calm quiet voice was almost snatched away by the wind. "The highest of us has requested your presence." She stepped out onto the bridge, feet light on the slippery surface. There were no railings—the bridge was perhaps as wide as one length of Asha's body lying down. And on either side, an immeasurable drop.

"Why?" Asha's voice was hoarse, shouting to reach Tecmessa.

"The level of energy generated by your reconstructed reality vision was anomalous, and . . . repercussive. Many of us felt it, including the Guild's leader. Relay what you saw, and if it is satisfactory, well . . ." She paused. "You will gain your freedom— here, at least, for as long as you wish. You will be treated not as an asylum-seeker but as a citizen."

A citizen. Asha could barely believe what Tecmessa was saying. There were privileges to that, even if they only applied within the walls of the Guild. This was something she could *use*.

And I'll have time, she thought, Obi's tired, beaten up face appearing in her mind's eye; Xavior's blood, splattering on the floor. *Time for them to rest. And time for me to figure out why Tecmessa was in my vision. Who Ishoal is. To take apart the computer I stole from Xesca and learn something—anything that will help me make sense of the last few weeks. That might point me in the right direction of my sister. I just need one week. One week to make my plan, and then I'll go.*

Asha took a deep, icy breath, and stepped onto the bridge.

They battled their way forward, snow blasting them from all sides. Asha huddled into her cloak and tried not to pass out whenever she caught a glimpse of the glacial ravine beneath, desperately trying not to envision what it would be like to fall.

Beneath the clouds, a frozen river carved a path beneath the mountains, its glass-like surface so blue, it seemed to glow faintly. As she stared, one of the shadows under its surface detached from the others and slowly began to glide downriver.

Asha nearly fell off the bridge when she realised it was a giant creature, swimming forwards under the ice.

Wrenching her gaze ahead, she put all the energy she had into trying to find purchase on the slick, icy ground. Snow spiralled down, hitting her face and melting against her skin, until her teeth were chattering, and the tips of her fingers were completely numb.

After what felt like an age, they stepped onto the solid ground of the other side, taking refuge in the doorway of the strange building set into the cliff face. Tecmessa knocked rapidly on the door, and it swung open almost immediately.

"Thank you," Asha gasped, stumbling into the dark passageway. But there was no one there.

They kept walking, down into the stony dark, and she got the distinct impression that they were descending into the centre of whatever building it was they were in. Out of the corner of her eye, shapes seemed to flicker in the burnished mirror glass.

"What is this place?" Asha murmured past frozen lips. Tecmessa did not reply.

Soon, they reached a nondescript door set into the end of a corridor. Tecmessa stopped. "Don't question him, don't talk back, and don't raise your voice. When you are dismissed, come back the way we came. I will meet you at the bridge."

She reached out to open the door.

"Wait," Asha said, impulsively. "When you saved us from Xesca, you said a name." She searched the woman's face for a shred of recognition. It was blank. "Ishoal."

Tecmessa's eyes darted into the darkness of the corridor, as she looked quickly around. "Do not say that name here again," she hissed. Asha took a step back. "In fact, you would do well to forget you ever heard it."

"I'm sorry—"

"You aren't. But if you run around the Guild asking questions about a man named Ishoal, you soon will be."

Asha was silent. At the last moment, Tecmessa seemed to soften slightly.

"He was an old friend, that's all. A very old friend." She shook her head, as though dispelling a memory she would have rather remained forgotten. Turning to the doorway in front of them, she pushed it open, revealing darkness. "Go," was all she said.

Compared to the bitter cold of the corridor, the room was a furnace. Asha's vision swam. The air was thick with heady incense, coils of smoke undulating through the space as though alive, so opaque they might have been made of charcoal silk.

"Hello?" she called.

"Hello." A candle flickered to life somewhere ahead of her,

throwing an impossible, monstrous shadow onto the canvas the smoke had made from the room.

Six arches loomed, spindly like spider's legs, a lumpy, bulbous body, and—

A face appeared out of the gloom, surging forward from within the smoke, on what appeared to be a neck of endless vertebrae. It stopped a hair's breadth from Asha's own. She didn't breathe. If she leaned forward just a fraction, their noses would be touching. Long white hair hung in clumps from its crown, swaying in the empty space beneath it—the empty space where its body should have been. Large, watery, eyes stared unseeing through obvious cataracts that shimmered strangely, like opals. Parallel turquoise lines ran from beneath the face's hairline, down the bridge of its nose, over its lips, and down its chin. Its skin was pale, sagging underneath its eyes as though pouches of liquid hung beneath the skin.

"How curious," the face said. "We thought you would be taller."

Asha forced herself to remain still.

"Nothing to say for yourself?" said the face, breath hot on Asha's skin. "You released unprecedented amounts of energy within our reconstructed reality simulation. We have not seen anything like it in a very long time."

Asha turned away from the face and vomited—her meal from earlier splattering onto the cold flagstones. Her heart was thudding in her chest, the sight of this creature was enough to have her considering the door, and what her chances would be like alone, out in the cold ruin.

The face tutted. "Impolite as well as unimpressive. Show some respect to your superiors."

She turned back to face it, dragging the back of her hand over her mouth. "What *are* you?"

"We are the Archivist, and you are so boring we are beginning to think we should kill you after all."

"You won't kill me," she said. "Not when you need something from me."

The Archivist's wet mouth stretched into a smile. "And who ever said that we needed something from you?"

Asha shrugged. "That's all anyone wants. To take things from other people." She looked into the Archivist's blind eyes. "And I bet you'd know all about that. Sitting here in this ruin among all these books and candles, *reading* and *thinking* when there's a war going on just outside the door." This place—seeing Tecmessa and Koshiro in their clean, warm robes and huge spaceship, talking about *diplomacy* like it was a calling and not a privilege.

"The war," said the Archivist, "is over. It has been over for one hundred years."

"You can't really believe that, can you?" she asked. "That a signed treaty could put an end to war when that same treaty created the Consortium?" She gestured around the room. "There must be something in one of these books about the cost of peace—who has to pay, and who gets to enjoy it?" She glared at the wizened face that hung in front of her. "Or maybe you'd rather those books were buried, all the better for you to sit here among relics and pretend everything is fine."

"Fighting words," the Archivist murmured. "Almost familiar in their fervour."

"What?" Asha said, wishing that for once, someone would say something that made even the tiniest bit of sense.

The face of the Archivist drew away, retreating into the folds of smoke like a snake into a craggy rock.

Asha felt ice cold and weary, and would have turned to leave, her life be damned, this whole stupid, journey be damned—*god* she was so *tired*—but Tecmessa's words rang in her ears like a portent.

Your freedom, here . . . for as long as you wish.

It was the *time* she needed, unhindered by life-threatening situations.

"Wait," she blurted out desperately into the dark. "Tecmessa said that if I— if I told you what I saw, you'd let my friends and I stay here."

There was no reply for a moment—only her, standing alone in a room of swirling smoke, distant shapes visible for mere moments before they vanished into the dark.

"And is that what you want?" came the Archivist's voice, finally. "To seek refuge among an order of shameful cowards?"

Asha flushed. "I don't feel as though I have any other choice."

"There is always a choice," was the reply. "Just as there is always a price."

She thought about Obi. All the things he'd been through with her these past few weeks, and the look in his eyes when they appeared in the ship's atrium after she'd gone back for that tech without telling him. She wondered if there'd been a moment when he had given her up for dead.

Why couldn't she do anything right?

"I'll pay it," she whispered into the empty space. "Whatever the price is, I'll pay it."

Asha had been paying prices all her life; the price for being human, the price for tentatively trusting, the price for believing that not everyone in this world was out to get her *all the time*. The price for being more than what they thought she was; the price for being less than the thing they wished she were. *So what was one more sacrifice*, she thought, *in a life filled to the brim with them?*

"Walk forward, then," said the Archivist's voice. "Walk forward and face us."

She did. Putting one foot in front of the other, she slowly made her way towards the back of the room, and the thing that sat there.

The Archivist's face was attached to a body, after all. A body with two long, long arms and four long, long legs with knobbly knees and elbows and far too many joints in between. The Archivist sat on a stack of books, legs bowed up in a crouch, the position reminding her again of an overgrown spider. Brittle looking arms were folded in front of the face—she was having trouble reconciling it with the body—fingers steepled pensively together. The face smiled.

"All we require from you is a memory," said the Archivist. "You will tell us what you saw in our reconstructed reality examination, allow us to archive the account, and we will grant you and your friends complete clemency."

"A memory? Is—is that all?"

"All?" The face echoed. "*All?*" A booming laugh echoed into the space between them, the face creasing with mirth, its mouth a gaping cavern. "Ignorant thing that you are, we will not hold that against you." Then the Archivist did move, scuttling, *springing* down from the throne, books slipping and falling, pages fluttering under the redistributed weight, until clawed toes were inches from her own, and the face was examining her again from horribly close quarters. "Knowledge is the Most Important Thing. We know that you understand this on a fundamental level, as you chose knowledge over ignorance not twenty minutes ago. And yet you ask, 'That's all?' as though a memory is nothing. As though a memory is even close to insignificant. As though your memories aren't the final pieces in a puzzle we've been playing for three hundred years." The head swung around, rolling in a full circle. "*Stupid.*"

Asha refused to flinch backwards. Instead, she swallowed rising nausea and stepped closer.

"I saw a young girl," she said. "I think she was my mother." She glanced at the Archivist's empty hands, at the elongated fingers. "You going to write this down, or what?"

The face smiled, turquoise lines stretching over wet lips. "We think we will remember just fine."

We remember how she looked, when she first came to us. A feral, half-wild thing, teeth constantly bared in what she likely thought to be mild smile. She first relayed to us her vision just after living it, and though we did not understand it, an old part of us remembered, we think . . . Remembered another feral, half-wild thing, his teeth bared in hunger for his people's lost mythos—a scholar turned apprentice, who seemed so promising before he fled into that comforting shadow.

Obscurity.

Ishoal Nisomn, we should never have let you go.

We know you believe yourself to be more soldier than scholar now, and that you stand watch over the prophecy rather than write about it . . . sentinel of the future . . . but your hero was here, you precocious child.

Just as you told us she would be.

Excerpt from the recorded notes of the Archivist.

Chapter Twenty-Eight

[planet: Aonia] + [location: The Diplomats' Guild] + [year: 6066]

After the simulation, Obi had woken lying in a dark room under soft sheets in a comfortable bed. And for a moment—one single, irretrievable moment—he had truly believed that what he had seen had been an awful dream.

Then he had taken in the black rock of the room's walls, and the rough-hewn circular window beyond which a mountain range extended, seemingly forever, into the distance. The sun was setting, casting everything into gloom.

Aonia.

It had all come back in one crashing wave.

So, I'll make do with dreams, and leave the loving of you to those who might do it properly.

Obi groaned and rolled over, smashing his head into the pillow. "No, no, *no*—"

"Erm, are you okay?"

"Eurgh!" Obi jumped, smacking his head, before turning around.

Xavior's little brother was staring at him from the doorway, a mixture of concern and fascination clear on his face. "Because 'Messa says dinner is ready, but if you're sick then I can eat yours—"

"Not sick," Obi replied quickly. Actually, he was starving. "Thank you. I'll be there in a moment."

343

Koshiro stared at him. The resemblance to Xavior was unmistakable when you got a good look at him—the same black
hair that was actually a little brown in the light, though Xavior's
was past his chin, and Koshiro's was far neater, cropped close to
his head. The pointed chin, the sparse eyebrows. But the younger
brother's eyes were so serious—dark and earnest, suspicious,
where Xavior's glittered with humour. Koshiro was shorter too,
and skinny in the way only fourteen-year-olds can be.

And I'm pretty sure he hasn't blinked in like five minutes.

Obi raised an eyebrow. "Are you okay? Can I help you?"

Clearly unable to help himself, Koshiro blurted out, "Is it true
that humans eat each other when—when they die?"

"Please get out of my room."

"Okay sorry."

Despite the precocity of Xavior's younger brother, dinner was
a subdued affair. None of them had eaten real food in weeks;
they shovelled Tecmessa's stew into their mouths like they didn't
know where their next meal was coming from. Unsurprisingly,
subsisting on a combination of long-hauler and prison rations
had the bonus effect of giving one a new appreciation for food
that didn't need to be re-hydrated in order to be consumed.
When the last of the plates were cleared, and Tecmessa had
excused herself (dragging Koshiro behind her), Obi looked
across the table at Asha. Her face was washed out, her eyes
darting from side to side as her mouth moved, like she was
muttering to herself. *What did you see in the simulation?* Obi
wanted to ask. *Was it as bad as mine?*

Oh, great, now he was thinking about it again. Resisting
the urge to gag, or find the nearest wall and slide down it in

abject agony, he settled for sighing. Deeply. *George. Married?* He wanted to think it was insane, that it was a betrayal to their relationship . . . But he should have seen it coming. He remembered George's face when he'd turned up at his residence.

I know things are different now, Obi had said. *Between us. That they have to be, because of who you are, and who I'm not. And maybe you don't feel as you used to, but I think—I think I do—*

What had George replied? *Obi, you have such terrible timing, but I do. I do.*

God, he was such an idiot.

Looking around the table to see if anyone had noticed his minor mental breakdown (they hadn't—he didn't know whether to be happy, or offended), he saw Xavior looking at Asha with concern, reaching out a hand to touch hers, before appearing to think better of it, and touching her shoulder instead.

Oh? Obi thought. *How interesting.*

"The tests can be difficult." Xavior whispered. "It's not your fault for finding them hard."

"It wasn't hard," Asha replied immediately. "I'm fine."

Obi resisted the urge to shake the poor girl. "Asha," he said gently, "we're your friends. You can tell us if you need help."

She looked back and forth between them, bewildered.

Xavior nodded. "He's right."

Asha stood, her chair scraping against the floor. Truly looking at her, anyone could tell she was exhausted. They all were. But between the dark bruises under her eyes, and the cuts and scrapes that littered her body, Asha looked like she was barely hanging on.

"I have to go." Her voice was strained. "Xavior, tell Tecmessa thank you for the meal, and for allowing us to stay. I think I— I need to sleep."

The door banged shut behind her. Xavior looked at it like a puppy might look at a person who had kicked it.

Though he hadn't thought it possible, Obi's heart sunk further—for all of them. "She'll come round eventually, Xavior. We just have to let her know we're here."

Xavior nodded, but his eyes were downcast. "I—" he sighed in frustration. "I wish there was something I could do. To make her feel better, to take some of the weight off."

"Be a friend," Obi said quietly. "I think that's what she needs right now. To know that somewhere in this godforsaken galaxy there are people who know how much she's going through. Who care."

"Of course, I care. But she's too stubborn, Obi, I swear—"

Obi wanted to laugh, but the memory of Asha, bloodstained and furious, running towards them on that rooftop wouldn't let him. "You don't know the half of it." Looking towards the door, he felt the exhaustion in his own body threatening to get the best of him. He struggled to his feet, calves aching. His head felt like it was full of rocks. "I'm going to head to bed as well." He grasped Xavior's shoulder on his way to the door. "She cares about you too, you know."

"Yeah, I know."

"I'll see you later."

"Yeah," Xavior said, his thoughts clearly elsewhere. "See you later."

Obi left the room, closing the door softly behind him.

Interesting, he thought again. *Very interesting.*

Obi sat up, blinking slowly in the dim light. A bleary glance at the clock told him he'd been asleep for six hours. It was nearly morning, but the sun had not yet risen, and the room was grey and eerie in the pre-dawn light. Unreal and alien. With its dark stone walls, and rough, circular window, it felt more like a painting of a room than a real place, and the bed was so obviously a stranger's, with its stranger's smell and too-thick pillow.

A dream had woken him, he was almost sure of it. The kind that feels so real it must be a memory in disguise. He remembered a vast field of ash. Dead trees like skeleton's fingers curling up from the earth. A scraping noise, like metal sliding over rock, sparks flying in his wake as he dragged something behind him, the hilt of it pressing into his wrist.

Suddenly, the room was too small, too dark, too much like a cave. Rubbing a hand over his face, he got out of bed. He slipped on his shoes, reaching for his coat where he had stashed it under the bed. Creeping past the locked doors of his sleeping friends, he sneaked out of the apartment.

The hallways of the Guild were deserted. Red moonlight spilling through the windows like blood, a bitterly cold wind blowing through the open windows and gusting snow through the colonnade of the inner courtyard. Obi briefly considered sitting outside, then thought better of it. *I don't want to sit on a bench and feel sorry for myself. I want to feel small. So small that my problems become small, too.*

His feet took him down the main corridor, the smooth stone floor absorbing the sound of his footsteps, so that only the noises of a great building at night remained. Wind whistled through windows he could not see, whilst the white snow-bats chittered softly in the roofs of the apse-like recess at the end of the corridor, its domed ceiling veined with white rock. When he reached it, he stood among the quiet bat noises and the gentle *drip-plink* of melting snow, and thought, *what am I, in the face of this?*

But George's pale, distraught face swam up through the gloom of his sorrow, and he didn't feel small enough.

He took the stairs down.

Below the Guild's upper levels, below the meditation rooms with their sacraria to knowledge, their books laid open on altars of black rock, below the choir halls and the observatories with their huge telescopes made of glass and alien metal, was a network of passageways, and lesser-used rooms. The windows were bigger here—so it was much colder, but also a little brighter.

Obi walked through the high-ceilinged hallways like a ghost.

How did I get here? Was all he found himself thinking. *How did I get here?*

He knew the literal answer.

Your father and mother had a baby. Your mother died, and it killed your father, but somehow, he kept breathing through the pain of a stopped heart. You grew up. He left. You got sick. And then you fell in love by accident with the worst person in the world you could have chosen if you wanted even the smallest chance of being happy. You ran away in every way a person can run. Through time, through space. Away from yourself. And it still didn't work, because you didn't like the person you were then, but you hate the person you are now. So really, it wasn't even worth it.

Trailing a hand along the black walls, he realised that the white striations weren't marbling at all, but fossils—great creatures preserved in the rock, a thousand years old. He looked at the opposite wall and saw a twenty-metre long spine, the delicate bones of a tail, fanning out behind it, flippers and fins like elongated hands, the long bones lying just as they had when this thing had perished on the ocean floor.

And now you're lying in the middle of a mountain.

He *almost* felt small enough, seeing that.

A shadow caught his eye. There was door, carved into the rock, just under the last of the spinal bones.

He walked over. The door was ajar.

Later, he would wonder if it had been left that way on purpose—if some ancient hand had reached through time, or space, descending from the clouds to push it open, just a crack, so that he might slip through it and find something to lay himself at the feet of, and feel sorry.

Placing one hand on the cool stone, he swung the door open.

At first, the space beyond was too large and strange for him to comprehend. He blinked a few times, and then, suddenly, his brain caught up with his eyes, and he could see it: a cavernous hall, great arches of stone rising into the dark that had gathered at their uppermost points like black smoke. Orange light pierced the dark at intervals, thrown up by the licking tongue of the brazier's flames. It was by the light of these flames that Obi saw the rest of the room.

A great lake spread out before him, the water so clear he could see the grey rocks at the bottom, and the pale, silvery fish that swam in the shallows, visible between the flashes of red, reflected fire that darted across its surface, cast by the braziers that burned, smokeless and bright in their stone-carved fixtures. And, stretching into the distance was a way across the water—stepping-stones like smooth pebbles, floating on the lake's crystalline surface.

Obi saw all of this. Saw that he could not make out the destination of the stone's straight path across the water. Saw the dark, and its infinite gloom. Saw, in his mind's eye, a memory, sparked by a familiar feeling. Lit like a matchstick struck against stone. Bright and swiftly burning.

You walked, one behind the other, through a cave. The shield glowed softly on Adesola's arm, lighting the way. The skeletons of leaves and

349

small animals crumbled and broke underfoot. Dandeyi's hair rippled against his back, the crown circling his brow like a band of light. The sword was so light in your hand, back then. Back when you were him.

The waves lapped the shore and whispered a name.

My name, Obi thought, nonsensically. *Once upon a time.*

Sensit.

Sword-bearer.

Obi felt the water lapping at his chest, and realised he was halfway submerged in the water of the lake.

He turned back slowly, loathe to make a sharp movement and disrupt the almost violent quiet—the ringing, expansive silence of this place. He saw his shirt and coat on the shore. His jeans were in a dark pile next to them.

I don't remember doing that, he thought, almost helplessly. *I think something is very wrong.*

The first stepping-stone was less than a metre away. Kicking over to it, he hauled himself up, water streaming off his body in great rivers, crashing into the still surface, sending ripples out into the dark.

It was colder in the air, so he began to walk in order to generate heat, stepping from stone to stone, descending deeper into the cave, leaving the light of the braziers behind.

It became colder and colder. He thought about turning back, but he had this sense, deep in his gut, that he wasn't *meant* to. So, he walked on, stepping from one stone to the next. It became like a meditation; right, left, right left, right—

His foot stepped onto nothing. Obi pitched forward, falling through the air—

He slipped under the skin of the lake without a sound.

Noise died. Light vanished. There was only this: a vast, directionless dark, in which he hung suspended, silently screaming.

And then, she came swimming toward him.

Her hair streamed behind her in slowly drifting coils, her dark skin gleaming in the places where the lace-like filigree of her armour had been torn, hanging off her like ribbons of glittering smoke. And on her arm, muscles rippling as she pulled herself through the water, was a shield. Circular and opalescent, gleaming with the lustre of the legends that had birthed it, engraved with a thousand scenes from myth that Obi had no hope of deciphering.

When she reached him, her voice rang out in his mind, deep and clear as the lake in which they were suspended.

Do you feel small enough now, Obi Amadi?

He was frozen—whether in shock, or with the cold, or due to forces outside of his control acting on his body, he did not know. He tried to breathe, couldn't. Tried to scream, couldn't open his mouth. Even his eyes wouldn't blink. They could only stare at the woman in front of him, the woman whose face looked so familiar—

Do you remember? Came her voice again. *Not yet? Alright. I will show you.*

Flashes of gold lit up the darkness around them.

There were three of us.

Obi watched as streams of golden light coalesced into images.

A woman, a man, and someone else, stood in front of him, shining against the darkness of the lake.

We were created to be Heroes. And we were, until we died, and the first prophecy was complete. The Second Prophecy was this: we would walk the earth again, re-incarnated in time of great need. The skin of the world would split into our doorways, and through them we would step, seeking our mortal counterparts. The Third Prophecy has been the bane of our existence—never arriving. But it is here now, and so, therefore, are we.

We? Obi thought, somehow knowing she would hear him.

Myself and my Heroes-in-arms.
Sensit and Dandeyi.
But one of them has wandered off the path.

The man made of golden light split from the others, walking away from them.

My brother, Sensit. He has been corrupted. His heroism fouled with ambition, with greed. It is not his fault. His mortal counterpart, of the Second Prophecy, the one that passed a hundred years ago when Chasca still stood—he did this to him. Became so ugly and evil that my brother's own soul—so closely tangled with that of his mortal charge—began to deteriorate. The gold of valour giving way to the tarnished grey of pride.

Now all my brother wants is worship, and he has entered your world, through a door of his own making, to get it.

The golden man drew a sword from the air and slashed a doorway into it, cutting through the fabric of the world with the same ease as someone slicing paper. Or skin.

He will destroy your city and then your world, if you do not stop him. And you are the only one who can.

Obi wanted to grab her and shout, '*What do you mean?*', but then the images of golden light danced and rearranged themselves. Obi watched as Sensit stepped through his makeshift door and into—

No.

One armoured foot met the cobbled street, greaves flashing in the low light. St Paul's Cathedral rose up in the distance, its ball and lantern piercing the sky, the smooth curve of its dome towering above the other buildings.

The back of Obi's neck prickled.

My brother Sensit sought out the soul of his mortal counterpart and landed on yours. But you aren't like us, or anyone else, are you? Your soul was split.

352

He followed the fragment of your soul that would grant him the most power. The one you Anchored in London. The gold ropes of power that hung around her disintegrated into luminescent powder that swirled around the room, forming huge, kinetic shapes—*a horse rearing on its hind legs, a clock face striking the hour, a crown falling to the floor, two hands that Obi had glimpsed in a dream once, straining towards each other, turning gold*—which then crumbled back into the currents of shining dust that eddied furiously around the figure at the centre of it all. Then the dust halted, hanging like so many stars in a vast universe of which the lost Hero was the centre.

Obi stood, transfixed, hyperaware of everything; the faint striations of light piercing the lake's depths, the cool water brushing his stomach, and the faint feeling that had pursued him ever since he'd returned to London, only to leave once more. The feeling of the timeline narrowing, focussing, converging on one point. *This point, I think.*

He closed his eyes.

George's face stared back at him from the blackness, reconstructed in the god's golden dust. He was looking past Obi, so Obi turned around, and came face to face with his father.

So it was true. He was alive.

"Dad?"

But his father couldn't hear him.

Then the darkness swallowed George and Alarick, and replaced them with the Hero, Sensit. Obi watched as he stepped out of a blazing rip in the air and ran towards a palatial mansion. Carlton House. Sensit disintegrated and reformed behind Obi, with a box in his hand—*the* box, the one with Obi's soul inside—and a ring on his finger. Then he looked upward at the Hero's face, but the body attached to the hand with the ring on it belonged to George, and he was staring at the ring with two faces. One of his faces was blank, so blank he could have been carved out of marble. The other face was screaming, eyes bloodshot, brow furrowed, a valley of fury in the crease between his eyebrows.

Obi turned away and Sensit rose up out of the dark water, seven feet tall, forming slowly out of the golden dust until they were eye to eye. Then he blinked, and the Hero's plan stretched out in front of him, as clear and obvious as though it had been written in his own hand.

He is only toying with them, Adesola said. *Leading them on a chase throughout the city while biding his time. They think they have him cornered, but he is far more slippery than even I anticipated. He will wait until the midsummer solstice, and then he will turn the people of the city into his subjugates. He will force worship upon them until they have torn down the old monuments and built temples to him in their place. Once he has that city under his control, he will move onto the next and the next . . . until the whole world loves him. That is all he has ever wanted. To be loved.*

Obi pictured a future where a crazed man forced a religion onto millions of people who had never asked for it, never wanted it, while taking away their freedom—freedom of speech, freedom of thought, freedom of faith—turning them into mindless slaves instead.

Asha's face flashed into his mind—her expression when she described the monotony of her life. The pain and degradation she suffered as a result of having her basic rights stripped away due to a lack of citizenship. He imagined being asked to worship the man who had done that. Tried to imagine what it might be like to be forced.

"He has to be stopped."

Yes, he does.

Your father and your lover and the city which means the most to you will burn if you do not help me find my brother and save him.

"And if I refuse?"

Sensit will need an immense source of pure power to facilitate this plan. Due to the huge amounts of energy your Anchoring required when it latched onto a person instead of a place, the largest, most volatile power source in the city is the piece of your soul that you left behind. The piece of your soul you left tangled up in the blood of the Prince Regent. I believe my brother's plan is to sacrifice him in order to release the energy he requires. But a soul's power is strongest when it is given willingly. Sensit will convince the prince to offer up his own life. And, though his own choices are driving him insane, he is nothing if not convincing.

The bottom of Obi's world fell away. Hollowness spread from his chest to his heart, from his lungs to his head. He couldn't breathe. Couldn't think.

Except—

"What do you mean, tangled up in his blood? I Anchored my soul to London. The fragment of my soul that I left there is tied to the *city*. A place. Not a person. What are you talking about?"

Adesola looked at him blankly. *Your soul is tied to Prince Augustine George Frederick of the United Kingdom of Great Britain and Ireland. Defender of the Faith, heir to the throne of Hanover, heir to the Dukedom of Brunswick-Luneburg—*

"Please, stop." Obi's heart felt ready to stutter out of his chest and fall, beating and bloody, onto the floor. "I don't understand. That—that isn't possible. The Book clearly states a Guide must Anchor their soul to a *time and place*. Well, I Anchored mine to London in 1802. That's where it will always be, because that's how this works."

I'm afraid not, Adesola replied, unsmiling. *There are things that I know to be completely, infallibly, true, and this is one of them. Prince Augustine is your Anchoring Place.*

355

Obi felt sick. His heartbeat thudded through his body. The darkness of the lake pressed in on every side.

Sacrifice him, Adesola had said. That meant *kill.*

"No," Obi said. "I—*No.*"

Adesola nodded. *You can stop it. You have to stop it. Without my brother vanquished, and returned to his normal state, the prophecy cannot be fulfilled. But you can only stop it if you return to London and face whatever you find there with a Hero's heart. But first there is something else you must do.*

"What?"

The Emperor has a weapon. A planet-killer. The prophecy dictates that it must be destroyed, before the next stage can begin. You must accompany Asha to A'lkari and see to it that one of you destroys it.

"Why?"

Because that is what the prophecy demands. And it is how you will go home. Currently, the prophecy forbids you from leaving this time—you have felt this. But if you fulfil what is foretold, the barrier will lift. You will be able to travel once more.

Obi remembered the moment he arrived in this future. He'd tried to leave immediately, but something had thrown him back.

Could this really be the reason? A prophecy stopping him from leaving until he had done—what? Fulfilled his fate?

Obi shook his head. "I'm not going to put my friends' lives in danger because you appeared to me in this lake and told me to do it. If what you say is true, then George needs me. My father needs me. But Asha also needs me—I can't let her walk into this alone, because I'm off, trying to find the Emperor's weapon and destroy it."

Adesola's bright eyes narrowed.

"So, I will help my friend, and then I will leave. I don't need to fulfil a prophecy to get my cure. I can use that to get home." He shook his head. "I'm sorry that I'm not the person that you want. But if you really knew me, you'd know I'm kind of a disappointment. I'm not a hero. I'm sorry."

He felt himself start to drift, away from Adesola, towards the dim light above.

The last thing he heard before he broke the surface was Adesola's voice, calm and terrifying, echoing in the dark.

"You might not be a Hero yet. But you will be."

There will be a touch of the divine in the story, when history repeats itself. The prophecy speaks of a goddess, and I can only assume this goddess will be Mother's counterpart. A sternly guiding hand. A force for good. Though, not always to be trusted.

'A Complete, Annotated History of Chasca, Including Relevant Translated Mythologies. Chapter: This Author's Informed Predictions' by I. Nisomn, ex-acolyte of the Aonian Archives.

Chapter Twenty-Nine

[planet: Aonia] + **[location: The Diplomats' Guild]** +
[year: 6066]

Asha did not know much about books, other than the fact she needed to find one.

It was night. She crept through the cavernous corridors of the Order's strange headquarters, her path illuminated by the bobbing spheres of light that floated in the hallways after dark, like miniature stars burning in the blackness of space. Keeping close to the cold stone wall, she ducked in and out of shadows, making her way to the enormous, gilded doors that led to the library.

It was time to take back control. Ever since she had left Gahraan, things had been happening *to* her. She felt like a puppet, or a rag doll, thrown from each insane scenario to the next. Meeting Obi, going to prison. Meeting Xavior, *going back to prison.* Barely escaping from Xesca with her life, then being thrown into her meeting the Archivist. And throughout it all, the events of her vision; each disorientating and horrible instance in which some image from it had seemed to leap from her mind and become reality. It was like walking through a dream. Like stepping into the pages of a story she'd already been told.

And what's worse is, I could have known that all of this would happen, if I'd just paid attention to the vision when I saw it weeks ago, the first time. When the Sentinel looked at me and started all of this. I can't keep being taken by surprise like a helpless child. I can't be scared anymore.

I have to find the next thing in the sequence. Before it finds me.

The library doors slid open with a faint hiss, their heavy wooden frames gliding along invisible tracks until they disappeared into the walls on either side, revealing the library.

The library was—much to Asha's surprise (not!)—a cave.

The walls were the same pure white stone she had seen in other rooms on this level, with the smoothness of marble and the reddish pink veins of iron and feldspar. When the globular lights drifted past certain sections, she could swear she saw veins of gold gleaming, too.

At this hour, the library was almost deserted. The only other patrons were faint noises in the distance—a low muttering, the scraping of a chair leg on white rock. But Asha had no hope of seeing them unless she bumped into them by accident—the library was as good as a maze. Carved directly from the rock, the stacks soared into the air, flowing seamlessly from the ground and back into the ceiling, stretching up into the soft-lit gloom of the cavern's roof, endless and mesmerizing. There had to be millions of books here. And not just books—the library was a historical repository of all kinds of knowledge. Ancient technologies preserved in glass cases decorated the entrance hall—whilst pre-historic pieces of fern and bone fossilised in alien rock were mounted on the walls. The first stories ever committed to physical material. Pedestals with faint spotlights trained on them from some invisible source displayed Artefacts so old and strange that Asha barely knew how to look at them, never mind how to figure out what they actually were.

Beside the entrance, a sheaf of papers sat on a shelf. Maps. Asha snatched one off the shelf and opened it up. The scroll unrolled past her feet, hit the ground, and then kept unrolling for a few metres. Locating the history section, she took note of a warning printed next to it. '*History, our most popular section, takes three days to cross on foot. Bring correct supplies.*'

"What the . . .?" she shook her head. Making her way to one of the faintly glowing screens by the first row of stacks, she let it scan her face, verifying her access rights, before swiping up to the search bar.

'*Chasca,*' she typed. And then, just to see what would happen, '*Ishoal*'. The page loaded. And loaded. And loaded.

After a few minutes, she was beginning to give up hope. Maybe if she removed one of the search terms, she could have better luck. She reached out to clear the search.

The page loaded. Asha sucked in a breath. A single hit. She looked at the title. It appeared to be a history of Chasca. There was no picture, or description. Just a section title and a number: 992. *Good thing I already know what it looks like.* Her head began to throb, just like it always did when she recalled the vision. Gritting her teeth, she ignored it. *Focus, Asha. What did you see?* She'd seen her own hands, turning the pages of a book by candlelight, the words written in an alien script. The shape of the words had been mesmerising. Like no language she had seen before.

Until her vision on the *Stayanax*.

That was the key—that was how she'd known the book she'd seen had to be related to Chasca. To the vision of her as a queen. To that woman, Adesola. Maybe it held the answers to all of this. Surely, she wouldn't have foreseen it if it wasn't important.

Squinting at the screen, she checked the reference number against the sections on the map. She saw it wasn't even in the history section—but in Myths and Legends of Dead Civilisations, just under an hour's walk away. She could do that. Next to the maps, a crate of small, handheld devices labelled, '*Use to access digital copies,'* stood, unattended. Snatching one up, she shrugged to herself. Who knew what she might need? Then, with a deep breath, and a wary look into the murky gloom ahead, she set off.

Forty minutes later, Asha was shivering. She had been tramping through the library while the sun had set, and now the large cavern was darkening, as the windows showed only a dark night sky, and the overhead evening lights took their time to turn on. The temperature was dropping too, for some reason, and more than once she was certain she saw something scurry inbetween the shelves.

Finally, she turned the last corner, arriving at the section on lost planets and their ancient civilisations. This stack was dusty, the bookshelf itself showing signs of erosion. The book closest to Asha was in terrible condition, spine peeling off like a lip of fungus hanging from a tree trunk. Praying she would find what she needed in good condition, she hurried down the aisle, eyes scanning spines and peeling labels. Luckily, the books were organised alphabetically.

"C for Chasca," she murmured. "Can't be too hard." She scanned the shelves.

Then scanned them again.

Nothing. There was absolutely nothing.

Maybe it had been wrongly re-shelved.

Stepping closer, she knelt down. She would search the whole shelf. Top to bottom. She was not walking out of this place without that book. Eyeing the place where it should have been, she looked from the number in her hand, and back to the shelf. The book definitely wasn't there.

Wait a moment.

Slightly further along the shelf than she anticipated two volumes leaned against each other at an angle.

She walked over. This was the place. Neither book was her book, but the numbers on their peeling spines read: 991 and 993. Hers was 992.

Briefly, Asha imagined running all the way back to the librarian's desk and beating the hell out of him. The book had clearly been taken by someone else. Her whole journey had been pointless.

She peered into the gap, trying to guess if the space left behind roughly matched the large book she'd seen in her mind.

That was when she saw it. Carved into the white stone of the shelves—a triangle with a circle at its centre.

Asha froze. Reaching out a hand, she brushed her fingers over the grooves. They seemed imperfect, and old. Like a long time ago, someone had chipped away at the stone with knife. Acting on impulse, she pushed on it.

With a great creaking groan, the shelf in front of her began to move. Sliding heavily a metre or so the left, white dust filtered into the air as the rock of the shelf ground against the floor.

Asha gaped.

In front of her was a slim, dark passageway that descended beneath the shelves. Beneath the library. *Into the mountain.* The air coming from it was cool and smelled like damp stones and clear water.

She heard Obi's voice in the back of her mind. *Please tell me you are not about to walk into a disgusting, though admittedly intriguing, hole. Tell me that's not what's happening.*

Sorry Obi, she thought, before gritting her teeth, and walking into the tunnel.

The passageway grew slimmer and slimmer the further down into the dark she descended. Her breath came out in clouds, harsh in the quiet. Distantly, she thought she could hear water dripping.

Claustrophobia squeezed at her stomach, she had to force her breathing to stay even as the tunnel got narrower still. Soon, she was walking sideways, rock scraping against her chest and back as she pulled herself through.

Then something changed—she couldn't pinpoint it exactly. Maybe it was the quality of the sound—echoing more, like it had reached a bigger space. Or maybe it was the air—growing more and more dusty the further down she went.

The tunnel was squeezing her from all sides now. She reached out a hand to grab the wall, and pull herself forward—

But her hand flailed into nothing. Asha stopped. She was pressed between two great slabs of rock. She couldn't turn her head to see what was coming, couldn't bend down and touch the floor to find out if there even *was* a floor beyond her next step. But there was no turning back now. She took a breath, and stepped forward.

She fell.

Almost immediately, her hands connected with the floor beyond the passageway.

Sighing in relief, she lifted her head with a groan, and looked around.

It was lighter here—fine cracks in the rock of the ceiling allowing thin shafts of sunlight to pierce the darkness.

It was a small room, carved out of stone, with nothing inside it but a pillar, waist-height—illuminated by a beam of light that fell across it, right at the room's centre.

And on the pillar, rested a book.

Struggling to her feet, Asha stood at the entranceway for a moment. Her heart pounded. The gold on the spine was the same as the gold on the spine of the book from the vision. The script the same script that she had seen all those weeks ago.

She approached the pillar like one would approach a cornered wolf.

Hesitating, she allowed her fingers to hover over the cover. She almost didn't want to touch it. Every time she'd seen an image from her vision, it had been followed almost immediately by tragedy, and she'd had to move on—to go somewhere new. And Aonia was comfortable. She knew she had to find her sister, knew she had to save her mother—it was the only thing she wanted. But she was so tired.

Sighing, she slid the book off the low column of rock, resisting the urge to cough as she blew the dust off it, clouding the air in great plumes like smoke.

The pages were wafer thin, so delicate they were almost translucent. And the *script* . . . Asha felt huge and ungainly even looking at it. The letters swooped and flew, looping together like wrought iron, both jagged and seamless all at the same time. Annotations were scrawled around the edges, messy and inconsistent. Her heart beat a ferocious rhythm in her chest; she yearned to read this text, to not only learn its secrets, but know them, too. It felt imperative, somehow. She turned a page, and a piece of paper drifted out, falling to the floor.

She picked it up. A drawing.

Scrawling handwriting had titled it: *A Meeting of Three*.

Asha held the paper to one of the brighter beams of sunlight, trying to make out the faces on it. When she did, her heart nearly skipped a beat.

Three people stood in a grey wasteland, dead trees decorating the horizon. All three wore a kind of engraved armour. So thin and ornate it looked like lace—made of metal, or crystal, or an impossibly delicate combination of both.

The woman named Adesola stood, tall and proud, her dark skin gleaming, the shield resting on her right arm like it weighed less than air. The skin around it was littered with pale scars. Next to her, stood a brown-skinned man whose grin remined Asha, somehow, of Obi. Loose red curls fell to his ears. He was laughing, leaning on an ornate sword like it was an extension of his body. Slightly apart from the other Heroes, someone else stood, slim and statuesque. Jet hair fell down their back in sheets like heavy rain, whilst their solemn blue eyes glittered under a pale brow upon which a crown sat, like a circle made of starlight.

Asha traced her finger over the image of Adesola and remembered standing next to her, inside a dream. And that man, with the long hair, he had been on the mural—embracing Adesola. Kissing her.

How is this possible?

From her pocket, she withdrew the small device she had taken from the crate by the Library's entrance, and held it over the ancient volume, watching as it scanned the number on the back, and loaded the digital copy, translated into Universal Standard.

A Complete, Annotated History of Chasca, Including Relevant Translated Mythologies by I. Nisomn read the spine.

A message flashed up: *retrieving translation from the personal library of the Archivist.*

Asha stopped breathing.

A photograph greeted her. It was simple, and judging by the black and white, incredibly old. It must have been taken of the author when he was a young man. He was handsome—long brown hair, tied low at his neck, some of it escaping to curl by his jaw. Dark eyes, a serious mouth. Human-looking, Asha noted. Just like the Chascans had been. But he would be long dead by now.

Her eye caught on the introductory paragraph:

Reader, be wary of all you read within these pages. I began this work clear in mind and sound in soul, but now, when it is done, I find myself scarcely able to recall my reason for starting at all. Is this a fiction, spawned from my own imaginings, or is it indeed, fact? I think the latter, as I was never much gifted at the spinning of stories. I was a scholar, once. I had a home, too, if the old diaries bearing my name are to be believed. I fear now I have become a fanatic, though many would say there is little difference between the two, and I am inclined to agree. Read on, then, and believe what I have written, or don't. But, above all, you must remember that so much of this story we are living has not yet come to pass.

There were notes, scrawled all over the text, written in a cypher unreadable to Asha. But there was only one person who could have annotated this text.

Retrieving translation from the personal library of the Archivist, the database had said.

The sense of foreboding that had followed Asha from the *Styanax,* to the Archivist's smoky room, to the library where she now stood, intensified, raising the hair on her arms.

She turned to the first page, and began to read. As she crouched there, devouring the words in the damp dark of the cavernous library's underground room, on a planet so very far from home, several disparate and terrifying thoughts solidified themselves in her mind. They became the same thought, the same truth, solid and inescapable, just like the future had been when she'd stared into the Sentinel's eyes and seen it.

As it turned out, the history of Chasca wasn't a history at all, but a myth. In the beginning, anyway.

And it went like this:

Long ago, before our civilisation had given this planet a name, having lost the name it had been given by the people who nearly killed it, Chasca was on the brink of dying. The ancient cities lay in ruins, their old technologies and once-green metropolises half-submerged by the sea. Sun shone on the tundra, whilst snow blanketed the deserts. The suns burned like dead, red eyes in the face of the sky. Grey ash fell and fell and fell, disappearing whole mountain ranges under its steady, submergent descent.

And underneath it all, blackened and burned but still alive, was our planet. It is said that in the silence before salvation, you could hear her dying breaths. Great gusts of dusty air that rushed through forests, uprooting their ecosystems; heavy sighs blew tsunamis into still water; ragged gasps shifting tectonic plates so that they bumped gently into one another and ripped deep trenches in her lithosphere.

But there was hope. Despite the advent of this apocalypse, there was hope.

From the last of the life that glimmered within her, from the rock and ash of its surface, from the magma of its mantle and the last of the magic at its core, three things were created.

We will call them Heroes.

"You will usher in a new age of prosperity. Of new life," they were told by the planet, who was their mother. "You will make ready for a new chapter in this planet's history. A golden age, unlike any that has been seen before, or will be seen after. The world I speak of does not yet exist, but you must save it. You must save this world by creating it." To each of them, she gave a weapon, as oftentimes, violence is a necessity when throwing off the chains of evil, though it pains many to admit this is true.

A sword. A shield. A crown.

So, the Heroes took up their arms, nodded in acknowledgment of the task that lay ahead, and began.

Three Heroes. One task: save the world.

This was the First Prophecy.

Many years passed. They did their work, and it was good work, and as they toiled, fighting the forces that threatened to overwhelm their planet and kill it, they had many adventures. They laughed and smiled for the happiness of their task, as it was great and beautiful. But they cried many tears of bitter hatred for it, too, as it was hard.

In the end, they succeeded though it cost all of them their lives. The cracked crystal of their bodies was subsumed into the earth that had birthed them, and from these remains, grew three doors of gold—great archways that led from the mortal realm they had saved, to the place they had gone after death. The place where they waited.

Their mother blessed their departure with these words:

"You will be back. This world will need its Heroes. I have made a place for you to wait, in the void between worlds, just behind the skin of this one. When the world cries out for its saviours three, you will find them, guide them. They will be you, and you will be them. And your souls will become one and the same. They will speak to you in dreams, see you in their reflections on still water, and they will know you are coming."

"When they call, screaming into the perilous dark for an answer, it is you that will answer."

This was the Second Prophecy.

Asha's heart thudded inside her chest like a drum.

The Third Prophecy is the last, and worst of them all.

It foretells a tyrant, with a great weapon. It warns that our holy objects, the crown, sword, and shield, having been lost, must be recovered. And it foretells that the fate of all worlds rests on the shoulders of our chosen three. For they alone have the power to save, or to destroy us all.

Asha ran through the library, the old book half hanging out of her bag as she sprinted down the slim corridors made by the shelves.

She burst into the foyer, and took a hard left, walking as fast as she could down the corridor that led in the opposite direction to Tecmessa's apartment. Because she wasn't going there.

The words of the book swam in her mind, repeating themselves over and over in a choir of whispers that sent chills down her arms, and anxiety jolting through her chest.

Before she knew it, she was at the door to the bridge. Snatching an outdoor cloak from a hook by the door, she pulled it on, shoving the door open with all her might.

The mountain range at night was eerie—mountains loomed, impenetrable crags of darkness standing tall against the sky. Snow fell, gently and steadily, muffling all noise.

Asha crossed the icy path along the bridge in a haze, staring rigidly ahead as her thoughts careened from one conclusion to the next, so many moments of the past few weeks taking on a new meaning.

Alighting on the other side, she strode up to the door and banged three times, just as Tecmessa had. Nothing. She banged again. Nothing.

Around her, the snow was picking up. For the first time, she doubted herself.

No. They will see me.

She was lifting her hand to knock for the third time when the door swung open. Storming through it, she walked down the corridor, all the way to the end.

Smoke curled out from under the door to the Archivist's room.

Asha pushed on it, and to her great surprise, it creaked open, revealing the dark cavern beyond. She gulped. They had obviously been expecting her. There was no other way she would have got this far unobstructed otherwise.

"Why did you want to record my vision?" she said quietly into the silence. Then louder, "*What did you take from me?*"

No reply from the silent gloom.

Asha felt her fury rising. "I didn't know what I'd seen, then. I didn't understand it. And you took it from me. No. *I gave it to you* because I didn't know any better. I thought it was nothing. But this isn't nothing," she yelled, brandishing the book. "This is—" she barely even knew how to articulate what it was. "This is—"

"The ramblings of a madman, nothing more," came the Archivist's voice. "Or so we thought, until you turned up." That strange voice seemed to come from everywhere and nowhere, all at once. Asha wheeled around, turning again and again, peering through the smoke, trying to find him. Her foot hit a pile of books, and they thudded to the ground.

"Watch out. Those are valuable. Unlike that glorified diary that you hold in your hands."

"But it must be valuable. You wrote all over this thing. Why?" She gritted her teeth. "Tell me the truth this time. Who is Ishoal?"

A laugh, echoing off the walls. Asha tilted her head. That noise had come from her right. She edged closer, watching for obstacles out of her peripheral vision. Dodging another precarious pile of books, she listened out for more sounds. *Talk*, she thought. *Get them to talk.*

"Did you know him? Did he work here?"

"Knew him? We took Ishoal in when he was a refugee, running from the ruins of a dead planet. We taught him everything he knows."

The ruins of a dead planet. That has to be Chasca, Asha thought with a thrill. Then she heard the last part of what they'd said.

"Knows?" Asha murmured. Then, louder, "He's alive?" She manoeuvred her way past an old chair, draped in a translucent cloth, and ducked under an archway made of books that appeared out of the smoke so quickly she was surprised she hadn't walked right into it.

"We assume so. Those Chascans live long lives. Too long if you ask us. And, after he left the Guild, disappearing into the night like a thief, he sent us a letter. Something about waiting for the end of the world. What did he call himself? A soldier? A scout? No that can't be right. Whatever it was, he said he was waiting for the prophecy to start, so that he could help the chosen ones, guide them, when the time came. Still bitter about the last time, we suppose."

The Archivist's voice was getting closer and closer. Then, through the smoke, Asha saw them, hunched over something, pulling off handfuls of it with the claw-like hands at the end of each one of their spindly spider's legs, and shovelling it into their mouth, the long spine curved over to get closer to the meal.

The Archivist continued speaking through the mouthfuls. "We recorded your vision because it was the first time any of Ishoal's ramblings had manifested true proof in real life. The prophecy he spoke of was terrifying. Truly. If it does come along, we wish to be prepared. We would not interfere with such a thing. But Knowledge must be known. Ishoal believed that, once." They sounded almost regretful. "He wrote that this prophecy was the final one. The one that signalled the end of the world—and not just of theirs. Of all of them. We don't know anything about it beyond that, and other, vaguer things he mentioned." Another wet tearing sound. "We don't know how you fit into it, yet. But you must. When Ishoal left the Guild, he burned all of his work. Set a match to his papers and closed the door to his study. Only a charred room remained by the time we discovered it. A charred room, and this." Metal scraped across the floor. A strange looking instrument slid into view. It looked almost like a triangular compass, with a needle in the middle that was whirring in all directions. Like it had been de-magnetised. Asha picked it up. The glass was still blackened slightly from the fire.

"What is this?"

"We believe it was a piece of equipment, built by Nisomn himself, that was able to detect the energy released by prophetic activity. When you strapped yourself into the simulation, all three needles started to behave in a way they never had before." As the Archivist spoke, Asha scrubbed her hand across the charred glass, scratching off the ash with her thumbnail. "That's why we recorded your vision. None of our scholars have been able to predict how it works. You can keep it. It is of no use to us here."

Asha's scraping had revealed two more needles. Both whirring round and round in the strange way the Archivist had mentioned.

But, as she watched, each needle began to slow down. Until the whirring turned to slow ticking, and then the revolutions stopped.

Two of the needles pointed vaguely east, in the direction of Tecmessa's apartment.

The other one pointed directly at her.

"He told me you'd pass through this place," came the Archivist's quiet voice, as Asha turned, heart thudding, ice in her veins, and stumbled towards the door, compass in pocket, head spinning. "I did not believe him. I know now I was wrong."

Enough is enough, she thought as she ran from the room. *I can't do this on my own. It's time to tell the others everything.*

The strength of the three Heroes will lie, above all in their unity. Their ability to act as one body, with one mind, and one goal. Free from secrecy, jealousy, and lies. They must trust one another, or there is no hope for the rest of us.

'A Complete, Annotated History of Chasca, Including Relevant Translated Mythologies. Chapter: This Author's Informed Predictions' by I. Nisomn, ex-acolyte of the Aonian Archives.

Chapter Thirty

**[planet: Aonia] + [Location: The Diplomats' Guild] +
[year: 6066]**

Asha made her way back to Tecmessa's apartments in a daze,
the compass clutched in shaking hands.

What did any of this mean?

First, on the *Stayanax*, she'd touched Xavior and seen a story
like something from a children's tale—a queen, a country at war
with itself, three young heroes, and a prophecy.

But that world had ended. She'd seen it. Seen it in the simulation, when she'd watched Tiwa, the queen of Chasca, give
birth to a baby, and send it out into the cosmos. A baby she
was sure had been her mother. The heir to the Chascan throne.
Then Iyanda had been captured, and brought to Gahraan, but
not before she'd had a child. Asha's sister. Who had been taken
by the Emperor.

And now, there was talk of a prophecy. A final prophecy.
Just like the one she'd heard in her vision. Not to mention that
Xavior had seen her and the warrior Adesola in his dreams.
And when Asha had met Obi, all those weeks ago, she'd shaken
his hand and seen a golden light and thought, *I know you. I've
always known you.*

She stopped, leaning against a wall, her breaths coming faster
and faster. How was any of this possible?

The memory of her mother's voice rang out inside her mind:

Find your sister. Find out where we came from. That's the key.

"The key to what?" she mumbled, frustration and exhaustion causing tears to well up behind her eyes. Had her mother known all this time? And kept it from her, just to protect her?

The importance of her mission threatened to crush her now, heavier than ever. If she didn't save her sister, she would never be able to talk to her mother again. Never get the chance to ask her what was happening.

She barely wanted to go back and see the others—she would have to tell them. Everything. Reveal all her suspicions, lay out all the puzzle pieces she'd been accumulating over these past weeks.

But how do you look someone in the eye and say, *I think we might be Heroes. I think the fate of the hundred worlds might soon come to rest on our shoulders, and I think we've fought together before, hundreds of years ago, when the galaxy was younger, and so were we.*

She felt so small and pathetic, in these ancient corridors of stone, so far from Gahraan and the box she called home. In that moment, she would have returned there in an instant just to feel like she knew where she belonged. So that someone could tell her what to do, and she could do it, without thinking. Without questioning her place in the universe, or the blood that ran in her veins.

The sun was coming up. Through the bare arches of stone, snowflakes flurried, the pale winter sunlight piercing the grey with soft violet. She sighed. Xavior and Obi would be furious with her for not telling them everything sooner. Xavior knew about the vision on the *Stayanax* because he'd been there, but she had been hesitant to tell Obi. Ever since their first night there, he'd been distant, like he was wrestling with his own problems. And she didn't want him to think of her as weak, or crazy. They had grown to rely on each other these past few weeks—she needed him to trust her, to be able to count on her. She hadn't wanted to put all that in jeopardy. And Xavior . . . her stomach flipped just thinking about it. What would he think of her, arriving at his home, charred compass in one hand, an ancient book in the other, talking about the end of the world? Would he care about what she had say? Especially after how she'd talked to him at dinner last night?

And why did she care so much about his opinion in the first place?

Arriving at the door to the apartment, she paused for a moment outside to breathe. Then she gritted her teeth and placed her palm on the scanner. The doors slid open with their usual faint hiss.

She tip-toed in. It didn't look like anyone was awake, thank God.

"You're up early," said a voice. Xavior was stood in the doorway to his bedroom, still in the shirt and shorts he had slept in, his hair sticking up at the back.

Asha blinked. She wasn't ready for this, for him.

He raised an eyebrow. "What's in your bag?"

"Library book."

"Cool—" he said, just as she blurted out, "Look, I'm sorry about last night. I was tired, and I didn't mean to be rude. There's just been . . . a lot going on."

He frowned. "Asha, it's okay. I get it. I mean—I don't get it. But what happened on Xesca was terrifying. And you can't expect yourself to be okay, after something like that."

"I'm fine." She hated the way his eyes softened.

"Asha, you don't need to act like it doesn't bother you." His expression changed, closing off. *No.* Why did she keep doing this? "Wait, Xavior, no—" She walked past him, into his room

376

and sat on his bed, motioning for him to join her. "Please, come and sit. I'll talk to you."

Warily, Xavior shut the door, and joined her. Immediately she wished she'd picked a less intimate place to do this. Being alone with him always made her stomach do flips. She took a deep breath. "I just found something—read it, in this book, that makes me wonder if maybe I actually died back on Xesca, and entered an alternate reality." Her breath came shallowly, and she felt vulnerable in a way she never had before in front of anyone. "If I tell you something, will you hear me out before telling me I'm crazy?"

Xavior nodded. He reached out briefly, as though moving to cover her hand with his, but thought better of it. The visions hadn't stopped, and now would be a terrible time for the past to rush in and spirit her away.

"I found this book in a secret room under the library, searching for information on the planet from my vision. Chasca." Xavior nodded—he remembered what she'd told him after she'd woken up from it. "It says that there's a prophecy. About the end of the world." She swallowed. "It says that there will be three Heroes, reincarnated from the Heroes of old, who will know they are Heroes from their dreams." Xavior's eyes widened. "From the feeling they get when they all meet. A recognition." She opened up the book, and pointed at Adesola's face. "There's a drawing in it. And in the drawing is the woman from my vision. The one who visits me. I saw her in the simulation too. And weeks ago, when all of this started, I heard her voice in my head. Saying *it* was starting again."

Xavior's eyes were transfixed on the drawing. With one hand, he reached out to touch it, his fingertips hovering millimetres away from the person to Adesola's left. The Hero who wore the crown. *Dandeyi.*

"That's you, isn't it?" Asha said, barely realising she had spoken. Xavior looked at her. The sunrise was peeking through the window now, bringing the brown-gold out of his eyelashes, his cheeks and nose smudges of sunlight and soft emerald darkness, whilst his hair fell over his forehead, casting his eyes into shadow.

When he spoke, his voice was gravelly with emotion. "This is the face. Of the warrior I saw in my dream. The one with the crown. The one who—" He faltered. And looked embarrassed suddenly. "The one who feels for you. Or for her, I mean." He pointed at Adesola. "That name you said. *Dandeyi.* That was the name I heard. Adesola whispered it in my ear. Hearing it now . . . I remember." Xavior looked at her, a helpless honesty in his eyes. "Ever since I met you, I've felt like I know you. Like we were supposed to meet. I didn't say anything because it sounded so stupid, but now . . ." He shook his head. "Asha, this can't be possible. You're saying we're them? The Heroes from a prophecy? That you, Obi and I were meant to meet, and what? Save the world?"

Asha inhaled shakily, her eyes searching his face. "Is it impossible?" she replied, and all she could think of was his mouth on hers, a couple of thousand years ago, their embrace immortalised in marbled rock and mosaic gold on an ancient palace's ceiling. *Yes,* she thought, with more clarity than she'd felt in months. *That was us.*

"Is it impossible if we both see the same things when I touch you?" Asha felt blood rush to her face, in shock at her own boldness, and wanted to look away, but Xavior's surprised her. His hand came up to touch her cheek, stopping just shy of her skin. If she turned, they would touch, and who knew what might happen then? She closed her eyes. "Is it impossible," she continued, "when I *know* you feel what I feel, even though we've never spoken of it?" She opened her eyes, and his face was seconds away. "That it's as though we all knew each other before now, when we were different people, with different names? As if we met, somewhere else a million years ago, and forgot?"

She realised her hands were screwed up in Xavior's shirt. An enormous feeling was creeping over her; like she'd slipped beneath the surface of dark water and was now drowning in a vast and ancient sea. She clutched him tighter. *You were there,* she thought nonsensically, *standing next to me, at the beginning. Don't you remember?* Her heart was hammering.

"Asha," Xavior said roughly. He was hot under her hands. She could feel his heart beating through the thin material of his shirt. "You make me feel like I could be something great." He swallowed roughly. "Or like I was, once, and when you look at me, when you touch me . . . I start to remember how."

His hand by her cheek was millimetres away.

They stared at each other, faces so close they were breathing the same air, and Asha was aware of nothing but the places where they touched, and of Xavior's hand, hesitant and trembling in the space by her cheek.

I want this. She ached. *I want to touch him. To be with him. To feel his skin on my skin, his mouth on my mouth. And I can have that. All I have to do is be brave enough to take it.*

She turned her cheek into his palm—

"*Stop!*" The door burst open, revealing Obi, his shirt and jeans soaking wet, a maniacal look on his face. He took in their position—Xavior's left hand around Asha's waist, his right millimetres from her cheek, and his eyes widened. "Or don't. I don't know why I yelled 'stop' I was just being dramatic. I can come back later—"

Asha and Xavior sprang apart. "No, no—" Asha said. Xavior

suddenly became incredibly interested in the sunrise outside his window.

Obi looked between the two of them, eyebrows raised, water dripping from his jeans into the carpet.

"Obi, why are you so wet?' Asha asked. "You look like you took a shower fully clothed."

"That's what I wanted to talk to you guys about, actually," he replied, closing the door behind him.

Xavior laughed nervously. "Your shower habits?"

"No, Christ. No. I—" He was opening his mouth to say something else when he stopped, something catching his eyes by one of the bed posts. He bent down to retrieve it—Asha saw a flash of white in his hands before he straightened up. It was the drawing from the book. Of the three Heroes. Adesola, Sensit, and Dandeyi. But he was holding it the wrong way round—staring with intrigue at the back of the page. He hadn't even seen the drawing of the Heroes. He brandished it at Asha. "Who drew this?" he asked. "It's not bad. But my eyes are not that far apart."

"What?" Asha took the page from him. Xavior bent over her shoulder to look at it, and she could feel his body heat, smell his hair. Her heart raced.

Then she saw the page.

On the pale yellow paper left exposed on the back of the painting, three faces stared out, all of them cast half in shadow, sketched frantically with crumbling charcoal. The artist, who Asha presumed to be this Ishoal Nisomn, had written: *The Faces in My Dreams*. Then smaller, *Next generation?*

One by one, Asha, Obi, and Xavior turned to each other.

"Those are our faces," Asha breathed. "That is me. And you, and you."

Obi looked at the two of them. "So, you're telling me this is not Koshiro's art homework?"

She felt choked and dizzy. "This drawing is nearly one hundred years old. I think."

A scrawled note covered the bottom of the page.

These faces came to me in a dream—I saw them again in the pool of an oracle. I believe they are the next of our Heroes, or at least, involved somehow in the prophecy. I will find them. I must find them, if this regime is to end. The Third Prophecy foretold a tyrant, someone who would rise from nothing, and gain mastery over the galaxy, at the cost of, well, everything. Of course, I know who that is. A part of me has known, I think, since we were boys. And now, I know the faces of the chosen three—the only people in the galaxy who may wield the weapons of old. The only people who have any chance at stopping him.

The paper grew clammy as she grasped it between sweaty fingertips, barely breathing. Seeing this felt like falling. Like hurtling towards something inevitable. The events of the past month had been rearranging themselves in her mind since she first read the book, hours ago in that underground cavern. Since she'd spoken to the Archivist and seen the compass. Seeing this was like slotting the final piece of the puzzle into place.

Asha remembered shaking Obi's hand and thinking, *I know you.* Remembered seeing the Sentinel and hearing Adesola's ancient voice awaken in her mind and say, *again?* This confirmed why she couldn't touch Xavior without being thrown backward into Chasca's past—reliving the events that led to its downfall.

That had led to this moment.

The start of the Third Prophecy, she thought.

Obi turned the page slowly. He raised a shaking finger and pointed at Adesola. "I just met her. She appeared from nowhere, and started talking to me about three heroes, and a prophecy. She said they were us."

Mutely, Asha pulled the compass from her pocket, and

set it in the middle of the floor. The needles whirred around, re-adjusting. When they stopped, one needle pointed at Obi, another at Xavior, and the final one, at Asha.

They all looked at each other. Goosebumps raced down Asha's arms.

Obi's voice was nearly hysterical. "What the hell do we do now?"

The one who will wield the crown must be in love—we can only fight for something—truly fight for it—if we love it. A country, equality, ourselves. Someone else who does not have the thing we fight, or labours under the constraints of the thing we are fighting against.

I know this now, though I did not before.

'A Complete, Annotated History of Chasca, Including Relevant Translated Mythologies. Chapter: This Author's Informed Predictions' by I. Nisomn, ex-acolyte of the Aonian Archives.

Chapter Thirty-One

**[planet: Aonia] + [Location: The Diplomats' Guild] +
[year: 6066]**

After the shock of seeing themselves in the drawing, of watching
the compass needles land unerringly on each of them, they'd
sat in stunned silence, before Asha had started to talk. It was
all Obi could do to listen, and then offer his own account of
events—Adesola, swimming towards him through the lake,
telling him that London and George were both in grave danger.
And before that, Qala, offering him the cure, and her strange
pronouncement: *There's something starting, out there in the universe.
All around us. Something is coming.* He almost told them both
about Adesola's order: that they find the Emperor's weapon and
destroy it . . . but something held him back. Maybe it was the
look on Asha's face that did it; like she was one more revelation
away from a mental breakdown.

In turn, Asha told them everything—from the vision she'd
had when she'd met the Sentinel, to the prophecy she'd heard
in the dream-like state she'd entered after touching Xavior.
Which was apparently a thing that happened. Asha's confession
did explain the conversation he'd overheard between her and
Xavior in the prison . . . and, as for the stuff about them being
re-incarnated Heroes, how could he not believe it, when he'd
seen his face drawn in charcoal set to paper a hundred years ago?
When he'd been visited by Adesola herself?

Her words still rang in his ears.

Sensit—or rather, the monster he has become—will destroy your city and then your world, if you do not stop him. And you are the only one who can . . . Without my brother vanquished, and returned to his normal state, the prophecy cannot be fulfilled. But you can only stop it if you return to London and face whatever you find there with a Hero's heart.

The prophecy. The one Ishoal Nisomn's tome said meant the end of the world.

"Obi," Asha said, breaking him out his reverie. "What are you going to do?" Obi shook his head. "I can't leave this time period. When I tried before, something stopped me. Threw me straight back here. At first, I thought it was a progression of my illness . . . but now I know it was the prophecy. Adesola told me. So, it's simple, really. The prophecy is leading us to A'lkari, where your sister is. Where you're risking your life to go. So that's where I'll go."

"Maybe there's a way you can go home, we can help you try—"

"I'm coming with you, Asha. End of debate." Obi shook his head, before looking her in the eye. "Everything in me wants to leave right now, the cure be damned. But I won't let you do this alone. Not after everything we've been through. You're my family now. And if all this is to be believed . . . you're part of my destiny too."

Opposite him, Xavior nodded. "I'm coming, too," his voice was quiet. "I couldn't live with myself if you had to do this on your own. I can't let that happen. Not after Isi betrayed you, which was my fault." He shook his head, likely still in disbelief at the revelations of the past few hours, just like Obi. But, despite the uncertainty, his expression was focussed, determined. "And just like Obi said . . . we're all connected. I think I'm meant to help you find your sister. I don't know why, and I don't know how we're going to do it. But you can count on me Asha," he looked at her, jaw set, and Obi realised, *he would do anything for her.* Asha smiled at him, so small anyone who didn't know her would likely have mistaken it for an involuntary twitch. He smiled back. "And you can't get rid of me that easily." He nodded. "Then it's settled, we're all going."

Asha closed her eyes, relief washing over her face like cool rain. "Thank you."

"So, what's the plan?" Xavior asked. "Between us, we have a lot of experience breaking out of prisons, but not much breaking in . . ."

Asha grabbed her tablet from the bed. "We have eight days left. For the next five, we'll stay here, and prepare. Xavior—" she bit her lip, looking at him apologetically "—could you write down everything you can remember about your time on A'lkari? I'll cross-reference it with any other information I can find on the prison in the library or digital archives. Even if I have to hack my way in, there has to be something."

Xavior nodded. "Of course."

"What can I do?" Obi asked. He was filled with a deep urge to be useful to her, to take as much of the burden from her shoulders as he could. To let her command him.

"What you do best," Asha smiled. "Talk. Make some friends around the Guild, get them to trust you. And then get any information that you can on out of them about transportation. How do people leave Aonia? It can't always be on fifty-person star-cruisers. There will be smaller craft—and I need you to find where they're kept. They'll likely be guarded. So ask about guard rotations—find out who is posted when and get to know them. Anything helps. We need a way to get off this planet—if I have a ship, I can do it. But if I don't . . ."

I can do that. Obi nodded. "Got it."

Asha stood up. Grabbing the book, she shoved it back in her bag.

"Where are you going?" Xavior asked.

"To take apart the computer I took from Xesca and see what I can find, or build. Anything I can salvage from it that will help us break into the Emperor's compound and steal my sister back."

I acknowledge the Archivist as my mentor. Without that fount of knowledge, I would not quite have known how to go about compiling this. Therefore, I will leave this work with the Guild. I carry this knowledge with me in my heart anyway, it is part of me now. And who can say? Perhaps when all is said and done, someone will have gleaned some measure of usefulness from its pages. If not, well, it cannot be said that I did not try.

'A Complete, Annotated History of Chasca,
Including Relevant Translated Mythologies. Chapter:
Acknowledgements' by I. Nisomn, ex-acolyte of the
Aonian Archives.

Part Three

'Arms! Arms!' he cries; 'the sword and shield prepare,
And send the willing chief, renew'd to war.
This is no mortal work, no cure of mine,
Nor art's effect, but done by hands divine.
Some god our general to the battle sends;
Some god preserves his life for greater ends.'

Virgil. *The Aeneid*, XII. 426-30, translated by John
Dryden, 1697.

Chapter Thirty-Two

The mirrored hallways of the Guild palace took on a different quality at night. Obi, Asha, and Xavior were dressed in dark clothes, bags slung over their shoulders, stealing their way towards the hangars.

"Here," Xavior said, motioning for them to stop. He had led them through the cold, stony hallways. Obi wondered what it had cost him to do so. He'd seen Xavior fold a small note under the door to his brother's room and then fastidiously pretended not to have noticed a thing when Xavior had looked up and told them it was time to leave.

Asha moved forward, darting into the shadows by the stone archway.

The fact that nothing was locked up in this place never ceased to amaze Obi. But trust was part of the mandate—that and the test to get here—and the acolytes didn't value anything material. Plus, Xavior had assured them the Guild didn't need a defence system, which just left the few Consortium guards stationed on Aonia, there to accompany Guild members travelling to A'lkari.

Of course, Asha had to have set her sights on stealing one of their ships.

She had been spying on them for the best part of the week now, and could report only that they were young, lazy, and bitter that their first post in uniform had been on a tiny planet of "creepy" pacifist monks. She had said with no small amount of confidence that wresting the ship from them would not be hard, though she had conceded that it might be a different story once they were in the air—with luck, no one would give chase. This seemed the most logical solution, as none of the Initiates seemed particularly inclined towards aerial warfare. But you never knew.

"That one," Asha breathed, as the boys joined her in the shadows. She was pointing to a small, sleek jet in the hangar's corner. She turned to him. "Obi, you're up."

It was the first part of their plan—and it rested on his shoulders. *Conjure a distraction.* He could do this—*had* done this, many times before. He nodded loosely, already evening his breathing pattern. The phantom didn't need to be completely solid—in fact, the more ghostlike it looked the better. Its only purpose was to distract. He had sat in front of the mirror for hours last night, trying to make it mean something, to focus on the fact of where he was, how he had got to be there, so that he could use that memory now. It wouldn't be strong, but it didn't have to be. He exhaled; closed his eyes, felt the memory rise in him—a boy in dark jeans and T-shirt standing in front of a mirror in the early evening, facing down a day in which he'd risk his life for a reason he didn't fully understand, but felt so much like destiny he couldn't refuse.

The soft glow started in his hands, wrapping around his arms and torso, up his neck, and head, and falling down around his feet. It lit up Asha's face—her expression one of wonderment and satisfaction—and threw Xavior's into shadow. He peeled his own ghost from himself like a pair of gloves, starting at the hands, loosening it, until he could take a handful of it at his chest, and wrench it free.

Memories came flooding towards him, as though passing

right in front of his eyes, shaken free by the power he needed to make the phantom appear.

His hand, shaking Asha's in a stolen ship. The fighting ring, appearing before him, before Asha's voice called out, like a gift from above, there to help him. The colourful, dirty streets of the NIS, strange people staring at him, with faces so different to his own—so profoundly alien. Sleeping in bunk beds, the stars drifting past outside the window, smiling as he listened to Asha sneak out to Xavior's room for the third night in a row. Then Xesca—the horror of it, the thunder crashing, the earth heaving under their feet as they ran through a prison collapsing on top of them, stepping into a column of light so white it looked like the heart of a flame.

The phantom staggered backwards, finally separate from him, and the memories ceased.

Obi grinned. The phantom grinned back, so Obi jerked his head towards the hanger doorway. In reply, the phantom gave a stupid salute—*Ha*, Obi thought. *I would totally do that*—and turned away, walking through the wall right next to the door.

"*Um*," said Xavior, who had never seen Obi use his powers before.

"Quickly!" Asha hissed.

They followed the phantom, watching as the glow dimmed, and it began to look like any person, any trespasser in the hangar late at night. Slipping behind the smaller craft, they watched as the phantom flickered its way towards their jet. They stalked closer to the guards, following the ghost's path at a parallel, hidden behind the assorted ships. When they reached them, Asha held up a hand. The boys stopped, and she gave a nod. Xavior went to her side, and together they slipped away, between the wing of a boxy jet, and its neighbour.

The guards standing by didn't notice Obi's ghost at first.

Then one of them jolted as the phantom moved, phasing into complete opacity for a moment. It was the distraction the others needed. Asha darted forwards from the shadows behind the smaller sentry, swiftly kicking the legs out from underneath him. He went down with a cut-off cry, and she wrenched his gun from his hands, swinging it down to crack against the side of his head. He went limp. Asha stood, frozen for a moment, looking at the prone body on the floor as though she couldn't believe what she'd done.

She hesitated for too long.

"*Behind you*—" Obi hissed, as the second sentry shouted in alarm, and raised their gun to fire—but then Xavior was there, knocking the weapon out of their hands with a clatter, and firing a bolt of bright light into their chest. The second sentry went down, mouth open in a shout that never sounded. Asha looked horrified—Obi couldn't tell if it was because she'd nearly been shot in the head, or because she couldn't believe she'd faltered long enough for someone to have to come to her rescue.

Obi watched Xavior touch her lightly on the shoulder, then hand her the gun he was holding. She stuffed it into her bag, alongside whatever other ridiculously dangerous weaponry she no doubt already had in there, and ran over to where Obi was now waiting by the jet.

"Hey," Obi said. "You alright?"

"Yeah," she said, and seemed to gather herself. She nodded her head at the limp bodies. "They'll come to eventually. We just have to be long gone. So get in," she said, dropping to the ground. "I'll complete pre-flight checks, and then we're leaving. Should be two minutes."

She passed Xavior as she ducked around to the back. He smiled at her, nodding his head, and she, like an animal caught in headlights, looked away, running around to the ship's tail. Obi barely restrained a cackle.

The jet was thin, almost identical to the model they'd stolen from the prison ship all those weeks ago, but larger. They'd chosen it for three reasons. Firstly, it was coated in the tessellating, slightly iridescent cladding that Asha had said gave it cloaking capabilities, which would be essential for their entry into A'lkari's atmosphere. Second, as an imperial grade ship, it could travel further distances, and had greater permissions in accessing alternate hyperspace routes. There were some equations only government-built ships were strong enough to handle—it was what set imperial ships apart from the rest. This one could get them to A'lkari in just under twenty-four hours. And, most importantly of all, it could fit four people; they would be leaving A'lkari with Asha's sister in tow.

"Okay," Asha whispered, climbing up into the cockpit, and taking her place in the pilot's seat. "Let's go."

They closed the hatch, Asha turned on the floodlights—

And suddenly, somehow, there was a small figure, standing in the beam, pale hands thrown up over their face to block the glare.

"*No*," Xavior breathed.

Koshiro's shoulders were heaving, his small, young face blotchy red with exertion. He'd run.

Obi had known the risk but couldn't bring himself to stop Xavior leaving that note. Clearly, the minute Koshiro had seen it, he'd guessed where they'd gone and torn out of the apartment, bare feet slapping on stone floors, thinking that if he could just talk to his brother, maybe he wouldn't leave again—

"Don't go!" Koshiro shouted. He was in his pyjamas. "*Please*."

Xavior looked undone. His hand was outstretched, halfway towards the domed glass of the cockpit window, as though he wanted to press his palm against it and communicate all the things he could not say. His jaw was clenched horribly, his lips a thin line of consternation, of complete regret. His jugular stood out in his neck.

"*I'm sorry,*" he mouthed, and it came out half whispered, a broken apology. Koshiro took a step forward—

The defence systems engaged automatically. Four huge guns swivelled around to point at the boy standing in the twin beams of converging light. He staggered back, staring at them in disbelief, though there was no way he could have seen their faces past the floodlights of the jet. Asha frantically tried to disable them, but they wouldn't budge. Koshiro's face, Obi realised with a jolt of horror, was wet with angry tears.

The brothers stared at each other. It felt like hours before Koshiro's shoulders slumped. Before he turned, defeated, and walked away.

"No," said Xavior. Then, "*Shit!*" as though he'd been broken out of some kind of trance. He lashed out, hitting the side of the jet. "I—" He stared after his brother, at his tiny retreating figure, already slipping back into the shadows of the palace, and his hand trembled against his thigh. He looked away from the window. Obi felt terrible—like he was watching something intimate, something intensely private, that he did not quite understand. *Betrayed by a brother*, he thought, and remembered how he'd felt the day he'd woken up to an empty house. *I bet this is worse,* he thought. *And it's not the first time.*

"Xav—" Asha said.

"No."

"*I'm sorry,*" she looked tiny and sad, and nothing at all like herself, and Obi realised that they were all thinking the same thing: *what am I doing?*

"It's okay. I made my choice," came the reply.

Asha was silent as she engaged the flight systems, and wheeled them around, rolling them out into the huge courtyard kept clear of snow to be used for take-off.

The jets whirred to life, and then they were rising up, faster and faster, past dark windows and stone towers, and there were wisps of cloud outside the window, and Obi could see the curvature of the strange world they'd taken refuge on, with its white sky, and frozen wastes, and the huge planets hanging on the horizon.

For a moment he was weightless, heart thudding in his chest.

It all went wrong pretty much immediately.

WHAM!

A bolt of light flew past the window, half a metre from their faces, and Asha yelled, slamming the joystick forward, and nose-diving towards the earth.

"What *was* that?" Xavior shouted.

"Someone's coming after us!" Asha replied, banking left hard, and slipping in between two mountain peaks, dodging rock and jutting cliffs. "If we'd carried on straight upwards, they would have shot us out of the sky." She shook her head. "It must be the guards. They woke up. They're the only ones posted out here, as far as I know." Another bolt slammed into the cliff face beside them, blowing chunks of rock into the gorge below with a sound like a bomb detonating. The low droning sound behind them grew louder, and Obi could see two shapes in the sweeping beam of the sensors on the dashboard.

"So much for pacifism. *Hang on,*" Asha said, and cut the engines.

"What the f—" Xavior started, eyes bulging.

They dropped like a stone, spiralling towards the ground. Obi thought he passed out for a second.

Behind them, the first craft kept going and slammed into the cliff. Bits of rock and flaming debris showered around them, as the ravine rushed up to meet them, snowy rock blurring past them. Suddenly, the engines cut back on and Asha righted them, shot them forward, and sped under a loop in the rock that Obi hadn't seen.

"'M gonna be sick," Xavior murmured, face pale.

The pursuer that remained was gaining, right on their tail, firing incessantly. Boulder-sized chunks of rock were blasted out of the valley's mountainous sides, missing them by metres.

They sped forwards and down, Asha taking them along the dark surface of the frozen river. There was a bridge up ahead that rose from the gorge, and Asha aimed for it, possibly hoping to use the huge stone arches that supported it to lead their pursuer on a perilous course, trick him into clipping a wing, perhaps, and spiralling down. But then Obi saw the huge icicles hanging from the snow drifts frozen to the lip of the edge of the bridge and realised what she was planning. She opened fire, aiming for the snow drift—perhaps hoping to separate the icicles from the drift and send them plunging down, just behind them, to bury the pursuing jet. For a moment, there was only the drone of two engines, the high-pitched whine of the other craft's gunfire.

Asha aimed them through the ancient arches of the bridge's underside, and for a moment they were in darkness, the bridge above them blocking the bright, wintry sun. Obi twisted in his seat, staring out the rear windows, waiting for the collision, for the explosion.

It never came.

Asha had fired too early—misjudged the distance.

He heard her curse, voice panicked, as the icicles fell, so huge they seemed to drift downwards in slow motion. They slammed into the river's blue-white surface, ice cracking and groaning on impact. The other craft sped onward, gaining on them, nearly at the bridge. If Obi squinted, he could see the person inside it.

Then, beneath them, the river erupted.

A creature heaved itself out of the gorge, fury in its glittering eyes, roaring at the disruption. All three of them screamed like little kids as glacier-sized chunks of ice were flung into the air, turquoise and sparkling. He saw a mass of flailing tentacles ringing a monstrous head like a mane, and past that, an immeasurably long, worm-like body, also ringed intermittently with tentacles, and banded with iridescence that glistened wetly in the sun. Its gaping mouth widened in a perfect circle, rings of teeth rotating like a grinding, devouring machine.

The other craft didn't stand a chance.

The creature's mouth was so huge, Obi couldn't even pinpoint the moment the other craft disappeared inside it.

From the other side of the bridge, they watched in silent horror.

The creature crashed back into the water; the valley rocked.

"What the *fuck*," Obi said, his voice strangled, "was *that?*"

Xavior shrugged. "I told you they didn't need a defence system."

Asha huffed a startled laugh, but her face in the reflection of the front window was kind of grey.

Mood, Obi thought.

As they watched, a stunning *crack* sounded, and the bridge collapsed, chunks of it tumbling into the ravine, smashing into the coldly rushing water made visible by the leviathan creature's rupturing of the river's frozen surface.

"Asha, we should go—" Xavior said, but Asha was already nodding, her eyes darting across each of the glowing screens set into the dashboard.

With a swipe of one trembling hand, she brought up one of the interfaces and began to tap in equations—lines of numbers filling up the holographic screen. Their jets rotated with a low grinding sound, and she guided them upwards, speeding towards the sky, until it grew dark around them and the atmosphere was straining against the nose of the jet, billowing past.

She barely gave them time to take in the view before she completed her equations with a final tap, setting their course, and firing them into a tunnel of light.

Adesola and Sensit recommended the next part of their journey together under the light of the stars. Sometimes they felt the spirit of Dandeyi walk beside them, though he remained physically far away. He gave them strength when they felt small in the face of the task, and though it was true that Mother had instructed them never to falter, sometimes the Hero in them seceded from the person in them, and they were scared.

'A Complete, Annotated History of Chasca, Including Relevant Translated Mythologies. Chapter: Scroll the Third' by I. Nisomn, ex-acolyte of the Aonian Archives.

Chapter Thirty-Three

[planet: Earth] + [location: London] + [year: 1812]

It's really better if I show you, Alarick had said.

Now George was standing in an alleyway behind an antiques shop, on the shadier, damper, decidedly more derelict side of town, waiting for Alarick to join him and finally reveal a key part of his plan. Which was apparently purchasable at an antiques store for the fairly modest sum of fifty pounds.

A pipe creaked, dripping grey water onto George's previously pristine boots. He had been waiting for nearly twenty minutes now and the damp was starting to seep into places damp should never seep.

"Ah, good, you're still here."

George turned around at the sound of Alarick's voice at the mouth of the alley.

"Lucky for you," he replied. "Could you have taken any longer?"

Alarick shrugged. "Artefact sourcing is a delicate business. I have to get acquainted with each item before purchasing. Rules out any room for error."

He pulled a notebook from the sturdy brown paper bag he held in his hands. It was crammed with handwriting, each page filled with the same faint, spidery scrawl. Alarick flicked through it, pausing on a few pages to read what was written there. George caught a glimpse of what looked like the draft of a letter. A love letter, if the blotchy tearstains and over-bold proclamations of dedication were anything to go by. It was addressed to one *John Seymour* and signed at the end by an *Emilia Ainsworth*. The faded date at the top read: the 15th of January 1752. It seemed to George like an intensely private thing, something that ought to be tied up with string and kept in the back of a bureau or a vanity table. Certainly not something to be unflinchingly scrutinised by two bedraggled strangers in a damp, grimy alleyway on the less reputable side of town. Although there was a strange delicacy to the way Alarick held it. Like a jeweller holding an uncut diamond, he seemed aware of an innate value in the object that remained indiscernible to the untrained eye.

Then Alarick whispered something that sounded like a question, and promptly set the notebook on fire.

George let out a strangled cry. "What are you *doing*?"

Alarick looked at him. "Wait and see," was all he said.

The letter crumbled to ash, smoke curling upwards into the grey sky until it was indistinguishable from the clouds. A gust of wind stirred the ashes, blowing them up into the sky.

Except, the air was still. It was a humid day, with damp in the air and rain gathering on the horizon. There was no wind to speak of, and yet . . .

The ashes whipped faster, spiralling upwards into the air like a contained hurricane.

A shape was forming from the ground upwards. Billowing skirts, a dainty hand, a laced-up bonnet and big, doe eyes. A woman rose out of the ash, her shape startlingly solid and corporeal. She was dressed in clothes that had been fashionable half a century earlier, and was looking at them serenely.

George's jaw dropped. "A ghost?"

"Memories, if there's a difference," Alarick said impatiently. "My lady." He tipped his hat. "We were hoping you could assist us in our effort to save the world."

The woman's eyes widened, her thick lashes fluttering in distress. "Whatever is the matter with the world?" she asked. "I do hope nobody is in immediate danger. How may I help?"

"We need time," Alarick replied, "as much as you can spare. But there are consequences—"

"Of which I am aware," she said, cutting him off. "I will cease to be, and therefore will at last be free to join my John in Heaven in my entirety. I have been waiting for this, and I thank you, kind traveller, for allowing me this opportunity."

Alarick bowed.

"I can offer you three days' worth of time," she said. "For that is how long it took me to fill that diary with letters after John was killed and I was left alone."

George felt choked with emotion. She looked so young, barely nineteen. "I am to be King of England one day," he told her. Her eyes widened further and she moved to curtsey, but George held up his hand. "I just wanted to thank you personally and commend you for your courage. This country will not forget you, Emilia, and neither will I."

Her chin trembled, but she did not let the tears fall. Instead, she held out one hand, offering it to Alarick. A pulse of pale light passed between the two, and Alarick's eyes glowed brightly under their lids, light spilling out from beneath his short eyelashes. He inhaled sharply and let go. When George turned back to Emilia she was fading. The ash that formed her skirts flaking away, crumbling on the nonexistent breeze to float upwards to the clouds. She waved at them, smiling, ashen tears finally spilling down her cheeks. Then she was gone, leaving only the faint smell of smoke and char, but also . . . wildflowers.

George turned back to Alarick, who did not appear quite as moved.

"It's not enough."

George sighed. *Time makes fools of us all*, Obi had once said. George was beginning to agree. "What next then?"

Alarick was smiling now, and—*oh no*, George did not like that look.

"Only one thing for it." His smile widened. He looked, for a moment, like Obi. "We raid the Tower of London."

"The amount of time a spirit is able to grant directly correlates to the power of the Artefact," Alarick had explained on their way to the Tower. "Which, as I told you, is generated by the amount of sentimental energy it possesses."

George had tried to protest. Tried to insist that the acting monarch of the country couldn't just steal diamonds from the Crown—let alone destroy them. But Alarick had pointed out the decades of time they'd get from one Artefact alone. That committing this one criminal act would be the difference between George losing his life, the city, the country, maybe even the world—and victory.

"We just need a year. One year. You gather all the defences you need and then *you* win. Which do you choose?"

It wasn't a choice, really. Victory or death. Not even peaceful death, but death lived in service to a god who saw him as nothing more than a curiosity. Something to be used.

I came to this place, this city, because I wanted more, Sensit had said. *And you look a lot like more to me.*

For whatever reason, having George was crucial to Sensit's plan. George would cut him off at every chance. He would do whatever it took.

"Alright," he had said. "On one condition."

Alarick lifted an eyebrow. "What?"

"We are *not* stealing the crown jewels."

Half an hour later, they were standing in front of the vault that held the symbols of an empire.

George had dismissed the guards easily—once they had recognised who he was—with a joke that nothing would end up missing or broken. But Alarick was already reaching into his pocket to withdraw a small silver device that looked like a pen. He clicked the top, and a slim groove in the side filled with turquoise light.

"Stand back," he said.

George didn't move. The light was mesmerizing.

"Your call," Alarick said, and pointed the pen at the door.

A thin beam of searingly bright light shot out of the end, colliding with the door and cutting through it. George flinched back from the light and the spit of the molten metal. By the time he looked back, there was a long, straight groove cut into the vault door.

George groaned. How would he ever explain this?

George blinked. Alarick proceeded to cut another three lines and then kick the door down. A loud, clanging thud echoed throughout the room, snapping George out of his reverie.

"We should try to be quiet—"

"You are lucky I've not decided to burn this disgusting place to the ground and dance on the ashes of it."

George didn't reply.

Alarick stepped through the smoking hole in the wall and strode in, disappearing into the gloom of the vault.

Resisting the urge to cross himself and beg the Lord (and his father) for forgiveness, George followed him.

By the time he reached him, Alarick had stalked over to the closest case and wielded his strange, powerful instrument. A small smoking circle later, he was reaching forward to grab what George soon realised to be the Crown of Mary of Modena.

Before George could protest, Alarick's hands blazed with light, and he barely had the presence of mind to throw his arms up over his eyes before the priceless, jewel encrusted crown melted into a puddle of gold and burning velvet. The diamonds loosened from their fastenings and crumbled to shining dust.

When it felt safe, George lowered his hands. Alarick was murmuring words George had never heard before in any language and could not understand. For a few tense moments, nothing happened. Then the diamond dust began to move, drifting in circles as though blown by a breeze neither of them could feel.

A figure began to rise out of the glittering diamond shards that littered the floor. A man. But something was wrong. He was hunched over, as though he carried a terrible burden. George had imagined his grandfather, or a great-grandmother, perhaps seated on a throne. Who was this?

Then the diamonds flurried faster, and the true owner of the priceless gems that had sat in this vault, collecting dust for decades, was revealed.

A man stood before them, his dark skin gleaming in the low light.

Rusted iron manacles circled his wrists, weighing down his arms. His feet were chained and shackled and bleeding. Bruises littered his face, his eyes were almost swollen shut.

George faltered. His first thought, simply, stupidly: *but those diamonds were sent here as gifts.*

Reason swiftly followed, like a blow. *Did you truly believe that? That a country would gift the largest diamonds discovered in centuries to a royal family that wasn't even theirs? A country that went on to enslave its people? To subjugate and destroy them?*

Next to him, Alarick swore once. Then, he knelt.

"Brother," he said. "I have come to ask for help."

The man started to speak. His language was not one George knew, but the harder he listened, the more he could understand. The strange syllables turned themselves inside out, trembling reluctantly into English:

"—must refuse. I will not serve them in death as I did in life." His voice, was hoarse, shaking with anger. "I have my dignity, now, in death. Will you wait until they kill you to find yours?

Alarick bowed his head.

"I am not asking for them," he said. "I am asking on behalf of your descendants; those who will walk the city as free men two decades from now. For their children, and their children's children. For all of us."

"It is not good enough."

"No," Alarick said. "It is not good enough. Nothing will ever be good enough to atone for what they did to us. For what they do to us every day." He exhaled. "But in a hundred years this city is *ours*. Whole boroughs of it belong to us, and yeah, it's not written anywhere, but *we* know. Everyone knows. You can *hear* it—" he closed his eyes briefly "—in the music. See it on the street. Generations of families will call this place home, and in doing so, they'll transform it."

The man remained unmoved. His sad eyes watched Alarick, filled with something that looked a lot like pity.

"They tried to break us," Alarick whispered. "When they stole us. When they threw us in boats and then threw us in chains. When they took our languages, and our homes, and our health, and the skin off our backs. But we put down roots into frozen ground and grew anyway," he said. "They forced their way into our imaginations, into the consciousness we shared, and took away all the hope. But we dreamed futures of our own. And then they tried to tell the world they didn't, but we sang songs about the things they did to us, and danced to them in town halls across this twisted country's capital city, and never forgot what they meant. Never." Alarick's eyes were squeezed shut. "We carved out space among the rubble of our dreams and our humanity, and used the stuff that remained to build something for ourselves." He grasped the knees of the apparition, and George realised with a jolt that he was supplicating the man to grant mercy to a city that had enslaved him and his descendants and had shown them nothing but violence and cruelty and the crack of bloody whips in return.

As Alarick knelt, supplicant to his ancestor who stood in chains, George was forcefully reminded of another supplication he had read about in the last pages of an epic. As the earth drank in the blood of the fallen, and the dust blew over frantic chariot tracks to settle in the cracks of the scorched debris that was once a great wall, an old and tired man, a *king*, begged for his son's mutilated body at the feet of the greatest warrior of the age.

Priam and Achilles.

Alarick and the . . .

George turned the word over in his mind. It was an ugly word that meant many things, but also nothing at all. It was an act of complete barbarism. It was a construct that killed and abducted and lied and destroyed. It was an arbitrary decision that was completely calculated.

It was slavery. The word, for the first time, took on meaning.

Alarick and the slave.

But that felt so wrong. That was not a title any man would choose, and so who was George to choose it for him?

Alarick and the man made of diamond dust.

Alarick and the warrior.

Alarick and the—

"I just wanted to live in the land I was born to," said the man. "And build a better future for my daughters and my sons. That was all I wanted; for them to surpass me, and to have the privilege of watching it happen."

Tears dripped from Alarick's chin, mixing with the dust on the floor that had once been the symbol of an empire. An empire built off the backs and the lives of those it had no right to.

Then the man's gaze moved away from Alarick, and landed on George, just for a moment. Their gazes met. And George saw it plain as day: pure, unadulterated hatred. The man hated him. Him and his family and everyone who had sat at home, profiting from his torture, telling themselves that they were better than the Americans, just because it didn't happen on their soil. Assuring themselves they were kinder than their forefathers, because they at least had had the decency to abolish the trade in slaves in 1807. As if there hadn't been mass resistance to the Bill, or widespread calls for compensation for slave-owners. Calls that had been obeyed. As if this did not forfeit and ignore the rights of the enslaved men, women and children suffering on plantations all over the world, and their desperate calls for freedom.

George looked into his shining, sorrowful face, and met his eyes just for a moment, before he had to look away.

He was ashamed. God, he was so ashamed that he thought he might fall apart with the horror of it, spreading through him like a sick poison.

I had to see you dead and hear the story of your torture from your mouth, see the remnants of it in your eyes, to feel this shame, this deep sorrow.

But he knew to be sorry wasn't enough—had known this for years. Had known that even if the trade in slaves was abolished, that didn't mean that slavery itself was illegal; had known that private, theoretical, moral disagreement with the crime was about as good as enthusiastic support of it; had known that however helpless he felt at the head of a parliament that would not listen, it was nothing compared to the helplessness and abuse and degradation of people who suffered as this man did.

The man looked back at Alarick. "I give this to you," he said, voice firm. "Not him. I give this to my brothers and sisters forced to live in this city, this country, against their will. They do not deserve any more suffering. They have had their share, and more. Save *them*." He spread his hands, and the chains clinked softly. "How much time do you need?"

Chapter Thirty-Four

Asha twisted around in her seat to face her two passengers, re-iterating the plan for the thousandth time. "We'll follow one of the supply ships in," she said, squinting at them to make sure they were listening, "we'll be cloaked the whole time."

She had pulled them out of hyperspace a few minutes ago, Xavior and Obi sitting in grim silence as they emerged a half-hour's flight from A'lkari's coordinates. Asha had rigged the stolen comms unit from Xesca into the dashboard display, and now, as they went over the plan, they were also listening in on the Consortium's private channels, trying to discern who would be landing on the planet and when.

Obi and Xavior nodded along as she spoke. "I'll shoot out the ship's communication dish, taking out a chunk of the hold with it. They won't be expecting an attack from one of their own ships. The convoy breaks formation—we slip inside the radar during the confusion, and hide, still cloaked, in the blind spot under the wing. They'll be on the lookout for intruders—but putting them on alert is a risk we have to take to have any chance of making it in. They'll be expecting another strike from the sky—but we'll already be on the ground by the time they realise there isn't one coming."

Xavior nodded. "But we have to assume the worst—that they

realise, turn their gaze inward, and up security in the compound significantly."

Asha nodded. "And that's where the cloaks will help us. Obi?"

"Here," he said, pulling the scarlet cloaks out of his bag. They'd stolen them from the laundry the night before they'd left, planning to disguise themselves as part of the group of Diplomatic Initiates stationed on A'lkari, charged with documenting Thracin's rule.

"Thank you." She nodded. "We'll put them on, and then split up—Xavior and I will go underground, find the prison complex, and Obi will stay with the jet, guiding us through our earpieces, staying ready for when we need to make our escape."

Obi nodded, but there was a pained look on his face. *He must be nervous,* Asha thought. *I don't blame him. I've never been more scared in my life.*

They'd been over the plan a thousand times, she knew. She'd been drilling it into the others every opportunity she got, making them answer questions on the finer points, and re-explain them back to her. But all their information had been gleaned from sources that were less than optimal. Xavior's memories from his time as a magical test subject being one of them. The other being documents Asha had been able to discover on Aonia—old building plans and proposals that went back sixty years, to when the palatial complex on A'lkari had been built. The best thing they had was the information she had been able to gather from the computer she had stolen from Xesca, which had gained her access to the closed security system of the Consortium—allowing her to view old records of surveillance footage and piece together a map of the basement level, and plan a route to the prison. They had contingencies and counter-contingencies; no possible scenario had been left unexplored . . . But that didn't erase the risk.

The radio crackled to life. "Cargo incoming, loading deck prepare for landing." They all sat up. It was an intercepted channel—the comm wasn't meant for them, but it was still their signal to move.

Asha flicked her eyes towards the radar, getting confirmation that a cargo-sized craft was approaching the tiny planet in the distance, preparing to land. She double-checked the cloaking and took a deep breath.

They all had to be confident—they couldn't afford to be anything else. If any of them wavered, even for a moment, it would be game over.

She urged them forward, slipping in behind the cargo ship as it sailed into view. Tiny jets flitted around it, moving in what looked like random patterns but that Asha could tell were calculated protective formations.

There was a moment of perfect silence. She thought, *here we go,* and then she opened fire.

To the convoy's pilots, the bright bolts would have appeared out of nowhere, sailing past the military escort to slam into the hull of the unprotected cargo ship. The section's communication dish was blasted to pieces, a hole blown into the bottom of the ship. Due to the craft's scale, this was fairly inconsequential for anyone aboard, but the section's convoy broke formation instantly, pilots swerving out of the way of the blast. She slammed the accelerator, urging them forwards towards the explosion, and then past it and up. She slipped the ship between frantic drones, coming to rest under the gigantic wing of the cargo craft.

"Phase one of the plan complete," Obi said, but almost immediately, Asha had noticed something out of the corner of her eye. There was a light flashing on the radar. A symbol she'd never seen—

More jets appeared out of thin air, formed in a perfect circle around their ship.

There was a short moment of stunned silence. Then the jet pilots opened fire, and Asha did the only thing she could: *fly*.

They shot forward, blasting through a ring of jets, laser fire missing them by inches, their cover blown to pieces. They passed so closely to one of the convoy jets that she could see into the cockpit.

Hold on.

There was no cockpit. The jets were empty. She looked around. No pilots. Which meant only one thing.

These were drones.

They were so sophisticated she hadn't recognised them at first—so terrified of the Consortium she had been convinced that the convoys around the ships would have been manned by real soldiers.

But if they were drones . . .

An idea came to her, fully formed and horrifying.

From this close, she could hack the drones' closed network and turn them off. She had no time for anything fancier, or more subtle, but it could work. And if she timed it right, if she struck just as they entered the planet's atmosphere, she could do a lot more damage to this base than simply breaking out a prisoner. The drones would drop—falling out of the sky and hitting the compound. Some of them would be caught and pulverised by the planetary security programme, but there were hundreds of drones surrounding this ship. If she could get all of them, she could as good as bomb Thracin's base of operations. The prison would be fine—it was deep underground, like a bunker. But the chaos and destruction this would cause on ground level would provide the perfect cover for them to slip in unnoticed.

But there was no way she could change the plan this late. The others would be blindsided—

A laser bolt slammed into the side of the ship, spinning them into empty space. Obi and Xavior yelled, looking at Asha with wide eyes.

Obi twisted around in the back seat, looking out the rear-view windows. "There are *so many*—"

"Warning," said the robotic voice of the system. "Shield capacity is now compromised at seventy-five per cent."

Asha swore, wrenching them to the left, blasting a line of drones to pieces. "They're drones—I—I think I can get us out of this. Change their chain of command so that it comes from me. But I can't fly and do that at the same time—*ah!*" She twisted them, turning the ship upside down to avoid being obliterated by drone fire. "I'm going to take out as many as I can. Then all you have to do is fly us away—"

"*What?*" said Xavior, then turned to Obi for support. "Obi—"

"Do *not* look at me right now!"

Asha could have screamed. *They didn't have time for this.* "It's a straight line," she said. "Unless we got shot at, which we probably will, but overall, just a straight line."

"I don't think—"

"You don't have a choice," she said, then she wheeled the jet around to face the veritable legion of guns facing her and opened fire.

Explosions of debris rocked their ship, whole clusters of drones going up as their neighbours were blown to bits by Asha's guns. But she barely had time to look before she was swerving back around and sliding the controls across the dashboard to sit in front of Xavior.

Immediately, she summoned extra screens with a swipe of her hand, her fingers flying over the keyboard in front of her.

"Go!" she said. "Straight line, remember?" In her peripheral vision, she saw him nod, wrap his hand around the steering controls, and push, urging them onwards.

"We need to stay within range of the drones' systems" she warned. They had exactly two minutes before they'd be too far away for her to even access the system she intended to infiltrate. Somewhere deep inside her, there was a girl who wanted to curl up on the floor and cry her eyes out. She felt her, she acknowledged her, and she shoved those feelings so far down they'd never see the light of day again. Then she got to work.

It took twenty-two seconds for her to bypass security, repurposing a similar code she used to get into Gahraan's flight networks, to study flight patterns and access other semi-private government resources.

Then thirty-four seconds to find the order to dispatch the drones and alter it—sweaty fingers slipping on her tablet's screen, hyper-aware of every single second ticking by.

It was messy, and improvised, and she was sure security on the ground was already onto her, trying to shut her down. But, if all went according to plan, there would no longer *be* any security on the ground—

"Come on," she said, paused and shaking, waiting to see if it would work, to see if she'd been *right*—

ACCESS GRANTED.

"*I did it.*" But there was no time for celebration. "Xavior—" He practically threw the controls at her, sliding them back across the dashboard with relief. "I'm turning around," she said. "*Hold on.*" The jet reversed, wheeling around, and shooting back towards what remained of their pursuers. At the last moment, she dived down, angling them back towards the planet looming hugely in the near distance. They shot forward, taking heavy fire.

"We can't keep going like this," Xavior said. "The shields are compromised—only at a quarter functionality, and it's dropping fast."

"I know," Asha gritted out, "hold on."

They were getting closer and closer, sparks flying off the outside of the jet. She returned fire as best she could, rear guns blazing as she urged them forward, faster, until she could see clouds on the surface of A'lkari. Navigation zeroed in on the buildings, identifying Thracin's stronghold in seconds. She locked on to the destination and kicked the speed up to maximum. They were nearly there—piercing the upper levels of the atmosphere—steam rolling off the jet as clouds vaporised on contact.

With one hand, she initiated an emergency protocol already programmed into the drones' systems.

The fire ceased. The drones went dead.

"Warning, shield capacity at three percent," said the system.

The drones began to fall out of the sky.

"Asha," Xavior said quietly. "Why wouldn't you kill the drones in zero gravity? Why wait until they would fall . . .?"

She looked ahead at the continents rushing up to meet them. "Hopefully they'll take out the planetary defence systems, and most of the facility too. By the time we get down there half of it will be ruined, and the rest will be in chaos." The air around them burned as they shuddered through the last of the atmosphere. "And I wanted him to hurt," she said, eyes ahead. "I wanted him to hurt like I've hurt."

"It's going to do more than hurt," Xavior said. "Asha, people will die."

"*Oh, please,*" she said, but she felt like she was going to be sick. "You don't think they knew there was a possibility they might die when they signed up to fight for the Emperor? To carry out his sick commands?" The planet grew swiftly closer, blurring towards them, green, and yellow. "You don't think I could have died any day working for him, breaking my body to service his empire, to keep it fed, and watered, and in surplus of weapons he'd ship right back round to *shoot us with*?" Her hands shook. "If you can't handle it, maybe you shouldn't have come. Maybe I should have done this by myself." The ground rushed closer, too close, and for a moment, she thought about her hand on the controls, not letting up, not slowing down, and the darkness, the relief she would feel just before she stopped feeling anything.

"Asha!" Obi said, and she pulled them up, metres from the ground, travelling at insane speed. There was a shocked silence.

Then they crashed into a forest.

The ship had ground to a halt about a mile from the treeline. Their entry into the atmosphere had been disguised by the falling debris—it was likely they'd been mistaken for one of the dead jet drones due to Asha's last-minute cut-on of the engines. No one had appeared out of the trees to shoot at them, so it was likely the ship would be safe there. Plus, they'd cloaked it again for good measure. That had taken Asha a good twenty minutes. She'd got straight to work after they'd crashed, ignoring her hands that shook from the adrenaline, desperately trying to control her thoughts, which were scattered from the fear of the chase.

Now she was sitting on a tree stump, re-packing the small bag containing the equipment they would need to break in. Obi was rummaging around in the jet, and Xavior was walking towards her, his own small bag over his shoulder.

"Are you sure you want to do this?" he said, sitting next to her. "There's still time to turn back." His voice was soft. She didn't know how he did it—remaining so calm and collected whilst all she wanted to do was run into the woods, bail on the whole mission, and never come out.

"You'd come all this way, just to do what? Turn around?" she tightened the bag strap, pulling on it viciously. "I knew you weren't the brightest but this almost takes it too far." She had aimed for levity and completely missed, too highly strung to make the joke sound anything but mean. She could have kicked herself.

"Yes," Xavior said, simply. "If you asked, I'd find a way to get us home. I'd find a way out of here. I'd do anything, if you asked me to."

The gentleness in his voice, pierced something in her chest. She felt tears prick behind her eyes. *No,* she thought. *No, no, not now. Over my dead fucking body am I crying in front of anyone. Get it together.* "Xavior—"

"Asha, you're the most incredible person I've ever met. And whatever happens today . . . well, I—" His hands twisted nervously in his lap. "I thought you should know that." Asha wanted to put her hands in his and let him hold them. Wanted it desperately. "Before I met you, I don't think I understood what bravery was. What selflessness was." He shook his head. "And you—you make me feel like myself. Like I'd forgotten who I was, but somehow, being around you helps me remember."

"I'm really glad you're here," she whispered, and grasped his wrist hard over his sleeve, trying to say everything to him that she wished she could have said out loud. *If I had to watch you walk away from me, everything would stop making sense. Do you understand? Everything. The only version of this world that I'll accept is the one with both of you by my side. Tell me you understand.*

He looked down at her hand on his wrist, smiling slowly, and a warmth spread through her as she gazed back at him. At his face, his beautiful face, silver and jade in the moonlight. Through her mind flashed a mural, one she'd seen in a dream, of two Heroes embracing, drawn in obsidian and gold. There were so many things she wanted to say to him . . . or maybe it was just one. *Maybe it's always been just one,* she thought, *ever since we met inside a legend, when we were other people.* But she had always been better at *doing* than *saying,* so she leaned forward.

Their mouths brushed, and Asha felt him brace, as she did, for a strange vision to flash across her awareness, but nothing did. Everything was quiet. His hand cradled the back of her head, and she could feel his nose touching hers, bumping against it as their mouths moved and opened against each other. In the darkness of her closed eyes, bright lights were bursting. And then it happened: she saw a pale blue sky, a field of flowers from a very long time ago, and a man walking towards her, a crown of gold and crystal flashing at his brow. *Dandeyi,* said Adesola's voice, *my love.* It felt like the ground underneath her had given way, and Xavior's hands—one on her neck, the other on her thigh, were the only things keeping her from falling.

Eventually they pulled apart.

Asha smiled, her cheeks hot. She opened her mouth to say something, but then Obi's voice was breaking the silence.

"Alright, everything is ready. It's time."

It took four days and four nights for horribly shining eyes to begin blinking their way out of the shadows between the trees. Adesola and Sensit walked back-to-back and planned at night how they would fight their way through the legions of clawed terrors. Adesola's shield shone in the dim light as she held it in front of her, Sensit's sword glinting behind her as he watched, ever vigilant.

'A Complete, Annotated History of Chasca, Including Relevant Translated Mythologies. Chapter: Scroll the Third' by I. Nisomn, ex-acolyte of the Aonian Archives.

Chapter Thirty-Five

**[planet: A'lkari] + [location: Emperor's Stronghold] +
[year: 6066]**

Plumes of smoke rose from Thracin's palatial compound, small fires blazing over broken metal structures that had once been the jet-sized drones Asha had commanded to fall out of the sky. Debris was scattered in places—walls that had collapsed on the drones' impact—and there was a smell in the air, like burning chemicals.

Asha and Xavior observed this all from the tree line, dark clothing blending in with the shadows. As they watched, soldiers streamed out of the facility, guns grasped in their hands, yelling commands to their dazed comrades who had been on the ground when the drones fell. They would have to pick their moment carefully—two figures darting forwards from the forest would arouse suspicion and likely result in their immediate death. *Or worse,* Asha thought, *we could be captured.*

"There'll be a gap in a moment," Obi's voice echoed in her ear, crackling through the small, wearable comms unit she'd fashioned out of a handheld device on Aonia. Obi was sitting a few miles away in the jet, tapped into the compound's surveillance footage—courtesy of the security codes that Asha had found in the computer she had stolen on Xesca—watching it and relaying back what he saw.

The craft had re-cloaked after some repairs Asha had sacrificed precious time to make, but it had been a quick fix—without the right tools, she'd only been able to guarantee a few hours of full concealment. They had to get in, free Aziza, get out, and go. Obi and the jet represented their only hope of a getaway outside of stealing a ship. They had to do everything in their power to ensure it didn't come down to that.

"*Put on your cloaks,*" Obi instructed. "*You'll be able to move in five.*"

Wordlessly, Xavior pulled the pieces of fabric out of his small duffel bag and handed one of them to Asha. The Initiate cloak was scarlet against the muted greens and browns of the forest. She slipped it on, and put up the hood.

The last of the soldiers jogged out of the compound. Their backs facing Asha.

"It looks like all other security has been diverted away from the tree line to protect what's left of the planetary defence systems," Obi told them as they walked. "If you can get to the opposite side of the compound, you'll be able to enter the chaos unnoticed. And then, if all goes to plan, the cloaks will do the rest."

He was right—as the last line of soldiers moved away from them, running from the back of the compound to the middle of it, no one remained. It would only be this way for a minute or two, before the groups sweeping the perimeter arrived.

"*Now,*" Obi said.

They ran out of the trees, feet silent on the concrete floor, two figures in billowing cloaks dark against the grey evening sky.

For those few seconds they were fully exposed, and they were the most terrifying of Asha's life.

Then she saw the body.

Someone lay still and unmoving under a slab of concrete, an arm and a booted foot all that was visible. A trail of darkening blood trickled from underneath them, staining the black and white of their uniform with scarlet. A soldier, from the looks of the uniform, hit by falling debris, and killed.

I did that, she thought, sick with horror. *It's my fault.* But immediately, her own words echoed in her ears. *No, not me. Him. Thracin killed them the moment he conscripted them into his army. The moment he ascended the throne and started building his empire. As soon as they put on that uniform, they were already dead.*

The body wore an armband—so white it almost glowed. Seeing the body had caused her to falter, but it was this that stopped her in her tracks.

One of the most tenuous assumptions they had made was that the cloaks, and their perceived status as Initiates would help them grant access to any doors that required codes, or scans, they had not been able to access through the stolen computer. But now, standing exposed in the concreate of the outer perimeter, Asha realised the body in front of her was the body of a Commander. A title that came with a high level of security clearance. She couldn't pass this up.

Breaking away from Xavior, away from the set route, she ran to the collapsed wall, crouching next to the dead soldier beneath it.

"Asha!" Xavior's voice was a strained whisper. *"What are you doing?!"*

No time to explain. She shoved her hand under the wall, pulling the arm out into the light. A scaled hand was revealed, the claws curling inward, relaxed in death. Asha pulled a knife out of her waistband and started sawing it off.

Blood splattered to the ground.

Xavior yelled, then clapped a hand over his own mouth—too much noise would give them away—and they'd already taken too long.

421

There. The hand fell to the floor. She grabbed it, shoving it inside her own duffel bag, and running for cover, Xavior just ahead of her.

They threw themselves behind the nearest wall, breathing hard, waiting for the alarms, for the gunshots, for the yells of *INTRUDER!*

But they never came.

They looked at each-other, pale-faced. Xavior's mouth was opening and closing like he wanted to berate her for being so stupid, but didn't know enough words to correctly convey the enormity of her stupidity.

He settled for saying. "Please don't do anything like that again."

Asha nodded.

"*Quickly,*" Obi's voice jolted them out of their daze. "*There's a door to your left, go through it.*"

Asha nodded, already scanning her memories for the blue-prints she had pored over for a week. They were on the south side of the compound. The prison was underground, beneath the western end of the facility. The majority of the commotion was to the north-east, and the soldiers were gathering there, as the command centre at A'lkari re-directed all efforts to protecting the Emperor's quarters, valuable weapons and ships. The safety of the prisoners was the least of anyone's worries—the carceral quarters would soon be operating on the bare minimum of staff required, as all protective efforts were re-routed elsewhere.

They pushed open the door to their left, and slipped inside.

Almost immediately, they heard footsteps. Drawing their hoods further over their heads, they began to walk down the corridor.

A platoon of soldiers jogged past them, Asha's heart jumped into her mouth as they passed. But they weren't stopped.

"Excuse me," said a voice. One of the soldiers had turned around. "You should really evacuate. Everyone is being moved to the hangars under the East Wing."

Asha's throat was dry. She tried to speak but realised she didn't know what to say. Her hand twitched, desperate to engage her gun and shoot her way out of this. But that would jeopardise the mission before it had truly begun.

Xavior's voice rang out, clear and assertive. "We are on Diplomatic business, soldier. We are to record the attack for our books." He hadn't even turned around.

From deep inside the hood of her cloakhood, Asha saw the soldier nod. "Of course, apologies." A salute. "Divine Might."

"Is Divine Right," Xavior completed. He must have remembered that from his time here. Asha tried not to stare at him.

"Come on," he said, as soon as the soldier had moved on. "They'll realise we were lying soon, and then put two and two together. We have to go."

Asha nodded. "Obi, where now?"

"*It's just here,*" Obi voice was a tinny murmur in her ear. He was tracking them using a combination of things that Asha had come up with; the blueprints she'd found on Aonia, and the compass, which seemed to point in the direction of all three of them, no matter the distance. "*Take the next right.*"

Asha made a discreet motion to Xavior, and he nodded. They moved towards a corridor that branched off from the others.

To Holding Cells, read the signage above the door in Universal Standard.

"Okay," Asha muttered. "Let's do this."

Now came the tricky part. The part most likely to get them discovered and shot.

Asha was to hack the surveillance cameras for this section

of corridor only, and feed back a continuous two-second loop of footage that would make the hallway seem unoccupied. This footage would play until the next patrol began and someone realised something was up—it should be enough to give them a head start.

It was all or nothing. There was too much riding on this to doubt it. Either she would be successful, and they would progress through to the holding cells to locate Aziza and extricate her, or Asha would trip the system, causing them to be found and executed.

Asha repressed the urge to wince. She must have subconsciously squeezed Xavior's hand, because he squeezed back, whispering, "Asha, whatever happens, we're together. And I won't let anything happen to you."

"I won't let anything happen to you, either."

She smiled, lips pursed, and nodded. Then she slipped into the corridor and got to work.

First, she removed the panel that covered the wiring she needed to reroute, before whipping out her screwdriver to repurpose a spare port hidden under a compressed cover.

It didn't take long to input the code and integrate it seamlessly with the existing programming, but her sweaty fingers were slipping on her tablet's screen, and she was hyper-aware of every single second ticking by. She messed up, and had to try again, heart in her mouth as she carefully undid the mistake and input it correctly.

It took a few more seconds to double-check her work, to triple check it, and then breathe. Once, twice. *Come on Asha. Calm down.*

She watched the light in the corner flashing as she screwed the panel back into place. Red, red, *green.*

For a moment, relief swelled in her chest—

Then the red light was back. *Manual override detected,* flashed a message. *Scan to approve.*

Scan to approve? Scan what?

Asha's heart dropped to her stomach. She didn't have anything—

The hand.

Asha had never moved so fast in her life. Pulling the bloody claw out of her bag, she tried not to gag as she pressed the palm to the scan panel attached to her keyboard. Blue lines scanned it, up and down, up and down. A white light flashed a few times in quick succession.

Then it turned green.

"Oh thank Thracin," she breathed out. Pure relief threatened to overwhelm her, but she did not have time for it. They could celebrate later, when her sister was safe and they were thousands of miles away.

With shaking hands, she unhooked her keyboard and hid the drive she had installed behind the jumble of pre-existing wires. The panel went on easily, screws twisting into place and sliding home.

The knot in her stomach unravelled. She'd done it. Resisting the urge to slide to the floor in relief, she signalled Xavior.

"Your trick with the drones has thrown the whole place into chaos," he muttered. "There should be more patrols out." His eyes darted to the next corridor. "It's too quiet."

"Well, I'm not complaining," Asha said. "Quickly, we've only got until the next patrol comes through here to get my sister and get out. Twenty minutes maximum. The chaos might mean we have longer, but we can't count on it—"

Asha experienced the next moment in startling clarity and strange stop-motion, turning the world to freeze frames around her.

As she spoke, a lone sentry rounded the corner, gun primed to shoot, barrel glowing, aimed directly at Asha's head.

They both froze. The sentry pulled the trigger.

The bolt of energy flew from the sentry's gun, Xavior's arm clawed at her own, shoving her sideways to crash into the wall, the subsequent momentum putting him directly into the line of fire. His chest absorbed the bolt and convulsed, his whole body going rigid. Asha's hands scrambled at her belt, drawing her own pistol and firing three bursts of laser fire into the exposed skin between the sentry's helmet and the shoulder plate of their tessellating robotic armour.

Xavior. Oh my god, Xavior.

She struggled towards him, crawling across the floor. Her head pounded, throbbing from where it had slammed into the wall, her vision spinning. Dimly, she registered footsteps, lots of footsteps, but she couldn't focus. Xavior's skin was warm under her hand. She placed her cheek over his mouth, her hand over his heart and—

Arms yanked Asha off the floor. The barrel of a gun pressed into her abdomen, the sharp prick of a syringe slid into the back of her neck.

Unconsciousness slammed into her like a freight train.

She felt nothing.

Obi was panicking. He'd seen the screen go blank as Asha had successfully hacked the surveillance system, looping the footage of an empty corridor. He couldn't believe she'd stopped to take the hand of the dead soldier—but it had saved her and Xavior in the end.

But now, they were both silent. He'd heard a scream—and

Asha's voice sobbing. *No, Xavior—*

And now one of the compass needles was spinning wildly, with no fixed direction.

Frantically, he tapped the screens, trying to understand what had happened. Had they been captured? He thought he'd heard the sound of a gun discharging but he couldn't be sure. He was readying himself to go in there and find them when Adesola's voice rang out in his mind like an alarm.

She is dying. You have to find her.

Outside the glass of the jet window, he saw someone walking towards him. They were tall, preternaturally so, with armour interlocked all over their body, shining dully in the evening light. The glimmer of the shield flashed on their back.

She was here.

On Aonia, she had told him that the prophecy wouldn't let him return to help George and save London until he had helped Asha destroy the Emperor's weapon. He remembered her final words to him. *You are not a Hero yet. But you will be.*

Had she come to enforce her order?

You must go to her. You must see for yourself.

Obi's heart dropped into his stomach as he clambered out of the jet to meet her. "What happened to her?" he said, not wanting to believe it, hardly understanding how Adesola could even be here.

She does not have long left.

An image flashed into his mind—or an impression, rather. Of someone in great pain, who had been in pain for a very long time, breathing weakly. *Asha,* he thought. *No, please, no.*

"Where?" he hissed, clambering out of the jet, and into the quiet of the forest.

I can take you, her voice was everywhere inside his head. *There isn't long.*

Obi was nodding before she'd even finished.

She turned from him and raised her hand. Then she brought it down in a slash, and suddenly there was a *cut* in the *air*, as though the space around them was made of some flimsy material like tissue paper, or skin.

Obi didn't give himself time to question it. Adesola grasped either side of the cut and wrenched them apart.

He stepped through.

When the monsters burst forth from the shadows and attacked, Adesola and Sensit believed themselves to be ready. Had they not planned for this? Were they not Heroes? Had Mother not told them they were invincible?

'A Complete, Annotated History of Chasca, Including Relevant Translated Mythologies. Chapter: Scroll the Third' by I. Nisomn, ex-acolyte of the Aonian Archives

My goddess tells me that I too am invincible. She visits me nightly now and reveals to me the secret machinations of this universe, and I love her. But, though I love her, she says she will not accompany me when the time comes. She says there is another she waits for, here at the Guild. I would know my adversary, so I ask her: *who is he?* She says she does not know. I ask her: *how old is he?* She says he is dead. I ask her: *when was he born?* She says he hasn't been born yet. I ask her: *how then can you await him? This man you do not know, who is not born but has lived a lifetime and is already dead?* She says, because time holds him to a different standard. She says, because I do not need to know him in order to use him. – I. Nisomn

Chapter Thirty-Six

[planet: A'lkari] + [Location: Emperor's Headquarters] + [year: 6066]

When Asha awoke, it was dark. The floor underneath her was hard and cold, leeching the heat from her skin like ink bleeding into clear water. Her breath ghosted through the air in clouds of vapour that dissipated into the eerie stillness without a sound. It was so silent she could hear the beating of her own heart.

She couldn't see a ceiling of any kind—the darkness hung above her like a weight, forcefully reminding her of the way the incense smoke had gathered on the roof of the temple back home as she said her prayers.

She wasn't praying now. Maybe she should have been, but Thracin had taken even that from her, too. Any god she might have laid claim to was long gone; burned along with the books that told the true history of the human race.

"Xavior?" she whispered.

No reply.

Panic thudded through her. The last she had seen of him was a body, lying still on the floor.

No, no, no, please, no.

Her vision swam as her eyes adjusted to the dimness. Faint shapes seemed to pierce the space in front of her, looming suddenly as she grew used to the low light and started to make sense of her surroundings.

Her skin prickled.

Pillars of thracinite soared into the sky, stalactites of it stabbing down from the cavernous ceiling. The floor was made from thracinite too, and inside it, set into the crystal-clear stone, were bodies. A screaming mouth gaped up at her. It belonged to one of the creatures she had seen on an Aonian index of conquered species, purple skin and milky-white eyes preserved forever in the castle of her conqueror. Other bodies were set into the stone, contorted and writhing, as though the crystal had once been water that held a thousand drowning bodies before it had frozen. Asha's hand lay on top of another body, its heads thrown back, eyes bloodshot and glazed over, doomed to stare at their fellow subjugates forever. Another, baring serrated teeth in a final howl lay stretched next to what looked like the remains of a woman with blue skin, and bright yellow markings. Asha turned away.

She had to get out of here. How much time had passed, though? Where was Xavior? Was Obi still waiting for them in the forest?

Their last conversation surfaced in her mind. *I want you to succeed, I want to help you succeed, dammit. You deserve this.* But she'd failed.

Turning around, her elbow slammed into something. A wave of light rippled out from the place where her arm had seemed to connect with empty air. She reached out a hand and pressed her palm against an invisible wall. Briefly, the entire cage was visible, pulsing gently in the air around her, light rippling outwards along the perimeters of a small cube. She let her hand fall away.

There was a jamming device sewn into the hem of her shirt. After they'd been captured on Xesca, she'd spent time building the little device—she would never be stuck in that position again, if she could help it. The cage looked similar to those energy fields, and she was sure that if she activated the device, she could get out. The question was *when*.

The click of boot heels on the crystal floor set her heart racing. She whipped her head around, trying to locate it. There was a faint swishing noise in the echo, too, like water, or rustling layers of fabric. A thin shadow stretched onto the wall.

Then someone strode into view.

Robes of gauzy white fabric that layered like mist swathed their thin frame, cinched in impossibly tight at the waist. A length of purple fabric streamed out behind them, and Asha could just about make out lines of strange, angry symbols picked out in the same deep violet as the cape, embroidered on the bright white hems and up the sleeves, circling around the collar that constricted their slim, pale neck like a vice. They carried a short staff in one hand, the end adorned with the outline of a triangle, wrought in some pale, dully gleaming metal. In the space at the centre, Asha thought she could see a faint blue-purple light crackling. A featureless mask covered their face, made of a shining white material that looked almost ceramic. The surface of it was completely smooth, save for a deep slash where the mouth should have been. From that thin sliver of darkness, a voice:

"So, this was what the people received," said the masked mage, "when they begged for the galaxy to birth them a Hero." A low laugh. Asha felt a powerful revulsion welling up in her. "I can't imagine they'd feel all that gratified if they were ever to meet you. I believe that we are doing our citizens a favour, then, taking you off the board."

Asha took a step back. Her spine hit the invisible wall of the cage.

The being advanced, cloak fluttering around their feet, emanating slow menace like a beacon. *Magekind*, she assumed, because she didn't know what else this person could be other than *magician* or *sorcerer*, and while she had thought fleetingly about these purported magi-scientists that walked at the right hand of the Emperor when Obi mentioned them, she had never stopped to think about what it might be like to face one, trapped in an invisible cage, unable to tear her eyes away from the staff-like instrument and its terrible crackling energy, like a little sphere of lightning called down from the sky.

"And I *know* that the Emperor told me not to underestimate you," said the assured voice from behind the mask. "That he told me you are more powerful than you look. But—" They broke off, and Asha could hear their smile in the silence. "You don't look like *much*, do you?"

Asha clenched her hands into fists, wanting to retaliate, wanting to smash her way through this cage and rip the mask right off their face. She was so sick of people talking to her like this—calling her *nothing* and *no one* by the tone of their voice; not only asserting their superiority with every word, but explaining explicitly that her inferiority was her *fault*, and expecting her to lie down and take it. "Maybe if you let me out of here," she grit out, "we can find out if he was right."

The Magekind laughed, harsh and dismissive, before bringing up one pale hand—one hand that looked astonishingly human as it emerged from the folds of the shimmering gauze—and waved it across the blank face of the white mask.

It melted away like mist, and beneath it, impossibly, was a human woman.

Her skin was white—almost unnaturally so, her cheekbones prominent above thin cheeks and a strong, pointed chin. The hair that Asha could see, scraped back from her face, was bright ash-blonde. Her eyes were large and liquid-looking, their irises a shocking shade of pale blue—almost lavender—just like the light that swarmed at the top of her staff.

"His Excellence doesn't know you're here yet," she said, as

Asha gaped, disbelieving. Her whole life, she'd been told humans were as good as mud on the bottom of a shoe, but here this woman was walking free in the palace of the Emperor. "He's off-planet on important business." She laughed again, and the sound was like broken glass falling to the floor. "So, you're all mine."

"How are you here?" Asha breathed, still caught up in the fact that this young woman was human, or something close to it, at least, and she was *here*, safe in the sanctum of the Emperor, exalted at his side.

The woman made a face, as though Asha had said something unbearably offensive. "No," she said curtly. "Not anymore." Her eyelashes were so blonde they seemed transparent. "I haven't been *that* since I was chosen to take up the staff and be remade; conduit to the power of the prophecy." A smiled stretched its way across her face. Asha could tell she didn't smile like that often—it ached with sincerity, like she truly was pleased to have been remade, whatever that meant. It was sickening. "I am Magekind now—component of a historic equation—thanks, of course, to the divine might of our god, may he rule these stars forever. You can call me Invidia—Third Tetrarch to the First of us, who is, of course, the Emperor."

Third Tetrarch? A human?

"How?"

"I replaced dear old Noeminus when he died from prophetic wounds. And I was handpicked by the Emperor as a child—taken away from that squalid planet you call home—and brought here to serve a greater purpose. And set an example to the rest of you. I was the natural choice for succession really. I'm the greatest Mage the Emperor's seen in a hundred years." She lifted her chin up, as though she not only believed what she was saying, but was proud of it.

433

Asha pursed her lips against a smile. She'd met girls like this before. The ones that guards took a liking to, who thought that meant they were somehow better than the rest of them. "I bet he said that to the last guy, too. You should ask him. Oh wait, he's dead."

There was a pause. Then Invidia said, "You don't look much like her, you know," as though she couldn't help herself. "Though she looks more like a corpse these days than a person, so I'm hardly surprised."

Asha's heart stopped, then restarted in a rush of fury. She slammed her hand onto the invisible walls of the cage, scarcely restraining a shout. A brutal, unnameable feeling was rising in her—it felt like *murder*, magma-hot and surging through her like something vicious.

"*Where is she?*" Asha said, voice low and shaking.

"You knowing that won't make any difference. You won't be seeing her. I've alerted the Emperor to your presence and received my orders. Within the hour, you'll be dead, and there'll be no touching reunions for either of you."

"Oh really?" Asha snarled. Then she put her hand over the tiny jamming device she'd slapped onto the wall behind her a minute earlier, hooked her thumbnail under the switch and slid it home. The cage froze—glitching into sight like a faulty hologram. There was a series of small beeps, and then a flash, and the cage around her died, flickering fully into perception. It was made up of a network of nodes, connected by wires, that had been broadcasting the invisible perimeters between them in the shape of a cube. It seemed the Magekind's 'magic' was just incredibly advanced technology. All she had to do was grab a fistful of wiring in each hand and yank them apart.

She stepped out into the cavernous room and activated the slim band around her wrist with a press of her fingers. The metal crawled down her hand, its tiny tessellating components flowing like water over her skin, constructing a gun out of nowhere, nestled in the clutch of her bent fingers. She levelled the barrel at the Magekind's cold, pale face.

"Take me to her," she said. "Take me to my sister—right now."

The Tetrarch raised an eyebrow, mouth curving into cruel and sadistic lines, as though Asha had impressed her the way one might be impressed by a small, domesticated animal that had learned a new way to beg for food. Lazily, she raised her staff, violet light crackling in the triangle's empty centre. For a moment Asha was mesmerised—the instrument seemed to pull threads of light from the air in glowing ribbons, sucking them into a swirling vortex of searing brightness. They wound together, coalescing into a tiny, sizzling sphere of energy that Asha had no doubt would kill her on impact.

"Stop that, ot I'll shoot," she said, "I'll shoot you right now."

"Oh please," Invidia said. Then she flipped the staff in a figure-eight so fast it was a blur in her hands, her eyes seeming to siphon the energy from the air too, blazing with purple light.

Fuck that, Asha thought, and shot her, squeezing the trigger—but Invidia just batted the bolt out of the air with one swift swing of the staff, rolling her eyes as she did so, and aiming it expertly to fly right back at Asha's hand. Asha yelped as the gun was snatched out of her grip, retracting back into the metal band, which was now searing hot against her wrist. If the bolt had touched her skin, she would have lost her hand.

Invidia smirked, before flinging a flaming ball of burning violet light straight at Asha's chest.

There was nothing she could do. The murderous light flew towards her, crackling through the air. With a yell, she flung her arm up, her scorched, numb hand covering her face.

Is this how I die? she thought, *is this—*

The world slowed.

As she stood there, terror coursing through her blood like a match touched to kerosene, she realised she could only think of one thing: all the people that were counting on her—the ones she swore she would protect every night when no one could hear. Her mother, captured by the Sentinel, alone and terrified. Her sister, who had been chained in a government cell since she was a child. Obi, waiting in the jet to take her to freedom so that he could get his cure and escape this time, so he could go home. And Xavior, collapsed in the hallway, not moving, maybe not even breathing. Captured, or—or dead—

She felt insane with grief. It was all she could feel—like a gaping hole inside her chest where her heart should have been, like someone had grabbed the vital organ and torn it clean out, and now her entrails were sliding out of her too, onto the floor. *I don't want to die. I don't want to die.*

Behind her closed eyes, golden light flickered. And into the gap where her heart should have been, something came rushing, filling her with fire.

The burning sphere of flame hurled at her from Invidia's staff slammed into her, shuddering through her frame, pushing her back along the floor.

She waited for the pain, for the descent of darkness, for the inevitable ceasing of her own heartbeat.

But it never came.

Then she heard Invidia gasp, and as she looked up, she saw why.

Something glimmered faintly in front of her, murky, almost, as though she were viewing it through a veil; two semi-translucent straps looped their way around her forearm, supporting a giant shield that shone like a ghost light, sparkling in the red sun of another realm, its interlocking plates of crystal and burnished gold carved with myriad images that Asha couldn't quite make out, or understand. *The shield of legend. Adesola's weapon.*

Asha looked over the top of it, scared, and alive, and so grateful, and felt like the world was ending.

And in a way it was—the confines of her tiny reality stretching and gaping around her, a vacuum of impossible things rushing in to fill the space.

Soon, you will understand, Adesola had said in her vision, standing there with her own shield. *This* shield.

"Holy shit," Asha murmured.

"How—" stuttered Invidia. "You can't have that *already*! The prophetic trajectory clearly states that—"

Asha stood up, jutting her chin, casting her eyes around the battlefield they'd made of this perfectly nice room, and finding it far more level with this shield of mass destruction in her hands. "Oh, shut up," she said. Then she launched herself, her arm already coming around on the downswing. It was faster than she'd ever moved in her life, and as her feet drove into the ground, propelling her forward, she remembered the arcs and turns of this violent dance in her muscles; memories of this ancient motion were stored somewhere inside her. Memories from long ago. Invidia swung her staff; time slowed, and Asha slipped passed it, coming up under her guard.

She slammed the shield into Invidia's head. There was no logical explanation for how she knew to do this. Though the shield barely seemed corporeal, her back muscles strained with the weight. She was already drenched in sweat. *This has to do some damage.*

Invidia staggered back a few paces, her pale hand coming up to slip through the blood sliding down her forehead.

There it is, Asha thought viciously. *We're all the same, under the surface.*

Invidia snarled at her, raising her staff, siphoning that crackling energy out of the air in huge ribbons, weaving it into a sphere on top of that pale, glimmering staff—

"Third, stand down," said a calm, deep voice. Chills erupted down Asha's arms. "I'd like to at least talk to her, before you kill her."

And then the Lord Emperor of the hundred worlds, First Tetrarch of the Council, and Chief Executive Officer of the Consortium, Ai'varek Thracin, stepped into the light.

Heroes they might have been, but ready they were not. The demons poured from within the forest's rotting heart, teeth clacking, necks writhing and snapping in animal fury. Jaws opened wide, gaping and red, and though Sensit slashed his sword in flashing arcs, the creatures did not abate. Barbed tails swung, lashing and jagged, and though Adesola threw her shield again and again with all her strength, lightning quick, its edges slicing underbellies open, the demons would not fall back. The two Heroes were soon separated, carried away on tides of blood that frothed in madness at the slaughter.

'A Complete, Annotated History of Chasca, Including Relevant Translated Mythologies. Chapter: Scroll the Third' by I. Nisomn, ex-acolyte of the Aonian Archives

Chapter Thirty-Seven

**[planet: A'lkari] + [location: Emperor's Headquarters] +
[year: 6066]**

Obi ran through the flickering gap that Adesola had torn in the
air and stumbled into darkness.

No. Not darkness.

His footsteps clanged on metal and he looked down. A thin
walkway stretched out on either side of him, as though he were
on a thin bridge, suspended in the middle of space. There were
pinpricks of light, hovering all around him like—*like stars*, he
realised. The lights surrounding him were stars, millions of them,
floating immobile in inky blackness.

As his eyes adjusted, more details revealed themselves. A
purple swathe of light to his left was a mass of dust and sparkling ice. A burst of pink and pale blue, edged in scarlet, was a
planetary nebula. A pinprick of dusky, wispy orange was a dying
star. It was mesmerising.

Where am I? Was his first thought. His second was, *Where's
Asha?*

He couldn't truly be standing in the centre of the galaxy—
he would have died as soon as he stepped through the gap.
Squinting downwards, he could almost make out some other
lights—blue-white and incongruent with the rest of the lights.
These were rectangular, with straight edges. *Screens.* A bank
of monitors glowed softly a way beneath the walkway he had

appeared on. Which meant this could be only one thing. A large-scale hologram—a simulated model of the galaxy.

As if to confirm his suspicions, the entire scene expanded, stars and planets rushing past. Vertigo nearly swept Obi to the floor but the swirling mass of stars beneath him wasn't actually moving. It really was a hologram; he could see that now. And it was focussing in on one particular star system.

But why am I here? Adesola told me Asha was hurt. I'm supposed to be helping her, but I can't even see her.

"Adesola," he whispered. "Where are you? Where's Asha?"

There was no reply.

Around him, the hologram slowed, its controller arriving at their destination. Obi did not know which system this was, or even which quadrant, but he could tell something was off immediately. Two of the six planets were blackened husks, scarred with craters and giant gorges slashed through the crusts right to their dead, icy cores. As Obi watched, the third planet in the system—a pale pink ball of cloudy atmosphere surrounded by three icy rings—tipped violently to one side and then began to spin. It was horrifying and unnatural, and made Obi want to reach out through the hologram and set it to rights.

"More," called out a voice. Obi nearly had a heart attack. Crossing the walkway as silently as possible, his mind raced as he tried to figure out where he was—and why he'd been brought there. The voices had come from the opposite side of the room. He peered over the edge. But he couldn't see anything—the hologram was too dark.

"More," the voice repeated. "They must pay for what they've done. Disobeying the Emperor comes at a cost."

Obi remembered a conversation, overheard on the NIS, about a planet destroyed, Ossock's calm, grave voice talking about the Emperor's power—about his destruction of entire worlds.

You three must destroy the tyrant's weapon, as was foretold. The prophecy has you where it needs. All you must do is bend to its will. Or you will be forced.

As he watched, heart sinking, the hologram of the planet stopped spinning.

Its atmosphere was gone, evaporated into nothing. Continents Obi had only glimpsed before the sickening spinning had started were cracked and drowning; no match for the centrifugal forces generated by such high-speed rotation. The oceans had gathered at the planet's equator, draining from its poles to drown the land masses at its middle.

For a single horrifying second, he was back on Xesca as it imploded, the ground convulsing and buckling under his feet, lightning striking the earth, and thunder shaking the sky. He remembered catching a glimpse of it through the window of the Guild ship. And it had looked just like this one—as though struck by the same force.

This was no simulation—this was truly happening, somewhere in the galaxy *planets was being destroyed.*

It was pure destruction. Murder on an epic scale. This was bigger than genocide, bigger than interplanetary war—

This was the Emperor's weapon.

This was where Adesola had taken him—not to Asha, not to save his friends, but to fulfil the instructions of what—a fairy tale? An ancient civilisation, long dead and gone?

"You tricked me," he hissed into the darkness, certain she was listening. "All I wanted was to help my friend. I trusted you, and you brought me here, against my will—"

"You have no will," Adesola said. "You are a Hero."

Obi turned.

She walked towards him out of the darkness, her golden eyes burning. "And I did not trick you. When we met, I told you what you were supposed to do. What you needed to do, so that the prophecy would let you leave this place and return to your home. As for trusting me . . . do you trust the turn of the clock's hands? The pull of gravity? Or do you recognise them for what they are: inevitabilities?" Obi could not speak. Adesola only smiled—though there was sorrow in it. "The prophecy is the same, and I was only ever its agent." She reached him and touched his shoulder. Pushing him backwards towards the railing of the bridge. "Besides, our missions were not so different. I wanted the weapon destroyed. You wanted it saved. Perhaps these aims have more in common than you think." She pointed over the edge. "Look."

His heart thudding, Obi turned. The hologram had shifted, revealing a dais, and a high-backed chair. There was a whimpering sound. As Obi strained his ears towards it, it grew steadily louder until he realised the high, keening wail he could hear was coming from whoever was seated in the chair. Then the wailing became words, and Obi's heart sank further with every single one.

"*No*," sobbed the voice. "Please, *no*, I don't want to anymore." It was a female voice, low and keening, like a kicked animal. "I'm sorry," she cried. "I'm so sorry,"

"You will obey the Emperor, child." The same monotone voice from before. "You know what will happen if you do not."

Another ragged cry, weak and reedy. Chills flashed down Obi's skin, raising the hair on his neck.

He remembered the feeling he'd had when Adesola had told him that 'she' was dying; of a person in terrible pain, who had been like that for a long time. He'd assumed it was Asha, in danger, but it couldn't be.

"Planet shaper," came Adesola's voice, soft, from behind him. "The last of my planet's people with the royal gift." Obi had never heard the shield-bearer angry before. Now, her voice was quiet with rage. "He took her so young. This life is all she's ever known. For this and for everything else, he must pay."

Who is she? Obi wanted to ask, but all the puzzle pieces were fitting together in his mind, answering his own question. *I wanted the weapon destroyed. You wanted it saved. He took her so young* . . . His blood ran cold.

"No," he murmured. "*No.* Adesola—" he turned to face her, but the walkway was empty.

She was gone.

Little Hero, said Mother into Sensit's mind. Little Hero, you are growing weaker.

Sensit did not reply.

Little Hero, do not ignore me. Little Hero—

"I know," said Sensit. "I know that I grow weaker, but I must persevere. It is what you ordered of me, and it is how I will reach Dandeyi. I cannot give up now, I do not have it in me to face what failure would make me."

'A Complete, Annotated History of Chasca, Including Relevant Translated Mythologies. Chapter: Scroll the Third' by I. Nisomn, ex-acolyte of the Aonian Archives.

Chapter Thirty-Eight

Asha trembled. The Emperor smiled, wide and clean and king of everything, his irises like black holes. She wanted to raise the shield, to warn him: *not another step*, but her whole body felt weak. Fear paralysed her limbs—her body wouldn't *move*. Horribly, it occurred to her that maybe all the years of deference, of obedience, that made up her entire life so far, were finally catching up with her—all the kneeling, bent at the waist, praying in a crystal cage to a ruler who saw her and didn't think *person*, or even *little girl*, but *object*, or *cost-efficient labour*, or *millimetre in a profit margin that should be wider*. Or maybe it was the violence enacted against her, or right in front of her upon every person she had ever loved, that had made her so scared. Maybe she *had* learned her lesson under the dome in that red desert, and that lesson had been *fear*. But there was another feeling, all Asha, that said maybe all the subservience and humiliation, all that suffering, would be worth it, if she could just get her hands around Thracin's neck and *squeeze*.

She blinked away tears of fear, clenching her hands into fists, but Thracin only smiled wider, pity touching the edges of his expression.

"There's no need to look so scared," he sounded regretful. "I won't hurt you. I can't." He raised a hand, and for a moment,

444

Asha could see through it to the other side of the room. *A projection*, she thought, and felt at once inexplicably safer, but also cheated. His hands looked just like hers—in fact, she was shocked to see that he appeared essentially humanoid; slim and broad-shouldered, with dark hair and pale skin. He looked false, almost. Like a high-definition simulation. A three-dimensional model made for virtual reality. Ageless. She couldn't have picked him out of a crowd back home, and for moment, she wondered how it was that she had never seen his face before.

But there *was* something different. Where it was clear that Invidia was all human, or had been, once, Asha's animal instincts were screaming at her that Thracin was something else.

He tilted his head, studying her with an expression of mild, detached interest, and suddenly, it was obvious.

Older, came the word, unbidden into her mind. *He's much older.*

She clenched her fists, not allowing herself to look away. The corners of his mouth lifted into a smile.

On the other side of the room, Invidia's expression was shifting between biting hatred for Asha and a sickly adoration of the Emperor. To her he was the sun, and in her expression, Asha saw the galaxy and its citizens. The ones who saw the Consortium as a force for good that sometimes had to make hard choices, who had not only saved the galaxy from the turmoil of a war and an old regime that had failed, but had bettered it, sweeping across the systems like a holy sunbeam, trailing prosperity and opportunity in its wake.

Thracin nodded his head, pointing at the shield. "Where did you get that?" he asked calmly. Amiably, even, as though they were friends and he was enquiring about something mundane.

Could it be that Thracin didn't know everything?

Asha forced herself to speak. "None of your business."

Invidia drew herself up, enraged, practically spitting, but the

Emperor leashed her with a flick of his hand, keeping the full force of his gaze on Asha.

"If you tell me," he said, unruffled, "I'll release your sister to you. That's why you're here, isn't it?"

Asha fought not to react. She dared a glance at Invidia, but the other girl's face was infuriatingly blank. "How do I know you won't just kill me?" she said.

"You would question the word of the Emperor?"

"You never gave me your word."

He nodded, conceding the point. "I give it to you, then."

She looked at the shield, her heart thudding. She could lie, reel off some random set of coordinates, or even say *Gahraan*, just to see the look on his face. But something told her he would know, and that he'd kill her for the deceit just because he could. So, she decided to rattle him a little instead.

"It appeared to me," she said. "I didn't go looking for it. It found me. Just like the—" She swallowed. "Like the prophecy did."

Silence. Then he nodded, as though she had passed some test that he hadn't expected her to. "So, it's true," he said plainly. In the corner, Invidia hissed like a feral cat, cornered. "It is starting." He was looking at her, contemplative and lightly intrigued in a way that made her feel as though he had only been observing her from the corner of his eyes before. He didn't seem afraid, or angry or surprised. There was only the small smile at the corners of his mouth, and an intelligent curiosity that chilled Asha to her core.

"In recent years I have found myself adjacent to this prophecy." His voice was measured and cold. "And it is . . . unbearable." His eyes were holes that went back forever. Sweat trickled down Asha's face. She felt primeval, distilled to her most basic instincts, *fight or flight* blaring like air raid sirens. And then Thracin said,

"I can't imagine you're enjoying it all that much either."

He smiled broadly, as though they shared some kind of inside joke, and the whole world of her terror rearranged itself around the lines of his placid laughter. He wasn't just going to kill her, he was going to delight in it. He would probably laugh as he drove the blade in, grin boyishly as he aimed the barrel of a gun between her eyes. She fought not to make a noise, but her horror was vacuous and gaping inside her chest, and something was bound to give. Her throat was closing up.

"All that responsibility!" He made a sympathetic face. "And why you? You aren't special. Just a girl, risen from nothing, supposed to save a hundred worlds." He *pondered* her, and there was something of the Archivist's philosophical wonderment in the tilt of his head—in the soft press of his fingers to his chin. "Often, I wonder if your death is supposed to teach me a lesson."

Behind him, Invidia nodded gravely. That curious light still shone in Thracin's awful eyes, and Asha did not doubt for a second that he meant every word of what he said. She was nothing but a game piece, perishable goods to be moved around the board of the galaxy, to be wrung out for energy and forward momentum, to be taken out of play, sacrificed for the greatest outcome, if that was what the hand in charge decided. And it had.

"So, my death is yours, too?" Asha said, helplessly, hating the crack in her voice, and the smooth assurance in his. "Just like my life was?" She searched his face, looking for something like shame, but all she could see was an easy superiority.

"It is an honour to contribute to the prosperity of the empire," Invidia said. "You should be grateful."

Thracin spread his hands as if to say, *there you go.* But there was something in his eyes that made Asha think he knew exactly what he had done. That he had calculated it—set the price of labour against the value of a good life and decided that for his purposes—exponential growth, a booming economy, straps by which he could pull a dying, war-ravaged galaxy from the brink of ruin and an age of crippling poverty—one could not justify the other.

She had wanted for so long to think of him as insane, as deranged and unhinged. A madman dictator whose commands were interpreted by soldiers who subsisted off violence and carried them out the only way they knew how: brutally and without compromise. This was the only way she could explain his actions to herself and have them make even the tiniest shred of sense. But, as she looked at him—at the serene edge of his smile, and the sharpened sword that hung by his hip, the military medals and the clean fold of his dress uniform across his chest, the way he held himself, like he truly was a god and everyone else his creation, existing at his mercy—and then downwards at the twisted bodies encased in the crystal of the floor, Asha realised he was just as sane as anyone else she had met, which was somehow infinitely worse.

"It isn't personal," he said, like he was delivering a lecture. "Although, in this case, I suppose it might be." An apologetic smile. "You were chosen by something, a long time ago, to be my enemy. You and I, we are different—of course we are—but also . . . not." He spread his hands. "You have great power buried inside you. Just like your sister did. Enough to pose a real threat, if I let you live past today. But I believe that the prophecy has not yet begun—it is close at hand, of course—but not yet started. So, I'll kill you, and prevent it, and you won't ruin this world that I have so carefully built in service of its citizens."

He smiled at her like that because she *was* nothing. A dat-apoint playing at being a saviour, at being a Hero. And maybe it *was* true that she had power, and a planet that in another life would have been hers, but this was *this* life, and that planet and its people were gone. Thracin held himself like he was a god because he was as good as. He killed entire planets, destroyed civilizations so that he could mould the galaxy into the shape that he wanted. Had she not prayed to him, sacrificed for him, however unwillingly? His soldiers died for him, wanted to die for him, and kept laying down their lives without question or hesitation. The Consortium didn't conscript, they *crusaded*; sentients the universe over believed in him, believed he was making a better one, but these people did not know the cost of a life, as they had always had one worth living and were so far removed from the bloodshed and the servitude that they could convince themselves that the people dying—the ones being killed by the life they were trying to live—somehow deserved it, that they were made for servitude and then death, just like Thracin said.

I'll kill you, she thought. *You will die at my hand. As of now, Ai'Varek Thracin is a marked man. I'll—*

There was a voice.

Whispering in her ear.

Softer than water over pebbles.

Lighter than air.

"Stay still. We must leave."

Asha's whole body tensed, ready for flight, but the voice—Adesola's voice, she realised dazedly—told her not to move.

"Not yet. Not yet . . ."

Thracin narrowed his eyes at her. Then the tranquil facade cracked, and his expression changed, something terrifying and ancient pushing forward, his eyes widening, mouth snarling—

"No!" he cried, and his black eyes were pure fury. He reached for his gleaming crystal sword at the same time that Asha felt a *body* materialise behind her. A hand with rich dark skin, armoured to the wrist. Thracin, seeming to remember he was

449

only present holographically, motioned sharply to Invidia, who was already moving, staff whirling in front of her, gathering light towards it like a black hole. She discharged a bolt of energy, flinging it towards Asha.

Time seemed to slow.

Asha heard herself suck in a breath, and then there was only a blanketed quiet, and the violet blaze of Invidia's eyes, and the answering echo in the comet of energy streaming towards them. Thracin stood impotent and furious behind her, hands flexing like claws, mouth a slash of anger.

Just before the bolt hit her, Asha saw him look behind her, as though he could see Adesola too, his eyes widening in something that looked a lot like fear.

"*Now,*" whispered the voice, and then she was falling.

Asha opened her eyes with a gasp and shudder as the world reformed itself around her. The shield still glowed faintly in front her, though it was growing less and less corporeal, like some unknown timer was running out.

She spun around—and came face to face with Adesola.

"I—" Asha said.

"Asha!" Obi's voice was hoarse and ragged. She whipped around, tearing her eyes from her apparent saviour to find him. *How was he here? How was* she *here?*

Asha, Obi, and Adesola stood on a narrow bridge, suspended in a dark, cavernous room. There was a hologram between them so complex that Asha's vision swam the second she tried to comprehend it.

"Don't look—" Obi was babbling, as though delirious. "Asha, I'm so sorry, I didn't know—*I didn't know.*"

Then she saw that in the middle of the hologram, past the solar systems made of pixels and the nebulae and the asteroid belts, sat a woman. At first, Asha thought she had tentacles sprouting from her head and her arms and her chest, but that didn't seem right. She blinked, squinting, and then bile rose in her throat

The tentacles weren't tentacles, but hollow tubes, and they were feeding the woman chemicals that raced and glowed in such a way that Asha thought she might be sick if she looked for too long.

Then she saw the woman's face. Truly saw it. And all the noise—Obi's frantic yells, the clanging of the stairs as every guard in the room ran towards them, alerted to their presence by the clang of Asha's arrival out of mid-air, and their crackling radios—all that noise faded to nothing, drowned out by the blood rushing in her ears.

The face of the woman controlling the hologram looked like her mother's; it looked like hers.

"*No*," Asha breathed, and then she was running.

Her footsteps shook the bridge, clanging against the metal, causing the support struts to creak and groan. A sentry loomed in front of her, his gun already firing, and she didn't even think before she raised the shield to block the shots and then slammed into him, the fading shield still solid enough, pushing his falling body over the side of the bridge.

Reaching the top of the steps that led to the floor, Asha crouched behind the phantom shield, covering her whole body with it, engaging her bracelet, and firing the gun over the top of the gold and crystal edge. Laser fire impacted the shield, but she drove her back foot into the ground and stayed stable. Her gunfire never stopped. Two shouts and the thump of bodies falling told her she'd succeeded. There must have only been three of them—*more than adequate intimidation for a malnourished, sick young woman,* Asha thought, rage turning the world around her to red.

She stood up, shield held over her stomach and face on the offchance she was wrong.

But the room was quiet.

The chair, when she reached it, turned with only a push. Her sister's hollow face greeted her, eyes closed in sleep, or at least the chemical imitation of one.

Aziza looked emaciated, and Asha was used to malnutrition, to hollow cheeks and dry, peeling skin, but they never starved on Gahraan, not really, because dead slaves were wasted money, so she had never seen this. Her sister's skin was thin and sallow, a yellowish membrane, where it should have been a lustrous brown. Her hair was gone, as if it had never existed, shorn to nothing but uneven black stubble. Her cheeks caved into her face, her skin clinging to her skeleton, sinking into the cavities of her eye sockets.

She was barely recognisable. In fact, Asha did not know how she had recognised her from the bridge. It was only now she knew it was Aziza that she could see similarities between the image she held in her head—the image she had fabricated—and this gaunt, skeletal ghoul of a woman.

Her sister sighed, eyelids fluttering, so thin they were almost translucent. Asha, compelled by the sight of her, so weak and sick, but still recognisably her sister, reached out a hand and touched her cheek.

This is it, she realised. *The final image from the vision.*

Bright, gold light flashed, shining through Asha's fingers. She knew what the gold was now—this strange light that had followed her from Gahraan all the way to A'lkari. It was the light of the prophecy, a sign of foretold events. It grew brighter and brighter, turning her vision to gold, then yellow, then pure white, until she was blinded. Yet in the oblivion of the light, she could somehow see everything that had ever been. She was deaf, yet she heard every word ever uttered, every song ever sang, every sigh that had ever fallen from forlorn and weary lips. She was incorporeal, yet she was certain she had a body, and that it was the universe.

When the images came, swarming around her, she knew what she was being shown before she saw it: the end of the story. Or one of them. The ending the prophecy had been guiding her towards this for weeks now. For her whole life.

The first memory was of a baby, and the day her mother left her, shivering in torn clothes, running out to find her freedom.

"Forgive me, please," Iyanda said, her face young and bruised. The baby didn't understand, and started to cry, howling louder as her mother darted a look towards the open door, and the bustle beyond it. "When you are old enough to know I left you, please forgive me for it. Please." She pressed a kiss to the baby's head and ran for her life.

They would never see each other again.

The second was of a spaceship and a journey that stretched forever into the heavens, until the heavens turned black and space turned blacker still, and she was told to call the dark planet in the distance *home.*

There were no stars in the sky above the dark planet. She had tried so many times to find them.

There was a monster, though, and he was king. As she grew, she visited him every day. Sat on his knee, even though his eyes were so cold and unfeeling she thought one day he might eat her, or worse, simply cast her aside. They told her to call him Emperor, or Exalted, and she did, even when her voice shook and her chin trembled. One day he told her to call him Father, though she did not know what that meant. Then he told her she was special, and that she would save the world.

The third memory was about a chair, and a game that she played and played and played, and always won, and about a throne and an offer to rule.

Her legs dangled off the edge of the chair that Father put her in. He stroked her face and told her not to worry as they slid lots of pointy, painful of needles under her skin and wriggled them into her veins. He told her it was all a game, even though it didn't look like any game she had played before, and that he just wanted to see if she was any good at it. He told her that in the game she was a god, just like him, and that he wanted her to find some rocks in space and make a planet out of them, just for fun. He flicked a switch and a model of the universe stuttered to life right in front of her eyes. A hologram that let her move planets and collect debris from space to make new ones. When she used the hologram, Father told her to imagine it was real. He told her that if she used it correctly, she would feel powerful. Like electricity in her blood, or pure light instead of bones.

The first time it happened she screamed so hard she threw up and burst a blood vessel in her eye.

Electricity in her blood, he'd said, and he'd been right.

Soon, the instructions became harder, but that was just because she was getting better at the game. She no longer felt sick. She felt okay. Sometimes she even felt good. Father didn't come and see her as much anymore. But he still gave her instructions. Make a planet with a breathable atmosphere. Make a planet that's all ocean, then freeze it. Make a planet out of gas and make it weightless. Make a planet of metal that stays molten. Make a planet with shining crystal strong enough to build palaces from.

Then, one day, Father told her that the game was different because the rules had changed. That the only way to keep playing was either to fix the planets that did not obey the new rules, or, to take them out of the game altogether. He showed her what these planets looked like, and when she pointed out that they were some of the most beautiful ones in the galaxy, he said that the only beautiful thing was power, and that these planets did not have that. He told her how he wanted them to be altered, and which ones he wanted destroyed, and if he wanted it to happen in a big explosion, or slowly, with lots of disasters and poisonous gases rising out of the planet's crust.

As the years passed, she became exceptional at this.

She became so incredible, in fact, that Father said if she agreed to do this for him all her life, she could have a throne next to his one day and be a real-life princess.

Then, she grew up.

The next memory was full of hatred. Hatred of the monster she called Father, of his sick game that she knew now to be terribly, tragically real. Hatred of herself for being so weak. For being so stupid. For genocide upon genocide committed unknowingly by her hand. The hatred was burning, so innate and so sickening that, as Asha felt it, even before she lived the memory, she began to cry uncontrollably.

She sat in the chair, sobbing as her hands moved over the hologram. She couldn't do this anymore, couldn't live with herself, couldn't—

But Father had told her what he would do with her, to her, if she didn't. That if she wasn't careful, that if she refused to play the game, he would—

Horror welled up in her, leaking out of her through the tears that fell weakly down her cheeks. She had been crying for days. Crying as she destroyed another planet at the request of a monster who had threatened nothing less than prolonged, agonising, chemical death if she didn't.

The first time she tried to kill herself she was twelve years old.

The next few memories sent Asha to her knees, sobbing and hugging her ribs so tightly she couldn't breathe.

The final undid her completely.

She sits in the chair, looking down at the tubes that slide under her sallow, wrinkled up skin, trying to remember her name. She blinks at the hologram that surrounds her, and thinks, 'I hold the fate of worlds in my hands, and yet I am powerless. I cannot even die. I'm too scared to refuse him. I cannot even do that.'

'What is my name? I—'

'Where did I come from?'

She remembers warm, brown hands, and a smile, but that is all.

'Who were you? My mother?'

'Did you do this to me? Did you give me this power?'

She thinks,

'He is nothing without me. And that is why I must die.'

She thinks,

'I couldn't live with myself, knowing what I've done, even if I tried.'

Asha shook her head.

"No," she whispered, and it echoed. "*No!*"

It was too much, this was all *too much*—

Then the memories fell away, and everything was dark except for the hologram, fading now, as the young woman in front of Asha blinked her eyes open and woke up.

Her sister's face hovered on the edge of fearful confusion, but any emotional response to Asha's presence was clearly dulled by the drugs. It was probably better that way. Asha looked again at the bones that poked through her skin, at the clear signs of muscle atrophy and malnutrition, and thought miserably that sedation had to be better than the pain one must incur as a result of dying slowly for nearly twenty years.

"I'm here, Aziza." Asha's voice trembled. "I'm your sister, Asha."

Aziza blinked slowly, her sclera shot through with burst blood vessels, her eyes large in sunken sockets.

"Sister?"

Asha's heart broke at the single, slurred word. A sob heaved through her chest. Aziza was frowning, her mouth turned down, her hand moving feebly, as though she wanted to reciprocate the gesture, but couldn't.

"Don't . . . don't cry," Aziza murmured, her voice rough and weak. "Don't cry."

"God." Asha could barely think past the pain in her chest. *Get it together. This was the point of everything, the reason you're here. You need to save her so that you can save your mother.* "We don't have much time," she sobbed. "I—I wish we could have had more time," she wanted to pull her sister from the chair, and escape, but she didn't know where to start—Aziza looked so fragile. Would she even survive the journey? "I'm going to kill the man who did this to you," Asha whispered, stifling another sob with the back of her hand. "You didn't deserve any of this. God, you're so brave. My brave sister. Braver than me." She gripped Aziza's thin hand in hers, felt the bones move beneath the skin. "In another life, we were all happy," she said fiercely, staring into her sister's eyes through the blur and sting of all the tears, as though she could fit a lifetime of happiness inside a single second. As though she could erase a lifetime of pain in the time it took to blink. "In another life, we were all free."

She looked into her sister's face and saw her struggling to speak, to form words. "A—are you," Aziza coughed, "free now?" Her voice rasped, as though sandpaper had been taken to her throat.

Asha's vision blurred. She nodded.

Aziza's eyes, huge in her thin, wasted face, were wet—glassy with emotion she was barely strong enough to feel. "What is it like?" she whispered.

Asha heard her unspoken words as clear as day. *I want to know what it could have been like. For me.*

"Let me get you out of here, and I'll show you—"

"No," Aziza's voice was stronger. "No, tell me."

Asha shut her eyes. "There's not time—"

"Please," Aziza whispered.

"I—"

Asha was crying so hard she couldn't see. She needed to pull it together, she needed to find the words.

"It's like flying," she said. "And it's terrifying. But I—I had friends." In her mind she saw a sphere of contained light spilling brightness across a classroom floor, and a hand, dark against the flames, stretched out in an offer she could not refuse. She saw a smile, pointed teeth sticking out of the corners—but it was so painful to think of him that she stopped. "They saved my life. They're the only people who have ever seen the truth in me."

Aziza nodded slowly, the tiny smile never leaving her face.

"It taught me a lesson, about love." She hung her head, tears rolling down her cheeks. "It's a great act of courage. To love someone enough to risk everything—to love yourself enough to go out into the universe and demand something better from it . . . You have to be brave. And if it refuses, you have to snatch it for yourself. Fight for it, hard, like your life depends on it, because it does. It does." Her sister closed her eyes, and Asha knew she understood. "And all this time . . . I—I loved you," she said, fresh tears falling faster, "even though I didn't know you. Because that's what family is."

She brought her sister's hand to her chest where her heart beat, strong and true.

"You were here the whole time. *Right here.*" She smiled wetly. "And now we're going to get you out."

Almost violently, Aziza shook her head.

"What . . .?" Asha said, but Aziza's hands were fumbling at the gun at Asha's wrist, the one she'd built on Aonia.

"No," Aziza murmured. "I can't go." She swallowed thickly, still grasping weakly at the gun. "Please—"

Asha moved to take the gun off her wrist, and hand it over—it made perfect sense that Aziza would want a weapon as they escaped. But her sister's hands closed around it, and then, slowly turned it inward, pressing the barrel against her own stomach.

Asha's heart seized.

"No," she said.

Aziza nodded. "He'll—" She coughed. "He'll never stop chasing me." The tears in her huge eyes finally spilled over. "He'll kill you. Everyone you love. And I don't want to go away from here. I've— I've hurt the world too much to deserve a place in it."

All Asha could see was the gun, nestled among the folds of cloth by Aziza's stomach. She realised she was shaking, all over, her whole body wracked with tremors.

"I can't," she said. "I can't do it. Don't make me do this—"

"Then help me do it," Aziza murmured. "Please." She gestured weakly to the tubes that snaked under her skin. "I don't know if I'd live without these. I don't know what they are. What he's made me into. But I don't want to be *his* anymore."

Aziza's fingers were already around the trigger. But she was too weak to pull it. With one hand, she tugged Asha closer, wrapped her fingers around the grip.

"Please." Her voice was ragged, desperate. "Sister." She leaned her forehead against Asha's, struggling to do even that. "*Please.*"

And all Asha could think of were memories—hers and Aziza's in parallel. All the times she'd wished for a sister and not had one; all the times Aziza had wished to die and been denied it.

I couldn't live with myself, Aziza had thought to herself, *knowing what I'd done, even if I tried.*

In the distance, a huge clang sounded. The doors, opening, Asha realised. *They've found us.*

Asha closed her finger around the trigger. Her sweaty hand clasped Aziza's brittle, papery one. She didn't want to let go. "Goodbye," she sobbed.

"Asha," Aziza whispered, "I loved you too." She was smiling. Together, they set her free.

Borne half a forest away on a tide of frothing blood, Adesola stood atop her shield and looked into the eyes of a Nightmare. Having cleared through legion after legion of monstrous beasts, she realised with a sinking heart that they had simply been a prelude to the main event. The Nightmare blinked open one sleepy eye, and in it, Adesola saw all manner of unspeakable things. She couldn't stand it.

When she dropped to her knees, she screamed.

'A Complete, Annotated History of Chasca, Including Relevant Translated Mythologies. Chapter: This Author's Informed Predictions' by I. Nisomn, ex-acolyte of the Aonian Archives.

Chapter Thirty-Nine

[planet: A'lkari] + [location: Emperor's Headquarters] +
[year: 6066]

Asha's world was blurry. Her cheek was buried in her sister's shoulder, her hand still clasped around the gun, around the gun she'd used to—

"Asha!" It was Obi, "Oh god, oh god—" He clattered to a stop next her, Adesola by his side. Asha blinked at them, barely seeing them.

"We must go," Adesola said. Obi looked almost hysterical. "There is a place, far from here, where they know of the prophecy and have tried to interpret it. There is a scholar there—an old friend—he has laboured his whole life over this future we find ourselves in now. We must—"

"STOP!"

They all turned.

Several figures stood in the arch of the doorway, the broken hologram throwing flickering light onto their robes of gauzy white, and their masks like smooth porcelain.

The Magekind.

Invidia.

She could feel Obi shaking her, but the world was far away. *What was the point? It was all over now, anyway.*

Would she ever get her mother back? She'd let down her side of the deal. But what other choice had she had?

461

"The Emperor told us you'd come to this place," Invidia called. "He's on his way back now. He'll want to view the bodies in person." She smiled. "And we've already got one."

Xavior, Asha thought dimly. *No, no, no—*

But then a voice yelled, "I'd like to see you try," and Obi was striding forward, trembling with rage and raising his hands, straining as though he held something heavy in each palm. It seemed to happen in slow motion, his eyes taking on a terrible white light, glowing brighter and brighter, until he resembled some kind of vengeful god, rather than the person Asha knew. The floor started violently shaking, throwing Asha off balance. She looked around and saw, incredibly, hairline fractures appearing in the crystal beneath them—

Bright, shocking light.

It *erupted* from the floor, a blinding flood, streaming upwards. And in the brightness, great moving shapes, like huge creatures summoned from a distant spirit realm. Obi gave a groan of exertion, and the floor rumbled again. Asha peered through the glare, past the quickening in the light, to the floor, where the bodies that had lain trapped in the crystal, like insects between microscope slides, seemed to writhe in place. The light was beaming out of them, rising into the air in slowly coalescing projections, and then the floor gave a great heave, and they surrendered their phantasmal images completely. With a shout, Obi threw up his hands, and the ghosts wrenched themselves free of their bonds. Malice rolled off them in waves, an anger so pure and distilled, Asha felt herself growing furious through the grief. They were a small standing army, a vengeful crowd of aggregate memory. She hadn't known he could do this on such a scale. It was terrifying to watch. She felt as though her skin was being melted from her skull with the sheer impossibility of it. The spirits glittered and shone. Then Obi said something, and they charged forward.

The Magekind moved into formation, and Asha could see that they all held instruments similar to Invidia's, but with key differences. Where hers was a staff, they held metal spheres made of concentric and overlapping rings of metal, that horrible violet energy gathering in the centre as they siphoned it out of the air, from some source that Asha could sense, somehow, but not *see*. For a wild moment, she wanted to reach into the air and grab some, and was convinced that she could, if only she knew *how*—

Then the two sides clashed, and light was flying everywhere, great spheres of crackling violet meeting translucent white and exploding, starry and horrible, like they were all stood in the sky during a storm, fighting amongst bolts of lightning.

She had to help. She couldn't just sit there, pathetic and wailing, while Obi risked his life for her and Xavior was already—

She squeezed her eyes shut. Then she pulled herself to her feet. This time, the shield was a ghost of its former self, fading fast, but she pulled it to her chest, and clutched her gun close with her other hand. She ran forward, dodging bolts of light, and shooting back wherever she could.

"*Asha!*" Obi shouted, his eyes still blazing with light as he ran towards her, his phantoms rearing up to block stray jets of power that flew his way. "We have to *go*, while they're distracted. There's no time. Adesola is calling to me—"

A masked mage was advancing on them, white cape billowing, strange instrument held high. Then they got closer, and Asha could see it was—

Invidia.

"*No*—" A bolt of light discharged from her staff, hurtling towards them, bright and burning like a comet, and Asha knew the shield wouldn't save her a second time, that it was already fading back into whatever mythical place it had descended from—

Obi's strong hand grasped the back of her shirt, pulled her away. She felt him twist, as though taking something out of his pocket. "Hold on!" he yelled, and Asha didn't have time to think so she obeyed, grasping his arm like her life depended in it.

Obi stepped backward through space and time, a small stone clutched in his fist, and then they were falling.

When Sensit did not yield, Mother yielded for him, sending wave after wave of vibration up through her crust, juddering through layers of igneous rock to shake the foundations of the place where he stood. The demons were emptied into a gorge that split the earth, screaming as they fell into hot magma. Sensit was raised on a pillar of rock that burst upwards under his feet, carrying him towards the sky and the darkening clouds. He raged at his removal from the fight, but part of him was glad. He wept.

'A Complete, Annotated History of Chasca, Including Relevant Translated Mythologies. Chapter: Scroll the Third' by I. Nisomn, ex-acolyte of the Aonian Archives.

Chapter Forty

[planet: unknown] + [location: unknown] + [year: 6066]

Asha's body slammed into the ground. The impact was enough to knock her breath from her lungs and dissolve her vision into shards of bright white light.

She heaved in a breath, her throat still searing and raw from her sobs. Everything hurt. She didn't want to move. Didn't want to think or feel or talk or even breathe ever again. Curling up into a ball, she hugged her knees to her chest and pressed her eyelids against her kneecaps so hard she saw white, but that did not—could not—vanquish the twin spectres that loomed in her mind like vengeful ghosts. Thracin, lips pulled back, teeth bared and eyes gleaming. And then her sister, skin sallow, fingers skeletal, looking so *used*, the soft glow of the gun's barrel against her stomach—

Another sob tore its way out of her throat.

She was a murderer.

Strong arms wrapped around her shoulders, and it was a testament to the overwhelming tide of her grief that she did not fight them off. She hung limp, as an arm slid under her knees and lifted her, the other carefully supporting her neck.

"It's okay, Ash. It's all going to be okay."

She didn't have the strength to reply.

He held her close, and started walking.

Dimly, she heard voices. She couldn't make out what they were saying. Not the Universal Dialect, then.

One of the voices addressed Obi directly, in UD this time, harsh and grating, old-sounding and scary. Vaguely familiar, too, but that didn't register until later. Asha pressed her face painfully into Obi's chest. She could hear his heart beating.

"Give us the girl," the voice said. "She must know of her fate, of all of your fates, as soon as possible! We must act now, or it will be too late. She needs to—"

Obi jerked to the side, as if shielding her with his own body.

"What she needs," he whispered, as though he thought she could not hear, "is rest and medical attention. She has been shot at, transported a great distance, and suffered severe loss. Get her to a medical facility or so help me *god*—" He broke off, his voice choked. "You don't know what I'll do."

"I know everything about you, Obi Amadi."

Asha felt his body stiffen. The familiarity of the voice grated at her.

"Order is the Architect," the voice continued. "And Order demands that she meets her fate."

Distantly, Asha felt Obi go completely rigid at those words. Then she felt him begin to shake. "Qala, what is this? I brought us here because you told me you had a cure . . . How do you know about her fate? Who are you?" He was barely holding *himself* together, but still he stood between her and them, whoever they were. A clear thought struck her through the hazy fog of her mind.

They were meant to be a team, weren't they?

Shaking her head more forcefully this time, she pushed at him, wriggling in his grasp.

"Asha, what—"

She slid out of his arms, landing on the floor. Dragging

herself to feet, she blinked blearily in the bright light. The walls of the strange room were made of a clear, glass-like substance that forced the light in at odd angles and made her head hurt even more than it already did. She cradled her right arm close to her chest, the wound in her shoulder pulsing sharply, and looked around. The assembled group could not have looked more shocked if they'd tried. They were a mismatched and motley crew of people, Asha thought. At least five distinct species stood before her, all wearing long black robes. The majority had drawn the cowls of their cloaks low, hiding their faces in shadow, but a few had elected not to, and she could see their faces.

Recognition slammed through her like a bullet.

"*You*," she said.

Suddenly, she felt infinitely younger, and a million worlds removed from this one.

The Sentinel bared his needle teeth in a smile. "Welcome to the Order, child."

Her temper snapped. Asha lunged, shoving obstacles out of her way that, she realised belatedly, were people. If she'd had a knife she no doubt would have used it to carve her path straight towards the Sentinel. She saw his eyes widen, but her arm was already swinging. A sickening crunch sounded as her fist connected with his face. Black blood smeared across her knuckles, her hand throbbed. She swung again, and again. She wanted to keep punching, keep swinging and connecting and hurting until she couldn't separate herself from her actions and the violence swallowed her whole.

"You *knew*!" she shouted at him, "You knew I would have to kill her, and you *let me do it*!" Her voice was hoarse and wild with savage, rabid *fury*—

Arms grabbed her, pulling her off and away. She kicked and struggled but whoever restrained her was far stronger. In the end, she hung limply, breathing harshly and glaring at the Sentinel with all the rage she had collected over the past weeks, months, *years*. He could have stopped all of this. It was his fault.

The Sentinel smeared the blood from his face with the back of his hand. "I didn't know. When I came to you that day, I had only an inkling of the events I would set in motion. I knew either you or your sister would prove central to the prophecy, but I had no way to tell, having seen your face only in dreams. So I sent you to find her, in the hope that all would reveal itself in time. And it did."

"Where is my mother?"

"I will take you to her shortly." Asha wanted to feel relief, to feel anything at all. But there was a terrible hollowness inside her, and it made everything dull. The Sentinel stepped closer. "It was regrettable, what you had to do. But I cannot say I'm sorry."

Asha looked at him. His patchwork face was blurry through the haze of her tears, eyes piercing like shards of sapphire.

He continued. "I have spent centuries poring over scraps of prophecy and listening to mere whispers carried on the winds of time," he said, in his voice like jagged rock. "Even before Thracin, I searched, back when I still believed that Knowledge on its own was enough to save us. I knew he was coming and that he would bring the end of life as we knew it, so I lay in wait, preparing. I studied under the Archivist in the Aonian Archives before leaving to found my own organization. The Order of Legends. We have dedicated eons to excavating and translating and preserving the little information we have left pertaining to our planet in the hope that when the end of days threatened, we'd be ready." His eyes, fixed on her, were hungry. "Now, we're ready."

"The Aonian Archives," Asha whispered, mostly to herself. "You knew the Archivist . . ."

A memory surfaced. Her, standing in the Archivist's smoke-filled room.

Those Chascans live long lives. Too long if you ask us. And, after he left the Guild, disappearing into the night like a thief, he sent us a letter. Something about waiting for the end of the world. What did he call himself? A soldier? A scout? No that can't be right. Whatever it was, he said he was waiting for the prophecy to start, so that he could help the chosen ones, guide them, when the time came.

She stared at him, a revelation dawning.

Not a soldier, or a scout. A *Sentinel.*

"Ishoal," she said. "You're Ishoal Nisomn."

For the first time since she had met him on Gahraan, the Sentinel's mask slipped. His lips parted in shock, eyes narrowing. Finally, he said. "I haven't heard that name for a very long time." There was silence. "Everybody get out."

The other cloaked people filed out of the room, leaving only Asha, Obi, the Sentinel, and the strange woman who looked just like him that Obi had spoken to. Tall, thin, and just as terrifying.

She stepped forward. "Obi—"

"I don't want to hear anything that comes out of your mouth unless it's to tell me that you weren't lying before. That you didn't string me along all in the name of this insane prophecy that everyone can't stop talking about—"

"The cure is real. We have it. That was never a lie."

Obi's face crumpled in relief. He brought a hand up to his face to cover his eyes, but Asha had seen his tears. He nodded, unable to speak for a few moments before wiping his eyes and pointing at the Sentinel. "I don't know who you are, or what you want with my friend. But there are two things that need to happen, or I will find a way to burn this place to the ground." The Sentinel did not react. "Number one, Asha needs to be taken to a medical facility. She needs to be looked at by a professional, and she needs food and rest." Reluctantly, the Sentinel inclined his head. "Number two, you will take her to see her mother. She has been through hell, carrying out your sick instructions, with the threat of her mother's death hanging over her head." She had never heard him this furious. "This might be a game to you—a fun puzzle to play. But she has nearly died, so many times, trying to do what you asked. Now you need to help her."

The Sentinel did not move for a moment. Then he motioned to Qala. "She will show you to the healing bay."

This time when Obi scooped her up, Asha did not struggle.

"Asha, I don't know what I've gotten us into here, but we'll be okay. If we're together, we'll be okay."

"I'm sorry," she mumbled, her strength fading fast. "I'm sorry for everything." She told him this even though she did not think her being sorry made any difference whatsoever. She told him this to convince herself that she was still human. That she was capable of emotions other than anger. That she wasn't a murderer, not really because—

I loved you, she had said to her sister, right before she killed her. *Even though I didn't know you. Because that's what family is.*

"Where's my mother?" she mumbled. "He said he would have her." She turned her face into Obi's chest, and let the tears fall. His arms tightened protectively around her even though they shook.

He's right, she thought. *At least we have each other.*

Then she stopped thinking anything at all.

I am so weary. It has been so long. I have preserved this body far past the point of what is natural, and it has made me monstrous. I want to rest, but I cannot. I want to die, but I cannot. I must guide

the chosen, as I am the only one who knows how, but I am so tired and it has made me mean. — I. Nisomn

A note, half-burned but legible, found in the ruins of Nisomn's work.

Chapter Forty-One

Wind whipped around George's face, tearing at his hair, slicing into his skin. His city was spread out before him, lights twinkling, river rushing, smoke and coal dust settled like a blanket over it all.

In the end, the man had given them a year. The time stretched out ahead of him, brittle and uncertain, a rope bridge strung across a perilous gorge, weighed down with uncertainty, barely high enough to escape the looming obstacles armed with gnashing teeth and flashing eyes that peered out from the dark, asking things of him he was not yet able to give.

A year. Anything could happen.

They were standing on the roof of Carlton House. After their destruction of the crown and their meeting with the ghost, they had returned here, "to watch the pausing of our world" as Alarick put it. George felt no vertigo, only a strange sense of calm. He could acknowledge that one chapter was closing on his life while another began—pages blank but for the numbers counting down.

"You feel it," Alarick said. "Time has us in her clutches."

George nodded. "I feel it."

"That man back there," Alarick said. "That was your fault. You and everyone like you, people born into power who do not use it for the right thing. People who could make a world of

472

difference, but turn a blind eye. Don't say anything. I don't care what you have to say on the matter."

George nodded. He wanted to crawl out of his skin, he was so ashamed.

"If I do this," Alarick continued, "we freeze the city for a year and three days. No undoing it. No stopping it. No turning back."

George nodded, breathed in. The sharp, chilling wind felt like knives in his lungs. He thought about the things that he had feared, the things that waited just out of sight, hidden within the year to come—war, France, his father's regency, *France*—and began to come to grips with the idea that they were now put off in favour of a two-man war against a god who wanted to turn the city into an underworld, and then rule it. It was a worthy cause, of *course* it was, and it wasn't as if he'd had much of a choice . . . it was simply very strange and so extraordinary that he considered again the idea that he might be living inside a dream. His hands shook.

Of course, they shook more often than they were still, these days, but he had so little left he wanted to hold on to.

"Do it," he said.

Alarick stretched out his hands, palms cupped together and glowing as though he held a firefly or a wayward fairy inside them. He started chanting, the words low and guttural.

Primordial, George thought.

Then Alarick opened his hands.

An orb of blue light drifted out, floating lazily towards the sky. It was impervious to the wind, and to gravity, and completely mesmerising to watch before it disappeared through the low, grey clouds, winking out like a star at dawn.

A distant *boom* sounded, sparking a crackle in the air like electricity gathering before a lightning strike, and then there was nothing, until—

Brightness. Cobalt blue and blinding as day, the light spread over the sky like the orb had turned into a firework, the dazzling offshoots of which blazed like shootings stars as they streaked towards the earth.

Is this what Lucifer looked like? George thought wildly. *Blazing holy fire like a comet's tail? Silent, as he fell from heaven?*

The lights connected with the ground, sinking into the earth around the perimeter of the city. A blue dome was visible above the clouds for mere moments, as though London had been miniaturised and imprisoned within a glowing sphere of blown glass, half of which lay buried below the soil.

At that moment, every face in the city was turned towards the stars.

When time stopped, George felt it. He felt the way the magic took root in the city and un-synced it from the rest of reality. He felt the magic look at him, consider his being, and then exclude him. He felt the city pause. Stopped, between one breath and another; the great beast London plunged into a year-long slumber. Buying them time.

His shoulders slumped.

"It worked," he said, and turned to Alarick, but the man was gone. He shook his head. There were footprints in the light dusting of frost that had gathered on the roof, so Alarick's path was easy to follow. It looked as though he had left in a hurry, scuffed and scattered ice detailing his escape.

George turned away from the soft dawn light—the dawn that would not break for a little over a year, now—and followed in Alarick's footsteps.

It seemed that was all he ever did these days, all he had ever done; follow in the footsteps of men named Amadi, and hope they cared enough to spare him, in the end.

474

Chapter Forty-Two

[planet: unknown] + [location: unknown] + [year: 6066]

Asha had been healing in a suspended animation pod for two days straight, and Obi hadn't left her side. He was going out of his mind. He hated it here—in this creepy place that resembled a huge, abandoned church. There wasn't even a way to get outside—all the corridors seemed to twist back on themselves, or lead to nowhere. And most of all, he couldn't stop thinking about George and his father, and everything that Adesola had told him was happening in London. He needed to go back. To see for himself. But to do that, he needed the cure.

It was desperation that had forced him to use the stone Qala had given him to transport them away from A'lkari. He'd had a feeling it would lead them to the Order, but he'd had no idea that the mysterious Sentinel Asha had mentioned was Qala's boss, and the leader of it.

Obi's fingers delved into his pocket and closed around a small glass jar, his fingers worrying against the ridges of the lid.

Qala had given him the cure this morning. It was a spell of sorts, she'd explained. Synthesised somehow into a small, white pill. They'd identified the key ingredient twenty years ago, after hearing of a drug used to treat a degenerative disease in a temporally sensitive and highly reclusive species that lived on the galaxy's fringes. He hadn't taken it, yet. Rattling it around in the jar slightly, he sighed, massaging his forehead. He could be cured and keep his powers. It had no side effects other than temporary fatigue. It wasn't necessary for the journey home—he had always been able to return to his Anchoring place, *to George*, he thought wryly, without losing anything. He had never had to mutilate himself just to come home. For a moment, he was overcome completely with emotion. Tears filled his eyes. *I'm going home.*

Without thinking about it, he unscrewed the cap of the jar, and put the pill in his mouth. It tasted bitter, like lemon-rinds. He swallowed, and waited for something to happen—a bright light in his vision, spontaneous levitation, maybe. But, of course, nothing did. He sighed.

After Qala had handed it to him, he had explained how Adesola believed the prophecy depended on him saving London from the corrupted Hero, Sensit, and somehow all of her conviction about how he should join the order dissipated. They must have wanted to recruit him to help them find the next generation of Heroes, not realising that he was one. Perhaps that was what his father had done for them. Obi didn't know.

A Hero. But what did that even mean? Shifting in the bedding that he'd dragged onto the floor of the medical bay, he propped his hands under his chin and looked at Asha. Clumps of glowing fluid were coagulating by all of her injuries, rendering her shape hazy amongst the thick blue liquid that submerged her body up to her chin. In the pocket of air at the top of the chamber, her face was serene. A small tube fed oxygen into her nostrils. Her closed eyes fluttered gently, like she was dreaming. The doctors were saying she would heal perfectly and be back to full strength after enough time in the pod, but had been infuriatingly vague about exactly how much time 'enough' was.

But it wasn't her physical condition Obi was most worried about.

I'm sorry, she'd said. *I'm sorry for everything.*

He buried his head in the blankets, closing his eyes. What a mess. What a colossally gargantuan unmitigated clusterfuck of a situation. *A prophecy? Re-incarnated Heroes? Ancient weapons? Seriously?*

He wondered whether Adesola would deign to show her face anytime soon. Back on A'lkari, Obi had grabbed Asha and left, sparing no thought for the ancient warrior—he had assumed she would find them, as she always seemed to when the time was right.

Soft footsteps sounded in the hall. Obi sat up, peering through the darkness, trying to make out the visitor.

The Sentinel stepped into the low light of the ward, dark cloak rippling with his movements, and bowed slowly, shallowly.

"Our little Hero is doing well," he said, in his voice like gravel. "She is much changed since the last time I saw her."

Obi stood up. "What do you want from her?" he asked quietly.

The Sentinel looked at him from under his heavy cowl. "I want her to fulfil her destiny. To save us. You heard what is to come. You know she is important."

"Why does it have to be her? Why can't you just save your-selves?"

"Because that is not what was foretold." The Sentinel's voice was infuriatingly calm. Dull, and bored almost, like he'd had this conversation—or every conversation, maybe—a hundred times already. Obi scowled, entirely unimpressed.

"You look just like him."

"Who?" Obi asked incredulously.

"Alarick. Your father. My right hand, my weapon. When you first appeared, I thought for a moment he had come back to us. Then I remembered that time ages you humans quickly and that he would be far older by now."

477

Now Obi was furious. Who did this guy think he was? Turning up out of nowhere to chat cosmic levels of shit about a destiny Asha had never asked for, telling her she *would* save the galaxy, and letting the 'or else' hang unsaid in the air like some kind of sideways threat. And now he was bringing up Obi's father for no discernable reason other than to rattle him, or get the upper hand, or have the last word like they were in a schoolyard fight, and not talking about *the fate of the universe.*

"Oh, give me a break," he sneered, glaring at the Sentinel. "Is this what you do? Is this, like, your thing? Manipulating people? Lying?" He took a step forward. If this was the game the Sentinel wanted to play, then he could play. "I know what you did, you know." he said quietly. "I figured it out."

The Sentinel didn't reply.

"The hologram. Asha told me about it when we first met, told me about the strange person who had delivered it." He crossed his arms. "It bothered me for a while . . . why now? Why her? And then we got here—" he looked around at the cavernous hall, the medbay in the middle of it "—and Asha said, 'you knew', and it all made sense." He stepped even closer, pointing at the Sentinel. "You did it all just to start this. You never cared about her sister. About how Asha and her mother suffered for all those years—all those years you could have helped them, broken them out of that awful place. Instead, you've been holed up here, standing watch over the prophecy like a glorified security guard for hundreds of years—I mean, *seriously*, get a real job—but I guess you got tired of waiting. Bored, maybe, and so you stole footage from the Consortium, of her sister, an abused little girl, and delivered it right to her doorstep. Baiting her into becoming the Hero that you needed." It felt absurd, saying it out loud.

"Bored?" came the reply, grating in the quiet. "No. We are desperate." His voice was a hiss. "Look around. The Emperor and

478

his regime are devouring this galaxy. Economic processes take precedence over the value of a life. He enslaves entire species, writes off the destruction of interstellar ecosystems as collateral. There is too much suffering, and he has too much power. He will never stop—he does not know how. That much I can be certain of." The Sentinel looked, all of a sudden, exhausted, and very old. "And around us all swarms the magic of the prophecy, growing more and more volatile without a vessel to conduct it. You and your friends are the only ones who could ever begin to hope to wholly control it. She is the last heir to the throne of the realm who started this cycle. We have been waiting for her. A very long time."

"She could die, doing this," Obi replied, fighting to keep his voice even. "Would it still be worth it?"

"She will not die," said the Sentinel simply. "Not until the prophecy wills it."

"The prophecy?" Obi said. "Are you kidding me?" If he hadn't been shaking with anger, he might have laughed. "You think some *poetry* written by *dead people* has enough innate power to guarantee a life?"

The Sentinel's voice was dull. "Clearly, it was remiss of me to expect you to grasp the gravity of this situation."

Obi did laugh at that. "Listen," he said. "That girl," he pointed to Asha where she floated in the healing chamber. "That girl is the bravest person I've ever met. She's been through more in eighteen years than anyone should go through in a *lifetime*, and now you're telling me she has to save a galaxy that's done nothing but make her life a living hell since the moment she was born?" He looked at the Sentinel, letting the derision show clearly in his face. "And maybe it said that she would in a prophecy, and *maybe* that prophecy is true. But regardless, I promise you there will be hell to pay for you and anyone else who thinks you can just sit back and watch her work." He clenched his jaw. "All she ever wanted was a place to be safe, and you—" he broke off. "You lured her here with false promises, and then gave her the fate of the world to carry on her shoulders like it was nothing." He breathed in deeply, breathed out. "And the worst part is, I don't think I can tell her what you've done because you'll need to work together when I'm gone, and you're the only person on her side right now in the entire world, and I—" he clenched his fists "—I don't want her to feel alone."

The Sentinel's expression had changed. He had seemed blank, before, with frissons of a deeper emotion intermittently visible under the mask of boredom. But now, he was looking at Obi almost smugly, that horrible, stitched together face searching Obi's like it saw something it recognised. "You *are* like him," he said finally, needle teeth glimmering in the low light. "To what extent remains to be seen, but you are his son. Of that I have no doubt."

"Fuck you," Obi said, feeling like someone had reached inside his chest and scooped out his most vital organs. "Just—" he flailed for something to say, but all he found inside himself was hollow space. "Just leave me alone." He turned away from the Sentinel, waiting to hear his footsteps retreating. There was no noise.

When he turned back, the Sentinel had gone.

A soft beeping accompanied by a low gurgling broke the silence. Obi went to the row of healing pods. Asha's chamber was draining of the blue, viscous fluid, the glowing clumps slowly seeping away.

A hissing sound signaled the dropping of the pod's screen, and another set of footsteps rounded the corner. The young medic who had overseen Asha's placement in the medical bay was coming to see her out of the pod. Obi gathered his blankets off the floor and moved to the side. Soon, Asha was laid out on a stretcher, her eyes peacefully closed, her breathing shallow and content, her hair still sticky with fluid. There was a metaphor about rebirth in there somewhere, but Obi was too tired to dig for it.

"Is she going to be okay?" he asked. He hadn't known precisely what her wounds were—the medics said she's been drawing on ancient powers, and it had taken too much energy from her.

"Yes. Now she must wake."

The medic pulled a short syringe from his bag and prepared it, before sliding it gently into Asha's arm and pushing the clear liquid into her bloodstream.

"Step back," he said.

Asha jerked awake with a start, her breathing ragged, eyes fluttering wildly—bloodshot and small-pupiled. Obi rushed forward.

"Asha," he whispered, "it's alright, you're alright, I'm here."

"Obi?" she sounded so young.

"I'm here, I've got you."

She grabbed onto his arms, pulling him in for a hug. Her body shook, her frame felt fragile.

The medic cleared his throat softly. "She is discharged now. You may take her to her room."

Obi nodded his thanks and hooked an arm around Asha's waist.

"I can walk on my own, thanks." Her voice was quiet, but much stronger than before.

He smiled in relief, rolling his eyes and gripping her waist tighter in support. "Of course you can. Welcome back."

And in the aftermath of the battle, as Sensit stood, weeping on his pillar of rock, and Adesola ran, stumbling and still screaming from the sight of a Nightmare that had now gone back to sleep, Mother settled into the earth of Herself and waited for the next trial that would test them. That there would be another one, she had no doubt. And they had so much left to learn.

'A Complete, Annotated History of Chasca, Including Relevant Translated Mythologies. Chapter: Scroll the Third' by I. Nisomn, ex-acolyte of the Aonian Archives.

Chapter Forty-Three

[planet: unknown] + [location: unknown] + [year: 6066]

Iyanda's face was serene behind the glass of the pod that she slept in. The Sentinel had informed Asha that she had been like this since he took her from Gahraan, unmoving. As though waiting to hear Asha's voice so she knew she could open her eyes. But she hadn't.

Asha thought she looked as though she had simply laid down to sleep, and not woken up. Her breath misted the glass, faint and weak, but still there. Asha had arranged a row of chairs by the pod's translucent side, so she could lie next to her, as though they were back home. She blinked, and her mother's face blurred, her eyes stinging. Curling up onto her side, she closed her eyes, letting hot tears leak down her cheeks. Her face felt scrubbed raw by the salt, as though the tears fell on open wounds. Despite the healing pod and the bed rest, her whole *body* felt like an open wound, as did her heart, and the tears weren't so much confirmation of this as they were a symptom of the loneliness she felt like a crushing weight.

Unclasping her fingers from the object she had carried since Obi had returned it to her a few days ago, she held it up to the light.

The compass.

Two needles, still and certain, one pointing at her, and the other at Obi, who had disappeared a few hours ago to talk with that strange woman, Qala. The other was wobbling, occasionally completing a full resolution before picking a new point and hovering there for a moment, before swinging away.

Xavior, where are you?

She wanted to break out of this strange place, get on a ship and go find him. But it was impossible. She was exhausted, ravaged by the energy taken from her when she had somehow summoned the shield—an incident that the Sentinel had made her describe several times, as he wrote in his notebook. She had never felt more desolate, more alone. All she had of him were memories. His laughter, his smile. Jokes they'd repeated until the words lost all meaning, faces he made, stories he told. The way he'd kissed her, in that forest, before everything had gone so terribly wrong.

Sadness had opened up like a yawning pit inside her and was destroying any other emotion besides the ones that fuelled it, the blackness swarming with things like guilt and regret and a shame so visceral she could barely stand it.

And all the while, the needle swung slowly, unsettled, and unfixed.

"Asha?"

Obi's voice drifted towards her through her fog-like thoughts, piercing the bubble of misery that had expanded around her. He was whispering. Asha realised slowly that it was the middle of the night.

"Yes?"

"Come with me, I want to show you something."

She shook her head, nodding at her mother. "I have to stay with her."

"Asha, do you trust me?" he asked.

She exhaled, watching her breath stir the short hairs on her forearm.

"Of course, I do."

"Then come with me."

The halls of the Order were silent. Silky, purple moonlight streamed through arching windows to pool on stony floors like puddles of liquid silver. Every step she took felt like it might be her last. It was like walking through treacle. *What was the point?* Obi shuffled next to her, matching her slow pace, step for listless step. *I hate this, I hate it here—*

"We've come a long way," he said firmly, interrupting her thoughts. "Both of us have. I can't tell for the life of me whether it's been for better or not, but we've done it." He looked at her sideways, then sighed heavily and came to an abrupt stop. "*Asha.* It's very easy to blame yourself for things you need not blame yourself for, and it's even easier to regret things you shouldn't, and be ashamed of things you shouldn't, and look back on the past with the benefit of hindsight and remake a single decision a thousand, thousand times until you're satisfied with it. Which you'll never be, by the way. That's not how it works."

She was holding her breath.

"The hard thing," Obi continued, "is acceptance. Forgiveness. You're allowed to accept your own apology. You will learn to live with the consequences of your actions. Which in this case, are terrible, but also . . . not." They had paused outside a door that Asha would have missed had Obi not singled it out. "You were merciful, Asha. She was suffering in incredible amounts, and you eased that suffering. You set her free. And, in doing so, you saved billions upon billions of sentient lives. Entire planets and civilizations and religions and—" He broke off, his voice choked with sudden emotion. "You're a hero, really," he whispered. "Not because you're unafraid or unmovable, but because you *are* afraid, and you *are* moved, and yet you constantly strive do the right thing, regardless of the consequences. I know you would not have pulled that trigger if you were not absolutely *certain* it was the right thing to do. I don't know the whole story, and I know there are things you've kept to yourself, but at the end of the day I trust your judgement. I trust it and I trust you so completely that I don't need to know everything. I just know you don't deserve a life of bitter self-hatred and regret because of an action that sounds so terrible on paper, but that was the only thing you could have done in the circumstances that would have made any difference." His eyes were bright and serious and, most importantly, familiar.

A tear rolled its way down her cheek. "I can't stop thinking about her. Seeing her face in my mind . . . " She wrapped her arms around herself. 'And Xavior." Obi nodded. "What if he's dead, and it's my fault?"

"He's not dead," Obi said firmly. "Thracin wouldn't kill him, not if he knew what he was. That he was a Hero. And don't you think we would have felt it?"

She shrugged. "The compass is still spinning, so I don't know."

He nodded. "Keep watching it."

Asha sighed. They stood in silence for a little longer, before Asha whispered, "Thank you. For everything. For trusting me. For caring about me, and—and braiding my hair, and laughing at me when I get mad. For saving my life."

"Asha." He pulled her into a hug, brushing a few stray hairs from her forehead. "I should be thanking you," he said, when they stepped apart. "You were the girl with the plan. I was just an accomplice."

She smiled. "Then you were the best accomplice I could ever have wished for."

Obi smiled back. "Sure, I was." He nodded his head at a small door, branching off the corridor where they stood. "Now come look at this."

He pushed open the door and Asha followed him into a room full of statues.

There were no windows—the click of the door plunged them into darkness.

Obi cursed, and a flare of blue light lit up the space, seeping into the cracks of the room, and illuminating the pale faces of the statues that had been visible moments before.

"Who are they?" Asha asked.

"I don't know," Obi admitted. "I can't read any of the inscriptions, but I think . . . I think they might be former Order members, or something. Look."

He walked to the far end, pushing past the solemn faced, empty eyed imitations of sentients that lined the wall, until he reached the end of the long room. Asha followed at a distance until he stopped, and she caught up. She felt keenly observed by the statues, like she was walking down an aisle in front of hundreds of spectators, even though there could not have been more than twenty sculptures in the whole room. The blue light shining from Obi's hand created a sphere of safety; Asha was sure that if she stepped out of the light's reach, the statues would grab for her, stony fingers wrapping around her throat, struggling limbs, stone lips widening into grimacing smiles, teeth glinting, razor sharp and bloodstained in the light—

"Asha?" Obi had been speaking.

"Sorry, I'm listening. What did you want to show me?"

He gestured to the statue in front of them. This one was carved from black marble and was the only sculpture that had its back to them. It was also undeniably human, or at least human-shaped. Its back was sculpted bare, so masterfully crafted that Asha could imagine reaching out to touch the skin and finding it warm and soft. She could see the sharp jut of the shoulder blades, and muscles cording under the skin. Vertebrae swelled smoothly, and then dipped, each bone like its own tiny mountain, tracing the spine downwards to the small divots at the base, and then . . . rough-edged, unrefined rock, untouched and crude, almost. It was as though the man had been waiting in the rock for someone to set him free, and then decided that reliance on others was overrated and began to haul himself out, limb by marble limb.

"It's unfinished," she said. It felt like a tragedy.

"I know," Obi replied. The quality of his voice told her that he was just as sad about it as she was. "Turn it around."

Asha moved forward, feeling more grounded in her body than she had since A'lkari.

Her hands met cool stone. She pushed with one hand and pulled with the other, Obi heaving it with both hands, until sweat beaded his forehead, both of them rotating the statue on its base until it wobbled to a stop, face bared to the light and so utterly shocking that Asha felt the blood rush from her head.

She gasped, unable to tear her eyes away.

"Obi? How is this possible?"

He was looking at his feet. "It isn't me," he said. "Don't worry. I think it's my father."

She looked back at the statue. It wore Obi's face, that much was true, except . . .

"He doesn't have your scar," she said. "And he looks a lot less kind than you."

"He looks very young," Obi said. "Looks my age."

Asha nodded. "You have . . . older eyes."

He turned to look at her, those same eyes creasing at the corners like they did when he was anxious.

"I have to leave, Asha." She could tell he hated to do this, that he knew just as she did that it was inevitable. A memory slid into her like a knife: a young man, flickering into being right in front of her, wearing a long, dark coat. He smiled, "They gave me my cure."

She gasped, and immediately burst into tears. Throwing her arms around his neck, she squeezed him. "Obi," she could barely talk. "Oh Obi." She could feel he was crying too, tears of relief and happiness and more relief, just so thankful to be alive. She had never been so overjoyed for another person.

When they finally separated, she felt the simple inevitability of time's passage all around, just like she had felt the prophecy so often the past few weeks, eddying past them like a strong current.

"What if I don't know how to be alone anymore?" she whispered.

Obi shook his head. "You're not alone. You will find Xavior, *alive*, and I will come back. You know I will."

She nodded, not trusting herself to speak. With shaking hands, she reached into her pocket, fingers scrabbling until she found what she was looking for.

"Asha, what—"

She glared at him, thrusting a robotic eyeball into his face, its wire still crusted with dried fluid from when she'd ripped it from the skull of the android on the prison ship, the pupil staring sightlessly.

"I held onto it. I don't know why, I just thought it could be useful. Couldn't it work as an Artefact? If you ever needed to return to this time?"

"Oh my god, that is disgusting. How do you even still have it?" He replied, grinning at her fondly.

"Take it," she said, placing it in his hands, and folding his fingers over it. "And come back."

He put it in one of his coat pockets, and Asha stared at him, as she realised she would miss him every single day that he was gone, and that if she was going to be saving even the tiniest part of this universe, she would be doing it for him, and for Aziza's memory, and for her mother, and for the way that they made this life so much brighter for everyone else.

They hugged again and didn't speak.

After a while, she detached herself from Obi, trying to control her breathing, to not cry.

Obi wiped the last tears from his eyes and squeezed her hand one last time. She found herself suddenly desperate to memorise every inch of his face. The scar that flicked wickedly from jaw to outer-eye; the white teeth and the wide nose; the grey eyes and the determination in them. His kind, *kind* smile and the way it did not weaken him but made him infinitely stronger instead.

"It was an honour," he said, as he let her hand go.

"I'll miss you more than I can say." she replied. Then, sternly, "Don't keep me waiting."

Obi smiled his brilliant smile, and sharply—acutely—Asha felt the version of herself that had been clinging to this life for so long disappear. She had been a stubborn, furious girl whose unquenchable anger had fuelled her every movement, who found it difficult to love anything without believing it made her weak. Now, as she looked at Obi's smile; winning and bright and so hopeful in the face of all this hardship, she realised he loved her without any kind of weakness involved, and that she loved him in the same way. It was at this moment that she felt another person step into herself; the next in an infinite line of selves that Asha would shed throughout her life as she grew. This person was more cautious, not because she was more afraid, but because she found she had significantly more to lose. She was angrier, too. She not only recognised the merit in doing good things for others regardless of how it might benefit herself, but she actively *wanted* to do them, especially if it meant people like Obi could live out their lives in happiness. This girl was not a murderer. She was just as human as she had been before. Perhaps more so.

"Wouldn't dream of it," Obi replied.

He made a fist with his metal hand, blue light shining from in between his fingers, then opened it, offering his empty palm to her.

I will survive, and so will you.

Rebellion.

Asha fought not to cry.

Then Obi stood back and closed his eyes. It was there, in the moment between his being and sudden, impossible *non*-being that Asha saw that look of calm and peace spread across his face; the very same look she would strive to wear herself one day and be honest and deserving in wearing it. The blue light vanished, plunging the room into darkness. Obi was gone.

Asha steadied herself on the arm of one of the statues and closed her eyes.

The road ahead was long, and it was perilous, and she was all alone. The darkness pressed in on every side, friend indistinguishable from foe, and ally a word she had known once, but that had become inapplicable to her life; both Obi and Xavior distant figures on distant shores, now shrouded in mist and indefinitely unreachable.

But Asha was an ancient Hero, she knew that now. Her life and deeds foretold in a prophecy written thousands of years ago. She had escaped the place she should have died in and travelled through the stars to save her family. She had run across rooftops on a dying planet and broken out of an imperial prison. Twice. She had fought the Mages of the Emperor with a weapon conjured from the air, a shield of shining crystal that was as familiar to her as her own reflection. She was the last of a line that had died long ago. And though her ancestors were lost, she would not be.

Her name was Asha Akindele. It was said that she would save the world.

From the ruins of the battle Adesola drew her shield and wiped the blood from it. The sun burst forth from the heavens, shining down upon her and the carvings that had littered the shield's surface since the beginning. Carved by Mother—with Her knowledge of prophecy, and of all that was yet to come—the shining furrows of crystal laid out the story of their planet, of the galaxy. The battle Adesola and Sensit had just fought stared out from the edge, two figures, shoulder to shoulder looking towards the rising sun. Various battles led on from this; wars she had not yet fought, victories she was yet to taste, and, jarringly, the defeat that would inevitably kill her. She saw an age of prosperity and peace, she saw their names pass into legend. She saw a civil war, and a desperate queen, and a hero whose pride would cost him his soul. And there, standing sombre in the centre, the girl who would end it all with a shield on her back, companions reminiscent of Adesola's own positioned behind her: a figure blurred around the edges, eyes blank, wicked-looking horns curving from his crowned head towards the sky, and a boy, cloaked in timeless shadow, hand resting on a sword hilt, light shining through the joints. Three Heroes, three weapons, one purpose: defeat the tyrant.

Humbled by this, and aching with the weight of inevitability, Adesola turned and lifted onto her arm the fates of those who would follow in her footsteps. The ones who would forever hold a piece of her inside them, without knowing it.

The ones who would too endeavour to save the world.

'A Complete, Annotated History of Chasca, Including Relevant Translated Mythologies. Chapter: Scroll the Third' by I. Nisomn, ex-acolyte of the Aonian Archives.

Chapter Forty-Four

[planet: Earth] + [location: London] + [year: 1812]

On the other side of the jump, Obi felt calm. Somehow, he knew the cure had worked. As his disease had progressed, time travel had begun to feel like trying to walk through a wire fence; he could push most of himself through, but there would always be *something* torn off, left behind.

But just then, as he had vanished from the dark chamber, statues looming all around . . .

Moving through time and space had been as easy as stepping through a doorway. It didn't require thought, only reflex. And there was, of course, no pain.

Obi opened his eyes.

His own face stared back, leaning over him, older, more lined with time. His reflection wore the same frown—though this one was nestled between two *whole* eyebrows—and the same smile, though one of his front teeth was slightly crooked and chipped in the corner. His scar was gone, his cheek relatively smooth. Smaller scars criss-crossed and slashed their way across his face and neck though. Silvery lines describing a life Obi had not yet lived. He closed his eyes.

"Dad?"

Alarick Amadi offered him his hand. Obi looked at him for a long moment before knocking it aside and standing by himself.

"You're alive," he said, and found himself unsurprised. He realised quietly that Alarick had never felt dead to Obi, not really—he had just felt *absent*. And now he realised that absence was not the same thing as permanent vanishment—

(*I'll miss you*, she'd said. *Don't keep me waiting*.)

—It couldn't be. *Not now*.

Alarick nodded. His face was impassive, his eyes carefully blank, every feature corralled and controlled to give nothing away.

"I'm glad you're here," he said. "I missed you, son."

"Don't," Obi replied. "Don't do this now." An unnamable feeling was welling up in him, like saltwater pushing through bedrock; fractious and briny and terrifyingly strong. He clenched his jaw. "You left me," he said, the saltwater growing to a tremendous and terrifying pressure inside his chest and pushing outwards—every tiny scrap of sadness and rejection, every plume of anger and all the carefully contained rage he had accumulated over the years was being forced to the surface. "And you didn't come back."

"There is an explanation."

"*I don't care*."

His father took that exclamation like a weathered cliff face takes a storm. Obi wondered how long he had until the mask eroded and crumbled into the waves. He wondered if he would live to see it. If anyone would.

"There's work to be done here, son." His father's face had turned unreadable. "And not much time at all to do it. London is in grave danger—"

"I know. I already know, that's why I'm here." He couldn't bring himself to talk to his father. How many times had he thought about this moment, deciding precisely what he would say, how he would say it? And now it had arrived all he wanted to do was get in Alarick's face and yell, *I did it on my own! I raised myself, made myself into a man. I got sick because of you. But of course, I had to find the cure on my own, too. Isn't it incredible that nothing I've done—no part of who I am—has anything to do with you.* But the words wouldn't come.

A moment passed before Alarick nodded simply and turned towards the door. Just before he reached it, he paused, rapping his knuckles lightly on the doorframe. "I know it's not my place to say it, but I'm proud of you. Of the man you've become." A pause. "And I'm glad to see you. Gladder than you can know."

Then he walked out, the door clicking softly behind him.

Obi had a moment to breathe, to collect himself, to set his mind straight and stop it from reeling, trying to answer questions he'd been asking since he was a lonely child.

The door cracked opened. Obi looked up. A hand curved round the door frame, pale fingers pausing at the edge. The chandelier's candlelight glinted off a golden ring and Obi's heart jump-started, thudding to a crescendo in his chest.

"Obi?" said a voice.

As George walked to the door of his rooms, he passed Alarick in the corridor. He had a strange look on his face, like he'd seen a ghost. As he passed George, he muttered, "He's back, by the way." But it wasn't until George was poised to enter his rooms that he realised who Alarick was talking about.

His heart stuttered.

Pressing one palm to the door, he quietly began to lose his mind. Reaching a hand into his hair, he withdrew the circlet of gold that rested there. He shrugged off his jacket, military medals he had never earned clinking to the floor. When he faced the man inside that room, he would face him as an equal. He looked at the ring on his finger. Considered removing it, then was immediately ashamed at having thought that. Keeping secrets from each other could no longer be part of the way this thing between them worked. From now on, it had to be the truth or nothing. Everything in, or nothing at all. Otherwise, what was the point?

He pushed open the door. Distantly, George heard Obi's name slip from his mouth into the space between them, like a prayer to a distant deity; unexpectant of an answer but wishing desperately for one regardless.

"You came back," he said simply. It was all he could manage.

"I—of *course* I came back. I said I would, didn't I?"

"No, you did not." George said. "You promised me you would say goodbye, and then I woke up alone. That whole day, I was *waiting*—" He broke off, realizing belatedly that he was furious. "You just *left*. Like you always do." George felt the calculated meanness surfacing in him, that forlorn and hurt part of him baring its teeth in answer to an attack from the only person truly capable of summoning it.

"It was an accident," Obi said, "you have to believe me. It was a mistake, this time. I didn't mean to leave without telling you, I swear."

But you did.

George's thoughts were mist, ungraspable, and in them he saw the shapes of things he had dreamed in Obi's absence. A man in hero's armour; the billowing sails of the ships at Troy; Achilles lying in a tent, waiting in vain for news of Patroclus' return; two hands that he had seen in a dream once, reaching towards each other, turning gold through blue flames.

"I stopped waiting," he said, which was a lie. "I—I'm *married*."

"I don't see what that has to do with anything," Obi said, but he wouldn't look George in the eye. "We always knew—"

"What?" George asked. "That there was no point in us hoping for anything real out of this because I'd have to marry one day?" He shrugged. "Well, I must be a fool because I hoped anyway." The room was silent. "Obi," he said, and there was, to his own surprise, a plea in his voice. "I have spent too long blaming myself for failings that I believe were perpetrated by us both." He couldn't believe he was doing this, but it was past time. "And I cannot pretend for a moment longer that this—" he gestured between the two of them "—is just about mutual satisfaction, and I believe it to be unconscionably cruel of you to ask it of me, even one more time." He felt unravelled; done with the artifice, done with all the emotions shoved violently down, and done with this brittle truce they'd erected between them like a wall that had turned out to be a mirror, reflecting their own desires back to them. They both knew what was coming; had both known for a while now, George thought. It wasn't as though he'd been particularly subtle. He took a step forward. "Obi, I—"

"*Don't—*"

"You are an ally to me when I feel deserted by every single other soul in this wretched, miserable world. You gave me a precious piece of you and bade me look after it like it was your life, *and it was*, and I did—*gladly*—because . . ." He screwed his eyes shut, grasping in the darkest corners of his mind for the words that might do this incredible, painful thing even a shred of justice. In the end, all that his mind could conjure was a dark hallway, and candlelight, and Obi's silhouette standing in front of a painting hung high on the wall. "You mean more to me than myself," he said. "You who are part of my very soul."

Obi closed his eyes.

"I think that I love you," George breathed, and felt something inside his chest unravel. "I think I've loved you since before I knew what it was to love, and what's more, I think you feel the same. And I want you to know that these past years have been like hell to me, all those minutes inside of all those hours I spent pretending otherwise." He smiled, though the amusement was aimed inward, at his own ruinous, meddlesome heart. "You can hit me if you'd like. I reckon I would almost deserve it."

Obi was silent, his face half in shadow. George could see his eyes were cast downward, and thought, *I will not be sorry for saying it, even if I was wrong. Even if it ruins everything. I think if I had kept it in, it might have killed me.*

"I'm not going to hit you, idiot," Obi said, finally. "I just hadn't expected this, and I hadn't expected you to say it like *that*."

"When it comes to you, I'm afraid I do not possess the restraint to say anything less than what I mean."

"I know," Obi said, and looked upward, at last. "I wish I could tell you how I felt, but I . . ." He sighed. "It's hard." He shot George a rueful smile, and George was reminded that Obi's life had been full of people who had left him—his mother, who had died, and his father, who had vanished into the night and never told him why.

He walked over to him, and they both sat down, backs against the wall, staring out of the window into the pale sky. George let his hand fall next to Obi's, so that the sides of their palms touched.

"I used to think that anyone who loved me would leave me one day," Obi said. "I was scared. I still am. *Terrified* of it—of driving people away. But I think . . ." He stopped, and George heard him make a concerted effort to even out his breathing. "I think there might be some things that only come around once in a lifetime." His voice was barely more than a whisper. "And I didn't want to tell you before, because I was scared of failing. Of messing it all up." He turned to George, his expression wide open. "But you're the only person I've ever met who makes me want to hold on. To life, to myself, to you." George thought—*Yes. It's the same for me. It's always been the same.* "So, I think I have to try anyway, even though I'm scared, because there's no me without you, not really, and I'm so tired of keeping myself away from the things that I want." George felt for a moment like his heart was made of the thinnest glass, and that if Obi tapped on it, just once, it would shatter.

"I love you too," Obi said, and then they were both leaning forward, mouths pressing together, slow and sure, like Obi's hands around George's blown glass heart.

It was gentle. George ached.

When they broke apart, he leaned his head on Obi's shoulder. "Things are different here now," he said quietly.

"I know."

George looked at Obi out of the corner of his eye, as if to say, *of course you do.* "How?"

For many minutes, Obi did not reply. Then he said, "I heard a prophecy, in the future, about me. And my friends. And this place. London. I think it's all connected."

"I didn't know you had friends."

"Oh, shut up," Obi replied. He was smiling but the smile faded quickly. "The monster that's here—he's not a monster at all. Just a man. Well. An ancient Hero with some fucked up superpowers and a sword."

"You really have such a way with words," George said. But then he was silent.

Obi said, "I think he was me. In another life."

George had no reply to that. So, he watched the frozen twilight until the candles burned down and went dark, whilst Obi relayed to him a tale like an ancient epic, one with monsters and great ships, with battles and huge sacrifice and three Heroes who risked everything for family, for a way back home, for love. And when he was finished, and George had no more questions, they sat there for a long while after, breathing into the silence, together. At last, they were together.

And after everything, the brutal fighting, the wild joy, the love, and the terrible hardship . . . at the curtain's close; beyond the final page; in the scarlet wake of the setting sun; at the end, what else will we have left, but a story?

Excerpt from marginalia found in the end-papers of 'A Complete, Annotated History of Chasca, Including Relevant Translated Mythologies' by I. Nisomn, located underneath the hastily handwritten title, 'Notes on the Second Prophecy'.

Acknowledgements

What was originally the first line of this book came to me, fully formed, in an ICT lesson when I was 16 years old. '*Once,*' I typed on the clunky black keyboard, expertly tuning out the voice of my poor teacher, '*there was a girl born amid chaos.*' The rest of the book took shape over the next two years, and I finished it in my A-Level English Literature class. I remember looking around stunned after writing *The End*, thinking, *none of you know what just happened*. But the truth was, neither did I. I had no clue what I was getting myself into, and no clue how many brilliant people I would meet on my journey towards publication and beyond.

To my wonderful agent, fellow Spider-Verse disciple, and dedicated champion, John Baker, *thank you* for seeing the potential in this book, and in me. There aren't words to describe how grateful I am for your consistent support, your truly unmatchable enthusiasm, and the level of care you have shown my characters.

To Bethan Morgan, editor-extraordinaire and champion of SFF, *thank you* for everything you have done to make me feel like such a valued member of the coolest club in the world. I will never forget the care and kindness you and the beautiful team at Gollancz have shown me. Thank you all. I must also say a special thanks for your dedication towards getting me this cover—I truly believe it is groundbreaking. A huge and heartfelt thank you as well to the artist. Waleo Molière, you have a heavenly talent.

To Sarah Nahid Shaffi and Andy Ryan at the Future Worlds Prize, as well as the inimitable Ben Aaronovitch and Adjoa Andoh, please accept my deepest thanks for your continued and much cherished support. I wouldn't be writing these acknowledgements today without it.

Thank you to Rachel Winterbottom, for your vision, and for bringing me into the Gollancz fold, as well as every wonderful English teacher I've ever had, and every adult who did not bat an eye when I told them I was writing a fantasy novel. It meant more to me at the time than it will ever be possible to say. Thank you as well to the city of London for welcoming me home, and being such a consistently beautiful, grimy, challenging, and ancient muse.

A million kisses to my gorgeous friends and their families; Lily for your love and eternal encouragement, Anya for reading all the Notes app excerpts I foisted upon you between Earl's Court and Parson's Green (sorry). Thank you to Soraya and the kindness of the Daya family, to Nell, Amy, and the whole Bevan family with your hearts of gold, thank you for always taking my aspirations so seriously. A truly heartfelt thank you to Faridah for the gift of your support and friendship, ever since I wandered into YALC with my mum and sat down at your table—thank you for always making space for me. To Ciannon—thanks a million times for those frank conversations about the industry, having my back in Cardiff, and telling me to travel—you are an angel. And Jade, for your advice, encouragement, and support, thank you.

This book—and probably every book I will ever write—is about love, so I want to thank the people who teach me every day what that is. Beeban and Aphra, my Beebs and my Flip—I'd fight my way across any and every galaxy to save you. You were my first confidantes, the first people who knew Asha and Obi's names. This book wouldn't exist without either of you and your patience. Parents, when I think about my real heroes, I think about you. Courage, sacrifice, and love are embodied in you both. M, I can't remember which lifetime it was where I met you the first time, but I'm so incredibly glad to have found you again in this one. Thank you for third year, for breathing with me, for everything.

And lastly, I thank my sixteen-year-old self, who sat down at the ancient family laptop with all her out of place feelings, her badly brushed hair, wild imagination, her anxiety and self-doubt, and poured everything she had into a Word document. Who stole her book title from a physics lesson, and then probably fell asleep on the desk. I know that all you wanted was to be seen and understood. I see you, and I understand. Look at what we made, incredible girl. You did it!

Credits

Esmie Jikiemi-Pearson and Gollancz would like to thank everyone at Orion who worked on the publication of *The Principle of Moments*.

Editor
Bethan Morgan

Copy-editor
Sharmilla Beezmohun

Proofreader
Andy Ryan

Editorial Management
Áine Feeney
Jane Hughes
Charlie Panayiotou
Lucy Bilton
Claire Boyle

Audio
Paul Stark
Jake Alderson
Georgina Cutler

Contracts
Dan Herron
Ellie Bowker
Alyx Hurst

Design
Nick Shah
Rachael Lancaster
Joanna Ridley
Helen Ewing

Finance
Nick Gibson
Jasdip Nandra
Sue Baker
Tom Costello

Inventory
Jo Jacobs
Dan Stevens

Production
Paul Hussey
Katie Horrocks

Marketing
Lucy Cameron

Publicity
Jenna Petts

Sales
Jen Wilson
Victoria Laws
Esther Waters
Tolu Ayo-Ajala
Group Sales teams across
Digital, Field, International,
and Non-Trade

Operations
Group Sales Operations team

Rights
Rebecca Folland
Tara Hiatt
Ben Fowler
Flora McMichael
Alice Cottrell
Marie Henckel